PENTECOST
ALLEY

PENTECOST ALLEY

Anne Perry

FAWCETT COLUMBINE

New York

A Fawcett Columbine Book
Published by Ballantine Books

Copyright © 1996 by Anne Perry

Grateful acknowledgment is made
to Harry Margary for permission to reprint
the endpaper maps from *The A to Z of Victorian
London*, published by Harry Margary,
Lumpne Castle, Kent, U. K.

Library of Congress Cataloging-in-Publication Data
Perry, Anne.
    Pentecost Alley / Anne Perry. — 1st ed.
        p.   cm.
    ISBN 0-449-90635-3
    1. Pitt, Charlotte (Fictitious character)—Fiction.
2. Pitt, Thomas (Fictitious character)—Fiction.   3. London (England)—History—1800–1950—Fiction.   4. Women
detectives—England—London—Fiction.   5. Police spouses—
England—London—Fiction.   6. Police—England—London—Fiction.   I. Title.
PR6066.E693P46   1996
823'.914—dc20   95-43557
                                                     CIP

Design by Holly Johnson

Manufactured in the United States of America

First Edition: March 1996

10 9 8 7 6 5 4 3 2 1

To Jonathan, Sylvia, Frances and Henry, with love

PENTECOST
ALLEY

CHAPTER
ONE

"Sorry sir," Inspector Ewart said quietly as Pitt stared down at the woman's body sprawled across the big bed, at her face swollen in the asphyxia of death. "But this one you ought to see."

"So I assume," Pitt said wryly. Since his promotion to command of the Bow Street Station, he no longer dealt with ordinary episodes of violence, theft and fraud. The assistant commissioner had directed that he reserve his attention for those crimes which had, or threatened to have, political implications; those which involved persons of social prominence and might provoke embarrassment in high places if not dealt with both rapidly and tactfully.

So his being sent for at two in the morning to come to this Whitechapel slum over the murder of a prostitute required some explanation. The pale-faced constable who had ridden with him in the hansom had said nothing as they clattered through the August night, the streets narrowing, becoming meaner, the smell of sour smoke, crowded middens and the sharp odor of the river stronger as they moved eastwards.

They had stopped at Old Montague Street opposite the cul-de-sac of Pentecost Alley. The light from the gas lamp on the corner did not reach this far. Holding his bull's-eye lantern high, the constable had led Pitt past refuse and sleeping beggars, up the steep, creaking steps of the tenement building, in through the deep-stained wooden door, and along the passage to where Ewart was waiting. The sound of weeping came from somewhere farther back, sounding frightened and carrying a rising note of hysteria.

Pitt knew Ewart by reputation, and he nurtured no doubts that there was some very real reason why he had been sent for, and so urgently. If nothing else, Ewart would be highly unwilling to yield command of his case to another officer, especially one who had risen from the ranks as Pitt had and who only a short while ago had been his equal. Like many regulars in the police force, Ewart believed that the only man with a right to such a position was one born to it, as had been Pitt's predecessor, Micah Drummond, a man of independent wealth and military experience.

Pitt looked at the woman. She was young. It was difficult to tell a prostitute's age. The life was harsh, often short. But the skin on her bosom where her dress was torn open was still unmarred by drink or disease, and the flesh was firm on her thighs where her red-and-black skirt had been lifted. Her left wrist was tied to the bedpost with a stocking, and there was a garter around her arm just above the elbow, a blue satin rose stitched to it. The other stocking was tied in a noose around her neck, tight, biting into it, almost cutting. The top half of her body, and all the bed around it, was drenched with water.

The sound of weeping was still audible, but it was quieter now, and there were other voices as well, and footsteps in the passage, light and quick.

Pitt looked around the room. It was surprisingly well furnished. The walls had been papered a long time ago, and though they were marked by the incessant damp and mold, and faded where the light had struck them, there was still a recognizable pattern. The fireplace was small, the dead ashes in it gray-white. The fire had been a gesture, something flickering and alive rather than a source of heat. The one chair was a cheerful red with a hand-stitched cushion on it, and there was a rag mat on the floor. An embroidered sampler hung over the shallow mantel, and the wooden chest for clothes and linens was polished. Even its brass handles gleamed.

The washstand held a single ewer and basin.

On the floor beside the bed were the girl's high black boots, not side by side, but half over each other. The round, shiny buttons of the left one had been fastened through the buttonholes of the right one. A bone-handled buttonhook lay beside them. It was a ridiculous, distorted gesture, and one that could only have been done deliberately.

Pitt drew in his breath and let it out in a sigh. It was ugly, and sad, but there was nothing in it to cause Ewart to have sent for him. Prostitution was a dangerous way to make a living. Murders were not unique, and certainly not reason for scandal in high places, or even in low ones.

He turned to look at Ewart, whose dark face was unreadable in the light from the bull's-eye, his eyes black.

"Evidence." Ewart answered the question he had not asked. "Too much of it to ignore."

"Saying what?" Pitt felt a chill beginning to eat inside him in spite of the mild night.

"Gentleman," Ewart replied. "Of very well connected family."

Pitt was not surprised. He had feared it would be something of the sort, pointless and destructive, something with which there was no graceful way to deal. He did not ask Ewart why he thought so. It would be better to see the evidence and make his own deductions.

There was a noise along the passageway, a creaking of footsteps, and another man appeared in the doorway. He was twenty years younger than Ewart, no more than thirty at the most. His skin was fresh, his hazel eyes wide, his face thin, aquiline. His features had been formed for humor and tenderness, but the marks of pain had scored them deeply already, and in the flickering light he was haggard. He brushed his hair back off his brow unconsciously and stared first at Ewart, then at Pitt. He carried a brown leather bag in his hand.

"Lennox. Surgeon," Ewart explained.

"Good morning, sir," Lennox said a little huskily, then cleared his throat and apologized.

There was no need. Pitt had little regard for a doctor who could look at violent death and feel no shock, no sense of outrage or loss.

He stood back a little so Lennox could see the body better.

"I've already examined her," Lennox declined. "I was called at the same time as Inspector Ewart. I've just been with some of the other women in the building. They were a bit . . . upset."

"What can you tell me?" Pitt asked.

Lennox cleared his throat again. He looked straight at Pitt, his eyes averted from the woman on the bed, even the spread of her hair and the bright rose on her arm. "She's been dead several hours," he answered. "I should say since about ten o'clock last night, not later than half past midnight. It's cool in here now, but it must have been warmer then. The ashes in the fire still have a little heat in them, and it's not really a cold night."

"You're very precise about ten o'clock." Pitt was curious.

Lennox flushed. "Sorry. There was a witness who saw her come in."

Pitt smiled, or perhaps it was more of a grimace. "And midnight?" he asked. "Another witness?"

"That was when she was found, sir." Lennox shook his head minutely.

"What else can you tell me about her?" Pitt continued.

"I would guess she was in her mid-twenties, and in good health . . . so far."

"Children?" Pitt asked.

"Yes . . . and . . ."

"What?"

Lennox's face was tight with pain. "Her fingers and toes have been broken, sir. Three fingers on her left hand, two on her right. And three toes dislocated. Left foot."

Pitt felt a shiver of ice inside him as if suddenly the temperature of the room had plummeted.

"Recently?" he asked, although he knew the answer. Had they been old wounds Lennox would not have mentioned them. He would probably not even have noticed them.

"Yes sir, almost certainly within the last few hours. Just before death, in fact. There's hardly any swelling."

"I see. Thank you." Pitt turned back to the bed. He did not want to look at her face, but he knew he must. He must see what and who she had been, and what had been done to her here in this shabby, lonely room. It was his job to learn why and by whom.

She was handsomely built, of roughly average height. As far as he could tell her features had been regular, pleasing in their way. The bones under the puffy flesh were difficult to see, but the brow was good, the nose neat, the hairline gently curved. Her teeth were even and only just beginning to discolor. In another walk of life she might have been a married woman looking forward to a comfortable maturity, perhaps with three or four children and thinking of more.

"What is this evidence?" he asked, still looking down at her. Nothing he had seen so far suggested anything more than some man's taste for pain and fear having gone too far.

"A badge from a gentleman's private club," Ewart answered, then stopped and drew in his breath. "With a name on it. And a pair of cuff links."

Pitt swiveled around to look at him.

Lennox was watching, his eyes wide, almost mesmerized.

"What name?" Pitt's voice fell into the silence.

Ewart put up his finger and eased his collar, his face white.

"Finlay FitzJames."

Outside the constable's footsteps creaked on the floorboards and river fog dripped beyond the dark windows. The weeping in the other room had started again, but fainter, muffled.

Pitt said nothing. He had heard the name. Augustus FitzJames was a man of considerable influence, a merchant banker with political ambitions, and a close friend of several noble families who had held high office. Finlay was his only son, a young diplomat rumored to be in line for an embassy in Europe in the not-too-distant future.

"And witnesses," Ewart added, his eyes on Pitt's face.

Pitt stared back at him. "To what?" he asked guardedly.

Ewart was obviously profoundly unhappy. His body was tense, his shoulders tight, his mouth dragged down at the corners.

"He was seen," he answered. "Not by people who know him, of course, and the description could fit more than him. Ordinary enough. But it was obviously someone of position . . ." He seemed about to add something more, perhaps about gentlemen who frequented such places, then decided it did not matter. They both knew there were men bored with their wives, frightened of censure or commitment if they used women nearer their own class, or simply excited by the forbidden, the frisson of danger. Or there were a hundred other reasons why they might choose to purchase their pleasures in alleys and rooms like this.

"And the cuff links as well," Lennox added from the doorway, his voice still husky. "Gold." He laughed abruptly. "Hallmarked."

Pitt looked slowly around the room, trying to imagine what had happened here only a few hours ago. The bed was rumpled, as though it had been used, but nothing was torn that he could see. There was a slight smear of blood close to the center, but it could have come from anyone, tonight or a week ago. He would ask Lennox, after he had examined it, if he thought it meant anything.

His gaze moved around the walls and the sparse furniture. Nothing else was disturbed. But unless a fight was very violent, and between people of something like equal weight or strength, it would hardly mark this ancient wallpaper or overturn the chair or the wooden washstand with its bowl and cracked and mended blue jug.

As if reading his thoughts, Ewart broke in.

"There's nothing interesting in the wardrobe, just half a dozen dresses, petticoats and an outdoor cape. There are underclothes, two towels, and a clean pair of sheets and pillow covers in the chest. Chamber pot under the bed, and one black stocking. Daresay she dropped it some time ago and couldn't see it in the dark. We wouldn't have found it without two of us, and the bull's-eye."

"Where did you find the cuff links and the badge?" Pitt asked. "Not under the bed?"

Ewart pushed out his lip. "One cuff link, actually—at least the two halves for one sleeve. Behind the cushion in the chair." He pointed towards it. "Jammed down between the seat and the upright. Suppose he took off his shirt and put it over the back, and maybe it got caught. Perhaps he sat on it or something. Left in a panic, and never thought of it until too late. Of course, there's nothing to say it was left here last night . . ." He looked at Pitt, waiting for his answer.

"Possibly," Pitt agreed. They both knew how unpleasant it would be if they had to pursue a man of FitzJames's rank. It would be so much easier if it could be some ordinary man, someone local, with no defenders, no power behind him.

Yet the evidence was there and had to be followed, and it was Pitt who would have to do it. Ewart's trying to evade the issue was understandable, but it was no real help.

"It proves someone was here with expensive tastes," Pitt said wearily. "And the badge proves either that FitzJames was here himself, at some time, or someone who knew him was. Where did you find it? Was that down the chair as well?"

Suddenly Ewart's urgency evaporated, leaving him sad and anxious, his face heavily lined, weariness in every crease. His dark eyes were almost black in the candlelight, puckered at the corners.

"On the bed," he replied, his voice little more than a whisper. "Under the body." There was no need to add that it could not have been there before. It was too wretchedly obvious.

Pitt put out his hand.

Ewart fished in his coat pocket and brought out a small, round piece of gold, enamel faced, a pin across the back of it. He dropped it into Pitt's open palm.

Pitt turned it over, looking at it carefully. It was about half an inch across, the sort of thing a man might wear on his lapel. The enamel was gray, discreet, easily lost against the fabric of a suit. On it were written in gold two words, "Hellfire Club," and the date "1881"—nine years ago. He turned it over towards the light. Even so it took him several moments before he could discern the very faint, hair-fine writing on the back, behind the bar of the pin—"Finlay FitzJames." But once he read it there could be no argument.

He looked up at Ewart, then at Lennox, still standing just inside the doorway, his face white, drained of life and color, his eyes full of pain.

"Did you find it?" Pitt asked Ewart.

"Yes. The constable didn't move her. He says he didn't touch anything. He could see she was dead and he raised the alarm."

"Why did he come in? What brought him here in the first place?" It might not matter, but he should ask. "Did he know her?"

"By sight," Ewart replied with a shrug. "Her name's Ada McKinley. Worked this area the last half dozen years or so. Constable Binns says he saw a man come running out in a panic and he stopped him. There could have been something wrong. Made him go back in, thinking he may have got mixed up in a scuffle, tried to cheat one of the girls, or something. Seems that he was a customer of one of the other girls, Rose Burke, and on his way out from her saw Ada's door open, and being a nosy sort of bastard, took a look in. Hoping to catch someone in the act, I suppose. Anyway, saw more than he bargained for." Ewart's nose wrinkled in disgust. "Came running out as if the devil were after him. But he couldn't have done it. He was with Rose till seconds before Constable Binns saw him. Rose'll swear for that. She's one of the witnesses who saw the man go in, whoever he was. We've got her waiting for you."

"And the man?"

"Him too." Ewart let out his breath in a little grunt. "Cross as two sticks, but still here. Swearing fit to turn the air blue. They're all cross, for that matter. Bad for business." He pulled a sour face.

"Isn't it a bit late for business?" Pitt asked ruefully. "When did all this happen?"

"When Binns saw him come out." Ewart's eyes widened. "About half past midnight. I got here just after one. I took a look around, then as soon as I saw that badge I knew we were going to have to get you in, so I sent Constable Wardle for you. Sorry, but the way I see it, it's going to get nasty whatever we do. No way out of it." He took a deep breath. "Of course FitzJames may be able to give us a proper explanation, and then we can look elsewhere."

"Maybe," Pitt said doubtfully. "What about money? Do you know if anything was taken?"

Ewart's face brightened. A light flickered for a moment in his eyes and he hesitated before he replied, considering as he spoke. "Her pimp? That would be a very much easier answer. I mean, easier to understand . . . to believe." He stopped.

"So was there money?" Pitt pressed.

"There was a small leather purse in the linen box," Ewart said reluctantly. "About three guineas in it."

Pitt sighed, not that he had really hoped. "If she'd been keeping it from him, it wouldn't be there now. First place he'd look," he said sadly.

There was a shrill whistle from a kettle towards the back of the house, and someone swore.

"Perhaps they quarreled and he killed her before he searched." Ewart's voice was keen again. "He panicked and ran. It'd make more sense. Teach the other girls a lesson they'd not forget. More reason to kill her than a customer like FitzJames."

"What about the boots?" Lennox asked from the doorway, his voice thick. "I could see him torturing her, but why would someone killing her for money fasten her boots together like that? Or put the garter 'round her arm?"

"God knows," Ewart said impatiently. "Perhaps that was the client before he came? He knew she was salting away too much of what she earned, and he came as soon as he saw the customer leave. She had no time to undo the boots or take off the garter."

"I can understand her not having time to undo the boots," Lennox said with harsh sarcasm. "But did the customer go, leaving her tied to the bed by one hand, and she stayed like that while she argued with her pimp?"

"I don't know!" Ewart said. "Maybe the pimp tied her up while he searched for money. He would do, to torture her."

"And didn't find it?" Lennox's eyebrows rose.

"Maybe there was more, perhaps under the mattress or something? Anyway, why would a man like FitzJames kill a woman like that?" Ewart eyed the body in the bed with a strange mixture of pity and distaste.

"Probably for the same reason he used her in the first place," Lennox said bitterly. He turned to Pitt. "I haven't moved her. Do you need to see her any more, or can I at least cover her?"

"Cover her," Pitt answered, seeing the urgency of distress in his face, and liking him so much more than he did Ewart, even though he understood Ewart's feelings, his weariness, his familiarity with such scenes and lives and the people who lived them. If he had ever had romantic delusions about young women in the streets, they were long since destroyed by reality. He was not unfeeling. It was simply that for his own sanity he must limit his emotions. And more immediate than that, to do his job and be of any use, his brain must be clear, driven by thought, not emotion. Ada McKinley was beyond human help, but other women like her were not.

But Pitt still preferred Lennox's vulnerability. It sprang from some kind of hope and a different sort of care.

Lennox shot him a look of gratitude, then came forward across the room. First he pulled down the dead woman's skirt to cover her legs, then took the quilt from the bed and spread it over her, hiding her distorted face as well.

"Did you find anything else you haven't mentioned yet?" Pitt asked Ewart.

"Do you want a list of her belongings?" Ewart said tartly.

"Not yet. I'll see Constable Binns, then the other witnesses in order."

"Here?" Ewart looked around, his eyes avoiding the bed.

"Is there anywhere else?"

"The other women's rooms, that's all."

"I'll see Binns here, and the women in their own rooms. I need some idea of the geography of the house."

Ewart was satisfied. It was what he would have done.

Binns was about thirty, fair-haired, blunt-faced, still looking shaken and rubbing his hands. He was not used to standing motionless on guard. His feet were numb; Pitt knew from the careful, clumsy way he walked.

"Sir?" He stood facing Pitt, his eyes studiously away from the bed.

"Tell me what you saw," Pitt directed.

Binns stood at attention. "Yessir. I were following me usual beat, which is Spittalfields, end o' Whitechapel Road, up ter beginnin' o'

Mile End Road, an' north ter 'Anbury Street and back again." He took a deep breath, still staring straight ahead. "I gets ter corner o' Old Montague Street and sees this feller come boltin' out o' the entrance o' Pentecost Alley lookin' like 'e'd seen a ghost or summink. 'E were abaht ter scarper orff westwards, towards Brick Lane way, but I reckoned as there must be summink wrong or 'e'd 'a' walked normal, instead o' keep dartin' a look over 'is shoulder like 'e were afraid someone was arter 'im." He swallowed. "So I nabbed 'im sharp by the back o' 'is collar and brought 'im up short. 'E squealed like the devil 'ad 'im. So then I knew 'e'd like seen summink bad. 'E were scared witless."

Pitt nodded in commendation. Neither Ewart nor Lennox moved, standing back in the shadows, listening.

"I made 'im go back," Binns continued, moving a little to ease his cramped feet as the circulation returned. "I thought it'd be one o' these rooms up 'ere. Other side's a sweatshop. 'E could 'a' nicked summink, but 'e didn't 'ave nuffink with 'im, so I came in 'ere." His eyes wandered momentarily, but ignored Ewart and Lennox as if he did not see them. "This is the first room. The door were 'alf open, so I come in." His voice dropped almost to a whisper and he glanced at the bed. "Poor little cow. I knew straight orff as she were dead, so I didn't touch nuffink. I shut the door an' took 'im wif me, and raised the alarm wif me whistle. Seemed like ferever till someone 'eard me, but I s'pose it weren't no more'n five minutes. P.C. Rogers were passing along Wentworth Street, an' 'e come runnin'. I sent 'im for Mr. Ewart."

"What time was that?" Pitt asked.

Binns flushed. "I dunno, sir. First I were too busy 'oldin' the witness ter take out me watch, and then w'en I saw 'er I never thought ter. I know that's right unprofessional, but I knew 'er, y'see, an' it fair shook me."

"What can you tell me about her?" Pitt asked, watching the man's face.

He shifted his weight, but still remained at attention.

"Bin 'ere six year, or thereabouts. Dunno w'ere she come from. Pinner way, I think. Country, any'ow. Miles from 'ere. Pretty she were, then. All roses and cream." He shook his head, his face crumpled. "Said she were a parlor maid in one o' them big 'ouses up Belgravia way. Lorst 'er character." He said it almost expressionlessly, as if it were an old tragedy, too familiar to arouse anger anymore. "Butler got 'er inter trouble. She told the lady o' the 'ouse, an' they kept the butler an' sent 'er packin'. Child come early. Didn't live, poor little beggar. Though that could 'a' bin fer the best." His face pinched and his eyes looked far away. "Death is better than the work'ouse, or some o' them baby farms. So she took ter the streets. Smart, she were, an' I guess she were bored and angry too." The gentleness ironed out of his features. His face set. "She'd 'a' liked ter've got even wi' that butler."

Pitt had no doubt that if she had, Binns for one would have been blind that moment. As a constable, Pitt might have too. Now he could not afford such a luxury.

"Maybe she tried blackmail on the butler?" Ewart spoke for the first time and there was a lift in his voice. "And he killed her?"

"Why?" Lennox said slowly. "His employer already knew her story and didn't care."

"It's irrelevant," Pitt cut across them. "No one would have taken her word against his. Not now." In a sentence he had reduced her to what she was, and he knew it. The only reason he had been called to her murder was because of Finlay FitzJames's name on the badge. Some men in Ewart's position would have suppressed it and gone through the motions of searching for her killer, then simply marked the case unsolved and left it. Perhaps if Lennox had not been there he would have. But Lennox had seen him find the badge under the body, and he would not have remained silent. There was no discretion in his face, no cynicism, only an aching, worn-out hurt.

There was silence in the rest of the house, but the sound of the first traffic could be heard in the street outside, and the smear of dawn paled a little beyond the windows.

Pitt turned to Binns. "Is that all?"

"Yessir. I waited till Mr. Ewart come, then I told 'im what I saw an' done, an' 'anded it over to 'im. That were a little arter one o'clock."

"Thank you. You acted well."

"Thank you, sir." He turned to leave with straighter shoulders, his head high, his feet still numb.

"We'd better see the witness." Pitt nodded to Ewart. "In here."

A few moments later another constable escorted in a lean, narrow-shouldered man with a brown jacket and dark trousers concertinaed over his boots, hand-me-downs from someone taller. His face was gray-white and twitching with fear. Whatever the pleasure he had purchased that night, it had been at a price he would never willingly have paid.

"What's your name?" Pitt asked him.

"Ob-badiah S-Skeggs," he stuttered, his face twitching. "I never touched 'er. I swear to Gawd I never did!" His voice was rising in what he intended to be sincerity, and was all too obviously terror. "Ask Rosie!" He gestured to where he imagined Rosie was. "She'll tell yer. Honest, Rosie is. She'd never lie fer me. She don't know me from nuffink." He looked at Pitt, then at Ewart. "I swear."

Pitt smiled in spite of himself. "Rosie doesn't know you?"

"No."

"Then how do you know her?"

"I don't! I mean . . ." He saw the trap, but he had already stepped into it. He breathed in and tried to swallow, choking himself.

"You don't have to make up your mind," Pitt said dryly. "I'll ask Rosie anyway. She'll no doubt know whether you're a regular or not."

"She wouldn't lie fer me," Skeggs said desperately, gasping between splutters. "She don't even like me."

"No, I don't suppose she does," Pitt agreed. "Do you know what time you got here?"

"No." He was not going to risk any more traps. "No. I were leavin' w'en that rozzer nabbed me. An' that were unjust, it were. I never done nuffink as is agin' the law." He became plaintive. "A man's allowed a little pleasure. An' I always paid fair. Rosie'll tell yer that."

"How would she know?" Pitt raised his eyebrows.

Skeggs's face tightened venomously.

"You thought you'd entertain yourself a little more," Pitt continued. "So when you saw Ada's door open, you peeped 'round. Only instead of finding her fornicating with a customer, you saw her lying dead, sprawled over the bed, tied to it, her stocking wound 'round her throat and the garter on her arm."

Skeggs let out an agonized blasphemy.

"And you fled, when Constable Binns caught you," Pitt finished.

"I were going ter raise the alarm," Skeggs protested, glaring at Pitt, and then at Ewart, as if to bear out his story. "Call the p'lice, like I should! Fast as me legs 'd carry me. That's why I were runnin'!"

"So why didn't you tell Constable Binns about Ada?" Pitt enquired.

Skeggs looked at him with murder in his eyes.

"Did you see anyone else?" Pitt went on.

Outside the light was broadening. There was more noise in the street. People coming and going, calling to each other. The sweatshop opposite was opening up.

"Yer mean like 'im wot done it?" Skeggs demanded indignantly. "Course I didn't, or I'd 'a' told yer. Fink I'd stand 'ere bein' suspected if I knew 'oo'd really done it? Wot yer fink I am, stupid?"

Pitt forbore from answering, but Skeggs read the silence as

affirmative and bristled with offense. He followed the constable out, glancing over his shoulder still searching for something cutting to say.

Pitt saw Rose Burke in her own room, two doors farther along. It was a different shape, and perhaps a foot or two wider, but essentially similar. A large bed occupied most of the space, also rumpled and obviously lately used. The sheets had a gray look down the center and were heavily creased. There was a stale smell of sweat and body dirt. Apparently Skeggs had had his money's worth, at least up to that point.

Lennox looked ashen-faced. There was no need for him to have followed, and Pitt wondered why he had. Perhaps he thought Rose might need him.

But Rose was of sterner stuff. She was broad-shouldered, handsome-bosomed, of no more than average height. Her hair was dark brown but had been bleached in a paler streak across the front. It was startlingly becoming. In fact she was a beautiful woman, even if her skin had coarsened from its youthful duskiness and her teeth were already going. She might have been anything between twenty-five and forty.

She was too composed to offer any remark before she was asked. She stood in the middle of the room ignoring Lennox and looking at Pitt, waiting, arms folded, only a slightly rapid rise and fall of her chest betraying that she was under any stress at all. Pitt did not know if it was indifference to Ada's fate or courage. He thought perhaps at least some of the latter.

"Rose Burke?"

"Yeah?" Her chin lifted.

"Tell me about your evening from eight o'clock onwards," Pitt commanded, then as her face lit with a contemptuous smile, "I'm not interested in doing you for prostitution. I'm after who killed Ada. He's been here once. If we don't get him, he could come again. You might be next."

"Jeez." She sucked in her breath, respect and loathing bright in her eyes.

"Do you want me to tell you it never happens?" he asked more gently. "It's not true. He broke her fingers and toes, then he strangled her with her own stocking, like a hangman's noose." He did not mention the garter or the boots. Better to leave something unspecified. "You think he'll do it just the once?"

Lennox winced and seemed about to say something, then changed his mind and silently went out, pushing the door closed behind him.

Rose breathed the Lord's name in what might even have been a prayer, because almost as if she did not register what she was doing, she crossed herself. Now the blood was gone from her face, leaving the rouge garish, though it was skillfully applied.

Pitt waited.

She began slowly. "I 'ad someone at ten. D'jer 'ave ter 'ave 'is name? S'bad fer business."

"Yes."

She hesitated only a moment. "Chas Newton. 'E were 'ere till near eleven."

"Generous, aren't you?" Pitt said dubiously. "A whole hour? Is business slow lately?"

" 'E paid double!" she snapped, her pride stung.

He could believe it. She was a handsome woman and there was an air of knowingness about her, as if little in the way of tastes or skills would be outside her capacity.

"And when he'd gone?" he prompted.

"I dressed an' went out, o' course," she said tartly. "Wot jer think I was gonna do? Go ter sleep? I went down ter the alley an' was turnin' ter go between the 'ouses ter Whitechapel Road, an' I saw this geezer comin' in on the other side—"

"The other end?" Pitt interrupted. "You mean Old Montague Street?"

"No, I mean the other side o' Ol' Montague Street," she said impatiently. "Could 'a' bin Springheel Jack or Farver Christmas from all I saw, if it'd bin the end o' the alley, w'ere I were. There i'nt no lamp there. Don't yer notice nuffink?"

"You saw him pass under the lamp?" Pitt's voice quickened in spite of himself.

"Yeah." She was still standing in the middle of the room with arms folded.

"Describe him," Pitt directed.

"Taller 'n me. Less 'n you. Bit more 'n usual, mebbe. Well built. Kind o' young."

"Twenty? Thirty?" Pitt said quickly.

"Not that young! Thirty. In't easy ter tell wi' a toff. Life in't so 'ard fer them. Live soft, live longer."

"How was he dressed?" He must not put words into her mind.

She considered for a moment.

"Decent coat. Must 'a' cost a quid or two. No 'at, though, 'cos I saw the light in 'is 'air. Fair, it looked, an' thick. Wavy. Wish my 'air waved like that." She shrugged. "Wouldn't want 'is face, though. Sort o' mean. Summink abaht 'is mouf. Good enough nose. Like a good nose on a man." She looked at Pitt speculatively, then changed her mind. Physical relationships were a matter of business for her. There was no pleasure in them.

"Ever seen him before?" he asked, ignoring the glance.

"Can't say."

"Why not?"

" 'Cos I dunno, o' course!" she snapped, her face pinched, fear and sorrow struggling with each other. "If I knew 'oo'd 'a' killed Ada, I'd tell yer. Be there ter watch yer string the bastard up. 'Elp yer, fer that. Poor little cow. She were a greedy bitch, and thought 'erself a bit above some o' us, but she din't deserve that."

"You don't know if you've seen him before," he challenged.

"In the dark all cats are gray." She made a gesture of disdain. "I'nt you never 'eard that before? I don't look at men's faces, only the money. But 'e don't jog me mem'ry none. I don't think as I've seen 'im. Sure as 'ell's on fire, I don't know 'is name, or I'd tell yer."

"Hell's on fire." He repeated the words carefully. "What makes you say that?"

" 'Cos it's abaht the one thing as I'm sure of," she retorted, looking him up and down. "Wot jer spec' me to say? Sure as 'eaven's sweet? I wouldn't know." She looked away from him at the tawdry, overfamiliar room. "Don't believe in it. In't fer me, fer Ada, if it was. Ask the preachers. They'll soon tell yer, women like me is gonna burn in 'ell fer corruptin' an' leadin' astray the likes o' gentlemen!" She gave an oath so coarse even Pitt was jolted by hearing it from her still-beautiful mouth.

"Have you ever heard of the Hellfire Club?" he asked.

Amusement flashed across her face. "No, wot's that? Them as is gonner burn—or them as is gonner stoke? Believe me, that sod's gonner burn, if I 'ave ter carry the coals meself—gentleman or no."

"Was he a gentleman?" he asked after a moment's hesitation.

Her eyes met his squarely. "Looked like it. 'E weren't 'ard up. An' as sure as 'ell's on fire, mister, 'e come just about the time poor Ada were croaked. I were along the Whitechapel Road fer 'alf an hour, an' I didn't see no one else go past, till I got another gent meself an' come in again."

"You didn't see the other end," Pitt pointed out.

"In't my pitch," she said reasonably. "Ask Nan about that."

"You said Ada was greedy," Pitt prompted. "Did she take from you?"

"I never said she stole." Rose was annoyed again. Her eyes were sharp and bright. "I said she were greedy. Always wanted more. Always thinkin' o' ways to get a bigger cut, not jus' for 'erself, but for us too. I never knew nobody so angry. Ate 'er up at times."

"Did she say who with?"

She shrugged and her lip curled.

"Lousy butler wot took 'er character, I s'pose. Then lied abaht it.

Dunno what she expected! Bit green, she were." Her face pinched and the sorrow returned. "Poor little cow."

There was a bang outside and a clatter of hooves. Someone shouted. There were footsteps in the corridor and a door slammed somewhere upstairs, the vibrations shivering through the room.

"Did she ever mention this butler's name?" Pitt asked.

Her eyes widened. "You reckon it was 'im as did 'er? Why would 'e? She couldn't do nuffink to 'im. Safe as Big Ben 'e were. Still is."

"No, I didn't think so," he conceded. "What time did you see this man?"

"Dunno. Ten p'raps."

"Then what?"

She was uninterested.

"I got another couple o' jobs, nuffin' special. 'Alf hour each, mebbe. The next were Skeggs, sorry little bastard that 'e is. Takes 'im an hour to get 'isself goin'. Likes ter look at other people." Her voice was thick with disgust. " 'E left me and went snoopin' on Ada ter see if 'e could catch some other stupid sod wif 'is pants orff makin' a fool of 'isself, and maybe doin' it good." She put her hands on her hips. " 'Oo knows? Anyway the little swine got more'n 'e bargained for. Saw Ada dead, an' damn near wet 'isself!"

"Time?"

"I know that 'cos this time I looked. I were 'ungry, and reckoned as I'd done well enough as I could get summink decent ter eat. I were goin' down ter the pie stand on the corner o' Chicksand Street, till the rozzer come back and all the row started. 'Ad ter stay 'ome, and I'm fair starvin' now."

Pitt said nothing.

She stared at him with sudden anger.

"Think I'm an 'eartless bitch, don'cher?" she demanded, her voice hard, full of resentment. "Well, I felt sick as you at first, but that's two hours ago, or like, an' I ain't eaten proper since yest'day. Death comes often 'ere, not like up west w'ere it's all soft an' folk die easy. An' that doc were real fair. 'E told me as she probably din't feel much fer long. Made Nan put on a kettle and get us all a cup o' tea. An' 'e laced it wif a drop o' brandy. Never known a bloke be so . . ." She was lost for a word. She had no term of praise to convey what she meant, the sudden warmth, the feeling that for a moment her emotions and her grief had been truly more important to him than his own. It eased the bitterness out of her face, till Pitt could see the woman she might have been had time and circumstance been different.

Nan Sullivan was at least ten years older than Rose, and long hours and too many bottles of gin had blurred her features and dulled her hair and eyes. But there was still a softness in her, some spark of memory left a gentleness behind it, and when she spoke there was an echo of the west of Ireland in her voice. She sat on her bed, frowsy, tearstained and too tired to care.

"Sure I was at the other end o' the alley," she agreed, looking at Pitt without interest. "Took me a while to find anyone. I had to walk along to Brick Lane." It was obviously a defeat she no longer bothered to hide. "I got back just as Ada come indoors."

"So you saw the man who went in?" Pitt said eagerly.

"Sure I did. Least I saw the back of his head, and his coat." She sighed and the ghost of a smile touched her mouth. "Lovely coat it was. Good gabardine. I know good gabardine when I see it. Used to work in a sweatshop. Master o' that had a coat o' gabardine. His was brown, as I recall, but it sat on the shoulder the same way. Neat and sharp it was, no rumples, no folds where there shouldn't be."

"What color was this one?" He was sitting in the one chair, about a yard away from her. This room opened onto the midden, and he could not hear the sounds of the street.

"This one?" She thought for a moment, her eyes far away. "Blue. Or mebbe black. Wasn't brown."

"Anything about the collar?"

"Sat fine. Sort o' curve you don't get in a cheap coat."

"Not fur, or velvet?" he asked. "Or lambskin?"

She shook her head.

"No, just wool. Can't see the cut with fur."

"What about his hair?"

"Thick." Unconsciously she brushed her fingers through her own hair, thinning with time and abuse. "An' fair," she added. "Saw the light on it from the candles in Ada's room. Poor little bitch." Her voice dropped. "Nobody should have done that to her."

"Did you like her?" he asked suddenly.

She was surprised. She had to think for a moment. "I s'pose I did. She brought trouble, but she made me laugh. An' I had to admire her fight."

Pitt felt a moment's irrational hope.

"Who did she fight with?"

"She went up west sometimes. Had nerve, I'll say that for her. Didn't often sell herself short."

"So who did she fight with, Nan?"

She gave a sharp, jerky little laugh.

"Oh, Fat George's girls, up near the Park. That's their patch. If it had bin a knife in her, I'd 'ave said Wee Georgie'd done it. But he'd never have strangled her, or done it in her own room either. He'd have done it in the street and left her there. Besides, I know Fat George when I see him, and Wee Georgie."

That was unarguable. Pitt knew them both too. Fat George was a mountain of a man, unmistakable for anyone else, let alone Finlay FitzJames. And Wee Georgie was a dwarf. Added to which, whatever the trespass into their territory, they would have beaten her, or crippled her, or even disfigured her face, but they would not have brought down the police upon themselves by killing her. It would be bad for business.

"You saw this man going into Ada's room?" Pitt returned to the subject.

"Yes."

He frowned. "You mean she opened the door for him. She didn't take him in? She didn't bring him from the street?"

Her eyes widened. "No! No, she didn't, come to think on it. He must have come here on his own—sort of reg'lar, or like that."

"Do you get many regulars?" Then he saw instantly from her face how tactless the question was. Ada might have, but she did not.

A flicker of understanding crossed her features, and knowledge of all the nuances of failure and his perception of what it meant, and his momentary regret.

She forced herself to smile, made it almost real. "Not reg'lar, like calling. See the same faces, but nobody makes appointments. Might come on the chance, sure enough. Ada was popular." Her face crumpled, her shoulders sagged, and suddenly her eyes filled with tears. "She was quick with her tongue, poor little beggar, and she could make you laugh." She took a deep, shaky breath. "And people like to laugh." She looked at Pitt. "She gave me a pair of boots once. We had the same size feet. They had a real pretty heel. She'd done better than me that week, and it was me birthday." The tears spilled over her cheeks and ran down the paint on them, but she did not contort her face. There was a strange kind of dignity in her, a genuineness of grief which made nothing of the shabby room with its unmade dirty bed, the garish clothes, the smell of the midden coming up from the yard, even her weary body, too often used, too little loved.

All Pitt could offer was to lend Ada McKinley the same worth.

"I'm sorry," he said quietly and without thinking, placing his hand for a moment over hers. "I'll do everything I can to find who did this to her, and I'll make him answer, whoever he is."

"Will you?" she asked, swallowing awkwardly. "Even if he's a gent?"

"Even if he's a gent," Pitt promised.

He went through the same questions with the third woman in the house, whose room was next to Ada's. Her name was Agnes Salter. She was young and plain with a long nose and wide mouth, but there was a vitality to her which would probably serve her well enough for at least another ten years. With the bloom gone from her skin and the firmness from her body, she might find it much harder to make her way. Most probably she was as aware of that as he.

"Course I knew Ada," she said matter-of-factly. She sat straight in a hard-backed chair, her skirts hitched up almost to her knees. Her legs were excellent, her best feature. No doubt she knew that too. She was not regarding Pitt as a man. He could see in the total disinterest in her expression that it was merely habit, and possibly quite comfortable. "Bit cocky, but not bad," she went on, referring to Ada. "Willin' ter share. Lent me a garter once." She smiled. "Knew I 'ad better legs 'n 'er. Not that 'ers were bad, mind. But money's money. I did well wi' that. Some geezers get 'igh on garters. Guess fancy ladies don't wear 'em. All whalebone stays and cotton drawers."

Pitt did not comment. It was now daylight outside and there was traffic on the street beyond the alley and the sweatshop opposite was hard at work.

"Can't tell yer nuffink," Agnes went on. "Don't know nuffink. I'd see the bastard quartered if I could. There's risks—and there's risks." Her fingers were clenched, knuckles white, belying her studied casual air. "Yer 'spect ter get beat up now'n again. It's part o' life. An' mebbe the odd cuttin', which can go too far if yer man's had a skinful. But this in't right, poor sow. She never asked fer this." She pushed out her large lower lip and her face was filled with anger. "Not that I s'pose any o' you lot give a toss. Just another tart got done. There's more'n enough tarts in London anyway. Mebbe it's some 'oly Joe cleanin' up the place?" She gave a laugh, a little high and sharp, and Pitt heard the fear in it.

"I doubt it," he said sincerely, although it was a possibility he had not thought of in this instance. It should not be ruled out.

"Oh yeah?" She was curious. "Why not? Ada were a tart, just like the rest of us."

He did not quibble the use of words. He answered honestly.

"There are evidences which suggest it could have been a man of wealth, and possibly position. She didn't bring him up. According to Nan, he came here and Ada let him in. Sounds as if he'd been here before."

"Yeah?" She was surprised, and at least to some degree comforted. "Mebbe 'e were someone as she knew?"

"Who did she know?"

She considered for a while. Pitt had asked only out of diligence. He still believed it would prove to be Finlay FitzJames. There was no other likely explanation for the Hellfire Club badge under the body.

"Someone as'd kill 'er?" she said thoughtfully. "I s'pose anyone 'oo quarreled wiv 'er. I'd 'a' said some other tart as she pinched a customer from, 'cept she'd 'a' fought and there'd 'a' bin one 'ell of a row, an' I never 'eard nuffink. Anyway . . ." She shrugged. "Yer might scratch someone's eyes aht. Or, if yer was real vicious, take a knife ter their faces ter mark 'em, but yer'd do it in the street, wouldn't yer? Yer'd 'ave ter bin a real mad bitch ter foller 'em 'ome an' do it cold, like. An' Ada weren't that bad."

"That bad?" he asked. "But she did take other people's customers?"

Agnes laughed sharply. "Yeah! Course she did. 'Oo wouldn't? She were pretty, an' smart. She 'ad a quick tongue, made 'em laugh. Some toffs like ter laugh. Makes 'em feel less like they're in the gutter. Feel like it's a real woman. Them as can't laugh wiv their la-di-da wives 'oo are all corsets and starch." She lifted her lip in a sneer which still had a remnant of pity in it. "Poor cows prob'ly never 'ad a decent laugh in their lives. Ain't ladylike ter laugh."

He said nothing. A dozen images crowded through his mind, but she would understand few of them, and it would serve no purpose trying to explain to her.

In the house, somewhere above them, a door slammed and feet rattled down the stairs. Someone shouted.

"And o' course there's them as likes the gutter," Agnes went on, frowning. "Like pigs in muck. Somethink in it excites 'em." The contempt was thick in her voice. "Jeez! If I din't need their bleedin' money, I'd stick the bastards meself."

Pitt did not doubt it. But it led him nowhere nearer to who had killed Ada McKinley without a fight. There was no blood in the room, and her body was hardly marked, except for the coldly, deliberately broken fingers and toes. There were no scratches, no bruising such as would have been caused by a drawn-out fight. One fingernail on her right hand had been torn, that was all.

"Who did she know that would have called on her here?" he repeated.

"I dunno. Tommy Letts, mebbe. 'E'd come 'ere. Or 'e would 'ave. She don't work for 'im no more. Got someone better, she said. Bragged about it, jammy bitch."

"Could the man you saw have been Letts?"

"Nah!" She swung her feet. " 'E's a dirty little weasel, black 'air like rats' tails, an' abaht my size. This geezer were tall, an' thick 'air, wavy, all clean like a gent. An' Tommy never 'ad a coat like that, even if 'e stole it."

"You saw him?" Pitt was surprised.

"Nah, I never did. But Rose did. An' Nan. Taken bad, Nan were. Soft cow. That doc were good to 'er. For a rozzer 'e were 'alf 'uman." She pulled a face. "Young o' course. 'E'll change."

There was little more to learn. He pressed her about having heard anything, but she had been busy with her own clients, and the fact that she claimed to have noticed no sounds at all was only indicative that there had been no screams or crashes of knocked-over furniture. Pitt had already assumed as much from the nature of the death and the comparative order of the room. Whoever had killed Ada McKinley had taken her by surprise, and it had been quick. It had been someone she had trusted.

Pitt left Agnes and went back to the corridor outside, where Ewart was waiting for him. Ewart glanced at him and saw from his expression that there was no escape, no new knowledge to free them from the necessity of going to Finlay FitzJames. A glimmer of hope faded from his black eyes and he looked smaller, somehow narrower, although he was a solid man.

Pitt shook his head fractionally.

Ewart sighed. The air blew up the stairs from the open door out to the alley. Lennox waited at the bottom in the shadows, his face lit yellowly by the constable's bull's-eye lantern.

"FitzJames?" he said aloud, a curious lift in his voice.

Ewart winced, as if he had caught an eagerness in it. His teeth ground together. He seemed on the edge of saying something, then changed his mind and let his breath out in a sigh.

"I'm afraid so," Pitt answered. "I'll see him at breakfast. There'll just be time to go home and wash and shave, and eat something myself. You'd better do the same. I shan't need you for several hours, at least."

"Yes sir," Ewart agreed, although there was no relief in his voice. The time was put off, not removed.

Lennox stared up at Pitt, his eyes wide, shadows on his face in the darkness, unreadable, but there was a tension in his thin body under the loose jacket, and Pitt had a momentary vision of a runner about to move. He understood. His own anger was intense, like a white-hot coal somewhere deep inside him.

He left Ewart to post a constable in Pentecost Alley. The room had no lock, and it would have been futile to trust to that anyway. There were enough picklocks within a hundred yards of the place to make such a gesture useless. Not that there was much evidence to destroy, but the body would have to be removed in a mortuary wagon, and Lennox would have the grim duty of a closer examination. It would be very unlikely to produce anything helpful, but it must be done.

He wondered as he rode home through the early-morning streets—hectic with traffic, drays, market carts, even a herd of sheep—whether Ada McKinley had any relatives to receive the news that she was dead, anyone who would grieve. She would almost certainly have a pauper's grave. In his own mind the decision was already made that he would go to whatever form of funeral she was given, even if it was simply an interment.

He rode west through Spittalfields and St. Luke's, skirting Holborn. It was quarter past seven.

Bloomsbury was stirring. Areaways were busy with bootboys and scullery maids. Smoke trickled from chimneys up into the still air. Housemaids were starting the fires in breakfast rooms ready for the day.

When he reached his own house in Keppel Street, and paid off the cabby, there was a streak of blue sky eastwards over the City, and the breeze was stirring. Perhaps it would blow the clouds away.

The front door was already unlocked, and as soon as he was inside and had hung up his coat, he smelled the warmth and the odor of cooking. There was a scamper of feet and Jemima arrived at the kitchen door.

"Papa!" she shouted happily, and started towards him at a run. She was eight years old now and quite conscious of her own dignity and importance, but not too ladylike to love to be hugged or to show off. She was dressed in a blue underfrock with a crisp white pinafore over it and new boots. Her hair, dark brown and curly, like Pitt's, was tied back neatly and she looked scrubbed and ready for school.

He held out his arms and she ran into them, her feet clattering with amazing noise for one so slim and light. He was still mildly startled by how loud children's feet were.

He hugged her and picked her up quickly. She smelled of soap and fresh cotton. He refused to think of Ada McKinley.

"Is your mother in the kitchen?" he asked, putting her down again.

"Course," she replied. "Daniel lost his stockings, so we're late, but Gracie's making breakfast. Are you hungry? I am."

He opened his mouth to tell her she should not repeat tales, but she was already leading him towards the kitchen, and the moment was gone.

The whole room was warm and full of the smells of bacon and new bread, scrubbed wood and steam from the kettle beginning to sing on the stove. Their maid, Gracie, was standing on tiptoe to reach the tea caddy, which Charlotte must inadvertently have put on the middle shelf of the dresser. Gracie was nearly twenty now, but had not grown appreciably since they had acquired her as a waif of thirteen. All her dresses still had to be taken up at the bottom, and usually lifted at the shoulders and tucked at the waist as well.

She made a final jump and succeeded only in pushing it to the back of the shelf.

Pitt walked over and picked it up.

"Fank you, sir," she said almost abruptly. She had immense respect for Pitt, and it grew with each new case; and she was perfectly used to being helped in such manner, but the kitchen was her domain, not his. One must keep an order in things.

Charlotte came in with a smile, her eyes bright to see him but also searching. They had been married too long and too closely for him to be able to hide from her the nature of the call he had received or how it had affected him. The details he could and would refuse her.

She looked at him carefully, his tired eyes, his unshaven cheeks, the sadness in the lines around his mouth.

"Can you eat?" she asked gently. "You should."

He knew he should.

"Yes, a little."

"Porridge?"

"Yes, please." He sat down on one of the smooth, hard-backed chairs. Jemima carried the milk jug over from the larder, carefully, using both hands. It was blue-and-white-striped, and the word *milk* was written on it in block letters.

The door burst open and six-year-old Daniel came in, waving his socks triumphantly.

"I've got them!" He saw Pitt with delight. Too often he was already up and gone before the children came for breakfast. "Papa! What's happened? Aren't you going to work today?" He looked at his mother accusingly. "Is it a holiday? You said I have to go to school!"

"You do," Pitt said quickly. "I've already been to work. I've only come back for breakfast because it's too early to call on the people I have to see. Now put your socks and boots on, and then sit down and let Gracie bring your porridge."

Daniel sat on the floor and pulled on his socks, then considered his boots carefully before deciding which one went on which foot. Finally he climbed onto his chair, still regarding his father. "Who are you going to see?"

Charlotte was looking at him too, waiting.

"A man called FitzJames," Pitt answered them both. "He has his breakfast later."

"Why?" Daniel said curiously.

Pitt smiled. Half of Daniel's conversation consisted of whys.

"I'll ask him," Pitt promised.

A marmalade-striped kitten came running in from the scullery, then stopped suddenly, its back arched, and took half a dozen steps crabwise, its tail bristling. A coal-black kitten charged in after it and there were squawks and squeals as they tumbled with each other, spitting and scratching harmlessly, to the children's entertainment. Porridge was ignored, and no one argued.

Pitt sat back as Jemima disappeared under the table to watch, and Daniel pushed his chair back so he could see too. It was all immensely comfortable, trivial and a different world from Pentecost Alley, and the people who lived and died there.

CHAPTER
TWO

It was nearly nine o'clock when Pitt alighted in Devonshire Street and went to the front door of number thirty-eight. The police station at Bow Street had sent him a messenger with FitzJames's address and a note from Ewart to say that he would inform Pitt of any further evidence, should he discover it. He was about to question Ada McKinley's pimp and see if he could locate her earlier clients of the evening, but he held little hope.

Pitt knocked on the door and stepped back. The wind from the east had risen and cleared some of the overcast. It was brighter, and warmer. The morning traffic was no more than the occasional hansom. It was too early for ladies to be making calls, even upon their dressmakers, so there were no private carriages out yet. An errand boy strode past, whistling and tossing a sixpenny piece, reward for his diligence.

The door opened to reveal a long-nosed butler with a surprisingly agreeable expression.

"Good morning, sir. May I help you?"

"Good morning," Pitt said quickly, taken aback by such pleasantness. He pulled out his card, more elegant than his old ones, stating his name but not his calling. Police were never welcome, no matter how senior. "I am afraid a matter has arisen in which it is necessary I see Mr. Finlay FitzJames most urgently," he explained.

"Indeed, sir." The butler offered his tray. It was small and of most exquisitely simple Georgian silver, and Pitt dropped his card onto it. The butler stepped back to allow Pitt inside into the magnificently paneled hall, which was hung with portraits. Most of them were grim-faced men in the dress of the previous century. There were also one or two scenes of farmland and cows grazing under heavy skies, which Pitt thought, if they were originals, would be extremely valuable.

"I believe Mr. FitzJames is taking breakfast, sir," the butler continued. "If you would care to wait in the morning room, it faces the garden and will not be disagreeable. Are you acquainted with Mr. FitzJames, sir?"

It was a polite way of asking if FitzJames had the slightest idea who Pitt was.

"No," Pitt confessed. "Unfortunately the matter is urgent, and unpleasant, or I would not have called without making an appointment. I regret it cannot wait."

"Just so, sir. I will inform Mr. FitzJames." And he left Pitt in the cool blue-and-brown morning room filled with dappled light while he performed his errand.

Pitt looked around. He had already been aware, even before he had come into the house, that the FitzJames family had a great deal of wealth. Most of it had been acquired through speculation by Augustus FitzJames, using the money his wife had inherited from her godmother. Pitt had picked up this piece of information from Charlotte's younger sister, Emily, who before her present marriage to Jack Radley had been married to the late Lord Ashworth. She had retained the money he had left her, and his aristocratic associates, and also an inveterate curiosity for details about people, the more intimate the better.

The FitzJames morning room was extremely comfortable, if a little chilly. It did not have the usual plethora of glass-cased trophies, dried flowers and stitched decorations which many families relegated to a room in which they spent little time. Instead there were two very good bronzes, one of a crouching lion, the other of a stag. Bookcases lined the farthest wall and the shafts of sunlight slanting in between the heavy brocade curtains showed not a speck of dust on the gleaming mahogany surfaces.

Pitt walked over and glanced at the titles. Probably the books FitzJames read were in the library, but still it would be interesting to note what he wished his guests to believe he read. He saw several histories, all of Europe or the Empire, biographies of politicians, religious discourses of an orthodox nature, and a complete edition of the works of Shakespeare, bound in leather. There were also translations of the works of Cicero and Caesar. There was no poetry, and no novels. Pitt smiled without being aware of it. This was how Augustus FitzJames wished to be perceived . . . a man of much learning and no levity or imagination.

It was no more than ten minutes before the butler returned, still smiling.

"Mr. FitzJames regrets he is extremely busy this morning, sir, but if the matter is as pressing as you say, perhaps you would care to join him in the dining room?"

It was not at all what Pitt wanted, but he had little alternative. Perhaps when he realized the nature of the enquiry, FitzJames would elect to discuss the matter alone.

"Thank you," Pitt accepted reluctantly.

The dining room was splendid, obviously designed to accommodate at least twenty people with ease. The velvet curtains framed three deep windows, all looking out onto a small, very formal garden. Pitt glimpsed topiary hedges and box trees, and a walkway paved in an exact pattern. The table was laid with silver, porcelain and crisp, white linen. On the sideboard were dishes of kedgeree; another of bacon, sausage and kidney; and a variety of eggs, any one of which would have fed half a dozen people. The aroma of them filled Pitt's nostrils, but his mind was forced back to Pentecost Alley, and he wondered if Ada McKinley had ever seen as much food as this at one time in her life.

He must remember FitzJames was not necessarily guilty.

There were four people at the table, and they commanded his attention. At the head sat a man of perhaps sixty years, narrow-headed with powerful features. It was the face of a self-made man, owing no obligation to the past and possibly little to the future. It was a face of courage and intolerance. He regarded Pitt with challenge for having interrupted the domestic peace of his breakfast.

At his side was a handsome woman, also of about sixty. Her features were marked by patience and a degree of inner control. She understood myriad rules and was used to obeying them. She might have assumed Pitt was a banker or dealer in some commodity. She inclined her head courteously, but there was no interest whatever in her wide-set eyes.

Her son resembled her physically. He had the same broad brow, wide mouth and squared jaw. He was about thirty, and already there was the beginning of extra weight about him, a fading of the leanness of youth. This must be Finlay, and his magnificent fair, wavy hair fitted exactly the description both Rose and Nan had given.

The last member of the party was quite different. The daughter must have inherited her looks from some ancestor further back. She had nothing of her mother in her, and little of her father except a rather long nose, but on her it was slender, giving her face just enough eccentricity to stop it from being ordinarily pretty. She had an air of daring and vitality. She regarded Pitt with acute interest, although that might be simply because he had interrupted the usual monotony of breakfast.

"Good morning, Mr. Pitt," the senior FitzJames said coolly, looking at Pitt's card, which the butler had offered him. "What is it that is so urgent you need to address it at this hour?"

"It is Mr. Finlay FitzJames I wish to see, sir," Pitt replied, still standing, since he had not been invited to sit.

"You may address him through me," the father replied without reference to Finlay. Possibly he had consulted him before Pitt was admitted.

Pitt controlled an impulse to anger. He could not yet afford to offend the man. This was just conceivably some form of error, although he doubted it. And if it should prove as he feared, and Finlay was guilty, it must be handled so that there would be not the slightest ground for complaint. He had no illusion that FitzJames would not fight to the bitter end to protect his only son, and his family name, and therein also himself.

Pitt began very carefully. He understood only too well why Ewart clung to the hope that some other evidence would be turned up to indicate any other answer.

"Are you acquainted with a group calling themselves the Hellfire Club?" he asked politely.

"Why do you wish to know, Mr. Pitt?" FitzJames's eyebrows rose. "I think you had better explain yourself. Why should we give you any information about our business? This . . . card . . . offers your name and no more. Yet you say your business is urgent and unpleasant. Who are you?"

"Has there been an accident?" Mrs. FitzJames asked with concern. "Someone we know?"

FitzJames silenced her with a glare and she looked away, as though to tell Pitt she did not expect to be answered.

"I am a superintendent in the Metropolitan Police Force," Pitt replied. "Presently in charge of the Bow Street Station."

"Oh my goodness!" Mrs. FitzJames was startled and uncertain what she should say. She had obviously never been faced with such a situation before. She wanted to speak, and was afraid to. She looked at Pitt without seeming to see him.

Finlay was also quite openly amazed.

"I used to be a member of a club which used that name," he said slowly, his brow furrowed. "But that was years ago. There were only four of us, and we disbanded about, oh, 'eighty-four, somewhere about then."

"I see." Pitt kept his voice level. "Will you give me the names of these other members please, sir?"

"Have they done something awful?" Miss FitzJames asked, her eyes bright with curiosity. "Why do you want to know, Mr.—Pitt, is it? It must be very terrible to have sent the head of a police station. I think I've only ever seen constables before."

"Be quiet, Tallulah," FitzJames said grimly. "Or you will excuse yourself and leave the room."

She drew breath to plead, then saw his expression and changed her mind, her mouth pulled tight, her eyes down.

FitzJames dabbed his lips and laid down his napkin. "I don't know why on earth you should concern me with such a matter at home, Mr. Pitt, and at this hour of the morning. A letter would have sufficed." He made as if to stand from the table.

Pitt said with equal sharpness, "The matter is a great deal more severe than you think. I thought it would be more discreet here. But I can deal with it at Bow Street if you prefer. It may possibly be explained without that necessity, although if that is what you wish, of course I shall oblige you."

The blood darkened FitzJames's narrow cheeks, and he rose to his feet, as if he could no longer tolerate Pitt's standing where he was obliged to look up at him. He was a tall man, and now they were almost eye to eye.

"Are you arresting me, sir?" he said through a tight jaw.

"It was not my intention, Mr. FitzJames," Pitt replied. He would not be intimidated by the man. Once such a pattern was set it would be impossible to break. He was in charge of Bow Street and he owed this man nothing but courtesy and the truth. "But if that is the way you care to view it, then you may take it so."

FitzJames drew in his breath sharply, was about to retaliate, then realized the matter must be far more serious than he had originally supposed or Pitt could not have had the audacity to speak so.

"I think you had better explain yourself." He turned to his son. "Finlay! We shall retire to my study. We do not need to trouble your mother and sister with this."

Mrs. FitzJames shot a pleading look at him, but she had been dismissed, and she knew better than to argue. Tallulah bit her lip in frustration, but she also kept her peace.

Finlay excused himself, then rose and followed his father and Pitt from the dining room, across the picture-hung hall and into a large book-lined study. There oxblood-red leather chairs surrounded a fireplace with a club fender in brass, leather bound also. It was a comfortable place for four or five people to sit, facing each other, and read or talk. There was a silver tantalus on a side table, and half a dozen books out of the glass-fronted cases.

"Well?" FitzJames said as soon as the door was closed. "Why are you here, Mr. Pitt? I assume there has been an offense or a complaint. My son was not involved in it, but if he knows anything that may be of assistance to you, then naturally he will inform you of such details as you require."

Pitt looked at Finlay and could not tell whether he resented his father's assumption of control or was grateful for it. His bland, handsome face revealed no deep emotion at all. Certainly he did not seem afraid.

There was no purpose in prevarication any longer. FitzJames had robbed him of any subtlety of approach and the surprise it might have given him. He decided to attack instead.

"There has been a murder—the East End," he replied calmly, looking at Finlay. "A Hellfire Club badge was found on the site."

He had expected fear, the flicker of the eyes when the blow falls, however expected, the sudden involuntary pallor of the skin. He saw none of it. Finlay was emotionally unmoved.

"Could have dropped at any time," FitzJames said, dismissing the news of murder. He indicated a chair for Pitt to sit in, then himself sat directly opposite. Finlay took a third chair, between them, to Pitt's left. "I assume you consider it necessary to speak to all those who are, or have been, members," FitzJames continued coldly. "I dispute the necessity. Do you imagine one of them may have witnessed it?" His flat eyebrows rose slightly. "Surely if that were so they would already have reported the matter to some police station or other?"

"People do not always report what they see, Mr. FitzJames," Pitt replied. "For various reasons. Sometimes they do not realize that it is important, other times they are reluctant to admit they were present, either because the place itself embarrasses them or else the company with whom they were there—or simply that they had said they were elsewhere."

"Of course." FitzJames relaxed a trifle in his chair, but he still sat forward in it, his elbows on either arm, his fingers over the ends. It was a position of command and control, reminiscent of the great statues of the Pharaoh Ramses, drawings and photographs of which were printed in the newspapers. "With what hours are we concerned?"

"Yesterday evening from nine until midnight, or a little later," Pitt replied.

FitzJames's face was under tight control, deliberately expressionless. He turned to his son. "We can end this matter very quickly. Where were you yesterday evening, Finlay?"

Finlay looked embarrassed, but resentful rather than afraid, as if he had been caught in an indiscretion, but no more. It was the first thread-thin whisper of doubt in Pitt's mind as to his involvement.

"Out. I . . . I went out with Courtney Spender. Went to a couple of clubs, gambled a bit, not much. Thought of going to a music hall, and changed our minds." He looked at Pitt ruefully. "Didn't see any crimes, Inspector. And to be frank, haven't had anything to do with the other club members in years. I'm sorry to be of no use to you."

Pitt did not bother to correct him as to his rank. He was almost certain Finlay was lying, not only because of the badge but because he so perfectly answered the description of the man Rose and Nan had both seen. There was a faint flush in his cheeks, and his eyes met Pitt's, steady and overbright.

FitzJames moved restively, but did not interrupt, and Finlay did not look at him.

"Would you be good enough to give me Mr. Spender's address, sir?" Pitt asked politely. "Or better still, if he has a telephone, we can clear up the matter instantly."

Finlay's mouth fell slack. "I . . . I . . . can give you his address. No idea if he has a . . . if he has a telephone."

"I daresay your butler would know," Pitt said quickly. He turned to FitzJames. "May I ask him?"

FitzJames's face froze.

"Are you saying that my son is telling you less than the truth, Mr. Pitt?"

"I had not thought so," Pitt said, sitting in a mirror position in his own chair, hands on the arms. Finlay sat upright, on the edge of his seat.

FitzJames drew in his breath sharply, then changed his mind. He reached for the bell.

"I . . . I think that may have been the day before. Is it yesterday evening we are enquiring about?" Finlay looked confused. His cheeks were red and he clenched his hands, fidgeting and moving uncomfortably.

"Where were you last night, sir?" Pitt could not afford to relent.

"Ah . . . well . . . to tell you the truth, Inspector . . ." He looked away, then back at Pitt again. "I . . . I drank rather too much, and I can't remember precisely. Around the West End. I know that. Weren't anywhere near the East End. No reason. Not my sort of place, you know?"

"Were you alone?"

"No! No, of course not."

"Then who was with you, sir?"

Finlay shifted in his seat a little.

"Oh—various people—different times. Good God, I don't keep a list of everyone I see! Most fellows take a night out occasionally. Do the odd club and hall, you know? No, I don't suppose you do know." He was not sure whether he intended it as an insult or not; the uncertainty was clear in his face.

"Perhaps you will let me know if you should be fortunate enough to remember," Pitt said with controlled politeness.

"Why?" Finlay demanded. "I didn't see anything." He laughed a little jerkily. "Wouldn't make a decent witness in my state, anyway!"

FitzJames finally broke in. "Mr. Pitt, you have come into my home unannounced and at a most inconvenient hour. You said there has been a new murder somewhere in the East End . . . a large and nonspecific area. You have not told us who is dead nor what it has to do with anyone in this house, beyond the fact that a badge has been found of some club or other of which my son was a member several years ago and is not presently. To the best of our knowledge, it no longer exists. You require some better reason to continue to take of our time."

"The murder was in Pentecost Alley, in Whitechapel," Pitt answered. He turned again to Finlay. "When did the Hellfire Club last meet, Mr. FitzJames?"

"For God's sake, man!" Finlay protested, still no more than irritated. "Years ago! What does it matter? Anyone could have dropped a badge in the street. Or—in a club, for that matter." He gestured with his hands. "Doesn't mean a thing! Could have been there for . . . I don't know . . . months . . . even years!"

"There's rather a sharp pin on it," Pitt pointed out. "I think a prostitute would have noticed it in her bed in quite a short time, say five minutes at the outside. Less, in this particular circumstance, since she was lying on it."

"Well, where did she say it came from?" FitzJames said angrily. "You aren't going to take the word of a common whore over that of a gentleman, are you? Any gentleman, let alone my son."

"She didn't say anything." Pitt looked from one to the other. "She was dead, her fingers and toes broken. She was drenched with water and then strangled with her own stocking."

Finlay gagged and went putty gray, his body slack.

FitzJames took a very slow, deep breath and held it while he steadied himself, then let it out in a sigh. He was white around the mouth and there were two spots of color in his cheeks. He met Pitt's eyes with a cold, defiant stare.

"How regrettable." He had difficulty keeping his voice level and under control. "But it has nothing to do with us." He did not take his eyes from Pitt's, as if by strength of will he could mesmerize him. "Finlay, you will give the Inspector the names and addresses of all those you know to be members of this unfortunate association. Beyond that, we cannot be of assistance."

Pitt looked at Finlay. "The badge we found has your name on it."

"He has already told you that he has not associated with them for years," FitzJames said, his voice rising. "No doubt the badge was handed back to whoever was the president in charge of the . . . club . . . and he has since misplaced it. It has nothing to do with the identity of whoever killed this unfortunate woman. I imagine with an occupation like hers it is a natural hazard."

Pitt waited to allow his anger to subside, to make some remark that would crush the unthinking arrogance of the man and make him see Ada McKinley, and the women like her, as he did himself: not beautiful, not witty or innocent, but at least as human as anyone else. She had been as capable of hope or pain as his own daughter sitting in the dining room in her gorgeous muslin dress with its lace embroidery, her life before her in which she would probably never know hunger or physical fear, and her worst social sin wearing the same gown as her hostess or laughing at the wrong joke.

But there was nothing he could say that would hold any meaning. In all the ways they could understand, Ada McKinley was exactly what FitzJames thought she was.

"Of course," he said coldly. "But police do not have the luxury of choosing whose murder they will investigate or where that investigation will lead them." He allowed it to be as double-edged as he intended, even if neither man grasped it.

"Naturally," FitzJames agreed with a frown. The conversation seemed to have become pointless. It was obvious from his expression. He turned to Finlay. "When did you last see this badge, if you can recollect?"

Finlay looked wretched. His extreme discomfort could be attributed to half a dozen possible reasons: his distress at being drawn into the murder of a woman of the streets, his embarrassment at having been so drunk he could not account for his movements last evening, fear at now being in a position where he was going to have to name his friends and draw them in also. Perhaps it was even the suspicion that one or several of them might actually be involved. Or simply anticipation of what his father would say to him once Pitt had gone.

"I . . . really . . . don't know." He faced Pitt squarely, but still sitting with his arms folded across his upper stomach. Perhaps it hurt after his indulgence. Certainly the skin around his eyes was puffy and Pitt could well believe his head ached. "It's years ago. I'm sure of that," he said unwaveringly. "Five at least." He avoided his father's cold gaze. "I lost it then. I doubt any of my friends had it, unless it was accidental, a jape or something."

Pitt was perfectly sure there was a lie in it somewhere, but when he looked at FitzJames he met a blank wall of denial. There was not a shadow or flicker of surprise in him. He had expected this answer as if he had known the precise words. Was it rehearsed?

"The names of the other members?" Pitt asked wearily. Now his lack of sleep was catching up with him, his inner tiredness from too much misery, dark streets and alleys which smelled of refuse and hopelessness. "I require their names, Mr. FitzJames. Someone had that badge last night and left it under the body of a woman he murdered."

FitzJames winced with distaste, but he did not move, except his fingers tightened a fraction on the arm of his chair.

Finlay still looked very pale, and white around the mouth, as if he might be sick.

In the corner a standing clock ticked steadily with a heavy, reso-nant tone. Outside the footsteps of a maid clicked softly across the parquet floor.

"There were only four of us," Finlay said at last. "Norbert Helli-well, Mortimer Thirlstone, Jago Jones and myself. I can give you Helliwell's last address, and Thirlstone's. I have no idea where Jones is. I haven't seen or heard of him in years. Someone said he'd taken up the church, but they were probably joking. Jago was a damn good fellow, as much fun as anyone. More likely gone abroad to America, maybe. He's the sort of chap who might go west—Texas or the Bar-bary Coast." He tried to laugh, and failed.

"If you would write the other two addresses for me," Pitt requested.

"I don't suppose they can help you!"

"Perhaps not, but it will be somewhere to start." Pitt smiled. "The man was seen, you know? By at least two witnesses."

He had expected to rattle Finlay, perhaps even to break him. He failed utterly.

Finlay's eyes widened. "Was he? Then you know it wasn't me, thank God! Not that I know such a woman," he added hastily. It was a lie, and not even a good one. This time he colored and seemed about to withdraw it.

It was FitzJames whose face tightened with a lightning flash of uncharacteristic fear, gone again the instant it had come. His look at Pitt now was one of anger, perhaps because he thought Pitt might have recognized it. After all, he had caused it, and that he would not forgive.

"I doubt it was Helliwell or Thirlstone either," Finlay went on to cover the silence. "But if you insist, then you'll discover that. Jago Jones I can't answer for, because you might find him a great deal harder to trace. I don't even know if he has family. One doesn't always ask these things, if it isn't obvious. Kinder not to, if a fellow comes from nowhere in particular, as he seemed to."

There was not a great deal more Pitt could do. He considered asking to see the coat Finlay had worn yesterday evening, but unless he destroyed it, the valet could always answer that later.

"There is the matter of a cuff link," he said finally. "A rather distinctive one, dropped down the back of a chair in the woman's room. It has 'F.F.J.' engraved on it, and is hallmarked. Not the sort of thing I think her average customers would possess."

FitzJames went white, his knuckles shone where he gripped the chair arms. He swallowed with some difficulty. His throat seemed to have contracted as if his collar choked him.

Finlay, on the other hand, was totally at a loss. His handsome, blurred face showed nothing but confusion.

"I used to have a pair like that . . ." he mumbled. "My sister gave them to me. I lost one . . . but years ago. Never liked to tell her. Clumsy of me. Felt a fool, because I knew they were expensive. Always meant to get another one made, so she wouldn't know."

"How did it get in Ada McKinley's chair, Mr. FitzJames?" Pitt said with a faint smile.

"God only knows," Finlay answered. "As I said, I don't frequent places like that! I've never heard of her! She is the woman who was killed, I presume?"

FitzJames's face was dark with anger and contempt.

"For God's sake, boy, don't be such a damn fool. Of course you've used women like that in your time!" He turned to Pitt. "But that cuff link could have been there for years! You can't connect it to last night or anything that happened then. Go and look for these other young men. See if you can find out something about the damned woman. She was probably killed in a quarrel over money, or by a rival in her trade. That's where your job is." He rose to his feet, his joints momentarily stiff, as if he had been constricting himself with such a tension of muscles his bones had locked. "We will write these addresses for you. Now I must be about my own affairs. I am overdue in the City. Good day to you, sir." And he walked out without looking behind him, leaving Pitt alone with Finlay.

Finlay hesitated awkwardly. He was embarrassed by having not only been caught in a lie but reprimanded for it in front of Pitt. It was stupid and he had no excuse. It was an instinctive act of cowardice, the instant will to deny, to escape, not something for which any man could be proud. Now he was about to give his friends' names and addresses to Pitt, and that also was something he could not avoid, and yet it sat ill with him. It would have been so much more honorable, more gentlemanly, to have been able to refuse.

"I've no idea where Jago Jones is," he said with satisfaction. "Haven't seen him for years. He could be anywhere. He was always a bit of an odd one."

"I daresay someone will know," Pitt replied with a bleak smile. "Army records, or the Foreign Office, perhaps."

Finlay stared at him, his eyes wide. "Yes, possibly."

"Mr. Helliwell?" Pitt pressed.

"Oh . . . yes. Taviton Street. Number seventeen I think, or fifteen."

"Thank you." Pitt took out his notebook and pencil and wrote it down. "And Mr. Thirlstone?"

"Cromer Street. That's off the Grey's Inn Road."

"Number?"

"Forty-something. Can't recall what. Sorry."

Pitt wrote that as well. "Thank you."

Finlay swallowed. "But they won't have had anything to do with this, you know. I don't know where that damned badge came from, but . . . but I'll swear it wasn't anything to do with them. It was a damn stupid club in the first place. A young man's idea of a devil-ish good time, but all very silly, really. No harm in it, just . . . oh . . ." He shrugged rather exaggeratedly. "A little too much to drink, gam-bling rather more than we could afford to lose, drinking too much . . . that sort of thing. Immature . . . I suppose. But basically quite de-cent fellows."

"I expect so," Pitt agreed halfheartedly. A lot of people one pre-sumed decent had darker, more callous sides.

"As I said, the badge could have gone missing years ago," Finlay went on, frowning, staring at Pitt with a degree of urgency. "I can't remember when I last saw mine. God knows."

"Yes sir," Pitt said noncommittally. "Thank you for the ad-dresses." And he bade him good-bye and took his leave, shown out by the still-genial butler.

Norbert Helliwell was not at home. He had gone riding in the Park early, so his butler informed Pitt, and after a large breakfast had de-cided to spend the morning at his club. That was the Regency Club, in Albemarle Street, although the butler expressed his doubt—not in his words, but in his expression—that it would be acceptable for Pitt to call upon him there.

Pitt thanked him and took a cab south, and then west towards Piccadilly. The more he thought about it, the less did he feel he would be likely to learn anything of use from Norbert Helliwell. There were aspects of his visit to the FitzJames house which had surprised him. He had expected evasion, anger, possibly embarrassment. He was not unprepared to find Augustus FitzJames a domineering man, willing to defend his son, guilty or innocent.

He sat back in the hansom as it bowled along the busy streets, passing all manner of other carriages in the mid-morning. It was now pleasantly warm, the breeze balmy. Ladies of fashion were taking the air, seeing and being seen. There was more than one open landau and several gigs. A brewer's dray lumbered past, great shaggy horses gleaming in the sun, brasses winking, coats satin smooth. Businessmen about their affairs strode along the pavements, faces intent, raising their tall hats now and again as they passed an acquaintance.

It was Finlay FitzJames who confused Pitt. He was lying, of that he had no doubt at all, but not as he had expected him to lie. Of course he had known women like Ada McKinley. To deny it was merely a reflex reaction, a self-defense in front of a stranger. And he was profoundly afraid, but not of the things he should have been. The mention of Ada's death produced no reaction in him at all, except the shallow regret such a thing might have evoked in any such young man. Could it really be that he regarded her as barely human, and the act of killing her produced no shame at all, not even the fear that he could in any way be brought to pay for it?

Was the use of a prostitute a little like riding the hounds, a gentlemanly sport—the chase was all, the kill merely the natural outcome? And perhaps foxes were vermin anyway?

His thoughts were interrupted by his arrival at the entrance of the Regency Club. He alighted, paid the cabby and crossed the pavement to go up the steps.

"Are you a member, sir?" the doorman enquired. His face was expressionless, but the overemphasized enquiry in his voice made it profoundly plain that he knew Pitt was not.

"No," Pitt replied, forcing himself to smile. "I require to speak to one of your members about a matter of delicacy and extreme unpleasantness. Perhaps you would convey that message to him and then find some place where I may do it in private, and avoid the embarrassment for him of approaching him in public?"

The doorman regarded him as if he were a blackmailer.

Pitt kept his smile. "I am from the police," he added. "The Bow Street Station."

"I see." The doorman did not see at all. Pitt was not what he expected of such persons.

"If you please?" Pitt said a trifle more sharply. "My business is with Mr. Norbert Helliwell. His butler informed me he was here."

"Yes sir." The doorman could see no other way of dealing with a deplorable situation which was threatening to get completely out of hand. He instructed the steward to show Pitt to a small side room, possibly kept for such needs. He could not be left in the hallway where he might speak to other members and make the matter even worse. The steward did so, then turned on his heel and went to inform Helliwell of his visitor.

Norbert Helliwell was in his early thirties, of very ordinary appearance. He could have been mistaken for any young man of good family and comfortable means.

"Good morning, sir." He came in and closed the door. "Prebble tells me there has been some unpleasantness with which you think I can help you. Do sit down." He waved directly to one of the chairs, and sat comfortably in the one opposite it. "What is it?"

Pitt had never seen a man look less guilty.

"I can give you ten minutes," Helliwell went on magnanimously.

"Then I am afraid I have to meet my wife and mother-in-law. They've been shopping. The ladies like to do that, you know?" He shrugged. "No, perhaps you don't. But they can get very upset if left waiting. Not proper at all. Gets oneself misunderstood. Sure you can see that. Only two sorts of women, what." He smiled. "At least waiting around the streets, there are. Remember that perfectly awful business of that perfectly respectable woman . . . arrested out shopping!" There was derision in his voice, and indeed the case did not reflect well on the police.

"Then I shall come immediately to the point," Pitt replied, aware that he was gaining an opinion of this man too rapidly. He was allowing the man's assumptions to make him also prejudge. "Were you once a member of a young gentlemen's association known as the Hellfire Club?"

Helliwell was startled, but there was no alarm in his bland, self-confident face.

"A long time ago. Why? Has someone resurrected it?" He shrugged very slightly. "Not very original, I'm afraid. Rather obvious sort of name, when one thinks of it. Speaks of Regency dandies a bit, don't you think?" He leaned back and crossed his legs. "Much more fashionable to be an aesthete now, if you have the emotional energy. Personally, I couldn't be bothered to stir up so much passion about art. Too busy with life!" He laughed very slightly.

Was there an edge to his voice, or did Pitt imagine it?

"Used you to have a badge, about so big?" Pitt held up his finger and thumb half an inch apart. "Enamel on gold, with your name engraved on the back?"

"I really don't recall," Helliwell said, meeting his eyes unblushingly. "I suppose we might have. Why? What on earth can it matter now? It was years ago. Haven't met since . . ." He drew in his breath. He was definitely a trifle paler now. "I don't know . . . well before I was married. Six years at least." He smiled again, showing excellent teeth. "Bachelor's sort of thing, you know?"

"So I imagine," Pitt agreed. "Do you still have your badge?" He overlooked Helliwell's uncertainty as to whether there had been one at all.

"No idea." He looked startled and even slightly amused. "Shouldn't think so. Why? Look, you'd better explain what this is all about. So far you haven't said anything remotely urgent or important. You told the doorman it was a matter of unpleasantness. Either come to the point or I shall have to leave you." He took out a heavy gold watch on an equally heavy gold chain and looked at it ostentatiously. "I must go in three minutes anyway."

"A woman was murdered last night, and a Hellfire Club badge was found underneath her body," Pitt replied, watching his eyes, his face.

Helliwell swallowed convulsively, but he did not lose his composure. It was a moment or two before he answered.

"I'm very sorry. But if it is my badge, then I can assure you I had nothing whatever to do with it. I was dining with my father-in-law and went straight home in the carriage. My wife will attest to that, as will my own servants. Who was she?" His voice was growing firmer as he continued. His color was returning. "Was it my badge? The least I can do is to determine where I lost it, or if it was stolen. Although I doubt it will be much use. It could have been years ago."

"No sir, it was not your badge. But . . ."

Helliwell rose to his feet, anger flushing his cheeks. "Then what in the devil are you doing bothering me?" he demanded. "This is outrageous, sir. So whose—" He stopped abruptly, one hand in the air.

"Yes?" Pitt enquired, rising to his feet also. "I'll walk with you. You were going to say . . . ?"

"Whose . . ." Helliwell gulped. "Whose badge was it?" He went a step towards the door.

"I understand there were only four of you," Pitt continued. "Is that correct?"

"Ah ..." Helliwell quite transparently considered lying, and then abandoned it. "Yes . . . yes, that's right. At least in my time! I left, Inspector . . . er . . . Superintendent. More could have joined after . . . of course." He forced a smile.

Pitt went to the door and opened it, holding it for him. "I mustn't delay you from meeting your wife and mother-in-law."

"No. Well . . . sorry I couldn't help." Helliwell went through and continued on across the hallway to the front door, nodding to the doorman.

Pitt followed him, half a step behind. "What can you tell me about the other members in your time?" he asked.

Helliwell went through the door and down the steps.

"Oh . . . nothing much. Decent fellows. All a bit older and wiser now, of course." He dismissed the whole idea. He did not ask again whose badge it had been.

"Mortimer Thirlstone?" Pitt increased his step to keep up with him on the pavement as Helliwell strode out in the sun along Albemarle Street towards Piccadilly, walking so fast he all but bumped into passersby. A landau with three ladies taking the air did not outpace him.

"Haven't seen him in a dog's age," Helliwell said breathlessly. "Really couldn't say how he's doing."

"Finlay FitzJames?"

Helliwell stopped abruptly, causing a gentleman in striped trousers two paces behind him to trip and cannon into him.

"I'm sorry!" the man said, although it was manifestly Helliwell's fault. "I say, sir, do take a little care!"

"What?" Helliwell was startled. He had been unaware of anyone but himself and Pitt. "Oh. In your way? For heaven's sake, go around me!"

The man set his hat straight, glared for a moment, then, swinging his umbrella, proceeded on his way.

"Finlay FitzJames?" Pitt repeated.

"You'll have to speak to him yourself," Helliwell said, swallowing again. "I daresay he lost his badge years ago. No need to keep it. Now you really must excuse me. I can see my family on the corner there." He swung his arm to where a carriage was indeed slowing up and a very well dressed young woman was looking towards them. An older couple of immense dignity sat well back, comfortably, in the seat beside her, the gentleman facing backwards, the ladies forwards.

Pitt inclined his head towards them and they nodded in reply.

Helliwell was left with no alternative but either to take Pitt forward and introduce him or to dismiss him with what could only be construed as the utmost rudeness, which he would then have had to explain.

Helliwell swore under his breath and made his decision. He strode forward, a fixed smile on his face, his voice artificially hearty.

"My dear Adeline. Mama-in-law, Papa-in-law. What an excellent day. May I introduce Mr. Pitt. We met by chance in my club. A few acquaintances in common—in the past, not the present. Mr. Pitt, my wife and my parents-in-law, Mr. and Mrs. Joseph Alcott."

Introductions performed, Helliwell made as if to climb into the carriage.

"And Mr. Jago Jones?" Pitt said cheerfully. "Can you tell me where I might be able to find him?"

"Not the slightest idea," Helliwell said instantly. "Sorry, old chap. Haven't seen him in years. A trifle eccentric. An acquaintance of chance rather than any common bond, you understand? Can't help you at all." He put his hand onto the carriage door.

"And Mr. Thirlstone," Pitt pressed. "Was he an acquaintance of chance also?"

Before Helliwell could answer, his wife leaned forward, looking first at her husband, then at Pitt.

"Do you mean Mortimer Thirlstone, sir? No, not chance at all. We know him quite well. Indeed, wasn't he at Lady Woodville's soirée the other evening? He was with Violet Kirk, I remember distinctly. There is some talk that they may become betrothed quite soon. I know that, because she told me so herself."

"You shouldn't speak of it, my dear," Helliwell said huskily, his face reddening. "Not until it is announced. It could cause profound embarrassment. What if it were not true, after all?" He opened the door and was about to climb in when his wife spoke across him again, still addressing Pitt. She had a charming face and the most beautiful brown hair.

"Did I hear you ask for the whereabouts of Mr. Jago Jones?" Adeline asked Pitt.

"Yes, ma'am," Pitt said quickly. "Are you acquainted with him?"

"No, but I'm sure Miss Tallulah FitzJames could tell you. He used to be a close friend of her brother, Finlay, whom we all know." She glanced at Helliwell, whose answering look should have frozen her. She kept her sunny smile on Pitt. "I am sure if you were to ask her, and explain to her how important it is to you, she would be able to help. She is a delightful creature, and most kind."

"She is a flighty young woman with whom I should rather you did not associate," Mr. Alcott said suddenly. "You are too generous in your opinions, my dear."

"You should listen a little more to what people say," Mrs. Alcott added. "Then you would know that her reputation is becoming less attractive as she grows older and does not marry. I am sure she must have had offers." She made a delicate gesture with one gloved hand. "Her father has money, her mother has breeding, and the girl herself is certainly handsome enough, in her way. If she does not marry soon, people will begin to speculate as to why not."

"I agree," Helliwell said hastily. "Far better you are no more than civil to her, if you should happen to meet, which is unlikely. She moves with a set you would have nothing to do with. I think 'flighty' is a very kind word, Mama-in-law. I should have chosen one less flattering." His tone was final. He turned to Pitt. "Delightful to have met you, sir." He swung up into the carriage and closed the door. "Good day to you." And he signaled the driver to proceed, leaving Pitt standing on the footpath in the sun.

Superficially, Mortimer Thirlstone was a vastly different man. He was tall and lean and affected a manner and dress of an artist. His long hair was parted in the center. He wore a soft silk shirt and widely flowing cravat tied meticulously, and a casual jacket. But he had the same easy air of confidence as Helliwell, as if he knew he looked well and was perfectly comfortable that his appearance would continue to earn him the courtesy to which he was accustomed.

He stood in the center of the pathway that wound gently through Regents Park towards the Botanical Gardens. He stared upwards into the hazy sunshine with a smile on his face. It had taken Pitt since mid-morning to find him, and only by dint of persistent enquiry had he succeeded.

"Mr. Thirlstone?" he enquired, although he was already certain of his identity.

"Indeed, sir," Thirlstone answered without lowering his gaze. "Is it not a magnificent afternoon? Can you smell the myriad aromas of the flowers, indigenous and exotic, which lie just beyond our gaze? What a marvelous thing is nature. We appreciate it far too little. She has given us senses, and what do we do? Largely ignore them, sir, largely ignore them. What can I do for you, apart from bringing you to mind of your olfactory perceptions?"

"Some years ago I believe you used to belong to an organization known as the Hellfire Club . . ." Pitt began.

"Organization." Thirlstone lowered his head, then looked at Pitt with amusement. "Hardly, sir. Organized it never was! I abhor organization. It is the antithesis of pleasure and creativity. It is man's puny attempt to lay his mark on a universe he cannot begin to comprehend. It is pathetic." A bumblebee meandered lazily by. He watched it with delight. "Nature organizes," he continued. "We merely watch in profound ignorance, and usually fear. Awe, sir, that is proper. Fear is stultifying. The difference is the span of all pure feeling. What about it?"

Pitt was lost.

"The Hellfire Club, sir!" Thirlstone explained. "What about it? Folly of youth. Personally, I have moved on, woken to the better pursuits of life. Did you want to join?" He shrugged, his face lifted again to the sun. "I cannot help you. Start one of your own. Don't wait for others. Begin anew! Try some of the gambling clubs, horse races, music halls, houses of ill repute and so on. You'll find like-minded men. Pick and choose as you will."

"That was the sort of place you frequented?" Pitt tried very hard to make his voice sound interested and yet not naive. He knew he failed. It was an impossible task.

Thirlstone lowered his gaze and stared at him as if he were some rare plant he had just observed.

"What else would you expect, sir? Horticulture? Poetry? If your taste is not to drinking, gambling, fine horses and willing women, what do you want with a Hellfire Club?"

The charade had been brief, and it was over.

"The names of the original members, a summary of their present whereabouts," Pitt replied, still a trifle mendaciously.

Thirlstone's eyes widened in amazement.

"My dear fellow, whatever for? It disbanded, or should I say dissolved of its own accord, years ago. It can be no possible use to you now."

A butterfly drifted past them, fluttering in the sun. Far in the distance a dog barked.

"A Hellfire Club badge was found under the body of a murdered woman last night," Pitt replied.

"Good God! How extraordinary!" Thirlstone's black eyebrows shot up, wrinkling his brow dramatically. "Why does it concern you?

Are you related to her? I'm fearfully sorry." He extended his hand in a gesture of sympathy.

"No. No I'm not," Pitt said with some awkwardness.

"Then . . . you're not police, are you? You don't look like police. You are!" He seemed almost amused, as if the fact had some esoteric humor of its own. "How unutterably squalid. What in heaven's name do you want from me? I know nothing about it. Who was she?"

"Her name was Ada McKinley. She was a prostitute."

Thirlstone's face showed a trace of pity, something lacking in Finlay FitzJames and Helliwell. Then suddenly he was absolutely sober. The slight air of banter vanished completely. Under his superficial manner his concentration was total. His eyes were narrowed, his body motionless, so that suddenly Pitt was aware of the breeze and the slight stirring of the flowers.

"There were only four of us, Superintendent, and each badge had a name on it." Thirlstone's voice was so level it was unnatural. "Are you saying it was my badge you found?"

"No sir."

Thirlstone's body relaxed and he could not keep a flood of relief from his face.

"I'm glad. I haven't seen it for years." He swallowed. "But one never knows . . ." He regarded Pitt with a mixture of curiosity and apprehension. "Whose was it? I . . . I cannot believe any of us would be so foolish as to . . ." He did not complete his sentence, but his meaning hung in the air, unmistakably.

A young couple walked past a dozen yards away, their footsteps crunching on the gravel.

"I have already spoken to Mr. FitzJames and Mr. Helliwell," Pitt said almost casually. "But I have not been able to find Jago Jones."

"It would hardly be Jago!" This time there was complete conviction in Thirlstone's voice.

"Why not?"

"My dear fellow, if you knew Jago you wouldn't need to ask."

"I don't know him. Why not?"

"Oh . . ." Thirlstone shrugged, spreading his hands helplessly. "Perhaps I don't know as much as I imagine. It's your job to find out, thank God, not mine."

"Where would I find Mr. Jones?" Pitt did not expect an answer.

He did not receive one, only a shrug and a bemused look.

"No idea, I'm afraid. None whatsoever. In the streets. In the slums. That's the last thing I remember hearing him say, but I have no notion if he meant it." Thirlstone lifted his face to the sun again, and Pitt was effectively dismissed.

He walked back past an army officer on leave, splendidly dressed in red coat and immaculate trousers, buttons gleaming, to the excitement of several young ladies in pastel dresses all muslin and lace, and the envy of a nursemaid in a white starched apron wheeling a perambulator. The noise of a barrel organ drifted from somewhere beyond the trees.

At four o'clock Pitt had eaten a late luncheon, but he was so tired his eyes felt gritty and his head ached from lack of sleep. He had no real belief that Jago Jones might somehow have dropped Finlay Fitz-James's belongings in Pentecost Alley, but he must prove it, were it only for elimination. It was not impossible.

He returned to Devonshire Street and asked the genial butler if he could speak to Miss Tallulah FitzJames. He knew it was a time of day when she might quite easily be at home, before dressing for the evening and going out to dine and be entertained.

She came into the morning room in a swirl of soft fabric of so pale a pink it was almost white, a blush pink rose at her waist, long satin ribbons hanging. Had her face been rounder, less full of intelligence and will, the effect would have been cloyingly innocent. As it was, it presented a challenging contrast, and from the way she stopped just inside the door and leaned against the knob, Pitt was quite certain she knew it.

"Well!" she said in surprise. "You back again? I heard about that poor creature's death, but you can't possibly imagine Finlay could have anything to do with it? It's too preposterous. I mean, why should he? Mama would like to think he never goes near such places, but then one's parents tend to be rather like the very best carriage horses, don't they? Work excellently together as long as the harness lasts, look very good in town, are the admiration of one's friends, and can't see a thing except what's directly in front of them! We blinker ours, to keep their attention from straying or have them take fright at things on the footpath."

Pitt smiled in spite of himself.

"Actually it was the address of Mr. Jago Jones I came for." He saw her body stiffen under its silk and muslin gown and her slim shoulders set rigid. He could imagine her hands clenched at the doorknob behind her. Very slowly she straightened up and came towards him.

"Why? Do you think Jago did it? You can't know how ridiculous that is, but I assure you, I'd sooner suspect the Prince of Wales. Come to think of it—much sooner."

"You have a very high regard for Mr. Jones?" Pitt said with surprise.

"Not . . . especially." She turned away and the sunlight caught her unusual profile—nose a little too big, mouth wide and full of laughter and emotion, dark eyes bright. "He's . . . he's rather proper, actually. Something of a bore." She still looked studiously out of the window at the sun on the leaves beyond. "But he couldn't do any-thing like that," she went on. "He's about Finlay's age, and when Finlay was in his twenties and I was about sixteen, Jago was fun. He could tell the best jokes, because he could make his face look like all the different characters, and his voice too." She shrugged elaborately, as if it could be of no possible interest to her. "But he's religious now. All good works and saving souls." She swung around to look at Pitt. "Why does the Church make people such crashing bores?"

"The Church?" Pitt did not hide his surprise.

"Didn't you know? No, I suppose you didn't. Finlay was stupid, pretending he didn't know the Hellfire Club anymore. I suppose it might be his idea of protecting them. It must be Norbert Helliwell or Mortimer Thirlstone, if it's any of them." She shook her head slightly. "It wouldn't be Jago, and of course it wasn't Finlay. Most likely the woman stole it, and then someone else killed her. It seems fairly obvious, doesn't it?" Her eyes challenged him. "Why would one of the other members have Finlay's badge, anyway? If they wanted one, they had their own."

"Not on purpose," Pitt explained. "But the engraving on the back is very small and very fine. It would be easy enough to pick up someone else's in error."

"Oh." She breathed in deeply, the sheer silk draped across her shoulders and bosom rising, the light gleaming in it. "Yes, of course. I hadn't thought of that."

"Where would I find Mr. Jones?"

"Saint Mary's Church, Whitechapel."

Pitt drew in his breath sharply. He knew St. Mary's. It was a few hundred yards from Pentecost Alley. Old Montague Street ran parallel to the Whitechapel Road before it turned into Mile End.

"I see. Thank you, Miss FitzJames."

"Why do you look like that? Saint Mary's means something to you, I can see it in your face. You know it!"

There was no point in lying to her.

"The woman was killed in an alley off Old Montague Street."

"Is that close?" She was too anxious to be offended that he might think her familiar with such an area.

"Yes."

"Oh." She turned away again, presenting a silk-swathed shoulder

to him. "Well, you won't find Jago Jones involved. He couldn't be after a woman like that except to save her soul." There was a sudden
hurt in her voice, almost bitterness. "I presume she wasn't bored to
death?"

"No, Miss FitzJames, she was strangled."

She winced. "If I could help you, I would," she said quietly. "But
I really don't know anything."

"You've given me Mr. Jones's address, which I appreciate. Thank
you for seeing me at what must be an inconvenient time. Good
evening."

She did not reply, but stood in the middle of the floor staring at
him as he went to the door and let himself out.

It took him until after six to get back to Whitechapel and the church
of St. Mary's. When he did, the verger told him the vicar was out,
somewhere down Coke Street way, helping the sick. If Pitt did not
find him there, he could go in the other direction and try Chicksand
Street.

The lowering sun was hidden by the high, grimy tenement
houses, but the pavements still gave back the claustrophobic heat
and the sour smells of the day. The gutters ran sluggish trickles of
waste. This was Whitechapel, where two years ago, about this season, a madman had murdered and ripped open five women, leaving
their bleeding bodies in the street. No one had ever found him. He
had disappeared as completely as if hell had opened up and swallowed him back.

Yet walking towards Coke Street Pitt could see women standing
in doorways and alleyway entrances with that peculiar air of readi-
ness that marked them as prostitutes. It was a directness in their eyes,
an angle to the hips quite different from the weary dejection of
women at the end of a day's labor in a sweatshop or factory, or bringing wet laundry in and out of boilers, twisting the dolly, and heaving
and wringing the sheets.

Were they afraid, but so hungry they did not care? Or had they already forgotten the Ripper and the terror of him which had paralyzed London?

A young woman approached him, her wide brown eyes looking him up and down, her skin still country fresh. He felt suddenly sick and angry for her that she was reduced to this, whether by circumstances beyond her or immorality within. He controlled himself with an effort.

"I'm looking for the Reverend Jones," he said grimly. "Have you seen him?"

Her face settled in resignation. "Yeah, 'e's 'round the corner." She jerked her hand to indicate the direction. "Want your soul saved too, do you? Good luck to yer—I can earn me own dinner, and cheaper at the price." And with that he lost her attention and she sauntered off towards the Whitechapel Road, and some likely custom.

Pitt did not know what he expected of Jago Jones—perhaps some dilettante priest, seeking a dramatic gesture; or a younger son unsuited for the military who had chosen the Church instead. This might be a first step towards a major preferment in the future.

Whatever dim prejudgment had been in his mind, he was unprepared for the man he met in Coke Street, ladling hot, thick soup out of a churn into tin mugs for a crowd of skinny children, several of them dancing from one foot to the other in anticipation.

Jago Jones was dressed in shapeless black clothes. No flash of white clerical collar was visible, but such things were immaterial anyway. His face was too arresting for a uniform of any sort to matter. He was lean to the point of being almost gaunt. His thick hair swept back above dark brows and eyes of extraordinary intensity. His nose was strong, high-bridged; his cheekbones accentuated by the deep lines around his mouth. It was the face of a man burning with his own emotions, and so certain of his course that nothing would deflect him. He looked across at Pitt with interest.

"Jago Jones?" Pitt asked, although he had no doubt.

"Yes. What can I do for you?" He did not stop ladling the soup and passing the full tin mugs to the children. "Are you hungry?" It was an offer, but not really an enquiry. One glance at Pitt's clothes, not only their quality but their cleanliness and the fact that they were in good repair, placed him beyond the kind of need Jones's parishioners knew.

"Thank you," Pitt said. "But it would be better used as it is."

Jago smiled and continued. He was nearly at the bottom of his supply and the end of his queue. "Then what is it you need me for?"

"My name is Thomas Pitt." Then the minute he had said it he wondered why he had introduced himself that way, as if it were a friendship he was expecting, not a policeman on duty interviewing a witness, possibly a suspect.

"How do you do?" Jago Jones bowed very slightly. "Jago Jones. Reverend, at least in spirit, if not in manner. You don't belong here. What brings you?"

"The murder of Ada McKinley in Pentecost Alley last night," Pitt replied, watching his face.

Jago sighed and dispensed the last of the soup to a grateful urchin. The boy's large eyes were on Pitt's face, but hunger was more pressing than curiosity, even though he could sense a rozzer when he saw one.

"I was afraid so," Jago said sadly, seeing the urchin off. "Poor creature. It's a hard occupation, destructive of both body and soul, although not usually as quickly or as violently as this. And it seems on this occasion, at least, as if it were someone else's soul in greater jeopardy than hers. She was not a bad woman. A little greedy at times, but she had courage, and laughter, and a kind of loyalty to her own. I'll see she has a decent burial."

"You'll bury her from Saint Mary's?" Pitt said with surprise.

Jago's face hardened. "If you object to that, Mr. Pitt, I suggest you take it up with God. He will decide who can be forgiven their faults and weaknesses and who cannot. It is not your prerogative, and I know it is not mine."

Pitt smiled quite honestly. "For which I am profoundly grateful," he said. "But you are unusual, Mr. Jones. I hope your parishioners will not cause you difficulty. But perhaps they are too close to the questionable lines of survival and morality to judge one another."

Jago snorted and made no comment, but his anger softened and he released the tension in his body as he put away the ladle and the soup container into the handcart behind him. Half a dozen urchins, mugs in hand, were creeping back to stand on the corner staring. The word had gone out there was a rozzer asking questions. Information was precious.

"Did you come to ask me about Ada?" Jago said after a moment or two. "I don't know what I can tell you that would be of use. It was probably some customer whose own inner devils broke from their usual control and temporarily overcame him. Many of us deal badly with our pain or our need to feel as if we are in control of the world, even if we cannot control ourselves."

Pitt was taken aback, not by the remark, but by the fierceness with which it had been made. There was a depth of feeling behind it, a perception, as if he were not angry with such a man for the senseless moment's outrage but from a deep thought which had lain within him a long time. Was it perhaps a self-examination? The idea was suddenly and violently repugnant to Pitt, but he could not avoid it.

"It could have been," he said quietly.

Jago was still looking at him, his eyes steady.

"Is that what you're following?"

"It seems the most likely."

"But not the only possibility?" Jago leaned against the cart. "Why are you telling me this, Mr. Pitt? All I can tell you about Ada is what you probably already guess. She was an ordinary prostitute, like a hundred thousand others in London. When girls are thrown out of domestic work, or unfit for it in the first place, can't take the sweatshops and match factories, or don't want to, then they sell the only thing they've got, their bodies." His eyes did not waver from Pitt's. "It's a sin to me, a crime to you: but to them it's survival. I don't know whose fault this is, and frankly I'm too close to it to care. All I see is individual women battling for the next meal, this week's roof, and not to get beaten by their customers or their pimps, or slashed by a rival from another patch, hope to God they can put off the time they get some disease. They'll probably die young and they know it. Society despises them, half the time they despise themselves. Ada was just one more."

A woman walked past with a bag of laundry on her hip.

"Did you know her personally?" Pitt moved over and leaned on his elbow, resting his weight on the other end of the barrow. He was appallingly tired. He should have accepted the soup.

"Yes." Jago gave a tight smile. "But I'm not privy to her client list. Most of them are casual anyway. The one you're looking for could be from anywhere. Occasionally she'd go to the West End. It's not so far. She was handsome. She could have picked up someone from Piccadilly, or the Haymarket. Or for that matter it could be a sailor from the Port of London, passing through."

"Thank you!" Pitt said tartly. It was time he said what he had really come for. The longer he evaded it, the harder it would be. "Actually, I came to you because you used to belong to a gentleman's association called the Hellfire Club. . . ."

Underneath his shapeless jacket Jago was rigid. His face in the waning light was curiously stiff.

"That was a long time ago," he said quietly. "And not something of which I am proud. What has it to do with Ada's death? The club disbanded six or seven years back. Ada wasn't even here then."

"When did she come?"

"About five years ago. Why?"

"I don't think it really makes any difference," Pitt confessed. "I think it is exactly as you say . . . a man whose violence and need is his own, and has nothing to do with her, except that she was the one to provoke it. Or perhaps she was merely there at the wrong time, and it would have happened to whoever the woman was. It might have been her face, her hair, a gesture, a tone in her voice that jarred loose some memory in him, and he lost control of the hatred there was inside him, and destroyed her."

"Fear," Jago said, his mouth tightening. "Fear of failure, fear of not being what you want, what other people want." He saw Pitt's face and thought he read something in it, or perhaps he expected to. "I don't mean a simple fear of impotence. I mean a spiritual fear of being weak, to the very soul, the fear which makes you hate, because you are too self-obsessed to love, too consumed by rage that you are not what you wished, that the road is harder, the price tougher than you thought."

Pitt said nothing. Ideas raced through his mind as to how much Jago Jones was speaking of himself, his demands and expectations of his role as priest. Had he needed a woman, and used a prostitute because all decent women were closed to him in his chosen role? Had she then mocked him in her own disillusion? He could hardly be the vehicle of God to her when she had seen his fall from his self-imposed virtue.

Was this strange confrontation a kind of admission of guilt?

"We found a Hellfire Club badge under her body," he said in the pool of silence in the street. Noises of wheels, horses and a man shouting from beyond the crossroads sounded remote, in another existence.

"Not mine," Jago said carefully. "I threw mine in the river years ago. Why have you come to me, Mr. Pitt? I don't know anything about it. If I did, I should have come to you. You would not have needed to look for me."

Pitt was not sure if he would or not. Jago Jones had the face of a man who followed his own conscience, whatever the law, and whatever the cost. Had it been one of his parishioners, confessing in terror or remorse, he doubted Jago Jones would have come with it to Bow Street, or anywhere else.

"I know it wasn't yours," he said aloud. "It was Finlay Fitz-James's."

It was too dark to see the color of Jago's face, but the sudden jerk of his head, the haggard look in his eyes and mouth betrayed the emotion which tore at him.

The silence was unbroken, heavy, like the gathering darkness. What horror was filling Jago's mind? The death of a woman he knew made suddenly more vivid? Fear for his erstwhile friend's peril, his embarrassment? Or guilt, because perhaps he had done as Thirlstone had suggested, and accidentally picked up Finlay's badge instead of his own and left it at the scene of the crime?

"You don't protest his innocence, Mr. Jones," Pitt said very quietly. "Does that mean you are not surprised?"

"It . . . it doesn't . . . ." Jago swallowed. "It doesn't mean anything, Mr. Pitt, except that I was grieved. I don't believe Finlay guilty, but I can't offer any explanation that would be of value to you, and certainly not any you won't already have thought of yourself." He shifted his weight a little. "Perhaps Finlay was there at some other time and dropped the badge, although I'm surprised he still wore it, very surprised indeed! Perhaps he even gave it to Ada in . . . in payment? The fact that she had it does not necessarily mean she obtained it that night."

"You are struggling to be loyal to a friend, Mr. Jones," Pitt replied wearily. "Which I respect, but I do not agree. Of course I shall pursue every piece of evidence, and every meaning it could have. If you should think of anything more about Ada McKinley, or anything that happened last night, please let me know. Leave a message at the Bow Street Station."

"Bow Street?" Jago's dark eyebrows rose. "Not Whitechapel?"

"I work from Bow Street. Superintendent Pitt."

"A Bow Street superintendent. Why are you concerned with the murder of a Whitechapel prostitute?" His voice dropped and there was a ripple of fear in it. "Do you fear we have another Ripper?"

Pitt shivered, cold in the center of his stomach.

"No. I was called in because of the evidence implicating Mr. FitzJames."

"It's too slender . . ." Jago swallowed hard again, his eyes on Pitt's face, almost pleading.

"A man answering his description was seen, by two witnesses, at exactly the right time, and with Ada."

Jago looked as if Pitt had struck him.

"Oh, God!" he sighed—a prayer, not a blasphemy.

"Reverend Jones, do you know something which you should tell me?"

"No." The word came from a dry throat, stiff lips.

Pitt wanted to believe him, and could not. The honesty which had been between them had vanished like the yellow in the sky over the rooftops. The lamplighter had passed unnoticed. The gas-lit moons made bright intervals along the way back towards the Whitechapel Road and the route home.

"Can I help you with the cart?" Pitt said practically.

"No . . . thank you. I'm used to it, and it isn't heavy," Jago refused, moving at last and bending to pick up the handles.

They walked side by side up Coke Street and turned the corner towards St. Mary's. Neither of them spoke again until they reached it and parted, then it was a simple farewell.

———

Pitt arrived home in Bloomsbury tired and unusually depressed. He ate the dinner which Charlotte had kept for him, then afterwards sat in the parlor with the French doors to the garden ajar, the warmth of the day fading rapidly and the smell of cut grass filling the air.

Charlotte sat under the lamp sewing. She had asked him about the case which had taken him out so early and kept him so late. He had told her only that it was a murder in Whitechapel and that the evidence implicated someone of importance and therefore was politically explosive.

He sat watching her now, the light on her hair, which was clean and bright, coiled on her head, shining like mahogany in the highlights, almost black in the shadows. Her skin was smooth, a faint blush in her cheek. She looked comfortable. Her gown was old rose, and became her as much as anything she owned. Her fingers worked, stitching and pulling, threading back into the cloth again, the needle catching silver as it moved. They were only a few miles from Whitechapel as the sparrow flew, yet it was a world so distant it was beyond imagination. Charlotte's world was safe, clean, its values secure; honesty was easy, and chastity hardly a challenge. She was loved, and she could surely never have doubted it. She had no compromises to make, no judgments of value against survival, no weariness of soul, endless doubt and fear and self-disgust.

No wonder she smiled as she sat! What would Jago Jones think of her? Would he find her unendurably self-satisfied—unforgivably comfortable in her ignorance?

Charlotte pulled the needle in and out, watching because she could not work otherwise. She wanted to have something to do with her hands. It was easier. The day had been long. She had woken when Pitt did, and not really gone back to sleep again.

Her sister, Emily, had called in the middle of the morning. She had said little of any importance, but there was a restlessness in her which was uncharacteristic. It was not one of unused energy but rather of seeking something she could not find, or perhaps even name. She was critical, and had taken offense at several remarks which were not meant unkindly. That was unlike her.

Charlotte had wondered if it was the difficulty of having their grandmother resident in the house since their mother had remarried. Grandmama had refused to stay under the same roof with Caroline's new husband. He was an actor, and several years Caroline's junior. The fact that they were extremely happy only added to the offense.

But Emily's dissatisfaction was not particular, and she left without explaining herself.

Now Pitt was sitting brooding silently, his brow furrowed, his mouth pulled down. She knew it was the case which troubled him. His silence had a particular quality she had grown used to over the years. He was sitting crookedly in his chair, one leg crossed over the other. When he was relaxed he put his feet on the fender, whatever the time of the year, and whether the fire was lit or not. On a summer evening like this, were he not absorbed in his thoughts, he would have walked to the end of the lawn, under the apple tree, and stood there breathing in the quiet, scented air. He would have expected her to go with him. If they had talked at all, it would have been of trivia.

Several times she had considered asking him about it, but his expression was closed in, and he had offered nothing. He did not want to speak of it. Perhaps he did not want its ugliness or its threat to intrude into their home. This was the one place where he could be free of it. Or if not totally free, then at least if it were mentioned at all, it would be of his own choosing, and not hers.

She knew he had been to Whitechapel, and she knew what it was like. He could not have forgotten the numerous times when she had seen slum tenements, smelled the stinking gutters, the dark, narrow houses with their generations of filth seeped into the walls, the tired, hungry and anxious people.

But in order to help, one had to keep one's own strength. Agonizing for people accomplished nothing useful. To help the masses one needed laws, and change of heart in those with power. To affect an individual one needed knowledge, and perhaps money, or some appropriate skill. Above all one needed nerve and judgment, one needed all one's own emotional strength.

So she sat quietly and sewed, waiting until Pitt was ready to share with her whatever it was that bothered him, or to deal with it by at least temporarily forgetting and allowing himself to restore his spirit with what was good.

CHAPTER

THREE

Emily Radley, Charlotte's sister, about whom she had been concerned, was indeed dispirited. It was not a specific problem. She had everything she considered necessary to be happy. Indeed, she had more. Her husband was charming, handsome, and treated her with affection. She was unaware of any serious fault in him.

When they had met he had been well-born, living largely on his value as a lively, delightful companion and guest, his exquisite manners and his ready wit. Emily had been fully aware of the risks entailed in falling in love with him. He might prove shallow, spendthrift, even boring after the first novelty had passed. She had done it just the same. She had spent many hours telling herself how foolish she was, and that there was even a high possibility he sought her primarily for the fortune she had inherited from her first husband, the late Lord Ashworth.

She smiled as she thought of George. Memory was very powerful, a strange mixture of sadness, loss, sweetness for the times that had been good, and a deliberate passing over of those which had not.

All her fears had proved groundless. Far from being shallow, Jack had developed a social conscience and a considerable ambition to effect changes in society. He had campaigned for a seat in Parliament, and after his first defeat had returned to battle, and at the second attempt had won. Now he spent a considerable amount of his time, and his emotions, in political endeavor.

It was Emily herself who seemed a little trivial, a little spendthrift.

Edward, her son and George's heir, was in the schoolroom with his tutor, and baby Evangeline was upstairs in the nursery, where the maid was caring for her, seeing to the laundry, the feeding, the changing. Emily herself was largely unnecessary.

It was late in the morning and Jack had long since departed to the City to various engagements before the House of Commons met. Watching him fight for his selection, then campaign, lose, and campaign again, she had gained a respect for him which added very greatly to her happiness. He was consolidating his position with skill.

So why was she standing in the sun in the great withdrawing room in her lovely town house, dressed in lace and coffee-colored tussore, and feeling such a sense of frustration?

Edward was in the schoolroom. Evie was upstairs in the nursery. Jack was in the City, no doubt fighting for reform of some law he believed outdated. Cook would be with the butler preparing luncheon; they would not need to serve dinner tonight. Emily and Jack were due to dine out. She had already asked her maid to prepare her clothes for the occasion. She had a new silk gown of dark forest green trimmed with ivory and pale gold flowers, which complemented her fair skin and hair. She would look beautiful.

She had seen the housekeeper. The accounts were attended to. Her correspondence was up to date. There was nothing to say to the butler.

She wondered what Charlotte was doing. Probably something domestic, cooking or sewing. Since Pitt's promotion she could afford more help, but there was still much she was obliged to attend to herself.

What about Pitt? His world was completely different. He would be investigating a crime, perhaps only theft or forgery, but possibly something much darker. His problems would be urgent, to do with passions, violence, greed. He would be using the skill and imagination he possessed, working until he was exhausted, seeking to unravel the tangle of events and find the truth, to understand the good and the evil, to bring some sort of justice to it, or at least a resolution.

In the past she and Charlotte had helped him. In the pursuit of the Hyde Park Headsman they had contributed a great deal.

She smiled without being aware of it. The sunlight streamed through the long windows onto a bowl of late delphiniums—the second blooming—catching their blue and purple spires. It had taken Jack a little while to forgive her for the risks she had run in that affair. She could hardly blame him. She could have been killed. She had known better than to offer any excuses, just apologies.

If only something would arise in which she and Charlotte could help again. Lately she had hardly even seen Pitt. Since his promotion he seemed to have been involved in cases which concerned more impersonal crimes, crimes whose motives lay outside her world, such as the treason in the Foreign Office just a month or two ago.

"What are we having for luncheon?" a querulous voice demanded from behind her. "You haven't bothered to tell me. In fact, you don't tell me anything! I might as well not be here."

Emily turned around to see the short, black figure of her grandmother standing just inside the doorway from the hall. The old lady had been obliged to move from her own home when Emily's mother had remarried, and since Charlotte had not room for her, and Emily had abundant room and means, there had been no reasonable alternative. It was not an arrangement either of them cared for, Emily because the old lady was extraordinarily ill-tempered, and the old lady because she had determined that she would not, on principle. It was not her own choice.

"Well?" she demanded.

"I don't know what is for luncheon," Emily replied. "I left it to Cook to decide."

"Seems to me you don't do anything around here," the old lady snapped, coming forward into the room, leaning heavily on her cane, banging it down. It was a border-painted wooden floor, and she disapproved of it. Too ornate, she said. Plain wood was quite good enough.

She was dressed entirely in black, a permanent reminder to everyone—in case they should forget—that she was a widow, and should be regarded and sympathized with as such.

"Cook rules your kitchen, housekeeper runs your servants," she said critically. "Butler runs your pantry and cellar. Ladies' maid decides what you'll wear. Tutor teaches your son, nursemaid looks after your daughter. All that done for you, and you still cannot find time to come and talk to me. You are thoroughly spoilt, Emily. Comes of marrying above your station first, and beneath it next. I don't know what the world's coming to."

"I'm sure you don't," Emily agreed. "You never did know much about it. You assumed one half and ignored the other."

The old lady was aghast. She drew herself to her full, but negligible, height.

"What did you say?" Her voice was shrill with indignation.

"If you wish to know what is for luncheon, Grandmama, ring down to the kitchen and ask. If you would care for something different, I expect they can accommodate you."

"Extravagance!" The old lady clicked her teeth disapprovingly. "Eat what's put in front of you, in my day. It's a sin to waste good food." And with that parting shot she turned and stumped out of the room. Her heavy feet echoed on the polished parquet of the hallway. At least this way they had avoided discussing Caroline's latest whereabouts, and the general selfishness of her having remarried and thrown everyone's lives into consequent disarray. Nor had there been another diatribe about actors in general, or Jewish actors in particular, and how they were, if such a thing were possible, socially even more of a disaster than policemen. The only thing good about it, in the old lady's vociferous opinion, was that at least at Caroline's age there would be no children.

No doubt at least one, if not all, of these subjects would arise over the luncheon table.

Emily spent the afternoon writing letters, more for something to do than any necessity, and then went upstairs to spend a little time in the nursery with Evie, and then with Edward. She heard from him of his latest lessons and his elaborate plans to build a model castle like the one the Knights Templar had built in the Holy Land during the Crusades.

Jack came home a little after five. He had been in the City all day, but there was still a spring in his step when he came into the withdrawing room, leaving the door swinging behind him.

"Excellent day," he said enthusiastically, bending to kiss her brow and touch her hair gently. "I think I might really have got old Fothergill on my side. I had luncheon with him today. I took him to that new restaurant in the Strand. More expensive than it was worth, but the decor is gorgeous, and he was suitably impressed." He sat sideways on the arm of one of the chairs, letting his leg swing.

"The thing is," he went on, "he actually listened to me. I was explaining about the importance of non-fee-paying education for the whole population as an investment in the industrial base . . ."

Jack had been fighting to obtain better education for the poor ever since his entry into Parliament. Emily had watched its future wax and wane.

"I'm very pleased." She was pleased, but she found it hard to invest her smile with as much delight as she should have. "Maybe he'll make a difference."

She dressed for the evening with great care, as a matter of self-esteem, and at half past eight was seated at an enormous dinner table between a large military gentleman with very forthright opinions on India, and a merchant banker who firmly believed that women were totally uninterested in anything except fashion, gossip and the theater, so confined his conversation accordingly.

Opposite her was a man of about thirty whose sole preoccupation was the breeding of fine bloodstock, but next to him was a most unusual-looking young woman whose nose was a trifle too long, her mouth a little wide and her expression one of such humor and vitality that Emily found herself staring at her often enough to catch her eye and let her know that they had exactly the same thoughts of exasperation and boredom at the same moment.

Jack was nearer the head of the table, as a matter of political duty, wooing people of influence who might be of further assistance with the education bill. It was important to Emily also, but the only part she could play here was to be decorative and charming, and the idea of doing that indefinitely was wearing very thin.

The dining room was sumptuously decorated in French blue and gold. The long windows were curtained in velvet, displayed in rich folds skirted out over the floor in the approved fashion, to show a wealth of fabric. The table glittered with silver and crystal. So many facets gleamed and glinted, it dazzled the eyes. One could barely see the faces of the people at the farther end for the reflected lights. Diamonds sparked fire around white throats and the luster of pearls shone softly.

Silver on porcelain clicked discreetly beneath the buzz of conversation. Footmen refilled glasses. Course after course came and went: entrées, soup, fish, removes, pudding, dessert, fruits. And then finally the hostess rose and invited the ladies to retire and leave the gentlemen to their port and the more serious discussions of the evening. It was, of course, the purpose for which they had come.

Obediently Emily rose and followed the ladies out in a rustle and swirl of gorgeous colored skirts. On the way she managed to fall in step with the young woman who had sat opposite her at the table.

She glanced sideways and caught her eye as they crossed the hallway and entered the ornate withdrawing room, decorated with portraits of family ancestors posed against unreal rural scenery.

"Isn't it ghastly?" the young woman whispered, raising her fan so her words were concealed from the ladies to their left.

"Fearful!" Emily whispered back. "I have never been more bored in my life. I feel as if I know what everyone is going to say before they say it."

"That is because it is exactly what they said last time!" the young woman replied with a smile. "Oscar Wilde says it is the artist's duty always to be surprising."

"Then it must be the politician's duty always to say and do precisely what is expected of him," Emily returned. "That way no one is ever caught off guard."

"And nothing is ever interesting, or funny! My name is Tallulah FitzJames. I know we haven't been introduced, but we obviously know each other in spirit."

"Emily Radley," Emily replied.

"Oh, is Jack Radley your husband?" There was a spark of appreciation in her eye.

"Yes," Emily acknowledged with satisfaction, then added honestly, "I wouldn't be here otherwise."

They walked over to a sofa just large enough for the two of them to sit side by side and be perfectly polite in including no one else.

"I can't think why I'm here!" Tallulah sighed. "I am with my cousin, Gerald Allenby, because he wanted me to, so he could pay court to Miss . . . I forget the name. Her father's got a huge place up in Yorkshire or somewhere. Glorious in the summer, and like the North Pole in winter."

"I'm here to be decorative and smile at the right people," Emily said ruefully.

Tallulah's eyes brightened. "Are you allowed to glare and make faces at the wrong people?" she said hopefully.

Emily laughed. "Possibly, if I could only be sure who they were. The trouble is one day's wrong people are another day's right ones. And you can't take back a glare."

"No, you can't, can you." Tallulah was suddenly serious. "In fact, you can't take back anything much. People remember, even if you don't."

Emily caught the note of pain underneath the light voice. Without warning, there was reality in the emotion. The rest of the room fell away from Emily's consciousness, the polite chatter, the tinkle of appropriate laughter.

"Some people forget," she said quietly. "It's an art. If you want to go on loving someone, you have to learn it."

"I don't want to go on," Tallulah said with a tight little smile of self-mockery. "I'd give a great deal to know how to stop."

Emily asked the next and obvious question. "Is he married?"

That seemed to Tallulah to be funny, in a bitter way.

Emily did not want to pry, but she sensed that the other woman had a need to share something which obviously hurt her and which perhaps she could not speak of to her family. They might not know . . . or if they did, maybe they disapproved. If he were married, they could hardly do anything else.

"No, he's not married," Tallulah answered. "At least he wasn't the last time I saw him. I don't imagine he'll ever marry. And if he does, it will be someone earnest and beautiful, with innocent eyes and hair which curls naturally, and a permanently sweet disposition."

Emily thought about it for a moment. She did not want to make a clumsy remark, and it was not easy to read through the flippant words the true nature of Tallulah's pain. She did not know whether to be witty in return, or to be noncommittal, or to show that she saw the depth if not the totality of the wound.

Over on the far side of the room a large woman with fair hair and magnolia skin tilted her head back and laughed daintily. The gaslight shone in a riot of beautiful colors, silk skirts spread out like poppy petals, oranges and plums and shot lavenders, a glory of gleam and shade. Beyond the windows the summer evening was barely dark, an afterglow still shooting shreds of apricot between the branches of the trees above the garden wall.

"I don't think I should like to be married to someone with a permanently sweet disposition," Emily said candidly. "I should feel intensely inferior. And I should also never be quite sure if they meant what they said."

Tallulah stared at her long, slender hands resting on her skirt.

"Jago wouldn't feel inferior," she replied. "He's the best man I've ever met."

Emily was at a loss to answer that. Jago, whoever he was, sounded like a bore, and more than a little unreal. Or perhaps that was unjust? It could be only the way Tallulah saw him. But looking sideways at Tallulah's unhappy face, it was hard to believe she would find someone she saw as so good of the slightest interest, except as a curiosity. Even deep in thought, her own face was full of vitality and daring. Her mouth was too wide, full of humor, her nose too strong and yet utterly feminine. Her eyes were lovely, wide and intelligent. It was the face of a rebel, unpredictable, far from wise, perhaps self-indulgent, but always brave.

"Best at what?" Emily asked before she thought clearly of her words.

Tallulah smiled in spite of herself.

"Best at honor, and caring for people, real people," she answered. "And at working all the hours there are, at giving away his goods to feed the poor, at giving his whole life in service. If he sounds boring, or unlikely, that's only because you don't know him."

"Are you sure you do?"

Tallulah looked up. "Oh, yes. He's a parish priest in Whitechapel. I haven't been there, of course. It's the most fearful place.

They say even the smell is enough to turn your stomach. Open middens everywhere. You can taste them in the air. All the people are dirty, and thin, and terribly poor."

Emily thought of her own experiences with poverty, the times she had helped Charlotte or Pitt and seen the reality of hunger: people crowded ten or twelve to a room, sleeping on the floor, always cold, without privacy even for the most intimate functions. She knew far better than Tallulah what they were speaking of. Perhaps this Jago really was good.

"How do you know him?" she said aloud. "He's not exactly your circle. I can't see him at something like this." Her eye strayed to the giggling women, their corseted waists, their flowing skirts, their gleaming white shoulders and necks colored with gems. If anyone here had gone hungry, it would be for vanity's sake. But to be fair, at least in the unmarried ones among them, beauty was survival.

"He used to be," Tallulah responded. She looked at Emily frankly. "You think I'm seeing him through a romantic haze, don't you? That I have no idea what the real person is like . . . that I only see his calling and his professional self." She shook her head. "That's not true. He's the same age as my brother, Finlay, and they used to be friends. Finlay's older than I am. Eight years. But I can remember Jago coming to the house often when I was about sixteen, just before I came out into society. He used to be awfully sweet to me then."

"But he isn't now?"

Tallulah looked at her with bitterness.

"Of course not. He'd be polite if we chanced to meet, naturally. He's polite to everyone. But I can see the contempt in his eyes. The very fact that he speaks at me, through a glass wall of good manners, as if I'm not a real person to him at all, says just how he despises me."

"Why should he despise you? Isn't that pretty intolerant?"

Tallulah's face set into misery again, losing all its brightness and courage.

"Not really. Perhaps 'despise' is too strong a word. He just has no time for me. I spend my life indulging myself. I go from one party to another. I eat wonderful food which I don't work to buy; I don't even cook it myself." She lifted one elegant shoulder. "To be frank, I don't even know where it comes from. I simply order it from the kitchen and it arrives, on the plate ready for me to eat. And when it's finished someone removes it and does whatever they do. Wash it, put it away, I suppose."

She smoothed her hands over the silk of her skirt, her fingertips caressing the soft, bright fabric.

"And I wear gorgeous dresses, which I don't make, and I wouldn't begin to know how to care for," she went on. "I even have a maid to help me put them on and take them off. She sends them to the laundry maid, who washes them, except the best ones, like this, which she will do herself. I think some of them even have to be unpicked to be cleaned properly, I'm not sure."

"Yes, they do," Emily told her. "It's a very long job."

"You see?"

"No. Lots of people live like that. Don't you like it?"

Tallulah's head came up, her mouth pressed into a thin line, her eyes fixed on Emily's.

"Yes, I do. I love it! Of course I love it. Don't you? Don't you want to dine and dance, look beautiful, spend your time in beautiful places, watch plays and laugh with witty people? Don't you want to be outrageous at times, lead fashion, say shocking things and spend time with marvelous people?"

Emily knew exactly what she meant, but she could not help smiling and allowing her eyes to wander to the group of staid and very proper ladies a dozen feet away who were sitting upright—a necessity in whalebone corsets—and discussing in hushed voices the very minor improprieties of an acquaintance.

"Perhaps his idea of marvelous people is not the same as yours?" she suggested.

"Of course it isn't," Tallulah said sharply, although the flash of humor in her face betrayed that she took the point. "I think Oscar Wilde is marvelous. He is simply never, ever a bore, and never speaks down to one, except artistically, which is quite different. And he is sincerely insincere, if you know what I mean?"

"I've no idea," Emily confessed, waiting for an explanation.

"I mean . . ." Tallulah searched for words. "I mean . . . he does not delude himself. There is no pomposity in him. He is so preposterous you know that he is laughing at everything, and yet it all matters intensely. He's . . . he's fun. He never goes around trying to improve other people or making moral judgments, and his gossip is always witty, and entertaining to repeat, and does no harm." She looked around the room. "This is so . . . crashingly tedious. Not one person has said a single thing worth remembering, let alone recounting to anyone else."

Emily was obliged to agree.

"So what is it about Jago that holds you? From what you say, he is as unlike Mr. Wilde as it would be possible to be."

"I know," Tallulah admitted. "But then I like to listen to Oscar Wilde. I wouldn't ever want to marry him—that's quite different."

Perhaps she did not realize what she had said. Emily looked at her and saw the earnestness in her face, the self-mockery lying just beneath it, and realized whether she had intended to speak it aloud or not, it was what she meant.

"I don't know why," Tallulah went on. "I don't think I want to know why."

They were prevented from discussing the matter any further by the arrival of the gentlemen. Jack looked very serious. He came in, deep in conversation with a heavily whiskered man with a ruddy complexion and the scarlet ribbon of an order across his chest. He glanced at Emily, held her eyes, then continued on. That moment was intended to convey that he could not be interrupted, and she understood.

She also understood nearly an hour later when he came over and told her, with much apology, that he was obliged to leave the party early and go to the Home Office with the gentleman of the whiskers, and he would leave the carriage for her to return home when she wished. She should not wait up for him, as he could not say when his business might be concluded. It was just conceivable that it might last all night. He was very sorry indeed.

So it was that twenty minutes later, so bored that it was difficult for her to make sensible answers to trivial questions, she was delighted to see Tallulah FitzJames again.

"I can't bear this anymore," Tallulah said in a whisper. "My cousin is apparently succeeding with Miss Whatever-her-name-is, and I can safely leave him to enjoy his victory." Her tone suggested how little she thought that was worth. "Reggie Howard has invited me to go to a party he knows of in Chelsea. The sort of people we were talking about will be there, artists and poets, people of ideas. They'll discuss all manner of things." Now she was full of enthusiasm. "Some of them have been to Paris and met the writers there. Indeed, I heard that Arthur Symons is just back, a month or two ago, and could tell us of his meeting with the great Verlaine. It has to be immeasurably more interesting than this!"

It was clearly an invitation, and Emily hesitated. She ought simply to excuse herself and take her own carriage home. She had acquitted her duty and it would be acceptable.

But she was weary of doing her duty to those who expected it and were barely aware of her. She was not needed by Jack or her children. The house ran itself; her decisions were merely a matter of form. She was asked only out of politeness. The cook, the butler and the housekeeper would all do precisely the same whether she was there or not. Her mother was remarried and far too absorbed in her own happiness to need either company or counseling.

Even Charlotte had not needed or wanted her help lately. Pitt had not had a case in which they could assist. She did not even know what he was involved with at the moment.

But Tallulah FitzJames had a grief to which she might offer some very good advice. It was there on the edge of her tongue as she thought about it. The answer was a matter of priorities and inner honesty. No one could have everything, and somehow choices needed to be made. One should make them with candor and courage, and then have the sense to see that one accepted the decision and realized the consequences.

And it might be great fun to hear what was going on in Paris, in the way of outrageous ideas.

"How exciting," she said with decision. "I should love to come."

"Reggie will take us," Tallulah said instantly. "Come on, Reggie. Do you know Mrs. Radley? The Honorable Reginald Howard." And without waiting for them to do more than nod to each other, she led the way to their hostess to say their farewells, and Emily sent her own carriage home without her.

The party in Chelsea was as different from the event they had left as it was possible to conceive. It was held in several rooms, all of them large, filled with books and comfortable chairs and chaise longues. The air was hazy with smoke, some of which had the peculiar sweetness of incense, quite unfamiliar to Emily. Everywhere people, a far greater preponderance of men than women, were engaged in intense conversation.

The first man Emily noticed individually had a dreaming face, large nose, humorous eyes and small, delicate mouth. His hair seemed fair in the gaslight, and he wore it long enough to touch the white, lace-edged collar of his velvet jacket.

"I think that's Richard Le Gallienne," Tallulah whispered. "The writer." She looked ahead to where another earnest young man, wavy hair parted in the center, rich mustache decorating a full upper lip, was describing something to his audience to their entranced delight. "And that's Arthur Symons," she went on, her voice rising eagerly. "He must be telling them about Paris. I hear he met simply everyone there!"

They were welcomed very casually by a middle-aged woman with powerful features and dressed in garb which could have come straight from an artist's impression of an Eastern traveler. It was flattering, but highly eccentric. She held a cigar in one long-fingered hand and seemed to know Tallulah, and therefore to be happy to accommodate anyone who accompanied her.

Emily thanked her, then gazed around with interest and a touch of apprehension. A large potted palm nearly obscured a corner of the room, where two young men sat so close to each other they were all but touching. One of them appeared to be reading to the other out of a very thin, leather-bound volume. They were oblivious of everyone else.

On a chaise longue near the farther wall a middle-aged man with a florid face was either asleep or insensible.

Arthur Symons was holding forth about his recent trip to Paris, where he had indeed visited Paul Verlaine.

"We went to his home," he said excitedly, gazing at his audience, "where we were most cordially received . . . Havelock Ellis and myself. I wish I could describe to you the atmosphere, everything I saw and heard. He entertained us with the last wine, all the while he smoked like a bonfire. I swear I shall never smell smoke again without it bringing to my mind that evening. Imagine it!" He held up his hands as if grasping a whole world, precious and complete.

Everyone within earshot was staring at him. No one made the slightest move to leave.

His face glowed with the rapture of the moment, although Emily wondered whether it was memory which burned so hotly in him or delight at being so absolutely the center of interest and the envy of his peers.

"Havelock and I sitting in the home of Verlaine himself. How we talked! We spoke of all manner of things, of philosophy and arts and poetry and what it is to be alive. It was as if we had always known each other."

There was a murmur around the small circle, a sigh of admiration, perhaps of longing. One young man seemed almost intoxicated by the very thought of such an experience. His fair face was brightly flushed and he leaned forward as if by being in such close proximity he could touch or feel it for himself.

"He invited us to return the following day," Symons continued.

"And of course you did!" the young man said urgently.

"Of course," Symons agreed. Then a curious expression crossed his features, anger, laughter, sorrow. "Unfortunately, he was not in."

Beside Emily someone drew in her breath sharply.

"We left in the utmost dejection," Symons went on, looking even now as if some tragedy had just struck him. "It was appalling! Our dreams crashed to the ground, the cup broken the very instant it was at our lips." He hesitated dramatically. "Then at the very moment we were leaving . . . we encountered him returning with a friend."

"And . . . ?" someone prompted vaguely.

Again the mixture of emotions crossed Symons's face. "He had not the faintest idea who we were," he confessed. "He had forgotten us completely."

This tale was greeted with a mixture of responses, including a gasp of amazement from Reggie Howard and an outburst of laughter from Tallulah.

But Symons had their attention, and that was all he required. He went on to describe in minute, witty and most colorful detail their earlier visits to cafés, theaters, concerts and various salons. They visited several artists and made a long trip out to the suburbs, where they went to the workshop of Auguste Rodin, who barely spoke to them—or to anyone else.

Utterly different, and holding his audience to even more rapt attention, was the tale of his visit to the Café Moulin Rouge, colorful, hectic and seedy, with its music and dancers, its mixture of high and low society. He told them of his encounter with the brilliant and perverse Henri de Toulouse-Lautrec, who painted the cancan girls and the prostitutes.

Emily was fascinated. It was a world of which she had barely dreamed. Of course she knew the names—everyone did, even if some of them were spoken in a whisper. They were the poets and thinkers who defied convention, who set out to shock, and usually succeeded. They idolized decadence, and said so.

From listening to Arthur Symons, she moved into the next room and eavesdropped on a conversation between two young men who seemed oblivious of her—an experience she had not had before, at least not at a party in her circle where politeness was exercised, often in defense of very obvious truth, and compliments were the usual currency of exchange.

This was outside all she knew, and invigorating because of it. No one mentioned the weather or who was courting whom. Politics need not have existed, or bankers or royalty either. Here it was all art, words, sensations and ideas.

"But he wore green!" one young man said in horror, his face twisted as if he suffered physical pain. "The music was the most obviously purple I have ever heard. All shades of indigo and violet, melting into darkness. Green was absolutely so insensitive! So utterly devoid of understanding."

"Did you say anything to him?" the other asked quickly.

"I tried," was the reply. "I spent ages with him. I explained all about the interrelationship between the senses, how color and sound are part of each other, how taste and touch combine, but I really don't think he understood a word." He gestured intensely with his hands, fingers spaced and then clenched. "I wanted him to grasp a complete art! He is so one-dimensional. But what can one do?"

"Shock!" his companion said instantly. "With something so sublime he will be forced to reconsider everything he has ever believed."

The first man dashed the heel of his hand against his brow.

"But of course! Why didn't I think of that? That's what dear Oscar says: the first duty of the artist is continually to astonish."

His friend leaned forward.

"My dear! Did you read *Lippincott's Monthly Magazine* last month?"

Both of them were completely unaware of Emily, a bare six feet away.

The young man thought for a moment.

"No, I don't think so. You mean July? Why? What was in it? Has Oscar said something outrageous?" He touched the other lightly on the arm. "Do tell me!"

"Absolutely! It's almost too marvelous." The reply was so eager the words almost fell upon each other. "A story of a young and beautiful man—guess who? Well anyway, he falls in with a depraved dandy, an older man with a wonderful wit, to whom he says one day that he wishes he could never grow old but would always have the looks and the youth that he has at that moment." His eyebrows rose. "He is very lovely, you understand?"

"So you said. What of it?" The young man leaned back, precariously close to the potted palm behind him. "We would all be delighted to retain such beauty as we have. Such a thought is hardly worthy of Oscar's invention, and certainly not shocking."

"Oh, but this story is!" he was assured. "You see, another man, a largely honorable man, paints a portrait of him—and his wish is granted! His face is beautiful!" He held up one long-fingered, white hand. "But his soul grows steadily more and more harrowed as he indulges in a life of utter pleasure seeking, regardless of the cost to others, which is high, even to life at times."

"Still ordinary, my dear. A mere observation of the obvious." He leaned back against the Chinese cushions behind him, exhibiting his boredom.

"Do you really imagine Oscar would ever be obvious?" The first man's high eyebrows rose even farther. "How unimaginative you are, and what a poor judge of character."

"Well, it may not be obvious to you, dear boy, but it is to me," his companion rejoined.

"Then tell me the ending!" he challenged.

"There is no ending. It is merely life."

"That is where you are wrong!" He wagged his finger. "He remains as young and utterly beautiful as ever. Years and years go by. His face is unmarked by the squalor of his soul and the viciousness of his life—"

"Wishful thinking."

"But the portrait is not! Week by week the face on the canvas grows more terrible—"

"What?" He sat suddenly upright, knocking off one of the voluptuous cushions. Emily suppressed her instinct to pick it up and replace it.

"The face on the canvas grows more terrible!" the man continued his tale. "All the sin and meanness, the disease of his soul, is stamped on it, till the very sight of it is enough to freeze the blood and make you lie awake at night for fear of sleeping and dreaming of it!"

He had his friend's total attention. He sat bolt upright.

"My God! Then what? What is the end?"

"He murders the artist, who has guessed his secret," the man said triumphantly. "Then at last, terrified at the hideousness of his own soul which he sees in the painted face, he stabs it."

Emily drew in her breath in a gasp, but neither of them heard her.

"And . . . ?" the man demanded.

"It is himself he has killed! He is inextricably bound with the painting. He is it and it is he! He dies—and the body takes on the monstrosity of the portrait, which now becomes again as beautiful and as innocent as when it was first painted. But the story is full of marvelous wit and wonderful lines, as Oscar always is." He shrugged and sat back, smiling. "Of course, there are those in the establishment who are furious, saying it is depraved, evil and so on. But what do you expect? A work of art accepted by everyone is damned from the start. There can hardly be a more explicit way of demonstrating that it has nothing whatsoever to say! If you don't offend anyone at all, you might as well not bother to speak. You obviously have nothing to say."

"I must get *Lippincott's* immediately!"

"There is talk he may publish it in a book."

"What is it called? I must know!"

" 'The Picture of Dorian Grey.' "

"Wonderful! I shall read it—probably several times."

So shall I, Emily thought to herself, moving away as the two men started to discuss the deeper implications of the story. But I shall not tell Jack. He might not understand.

She was beginning to feel a little dizzy, and certainly very tired. She was not used to so much smoke in the air. In polite society gentlemen retired from the main apartments in order to smoke. There were rooms specifically set aside for it, so as not to offend those who did not, and special jackets worn, not to carry the smell back into the rest of the house.

She looked across and saw Tallulah. She was flirting with a languid young man in green, but it seemed more a thing of habit than of any real intent. Emily had no idea what time it was, but all intelligence said it must be very late indeed. She had no way of going home, except with Tallulah. She could not leave alone and wander the streets looking for a hansom at this hour of the morning. Any men around, any policemen, would take her for a prostitute. Since the uproar four years ago about prostitution generally, and the purge on pornography, all sorts of decent women had been arrested walking about in daylight in the wrong areas, let alone at this hour.

A fraction unsteadily, she made her way across the room, stopping by the chair and looking down at Tallulah.

"I think it is time we excused ourselves," she said clearly, at least she meant it to be clear. "It has been delightful, but I should like to be home in time for breakfast."

"Breakfast?" Tallulah blinked. "Oh!" She sat upright sharply. "Oh yes, the mundane world that eats breakfast. I suppose we must return." She sighed. It seemed as if she had already forgotten the young man, and he did not seem disconcerted. His attention turned as easily to someone else.

They found Reggie quite quickly, and he was amiable enough to be willing to leave, wandering outside with Emily on one arm and Tallulah on the other. He woke his coachman and they all climbed into the carriage, half asleep, Reggie closing the door behind them with difficulty. There was already a pale fin of light in the east, and the earliest traffic on the roads.

No one had asked Emily where she lived, and as she sat jolting gently as they moved along the riverbank, then turned north, she looked at the sleeping figure of Reggie Howard in the light of the lamps they passed under, and hesitated to ask him to take her home first. They were going in the wrong direction. She would have to wait.

They stopped rather abruptly in Devonshire Street. Reggie woke with a start.

"Ah. Home," he said, blinking. "Let me assist you." He fumbled to open the door, but the footman was there before him, offering his hand to Tallulah, and then to Emily.

"You'd better stay with me tonight," Tallulah said quickly. "You don't want to arrive home at this hour."

Emily hesitated only a moment. Perhaps this was also a polite way of allowing her to know that Reggie's carriage was not available for her any further. It was quite true; it would be easier to explain to

Jack that she spent the night with Tallulah than that she was out until four in the morning at a party in Chelsea with artists and writers of the highly fashionable decadent school.

"Thank you." She scrambled out with more haste than grace. "That is most generous of you." She also thanked Reggie, and the footman, and then as the carriage rumbled away, she followed Tallulah across the pavement, through the areaway doors and into the back yard, where the scullery entrance was apparently unlocked.

Tallulah stood in the kitchen. She looked surprisingly fragile in the first cold daylight, away from the gas lamp's glow and the velvet hangings. She was framed instead by the wooden dresser with the rows of dishes, the copper pans hanging on the wall, and the flour bins, the black kitchen range to the left. Clean linen hung on the airing rack above, and there was a smell of dried herbs and strings of onions in the air.

It would not be long before the first maids were up to clear out the stove and black it and light it ready for Cook to begin breakfast.

The same would shortly be happening in Emily's own home.

Tallulah took a deep breath and let it out soundlessly. She turned to lead the way up towards the stairs. Emily followed, tiptoeing, so as not to be heard by the early-waking servants.

On the landing Tallulah stopped outside a guest room door.

"I'll lend you a gown," she said very quietly. "And I'll send my maid in the morning." She winced. "At least about eight o'clock. Nobody'll breakfast very early . . . I don't think. Actually . . ." She looked at Emily with a sudden misery in her face. "Actually, it's not a very good time, at the moment. Something rather wretched has happened." Her voice was no more than a whisper. "A woman of the streets was murdered off the Whitechapel Road somewhere, and the police found an old club badge there that belonged to my brother. They actually came to the house asking questions." She shuddered. "Of course he didn't have anything to do with it, but I'm terrified they won't believe him." She stared at Emily, waiting for her to say something.

"I'm sorry," Emily said sincerely. "It must be awful for you. Perhaps they'll discover the real person quickly." Then her habitual curiosity broke through. "Where did they find the badge?"

"In her room, where she was killed." Tallulah bit her lip and her fear was naked in her face, accentuated in the sharp shadows cast by the faint light of a gas lamp glowing dimly at the stairhead and the daylight beginning to show through the landing windows.

"Oh." There was nothing comforting Emily could say to that. She was not shocked that Tallulah's brother should use a prostitute. She was worldly enough to have known such things for years. It was not even impossible that he had actually killed her. Somebody had. Perhaps he had not meant to. It could have been a quarrel over money. She might have attempted to rob him. Emily knew from Pitt that such things happened. It did not take a great deal of imagination to think how it could come about: a rich young man, expensively dressed, gold cuff links, gold watch, perhaps cigar cutter, card case, studs, money in his pocket to spend on satisfying his appetites . . . and a desperate woman who was tired, hungry and not even certain of a roof over her head next week. She might even have had a child to feed. It was only surprising it did not happen more often.

But that was hardly the thing to say to Tallulah. Although perhaps—looking at her pale face, tiredness smudging shadows under her eyes, fear bleaching the vitality and the spark from her—it was something she already knew.

Emily forced a smile, bleak and a little shaky.

"There must have been lots of other people there too," she said hopefully. "It was probably someone she knew. They have men who take their money and look after them, you know. It was more likely he. The police will know that. I expect they only came here as a matter of form."

"Do you?" Tallulah asked. "He was very polite. He spoke beautifully, I mean like a gentleman, but he was rather scruffy to look at. His collar was very clean, but crooked, and his hair was all over the place. If I didn't know he was a policeman, I would have thought he could have been an artist, or a writer. But I don't think he was a fool. He wasn't afraid of Papa, and most people are."

Emily had a sudden feeling of chill, a ripple of familiarity, like a scene from a dream, when you know what is going to happen before it does.

"Don't worry," she said as confidently as she could. "He'll find the truth. He'll never charge the wrong person. Your brother will be all right."

Tallulah stood motionless.

Outside a cart rattled along the street and someone on the footpath was whistling as he walked. It was almost daylight. The scullery maid could be coming down the back stairs any minute.

"Thank you," she said at last. "I'll see you at breakfast. I'll fetch the nightgown."

Emily smiled her gratitude and determined to find a telephone the moment she could, and at least inform her ladies' maid that she was perfectly well and spending the night with a friend. If Jack was home, that would serve for explanation to him as well. If he should rise in the morning and find her late for breakfast, he would understand.

Emily woke with a start. The sun was streaming through the open curtains into a room she had never seen before. It was all yellow florals with a little gray and blue. There was a maid pouring hot water into a large china bowl and fresh towels over the back of the chair.

"Mornin', miss," the girl said cheerfully. "Nice day again. Looks to be set for sunshine and warm. Miss Tallulah said as if you'd care to borrow one of her dresses for the time bein', you'd be welcome. Seein' as your gown's a bit formal for breakfast." She did not glance at Emily's green dinner gown with its ivory and yellow roses spread over the chaise longue, its skirts fanned out, its deep-cut bodice and flimsy sleeves looking like wilted flowers in the sharp morning light. Nor was her expression anything but politely helpful. She was a very good maid indeed.

"Thank you," Emily accepted. She would dislike intensely turning up at Augustus FitzJames's breakfast table looking as if she had been up all night. And the cream muslin dress offered was certainly very attractive. It was a trifle young for her, but not unsophisticated with its swathed bodice and delicate embroidery.

She went downstairs with Tallulah, in order that her presence might be duly explained and she be properly introduced.

The dining room was large, formal and extremely attractive, but she had no time to do more than notice it momentarily. Her attention was taken entirely by the three people who sat around the table. At the head of it was Augustus FitzJames, his long, powerful face set in lines of severity as he studied the morning newspaper. He had it folded in front of him, but he did not look up when the two young women came in until he realized that there was someone present he had not expected.

"Good morning, Papa," Tallulah said cheerfully. "May I present Mrs. Radley? I invited her to stay the night with us because the hour was late and her husband had been obliged to take their carriage on an urgent call of government business." She lied quite adroitly, as if she had considered the matter beforehand.

Augustus regarded Emily with a slight frown, then as he connected the name with a member of Parliament, he inclined his head in acknowledgment.

"Good morning, Mrs. Radley. I'm delighted we were able to offer you hospitality. Please join us for breakfast." He glanced at the woman at the foot of the table. Her hair was perfectly coiffed, her morning gown immaculate, but her face was creased with tiny lines of anxiety. "My wife," he said expressionlessly.

"How do you do, Mrs. FitzJames," Emily said with a smile.

"Thank you for your kindness in allowing me to stay here." It was a formality, something to say in the stiff silence. Aloysia had been totally unaware of her presence.

"You are most welcome," Aloysia said hastily. "I hope you slept well?"

"Very, thank you." Emily sat on the chair indicated for her, while the maid set an extra place for Tallulah.

"My son," Augustus continued, gesturing with his rather bony hands to the young man who sat opposite Emily.

"How do you do, Mr. FitzJames," she responded, looking at him with a far greater interest than she could ever have had, had Tallulah not confided in her his disastrous connection with the murder in Whitechapel. She tried to smile brightly, noncommittally, as if she knew nothing, but she could not help trying to read his face. He was handsome; he had a good nose, a wide mouth, and a broad, firm jaw. His hair was beautiful. It sprang back from his brow in thick, fair waves. It was the face of a man who would never be lost for female admiration. What uncontrolled appetite or unseen weakness had taken him to find a prostitute in Whitechapel, of all places? Looking at him across the family breakfast table, she thought how little of a person one sees in the inbred manners and the traditional dress, the neatly barbered hair.

"How do you do, Mrs. Radley," he replied without interest. "Morning, Tallulah. Have a good evening?"

Tallulah sat down next to Emily and picked at a bowl of fruit, then set it aside and chose toast and apricot preserve instead.

"Yes, thank you," she replied noncommittally. He was not asking with any interest.

Emily was offered smoked haddock or eggs and declined both. She too said toast would be sufficient. She must return home as soon as she decently could. It would be difficult enough to give a satisfactory explanation of her night's absence as it was.

"Where did you go?" Augustus asked Tallulah. His tone was not peremptory, but there was an underlying assumption in it that he would be answered, and answered truthfully.

Tallulah did not look up from her plate.

"To Lady Swaffham's for dinner. Did I not mention it?"

"Yes, you did," he said grimly. "And you did not remain there until after two in the morning. I know Lady Swaffham better than that."

They had not mentioned the time they came in. Presumably two was the time he had gone to bed himself, and knew she was not home.

"I went on with Reggie Howard and Mrs. Radley to a literary discussion in Chelsea," Tallulah replied, glancing up at her father.

"At two in the morning?" His eyebrows rose sarcastically. "I think, madam, that you mean a party at which certain young men who imagine themselves writers sit around striking poses and talking nonsense. Was Oscar Wilde there?"

"No."

He looked at Emily to confirm or deny the statement.

"I don't believe any of his set were there," she said with complete honesty. Actually, she was not sure who his "set" were anyway, and she resented being put in the position of having to answer for Tallulah or make her a liar.

"I don't care for young Howard," Augustus continued, taking another slice of toast and pouring himself more tea. He did not look at his daughter. "You will not go out in his company again."

Tallulah drew in her breath and her face hardened.

Augustus faced his wife.

"It is time you took her to more appropriate places, my dear. It is your job to find her a suitable match. This year, I think. It is past time you did so. As long as she does not jeopardize her reputation too far by wasting her time in loose company, then she is eminently eligible. Regardless of behavior, she will not remain so indefinitely." He was still looking at Aloysia, not Tallulah, but Emily saw Tallulah's cheeks flush with humiliation. "I will make a list of desirable families," he concluded, and bit into his toast, his other hand reaching for his cup.

"Desirable to whom?" Tallulah said hotly.

He turned to her. There was not a shred of humor or light in his eyes.

"To me, of course. It is my responsibility to see that you are well provided for and that you make a success of your life. You have everything that is necessary, except self-discipline. You will now apply that, beginning today."

Had she thought anyone was taking the slightest notice of her, Emily would have been embarrassed, but even Finlay seemed absorbed in what his father was saying. Apparently such total command did not surprise any of them. She did not need to look at Tallulah's downcast head to know that Augustus FitzJames's list of acceptable suitors for his daughter's hand would not include the "Jago" she had referred to. The virtue she was so sure he possessed would not endear him to a socially ambitious father.

Tallulah needed to do some very serious evaluating of her own desires, and some weighing of costs and rewards, if she were to have any chance of happiness.

Emily looked across at Finlay, still eating toast and marmalade and finishing his last cup of tea. Any sympathy he might have felt for his sister did not register in his face.

Without warning Augustus turned on him.

"And it is past time you found a suitable wife. You cannot take up an embassy post of any importance unless you have a wife capable of maintaining the position. She should have breeding, dignity, the capacity to hold intelligent conversation without forcing her own opinions into it, and sufficient charm to appeal, but not so much as to cause gossip and speculation. Wholesomeness is preferable to beauty. Naturally her reputation must be impeccable. That goes without saying. I can think of a dozen or more who would be suitable."

"At the moment—" Finlay began, then stopped abruptly.

Augustus's face froze. "I am quite aware that at the moment there are other matters to be cleared up." His face was tight and hard, and he did not look at his son when he spoke. "I trust that that will not take more than a few days."

"I should think not," Finlay said unhappily, staring at his father as if willing him to look up and meet his eyes. "I had nothing to do with it! And if they have any competence at all, they will soon know that." He said it as if it were a challenge, and he did not expect to be believed without proving it, and yet Emily heard the sincerity sharp in his voice.

Tallulah ignored her unfinished toast, and her tea grew cold. She looked from her father to her mother, and back again.

"Of course they will," Aloysia said meaninglessly. "It is unpleasant, but there is no need whatever to worry."

Augustus regarded her with a world of contempt in his eyes and the tired lines around his mouth deepened.

"No one is worried, Aloysia. It is simply a matter of dealing with things so that nothing unpleasant does happen as a result of . . . incompetence, or other misfortune we cannot prevent." He turned to Tallulah. "You, madam, will deport yourself in a manner which raises no eyebrows whatsoever and gives no malicious tongues the fuel with which to spread gossip. And you, sir"—he looked at Finlay—"will conduct yourself like a gentleman. You will confine your attentions to your duty and to such pleasures as are enjoyed by the sort of young lady you would wish to marry. You might escort your sister. There are soirées, exhibitions and other appropriate gatherings all over London."

Finlay looked desperate.

"Otherwise," Augustus continued, "this matter may not be as easily contained as you would wish."

"I had nothing to do with it!" Finlay protested, a rising note of desperation in his voice.

"Possibly," Augustus said dryly, continuing with his breakfast.

The discussion was over. He did not need to say so in words; the finality in his voice was total. Argument with it would have been useless.

Tallulah and Emily finished the remains of their meal in silence, then excused themselves. As soon as they were in the hallway and out of earshot, Tallulah turned to Emily.

"I'm sorry," she said with distress. "That must have been dreadful for you, because I'm sure you know what he was talking about. Of course they will clear it all up, but it could take ages. And what if they never find out who it was?" Her voice sharpened as panic mounted inside her. "They never found the other Whitechapel murderer! He killed five women, and that was two years ago, and still no one has the faintest idea who he was. It could be anyone!"

"No it couldn't," Emily said steadily. She was speaking empty words, but she hoped Tallulah would not know it. "That other failure had very little to do with this." She believed Pitt could find the truth, but probably all the truth, which even if Finlay were as innocent as he claimed, might include a few facts about him which were embarrassing or painful, or both. The trouble with an investigation was that all manner of things were discovered, perhaps irrelevant to the crime, private sins and shames which it was afterwards impossible to forget.

And when people were afraid they too often behaved badly. One might see them far more clearly than one ever wished. There was more to fear than simply a discovery of guilt.

"It is probably someone in her daily life," she went on very steadily, thinking even as she was saying it that Augustus FitzJames was not certain of his son's innocence. Emily knew from the edge in his voice, the way he overrode his wife's comfortable words, that a needle of doubt had pricked him. Why? Why would a man have so little confidence in his own son as to allow such an awful possibility into his mind?

"Yes, of course it is," Tallulah agreed. "I'm just upset because

Papa is going to try to force me to marry some bore and become a bland, uninteresting wife sewing useless embroidery and painting watercolors no one wants to look at."

"Thank you." Emily smiled at her.

Tallulah blushed scarlet. "Oh God! I'm so sorry! What an unpardonable thing to say! I didn't mean it like that!"

Emily blinked at the blasphemy, but said frankly, "Yes you did. And I don't blame you. Plenty of women spend their whole lives doing things they despise. I bore myself to tears sometimes. And I am married to a politician, and usually he is very interesting. I was bored last night because he has been so busy I have seen little of him lately, and I have done nothing to interest myself. I need a good issue to fight for."

Gradually the color subsided in Tallulah's cheeks, but she still looked mortified.

Emily took her by the arm and led her back up the stairs towards her temporary bedroom.

"I have a great-aunt by marriage," she continued, "who is never bored a day in her life, because she is always concerned with something, usually battling some injustice or ignorance. She doesn't take on anything easy, so everything tends to last." She could have mentioned that she had a mother who had just married a Jewish actor seventeen years her junior, and a sister who had married beneath her, to a man in the police force, and brought drama into all their lives by becoming involved in the worst of his cases. But just at the moment that would be tactless, not to mention overwhelming.

"Does she?" Tallulah said with a flicker of interest. "Her husband doesn't mind?"

"Actually he's dead, and he doesn't count," Emily conceded. "If he were alive that would make it harder. What about this Jago that you mentioned?"

"Jago!" Tallulah laughed jerkily. "Can you see Papa allowing me to marry a parish priest in Whitechapel? I should end up with about two dresses to my name, one to wash, one to wear, and live in a drafty room with cold water and a roof that leaked. Socially I should cease to exist!"

"I thought priests had vicarages," Emily argued, standing at the top of the stairs on the bright sunlit landing with its yellow carpet and potted palms. A housemaid in crisp lace-trimmed cap and apron walked across the hall below them, her heels clicking on the parquet. There might be vicarages in Whitechapel, but they were still another world from this.

Tallulah bit her lip. "I know that. But I would have to give up so much. No more parties. No more beautiful gowns, witty conversations that last all night. No more trips to the theater and the opera. No more dinners and balls and coming home in the dawn. I wouldn't even be warm enough half the time, or have enough to eat. I might have to do my own laundry!"

It was all perfectly true.

"Do you want to change Jago into something he isn't?" Emily asked her.

"No!" Tallulah drew in her breath slowly. "No, I don't. Of course not . . . I . . ." She stopped. She did not know what she meant. The decision was enormous.

"No one gets everything," Emily said softly. "If what you care for in him is that part which clings to his own values, then you have to accept all that goes with it. Perhaps it is time to weigh up exactly what life with him would mean and what life without him would be for you, and then decide what you really want. Don't let it go by default. It is too important for that. It could be your whole life."

Tallulah's curious face was twisted in self-mockery, but there were tears in her eyes.

"There's no decision for me to make. Jago wouldn't even look at me in that way. He despises everything I am. It's just a matter of trying to help Finlay through this, and I can't even think of a way to do that. And then not letting Papa marry me to anyone too stultifyingly tedious." She sniffed. "Maybe he'd marry me to someone very old, and they'd die. Then I can be a widow, like your great-aunt, and do as I please."

Below them the dining room door opened again and Finlay came out, walking quickly and a little angrily towards the front door.

"Jarvis!" he shouted. "Where's my hat and my stick? I left them in the stand last night. Who's moved them?"

A footman materialized, duly deferential.

"Your stick is there, sir, and I took the hat to brush it."

"Oh. Thank you." Finlay reached for the stick. "Well, fetch the hat, Jarvis. Why did you take it anyway? I don't need a hat brushed every time I wear it."

"A bird unfortunately . . ." Jarvis began.

Tallulah smiled in spite of herself and took Emily by the arm to guide her back to the room to make the necessary arrangements to have her own dress packed so she could take it with her on her return home.

Emily made her farewells, then rode home in the FitzJameses' second carriage, Augustus having taken the first. Her thoughts were engaged in Tallulah's problems. Was it possible that Finlay was guilty?

Why would he do such a thing? What was there about him that his father knew, or suspected, which made him so cold, so uncertain, and yet unhesitant to defend him?

Or had she misread the emotions in his face? She had been an onlooker at one meal. Perhaps she was being foolish, absurdly overrating her own judgment.

She wondered idly what Jago was like that he could have captured Tallulah's dreams so completely. Apparently he was the opposite of everything she treasured in her present life. Perhaps that was it? Not reality at all, simply an enchantment with the idea of the different. Whatever it was, she liked Tallulah, liked her vividness, her ability to care, and the fact that she was teetering on the edge of dreams for which she would have to pay for the rest of her life. She was worthy of all the help Emily could give her. There was no decision to be made about that.

When she arrived she thanked the FitzJameses' coachman, alighted and went up her own front steps. The butler opened the door to her without raising his eyebrows.

"Good morning, Jenkins," she said calmly, walking in.

"Good morning, ma'am," he replied, closing the door behind her. "Mr. Radley is in the study, ma'am."

"Thank you." She passed him the package containing her dinner gown with instructions to give it to her ladies' maid. Then, feeling a trifle odd in Tallulah's muslin morning dress, she walked, head high, to the study to explain herself to Jack.

"Good morning," he said coolly when she opened the door. He was sitting at the desk with a pile of papers, a pen in his hand, his expression unsmiling. "I received your message. Rather incomplete. Where were you?"

She took a deep breath. She found herself resenting the need to account, but she had known it would be unavoidable.

"I accepted a ride to another party, and did not realize how late I had stayed. They were interesting people, and I met someone . . ." She still had not made up her mind whether to pass it off as help to a friend in trouble or enquiring into Pitt's current case. Looking at Jack's displeased face did not assist her. Whatever she said, it had better be something she could substantiate.

"Yes?" he prompted, his eyes chilly.

She must decide immediately, or it would look like a lie. He was not as easy to mislead as she sometimes wished. She had once assumed that his attention could be diverted by a smile, and she had been wrong.

"I'm waiting, Emily . . ."

"I met a young woman I liked very much, and she was in great distress because her brother has been accused of murder . . . Thomas is investigating the case. I couldn't leave it, Jack! I had to find out all

I could about it . . . for her sake, and Thomas's . . . and for the truth itself!"

"Indeed . . ." He sat back in his chair, regarding her skeptically. "So you stayed the night in her home. What did you learn in this generous effort? Is he guilty?"

"Don't be sarcastic," she replied tartly. "Even I can't solve a murder over breakfast." She looked at him with a hesitant smile. "It will take me at least until dinner . . . maybe even longer." And with that she met his eyes for an instant, saw the beginning of humor in them, then turned and went out, closing the door behind her.

In the hall she gave a sigh of relief and ran swiftly upstairs to change.

CHAPTER

FOUR

At the time Emily was talking to Tallulah at the stairhead, and Finlay was taking his hat and stick from the footman and going out of the door, Pitt was sitting in a hansom on the far side of Devonshire Street with Rose Burke beside him. As the door to number thirty-eight opened and Finlay came out, she leaned forward, peering out of the side, her body stiff. She remained watching, her head turning very slowly to follow his path along the pavement until he disappeared around the corner of Upper Wimpole Street, then she sat back again.

"Well?" Pitt asked. He did not know what he wanted her to say. If she identified him it would be the beginning of a very unpleasant gathering of facts for an arrest and prosecution. The FitzJames family would muster all its resources to fight back. There would certainly be accusations of police incompetence. Rose herself would be attacked and every attempt would be made to undermine her resolve, slander her character—which would not be hard—and generally discredit her testimony.

On the other hand, if she did not identify him (or worse than that, said it was not him), then they were thrown back to the cuff link and the badge, and to searching for any resolution which explained their presence but excluded Finlay from the murder itself.

Rose turned and looked at him. She might have relished her moment of power. He expected to see it in her eyes. Instead there was only anger and a bright, hard hatred.

"Yeah, it was 'im," she said in a tight, harsh voice. "That's 'im wot I saw goin' in ter Ada just afore she were killed. Arrest 'im. Get 'im tried so they can 'ang 'im."

Pitt felt his chest constrict and his heart beat harder.

"Are you sure?"

She swung around to glare at him. "Yeah, I'm sure. You gonna argue, 'cos 'e lives in a posh 'ouse in a fancy street an' got money ter pay 'is way abaht?" Her lip curled with disgust close to hatred.

"No, Rose, I'm not," he said softly. "But when I go after him, I want to be sure I have everything exactly right. I don't want any clever lawyer finding mistakes and getting him off because of them."

"Yeah . . ." She settled back, mortified. "Yeah . . . well . . . I suppose so. But yer got 'im this time."

"This time?" he asked, although with a little twist of misery he knew what she was going to say.

"Yeah. Well, yer never got Jack, didjer?" Her body was stiff, her shoulders rigid under her shawl. " 'E's still around, fer all we know, waitin' in some dark doorway ter cut someone again. Well, get this bleedin' murderer an' top 'im before 'e does another poor cow."

He would have liked to tell her this was not another serial murderer, that that would never happen again, that it was only one hideous aberration. But he was not sure. There was an air of compulsion about this murder, an inward rage that had been momentarily beyond control. If it could happen once, it could, perhaps would, happen again.

"It's no help to you, Rose, if we get the wrong man," he said, watching her face. Its hard, handsome lines were set rigid with hate and fear, her skin still smooth across her cheekbones. If it were not for a certain brashness in her expression, and the quality of her clothes, she could have been a lady like any of the others along Devonshire Street, or this part of Mayfair.

" 'E in't the wrong one," she replied. "Now I in't got all day ter sit 'ere talkin' ter you. I charge fer me time."

"You charge for your services, Rose," he corrected her. "And I don't want them. You'll give me as much time as I need. I'm taking the cab back to Bow Street. You can have it from there, if you want."

" 'Oo's payin' fer it?" she said immediately.

"I will," he offered with a smile. "This once. You can credit me, for next time I want to speak to you!"

She said nothing. She would not commit herself to words, but there was the slightest of smiles.

He leaned forward and gave the driver instructions, and when they were at Bow Street he alighted and paid for the rest of the way to Whitechapel.

He had learned nothing more from Rose on the journey. She was frightened. She remembered the outrage of 1888 far too sharply, the fear that had gripped London so tightly that even the music halls, which laughed at everything and everyone, made no jokes about the Whitechapel Murderer. She needed the police, and she hated that. She saw them as part of an establishment which used her and at the same time despised her.

Four years ago new laws had been passed, initially intended to protect women and curb pornography and prostitution. In effect they had only meant that the police had harassed and arrested more women, and while some brothels had been closed down, others opened up. Many men still believed that any woman who walked along in certain areas, including some in the West End, was by definition doing so to invite trade. Pornography flowed as freely as ever. It was all one giant hypocrisy, and Rose saw it as such and hated all those who supported it or benefited from it.

Pitt went into Bow Street Station, nodded to the desk sergeant, and went on up to his office. Tellman was waiting for him, his lantern-jawed face sardonic, his eyes hard.

"Morning, sir. There's a report from a Dr. Lennox on your desk. Came about fifteen minutes ago. Couldn't tell him when you'd be in, so he didn't stay. Looked wretched, like he'd got an invitation to his own funeral. It's this Whitechapel murder. I s'pose yer toff is guilty?"

"Looks like it," Pitt agreed, reaching across his desk with its beautiful green leather inlay and picking up the sheet of paper covered in generous, sloping handwriting.

Tellman shrugged. "That'll be ugly." There was some satisfaction in his voice, although it was not possible to judge whether it was at Pitt's discomfort or at the prospect of a family like the FitzJameses being exposed to such a public indignity. Tellman had risen from the ranks and was only too familiar with the bitter reality of hunger, humiliation and the knowledge that life would never offer him its great rewards.

Pitt sat down and looked at the report Lennox had left him. Ada McKinley had died of strangulation between ten o'clock and midnight. There were no bruises or scratches to indicate that she had fought her attacker. Her fingers had been broken, three on her left hand, two on her right. Three toes had been dislocated on her left foot. On her right hand one fingernail was broken, but that was probably from her attempt to tear the stocking from around her neck. The only blood under her fingernails was almost certainly from the scratches on her own throat.

There were stretch marks on her abdomen from the child she had borne, one or two old bruises on her thighs and one on her shoulder which was yellowish green, and obviously had predated the night of her death. Other than that, she was in good enough health. As far as Lennox could judge, she was in her middle twenties. There was little else to say.

Pitt looked up.

Tellman was waiting, his long, harsh face grim.

"You're still in charge here," Pitt said dryly. "I'm going to see the assistant commissioner."

"Enough for an arrest?" Tellman asked, looking very directly at Pitt, an edge of surprise and challenge in his voice.

"Close," Pitt replied.

"How difficult for you," Tellman observed without sympathy. He smiled as he turned and went to the door. "I suppose you'd better be sure. Don't want it to fail in court because you didn't get everything right." He went out with his shoulders square and his head high.

John Cornwallis had been assistant commissioner a very short time—in fact, a matter of a month or so. He had been appointed to fill the vacancy left by the dramatic departure of his predecessor, Giles Farnsworth, at the conclusion of the Arthur Desmond case. He was a man of average height, lean, broad-shouldered, and he moved with grace. He was not handsome. He had strong brows. His nose was too powerful, his mouth too wide and thin, but he had a commanding presence, a quality of stillness which was a kind of inner confidence. One barely noticed that he had no hair whatever.

"Good morning, sir," Pitt said as he closed the office door and walked in. This was only the second time he had been back since his battle with Farnsworth. The room was the same in all essentials: the tall windows facing the sun, the large polished oak desk, the armchairs. Yet the stamp of a different personality was on it. The faint odor of Farnsworth's cigars was gone, and in its place was a smell of leather and beeswax, and something vaguely aromatic. Perhaps it came from the carved cedarwood box on the low table. That was new. The brass telescope on the wall was also new, and the ship's sextant hung beside it.

Cornwallis was standing as though he had been looking out of the window. He had been expecting Pitt. He was there by appointment.

"Good morning. Sit down." Cornwallis waved towards the chairs spread out comfortably, facing each other. The sunlight made a bright pool on the red patterned carpet. "I'm afraid this business in Pentecost Alley is turning very ugly. Did he do it? Your opinion . . ."

"Rose Burke identified him," Pitt replied. "The evidence is strong."

Cornwallis grunted and sat down.

Pitt sat also.

"But not conclusive?" Cornwallis asked, searching Pitt's face. He had caught the hesitation in his voice and was probing it.

Pitt was not sure what he thought. He had been turning it over in his mind since leaving Rose. She had seemed certain beyond doubt at all. She had described him before she had seen him again in Devonshire Street; so had Nan Sullivan. There were the cuff link and the Hellfire Club badge.

"It's pretty tight," he answered. "And so far there's no one else indicated."

"Then why do you hesitate?" Cornwallis frowned. He did not know Pitt except by reputation. He was seeking to weigh his judgments, understand what held him from a decision. "Never mind the ugliness. If he's guilty I'll back you. I don't care whose son he is."

Pitt looked at his tense, candid face and knew it was the truth. There was none of Farnsworth's deviousness in him, none of his evasive self-interest. But it was possible there was also not his diplomatic skill either, or his ability to persuade and cajole those in power. Because Farnsworth was ambitious and capable of lies, he understood others who had the same nature. Cornwallis might be more easily outflanked and misled.

"Thank you," Pitt said sincerely. "It may come to that, but I'm not sure yet."

"She identified him," Cornwallis pointed out, sitting forward in the chair. "What worries you? Do you think the jury will disbelieve her because of what she is?"

"It's possible," Pitt conceded thoughtfully. "What worries me more is that she may be overkeen to catch a man because she's afraid and angry, and she'll identify anyone, out of her own need. Whitechapel hasn't forgotten the Ripper. Two years is not long. Memories come back too easily, especially to women of her trade. She may have known Long Liz, or Mary Kelly, or any of his other victims."

"And the badge you found?" Cornwallis pressed. "She didn't imagine that."

"No," Pitt agreed cautiously. "But it is possible someone else left it there, or he lost it at some other time. I agree, it's not likely, but that is what he is claiming . . . that he has not had it in years, or the cuff links either."

"Do you believe him?" Cornwallis's eyebrows were high, his eyes wide.

"No. He's lying. But he's not as afraid as I would have expected." Pitt tried to analyze his impressions as he spoke. "There is something I don't yet know, something important. I want to investigate it a little further before I arrest him."

Cornwallis sat back. "There's going to be a great deal of pressure, of course," he warned. "It's already started. I've had someone from the Home Office calling this morning, half an hour ago. Warned me about making mistakes, being new to the position and not understanding things." His lips tightened and there was anger in his eyes. "I understand a threat when I hear it, and the sound of the establishment closing ranks to protect one of its own." He pressed his lips together. "What do you know about Finlay FitzJames, Pitt? What sort of a young man is he? I don't want to press charges, then discover he's a model of every virtue. Perhaps we need more than the circumstantial evidence of his presence at the scene. Is there any suggestion of a motive, other than the private vice of a weak and violent man?"

"No," Pitt said quietly. "And if it is FitzJames, I don't imagine

we'll ever find anything. If he's ever abused a woman before, or indulged in a touch of sadism, the family will make very sure there is
no evidence of it now. Anyone who knew will have been paid off, or
otherwise silenced."

Cornwallis stared across the room at the empty fireplace, his
brows drawn down in thought. The August sun was hot in the
bright patch between them and a wasp bounced furiously on the
windowpane.

"You're right," Cornwallis agreed. "Anyone involved, anyone
who knew, would be in his own circle, and they wouldn't betray him
to us." He looked at Pitt suddenly. "What did you think of his father?
Does he believe him innocent?"

Pitt paused for a moment, remembering Augustus's face, his
voice, and the speed with which he had taken control of the
interview.

"I'm not sure. I don't think he's convinced of his innocence. Either that or he has no trust in us at all, and believes we may lie or
misinterpret the evidence."

"That surprises me," Cornwallis admitted. "He's a self-made
man, but he has great respect for the establishment. He should have.
He has a great many friends highly placed in it. I've heard it said he
expects Finlay to achieve supreme office, even possibly the premier-
ship one day. He'll want him cleared of even a whisper against his
name. It will be the destruction of his dreams if this goes against him.
It could be that fear you saw."

"Or the will to protect him, regardless," Pitt pointed out. "He
may consider the death of one London prostitute no more than a regrettable accident in an otherwise well-planned life. I don't know.
You say he has powerful friends?"

Cornwallis's expression quickened. "You think he might have
powerful enemies as well?"

Pitt sighed. "Finlay? No. I think he's an arrogant young man who
takes his pleasures whenever he wants to," he answered. "One night,

in his hunger to feel powerful, in control of other people, he went a little too far and killed a prostitute. When he saw what he had done he panicked and left her. I think he's not as frightened as he should be because he imagines his father will somehow get him out of it in order to preserve his own dreams." His voice hardened. "He doesn't feel the guilt he should because he barely thinks of Ada McKinley as of the same species as himself. It's a bit like running over a dog. It's regrettable. You wouldn't do it on purpose. But then neither would you allow it to ruin your life."

Cornwallis sat motionless for several moments, his face filled with thought and a certain sadness.

"You are probably right," he said at last. "But my God, if we charge him we'd better be sure we can prove it. Is there anything more I should know?"

"No sir, not yet." Pitt shook his head.

"Where are you going next?"

"Back to Pentecost Alley. If the evidence still stands up, and it's a slim hope there's anything new, then I'll start enquiring into the character and the past of Finlay FitzJames. I don't want to do it until I have to. He's bound to learn of it."

Cornwallis smiled bleakly. "He's already expecting it, and he's begun taking appropriate steps."

Pitt was not surprised, although it was sooner than he had foreseen. Perhaps he should have. He rose to his feet.

"Thank you for warning me, sir. I'll be careful."

Cornwallis rose also and held out his hand. It was a spontaneous gesture, and one Pitt found peculiarly attractive. He grasped Cornwallis's hand hard for a moment, then turned and left with a new warmth inside him.

Ewart was already at the house in Pentecost Alley. In the daylight he looked tired and harassed. His receding hair had gray threads in it and his clothes were crumpled, as though he had had no time or interest to spend on his appearance.

"Anything new?" Pitt asked as he joined the inspector on the steps going up to the door.

"No. Did you expect anything?" Ewart stood back for Pitt to go up first.

"Rose Burke identified FitzJames," Pitt said as he reached the top. It was hot, the air stale, smelling of old food and used linen.

Ewart climbed up behind him in silence.

"Are you going to arrest him on that?" he said when they were inside the door. His voice was tense, rasping, as though he were out of breath. "You shouldn't. The jury's not likely to believe her over a man like FitzJames. We'll lose."

Pitt faced him. In the dim light of the passage it was harder to see, but there was no mistaking the urgency in him, almost panic.

"Do you think he's guilty?" Pitt asked, almost casually.

Ewart stared at him. "That isn't the point. What I think is irrelevant . . ."

There was a bang as someone slammed a door at the end of the passage, and behind them in the street a carter was shouting at someone who was blocking his way.

"Not to me . . ." Pitt said quietly.

"What?" He looked disconcerted.

"It's not irrelevant to me," Pitt repeated.

"Oh . . ." Ewart let out his breath in a rush. "Well, I don't know. I just go by the facts. So far it looks as if he did, but we don't have enough yet. I mean . . . why would he? Far more likely someone she knew personally." His voice gathered conviction. "You've got to consider the life of a woman like that. She could have made all kinds of enemies. They told us she was greedy. She changed her pimp, you know? And one should look more into money, property. Who owns this house, for example?"

What Ewart said was true, but Pitt felt it was irrelevant in this case. Of course prostitutes got killed for a variety of reasons, most of them to do with money, one way or another, but the broken fingers and toes, the water and the boots buttoned together had no part in a crime of greed. Surely Ewart must know that as well?

"Who does?" he asked aloud.

"A woman called Sarah Barrows," Ewart replied with satisfaction. "And three other houses too, farther west. This is just rented out, but at least two of the others are run as regular brothels. She rents the dresses out as well in them. The women here say they don't rent their clothes, but that's beside the point. Ada didn't have to work only from here. Several of them don't, you know? They live one place and use shilling-an-hour rooms up the Haymarket and Leicester Square area. She could have skipped from there, with dress, money an' all."

"And some man followed her here and strangled her?" Pitt said with disbelief.

"Why not?" Ewart retorted. "Some man followed her from somewhere and strangled her. What is more likely: a pimp she bilked or a gentleman customer like FitzJames, I ask you!"

"Let me put it differently," Pitt answered, still keeping his voice low. "Which is more likely: that she used other rooms and cheated the owner, who then followed her—and I grant that brothel owners do have people hired to follow girls . . . although it's more often a prostitute past her working days than a young, strong man."

One of the women came out of a door to their left and looked at them curiously for a moment, then walked past and disappeared around the corner at the end of the passage.

"But let us grant that she took a dress," he continued. "And her earnings, and came back here, and was followed. This man, instead of warning her, taking the money and the dress, perhaps knocking her around a bit to teach her a lesson, he breaks her fingers and toes . . ." He noticed Ewart wince and saw the distaste in his face, but ignored it. "He takes off the stocking and strangles her with it," he went on. "He ties her garter 'round her arm and then, after she is dead, buttons her boots to each other, throws a pitcher of cold water over her, and leaves?"

Ewart opened his mouth to protest, but was too filled with disgust and confusion to find the words.

"Or alternatively," Pitt suggested, "a customer does these things as part of his particular fetish. He likes to threaten, cause a little pain or fear. That's what excites him. But this time it goes too far, and the girl is really dead. He panics and leaves. What do you think?"

Ewart's face was sullen and there was a flicker of unmistakable fear in his dark eyes. The passageway was hot and the air close. There was sweat on his skin, and on Pitt's also.

"I think we've got to be damned careful we don't make a mistake," he said harshly. "FitzJames won't deny he was here sometime, if it comes to facing him with it. His lawyer'll advise him to do that. Lots of respectable men use prostitutes. We all know it. You can't expect a young man to curb his natural feelings all his youth, and he might not be able to afford a good marriage until he's in his late thirties, or more. It's better not talked about, but if we force it into the open, no one'll be surprised, just angered by the bad taste of speaking about it." He took a deep breath and rubbed the back of his hand across his brow. The carter was still shouting outside.

"He'll say he was here, but not that night. She must have stolen the badge. He'd not be the first man to have something pretty stolen at a brothel. Good God, man, in times past there were places in Bluegate Fields and Saint Giles where a man'd be lucky to get out with his skin whole!" He gestured sharply with his arm. "I've seen 'em running out without shirt or trousers, naked as a jaybird and scared out of their wits. Covered in bruises and scars."

"Nor would he be the first to go back in a temper and beat the thief," Pitt pointed out. "I don't think he'd be well advised to try that story."

"But there wasn't a fight," Ewart said with a sudden smile. "Lennox said that, and we saw it for ourselves."

"Which proves what?"

Ewart's eyes opened wide.

"That . . . that he took her by surprise, of course. That he was someone she knew and wasn't afraid of."

"Not a customer from whom she'd just stolen something."

Ewart was losing his patience. "I don't know what it proves, except we've a long way to go yet." He turned away and pushed the door to Ada's room. It swung open and Pitt followed him inside. It was exactly the same as when they had first come, except that the body of Ada was no longer there. The window was closed and it was oppressively hot.

"I've searched right through it," Ewart said wearily. "There's nothing here except exactly what you'd expect. It doesn't tell us anything about her. No letters. If she had anyone, either they didn't write or she didn't keep them."

Pitt stood in the middle of the floor.

"They probably couldn't write," he said sadly. "Many people can't. No way to keep in touch. Any pictures?" That was a forlorn hope too. People like Ada would have little money for photographs or portraits.

"No." Ewart shook his head. "Oh, there's a pencil sketch of a woman, but it's fairly rough. It could be anyone. There's nothing written on it." He walked over and took it out of a small case inside the chest where it was kept with a few handkerchiefs, pins and a comb. He gave it to Pitt.

Pitt looked at the piece of paper. It was bent around the edges, a little scarred across one corner. The sketch was simple, as Ewart had said, of a woman of perhaps thirty with a gentle face, half smiling, her hair piled on her head. It had a grace in the lines, but it was only a rough sketch, the work of a few moments by an unskilled hand. Perhaps it was Ada's mother . . . all she had of her past, of a time and place where she belonged.

Suddenly he was so choked with anger he could have beaten Finlay FitzJames black and blue himself, whether he had killed Ada or not, simply because he did not care.

"Sir?" Ewart's voice broke across his thoughts.

"What?" he said, looking up sharply.

"I've already asked around and learned a lot about her life, the sort of customers she had, where she went regular, if she could have crossed up someone. It's always possible, you know, that the boots and the garter were from her last customer, and not necessarily to do with whoever killed her."

"Have you!" Pitt asked. "And what did you discover?"

Ewart looked profoundly unhappy. His face was puckered and the sweat on his skin gleamed wet.

"She was cheeky. A bit too much brass for her own good," he said slowly. "Changed her pimp a short while ago. Chucked him over and got someone new. Now he could be taking it hard. She was a nice bit of income for him. And he could have had a personal interest. Not impossible. She was handsome."

"What did he look like?" Pitt asked, trying to quell the flicker of hope inside him.

Ewart's eyes avoided his. "Thin," he answered. "Dark . . ." He tailed off; the pimp was nothing at all like the man Rose Burke and Nan Sullivan had described. It was pointless to discuss it any further. Of course they must know all they could about Ada's life, and then about Finlay FitzJames's as well.

"Well, you'd better follow up the new pimp," Pitt said wearily. "I'll speak to these women again."

In fact, Pitt had considerable trouble raising anyone, but a quarter of an hour later he was sitting on a hard-backed wooden chair in the kitchen with Nan Sullivan, who looked exhausted, blowsy and bleary-eyed. Every time he changed his balance the chair tilted and threatened to tip over. He asked her to tell him again what she remembered of the night Ada had been killed. It was not that he expected any new evidence; he wanted to weigh up what impression she might make on a jury and whether anyone would believe her rather than Finlay FitzJames.

She stared at Pitt, her eyes blinking, unfocused.

"Describe the man you saw going into Ada's room," Pitt prompted, steadying himself on the chair again. A couple of flies droned lazily around the window. There were two pails standing with cloths over them. Probably water.

"Fair hair, he had," Nan answered him. "Thick. And a good coat, that's all I can say for sure." She looked away, avoiding Pitt's eyes. "Wouldn't know him again. Only saw his back. Expensive sort of coat. I do know a good coat." She bit her lip and her eyes filled with tears. "I used to work in a shop, making coats, after me man died. But you can't keep two little ones alive on what they pay you. Worked all day and half into the night, I did, but still only made six shillin's a week, an' what'll that get you? Could've kept me virtue, an' put the baby to one o' them farms, but I know what happens to them. Sell 'em they do, into Holy Mother knows what! Or if they're sickly, let the poor souls die. Leave them to starve, so they do."

Pitt said nothing. He knew what she said was true. He knew sweatshop wages, and he had seen baby farms.

There was no sound in the rest of the house. The other women were out or asleep. From outside in the street came the distant noise of wheels and hooves on the stones, and a man calling out. The sweatshop opposite was busy, all heads bent over the needle. They were already five hours into their day.

"Or I could have gone to the workhouse," Nan went on slowly. "But then they'd have taken the little ones away from me. I couldn't bear that. If I went on the streets I could feed us all."

"What happened to your children?" he asked gently, then instantly wished he had not. He did not want to be compelled to share her tragedy.

She smiled, looking up at him. "Grew up," she answered. "Mary went into service and done well for herself. Bridget got married to a butcher out Camden way."

Pitt did not ask any more. He could imagine for himself what two girls would do to keep the precious gift their mother had given them. They might think of her now and again, might even have some idea of what their well-being had cost, but nothing would bring them back here to Pentecost Alley. And it was probably better so. She could imagine their happiness, and they could carry only early memories of her, before she became worn out, shabby and stained by life.

"Well done," he said, and meant it profoundly, steadying himself on the chair as it tilted dangerously.

"Ada's child died, poor thing." She did not say whether her pity was for the child or for Ada herself. "I'd tell you who did it, if I knew, mister, but I don't. Anyway"—she shrugged her wide shoulders—"as Mr. Ewart said, who'd believe me anyway?"

Pitt felt a wave of anger again.

"Did Mr. Ewart say that?"

"Not in them words, but that's what he meant. An' he's right, in't he?"

"That depends on several things," Pitt said, evading the question. He could tell the truth; she would not have thanked him for it. "But if you aren't sure, then it doesn't matter anyway. Tell me more about Ada. If it wasn't FitzJames, who do you think it was?"

She was silent so long he thought she was not going to answer. Flies droned against the glass. There was a banging upstairs and along the corridor someone swore.

Finally she spoke. "Well, if it weren't for the boots all buttoned up, I'd have said Costigan, he's her new pimp. Nasty piece of work, he is, an' no mistake. Pretty." She said the word with condemnation. "Thinks every woman should want after him. Temper like a mousetrap. All cheese one minute, an' then bang! Takes off your legs." She shrugged. "But he's a coward. I know that sort. The moment he'd seen she was dead, he'd have taken off, scared for his life. He'd never have stopped to do up the boots an' put the garter 'round her arm." She looked at Pitt blankly. "So I reckon as it was her customer, Fitz-James or not."

She had not mentioned the broken fingers and toes, but then she did not know about them.

"Perhaps it was the customer who did the boots and the garter?" he suggested. "And then Costigan came in before she had time to undo them?" It was a reasonable thought.

Nan shook her head. "Me or Rosie'd have seen him, if there'd have been two. Or Agnes. It may look as if no one sees who comes and goes in these rooms, but it isn't that way. We look out for each other. Have to. Mostly it's old Madge who watches. Never know what a customer might do. Some of them have too much to drink and get nasty. Some want you to do things a sane person wouldn't ever think of." She blinked and sniffed hard, wiping her nose on a piece of rag. "That's what's funny about it. You'd have thought she'd have shouted out, wouldn't you? She can't have had any idea until the stocking was 'round her throat, poor little bitch."

"That doesn't sound like a first-time customer," Pitt reasoned. "Rather someone she'd had before, and expected to do something odd like that. Was Costigan her lover as well as her pimp?" He leaned forward, forgetting the chair, which tipped violently.

"He'd like to have been," she said with a curl of her lip. She ignored the chair. She was used to it. "Don't think he was, but then I don't know everything. Maybe. But if she let him, why'd he kill her?"

"I don't know. Thank you, Nan. If you think of anything else, tell me—or Mr. Ewart."

"Yeah, yeah, course I will." She watched as he stood up and the chair righted itself with a clatter.

Pitt spent several hours tracing all he could of Ada's daily life, and found nothing different in it from the pattern of most women who made their living on the streets. She rose in the middle of the afternoon, dressed, ate her main meal, then started to walk the pavements. Very often she stayed in the Whitechapel area. There were plenty of customers. But sometimes if it was a fine evening, and especially in the summer, she would go up to the traditional areas for picking up wealthier men: Windmill Street, the Haymarket, Leicester Square. There the theater crowds, elegant ladies and men about town, paraded side by side with prostitutes of all classes and ages, from the well-dressed, expensive courtesans down to the ten- or twelve-year-old children who ran along, tugging at sleeves, whispering obscene offers, desperate for a few pence.

Ada had been beaten the occasional time, usually by her former pimp, a man named Wayland, a mean-faced, part-time drayman who supplemented his income by sometimes bullying, sometimes protecting, girls in the Pentecost Alley area. He had lodgings opposite and spent much of his time lounging around, watching to see that the girls were not actually molested in the open. Once they were inside, any restraint of a violent or dishonest client was up to them. There was a woman, old Madge, the one Nan had referred to, who had been a prostitute herself in her better days and who roomed in the back of the house, and she would come if anyone screamed. Her sight was poor, but her hearing was excellent, and she could wield a rolling pin with accuracy and the full benefit of her twenty stone. She had half killed more than one client whose demands she had considered unreasonable.

But like anyone else, even Agnes in the next room, she had heard nothing from Ada the night of her death.

Wayland could be accounted for all that night by one of his new acquisitions, a plain-faced girl of eighteen or so whose extremely handsome figure earned them both a comfortable income. And as Ewart had admitted, he looked nothing whatever like the man Rose and Nan had described. He was small and thin, with dark straight hair like streaks of black paint over his narrow skull.

There had been hasty quarrels in Ada's life, flares of temper, and then quick forgiveness. She had not been one to hold a grudge. There were impetuous acts of kindness: the sharing of clothes; the gift of a pound when times were hard; praise, sometimes when it was least merited.

She had sat up all night with old Madge when she was sick, fetching and carrying for her, washing her down with clean, hot water, emptying slops, all when she could have been out earning. And sitting back in the kitchen again on the same rickety chair, looking at Madge's worn-out, red face, Pitt thought that if they found who had killed Ada, he would be better off with the law than left to Madge.

"Looked arter me good, she did," she said, staring at Pitt fixedly. "I should 'ave 'eard 'er! W'y din't I 'ear 'er call out, eh? I'd 'a' killed the swine afore I'd 'a' let 'im 'urt 'er. I in't no use no more." Grief puckered her huge cheeks, and her voice, high for so vast a woman, was thick with guilt. "Look wot I done for 'er—nuffink! W'ere were I w'en she needed me? 'Ere, 'alf asleep, like as not. Great useless mare!"

"She didn't cry out," Pitt said quietly. "And it could all have been over quite quickly anyway."

"Yer lying ter me," she said, forcing a smile. "Yer mean ter be kind, which in't nuffink bad, but I seen folk choked afore. They don't die that quick. An' leastways I might've caught the bastard. I'd 'ave finished 'im with me pin." She gestured towards the rolling pin on the table near her right hand. "Then you could've topped me fer it, an' I'd've gorn glad."

"I wouldn't have topped you for it, Madge," he said honestly. "I'd have called it self-defense and looked the other way."

"Yeah, mebbe yer would an' all."

But even though he also went and found Albert Costigan—a brash man of about thirty, sharply dressed and with thick, brown hair—Pitt learned nothing either to confirm or disprove his belief in Finlay FitzJames's guilt.

Pitt decided to learn all he could about Finlay himself. It would be difficult, and he was afraid of prejudicing any information he might acquire simply by the act of having sought it. Had there been time, it was the type of investigation Charlotte would have helped with, and had done so excellently in the past. It needed subtlety and acute ob- servation. Simple questions were not going to uncover what he wanted to know.

Pitt had already asked discreetly in the Force about Finlay— and learned nothing. Other police superintendents knew only his name, and then only in connection with his father. Pitt had made an appointment to see Micah Drummond, who had been his su- perior before he had inherited the position. Drummond had gone to live abroad with his new wife, finding London social life intol- erable for her after the scandal of her first husband's death. Micah returned home from time to time, and fortunately this investiga- tion coincided with one of those occasions. He would at least be honest with Pitt and have the courage to disregard the political implications.

Perhaps Emily was the one to ask. She moved in society and might hear whispers which would at least tell him in which direction to look. Jack would not be pleased that she should be given even the slightest encouragement to meddle again. But all Pitt wanted was information.

He thought of Helliwell and Thirlstone. They were the ones who would know Finlay best, but they would close ranks, as they had begun to already. It was part of the creed of a gentleman that he did not betray his friends. Loyalty was the first prerequisite. Pitt was an outsider. They would never speak ill of Finlay to him, no matter what they thought privately, or possibly even knew.

At the Foreign Office he went in and gave the name of the man with whom he had made his first appointment. He was shown upstairs and along a wide, gracious corridor into an outer office where he was obliged to wait for nearly a quarter of an hour.

Eventually a handsome gray-haired man came in, his face composed, his dress faultless. He closed the door behind him.

The room was charming. A French Impressionist painting, all sunlight and shadows, hung on one of the paneled walls. There was a tree beyond the window.

"Do sit down, Superintendent Pitt. I'm so sorry for having kept you waiting, but you explained your errand in your letter, and I wished to have ready for you all the information you could possibly find useful." He looked at Pitt pointedly. "I do hope you will be able to clear up this matter quickly. Most unfortunate."

Pitt sat down, as if he had every intention of remaining for some time.

"Thank you, Mr. Grainger. I hope so too." He crossed his legs and waited for Grainger to sit also.

He did so reluctantly, towards the edge of his chair.

"I don't know what I can tell you of relevance," he said, frowning. "Mr. FitzJames has never given cause for anxiety as to his private life. Of course, before considering him for an ambassadorial post it would be most satisfactory if he were to make a fortunate marriage." He shrugged very slightly. "But no doubt he will. He is young . . ."

"Thirty-three," Pitt pointed out.

"Quite. A good age to consider such a step. And he is most eligible. What has any of this to do with your investigation?"

"You are considering him for an ambassadorial appointment?"

Grainger hesitated, unwilling to commit himself when he was beginning to sense the possibility of something embarrassing.

"You are not?" Pitt concluded. "You have found him not entirely suitable after all?"

"I did not say that," Grainger replied tartly, stung to be so bluntly interpreted. "I really do not wish to discuss it with you so freely. It is a highly confidential matter."

Pitt did not move. "If you considered him, Mr. Grainger," Pitt went on, "then you will have made your own enquiries into his personal life." He made it a statement, not a question. "I realize your findings are confidential, but it would be a great deal pleasanter for Mr. FitzJames if I were to learn what I need from you, who enquired for the most honorable of reasons, rather than on my own behalf, when I am investigating a particularly sordid murder in Whitechapel."

"You make your point, Mr. Pitt," Grainger said with a sudden tightening of his face. "I should be reluctant to have you do that, for the embarrassment to his family and for the shadow it would cast on his career . . . which I am sure you understand?"

"Of course. That is why I came to you."

"Very well." Grainger began resignedly. "Six or seven years ago he was a very raw and arrogant young man who took his pleasures wherever he wished. He drove far too fast. His father had bought him a very fine pair of horses, which he raced against other young men, frequently in the public streets." He stared at Pitt with cold, blue eyes. "But no one was ever seriously hurt, and it is something many rich young men do. Hardly a matter for comment." He made a steeple of his fingers. "He gambled, but always paid his debts—or his father did. Anyway, he left no dishonor, no one with ill feeling. And he certainly never cheated, which of course would be unforgivable."

"I assumed that," Pitt agreed with a smile. "What about women?"

"He flirted, naturally, but I never heard that anyone had cause for offense. Left a few broken hearts, and was occasionally disappointed himself. At one time his name was linked with one of Rutland's daughters, I believe, but nothing came of it. But there was no talk, nothing against either of them. I daresay she just received a better offer."

"Altogether a faultless young man," Pitt said a trifle sarcastically.

Grainger drew in a deep breath, keeping the irritation from his features with an obvious effort. "No, of course not. You know, Mr. Pitt, that that is not so, or I would merely have stated it and left you to your investigation. He frequented a good few houses of ill repute. He spent his share of time in the Haymarket and the surrounding areas, and a lot of nights a great deal more drunk than sober. His tastes were at times rather more lurid than one would wish, and his self-indulgence something better forgotten." He leveled his stare at Pitt. "But it has been forgotten, Superintendent. I daresay as a young man you had a few episodes you would prefer were not raised again, and perhaps of which your wife remains ignorant? Of course you have. So have I." He said it like a rehearsed speech, without a shadow of humor.

Pitt felt himself blush and it surprised him. There was nothing in his past which was shocking—simply clumsy and extremely selfish, things he would far rather Charlotte never knew. They would alter the way she saw him.

Could that really be all there was to Finlay FitzJames?

As if reading his thoughts, Grainger went on. "You understand, Superintendent? There are parts of all our lives which fate usually allows us to bury decently. It is only when some other circumstance arises which compels us to face examination that they can be raised again, for a few of us unfortunate enough to be at the wrong place at the wrong moment. Or, of course, to have enemies . . . ?" He left it in the air, more than a suggestion, less than a statement, something Pitt could complete for himself more effectively in his own imagination.

He thought about it for a moment. Was it conceivable that Finlay, or his father, had enemies clever enough and unscrupulous enough to have planted Finlay's badge at the scene of a murder? It would be an extraordinary coincidence.

He looked at Grainger's smooth face. He was a diplomat, used to thinking of death far away, in other countries, of other sorts of people whom he never saw. Perhaps to a man like him, dealing with men only as names and pieces of paper, such an enemy was not unimaginable.

There was a bird on the tree he could see through the window.

"Enemies who would murder a woman in order to embarrass Fitz-James?" he said with heavy doubt in his voice.

"Not Finlay, perhaps," Grainger conceded, "but his father. Augustus FitzJames is a very wealthy man, and he was ruthless in the early days of his climb. I agree that to murder someone simply to incriminate someone else is very extreme, but it is not impossible, Mr. Pitt, if hatred and ambition both run deep enough." He held his hands apart, then put them together again gently. "It seems to me at least as likely as the probability that a man such as Finlay FitzJames, who has everything to lose and nothing whatever to gain, should visit a Whitechapel prostitute and murder her, Superintendent. I am sure you want to see justice done as much as I do, not only in the courts but in the broader sense as well. A reputation ruined, a promotion lost, cannot be set right again with an apology or a retraction. I imagine you are as aware of that as I?" He stared at Pitt with wide eyes and a very slight smile.

Pitt left the Foreign Office with new shadows in his mind. He lunched with Micah Drummond, then the two of them walked slowly up the Mall past ladies in beautiful dresses with narrow, almost nonexistent bustles; just a clever draping of the fabric. That was the fashion of the moment. Their sweeping hats added an impossible grace. Parasols were folded and used elegantly, almost like sticks. He was here to talk about Finlay FitzJames, but even so he could not help occasionally glancing sideways with admiration and a distinct pleasure.

Other men did the same, gentlemen in beautifully cut suits and tall, shiny hats, soldiers in uniform, ribboned and medaled. There was laughter in the warm air, and faraway snatches on the breeze of a barrel organ, and children shouting in the park. Their feet made a slight crunch on the gravel.

"A ruthless man," Micah Drummond said, using the same word Grainger had. He was speaking about Augustus FitzJames. "Of course he had enemies, Pitt, but hardly the sort who would frequent Whitechapel, or find themselves in a Pentecost Alley tenement. Most of them are his own age, for a start."

"Elderly gentlemen use prostitutes as much as anyone else," Pitt said with impatience. "And you must know that!"

"Of course I know it," Drummond conceded, wrinkling his nose. He looked extremely well, not quite as thin as in the past, and his skin had the warmth of the sun on it. "But not in the Whitechapel area. Think about it, Pitt!" He raised his hat as he passed a lady who was apparently an acquaintance and then turned back to Pitt. "If the sort of man you are describing were to kill a prostitute in order to implicate FitzJames, he'd choose one of the better class of women, the sort he would use himself, around Windmill Street or the Haymarket. He wouldn't enter into an area he didn't know and where he'd be remembered as different."

"But he was remembered." Pitt half turned towards him. "That's just the point! Perhaps he was afraid he'd be recognized in his own haunts?"

"And when did he get the Hellfire Club badge?" Drummond added.

"I don't know. Perhaps he got it by chance, and that gave him the idea?"

"Opportunism?" Drummond was skeptical.

"Perhaps," Pitt agreed. "And maybe the chance to use the murder was opportunism as well?"

Drummond looked sideways at him, his long face full of wordless disbelief.

"Although," Pitt conceded, "I'm listening to the evidence. It probably was Finlay. I daresay he has a vicious streak in him which he's kept under control pretty well until now, and this time he went too far. He wouldn't be the first well-bred man to enjoy hurting people and be willing to pay for his entertainment." He took a deep breath. "Or the first to lose control and end in killing someone."

A small black dog trundled past them, nose to the ground, tail high.

"No," Drummond said sadly. "And I'm afraid it fits in with what little I know of him from my days in Bow Street."

Pitt stopped abruptly.

Drummond put his hands in his pockets and continued walking, but more slowly.

Pitt increased his pace to catch up with him.

"We had to cover up one or two unpleasantries a few years ago," Drummond went on. "Seven or eight years, almost. One incident was a brawl in one of the alleys off the Haymarket. Several young men had drunk too much and it ended in a very nasty affray. One of the women was fairly badly beaten."

"You said one or two," Pitt prompted.

"The other I recall was a fight with a pimp. He said FitzJames had asked for something unusual, and when it wasn't given had refused to pay. Apparently he'd already had the regular services, and when she wouldn't do whatever it was, he became very unpleasant. Unusually, the pimp came off quite badly. There was a knife, but both of them seem to have been cut with it. Not seriously."

"But that was hushed up too?" Pitt was not sure whether he was surprised or not. The picture was becoming uglier, more into the pattern both he and Ewart feared.

"Well, there wasn't a crime," Drummond pointed out, touching his hat absentmindedly to another acquaintance passing by. "Unless you want to call disturbing the peace a crime. It didn't seem worth a prosecution. He'd have fought against it, and the pimp was hardly a good witness."

"What was it FitzJames wanted the girl to do?" Pitt remembered the boots buttoned together in Pentecost Alley, the cold water and the garter around Ada McKinley's arm. He assumed the broken fingers were a cruelty peculiar to this particular incident.

"I don't know," Drummond confessed.

"What was the pimp's name?" Pitt went on. "What date was it? I can look it up in the records. You did keep a record, didn't you?"

"No I didn't." Drummond looked uncomfortable. "I'm sorry, Pitt. I think I was a little more naive then." He did not say any more about it, but they both knew the world of experience they had seen since then, the corruption and the ugliness of influence misused, the inner dishonesties.

They walked in silence for fifty yards, no sound but their feet on the gravel of the path.

"Do you remember his name?" Pitt asked at length.

Drummond sighed. "Yes. Percy Manker. But it won't do any good. He died of an overdose of opium. The river police pulled him out of Limehouse Reach. I'm sorry."

Pitt said nothing. They walked a little farther in the sun, then turned and retraced their steps. They did not speak any more about FitzJames, choosing instead to think of pleasanter things, domestic and family matters. Drummond asked after Charlotte, and told Pitt about his own wife's happiness in their new home and the small businesses of daily life.

Pitt had no hope of learning anything of value about Finlay Fitz-James from Helliwell or Thirlstone. He had thought he might persuade Jago Jones that truth, in this case, was a higher good than personal loyalty. Jones's parishioners had the right to expect a certain loyalty from him as well, and Ada had been a parishioner, in however loose a sense.

He found Jago alone in the church itself, the sunlight streaming in through the windows into bright patterns on the stone floor and across the worn pews. He turned in surprise when he saw Pitt walking up the aisle.

"Thank you for coming," he said. Pitt knew he did not mean this occasion but the brief half hour he had spent at Ada's funeral two days before.

He smiled. There was no answer to make.

"What brings you now?" Jago asked, walking down towards where a long-handled broom was resting against the first pew. "Do you know who killed Ada?"

"I think so . . ."

Jago's eyebrows rose. "But you are not sure? That means you don't have proof."

"I have a very strong indication, it just seems such a stupid thing to have done. I need a clearer picture of the man in order to believe it. I already have a picture of Ada."

Jago shook his head. "Well, Ada I could have helped you with. The man I doubt I know." He picked up the broom and began to sweep the last area of the floor which still needed doing. "You don't mind?"

"Not at all," Pitt conceded, sitting on the pew and crossing his legs. "You're wrong. You do know the man, or at least you did."

Jago stopped, still standing with the broom in his hands, his shoulders back. He did not turn to look at Pitt.

"You mean Finlay?"

"Yes."

"Because of the badge? I told you, he could have lost that years ago."

"Possibly. But he didn't leave it in Ada McKinley's bed years ago, Reverend."

Jago said nothing. The unlikelihood of someone else's having stolen the badge, or found it by accident, and chancing to have left it by the dead woman's bed, and the cuff link also, lay unspoken between them. Jago continued sweeping the floor, carefully directing the dust and grit into a little pile. Pitt watched him. The sunlight slanted in through the windows in bright, dusty bars.

"You knew him well a few years ago," Pitt said at last. "Have you seen him at all since then?"

"Very little." Jago did not look up. "I don't frequent the places he does. I never go to Mayfair or Whitehall, and he doesn't come to Saint Mary's."

"You don't say that he doesn't come to Whitechapel," Pitt pointed out.

Jago smiled. "That's rather the matter at issue, isn't it?"

"Have you ever seen him here?"

"No."

"Or heard that he was here?"

Jago straightened up. "No, Superintendent. I have never heard of Finlay being here, nor have I reason to suppose that he has been."

Pitt believed him. Yet there was something in Jago's attitude which disturbed him. There was a pain in him, an anxiety which was more than merely sadness for the violent death of someone he had known, however slightly. When he had first told him they had found Finlay's badge he had looked like a man in a nightmare.

He changed his approach. "What was Finlay like when you knew him?"

Jago swept up the dust in a pan and set it aside before he answered, propping the broom up against the wall.

"Younger, and very much more foolish, Superintendent. We all were. I am not proud of my behavior in those times. I was extremely selfish, I indulged my tastes whenever I could, with disregard for the consequences to others. It is not a time I look back on with any pleasure. I imagine it may well be the same for Finlay. One grows up. One cannot undo the selfishness of youth, but one can leave it behind, learn from its mistakes, and avoid too quick or too cruel a judgment in those who in their turn do likewise."

Pitt did not doubt his sincerity, but he also had the feeling it was a speech he had prepared in his mind for the time he should be asked.

"You have told me a lot about yourself, Reverend, but not about Finlay FitzJames."

Jago shook his head very slightly.

"There's nothing to tell. We were all self-indulgent. If you are asking me if Finlay has also changed, grown up, then since I have not seen him above a couple of times in the last three years, I cannot answer you from my knowledge. I imagine so."

"I learned where to find you through his sister. Presumably you are still acquainted with her?" Pitt pressed.

Jago laughed very slightly. "Tallulah? Yes, in a manner of speaking. She is still in that stage of selfishness and the all-consuming pursuit of pleasure that the members of the Hellfire Club indulged in six or seven years ago. She has yet to see the purpose of any other kind of existence." He said no more in words, but the expression of weariness in his face, the slight tightness to his lips, showed vividly how little regard he had for her. It was as if he did not wish to despise her but could not help himself. He despised his own past life at the same time as he asked compassion for Finlay.

Why? Was it a fear that Finlay had not, in fact, grown beyond it at all but, like Tallulah, still placed his pleasures above honor or responsibility?

"Why has your friendship lapsed so completely?" Pitt asked as if he were no more than mildly curious.

Jago did not move. He stared at Pitt without speaking. He drew in his breath as if to reply, then let it out again.

Somewhere beyond the church a woman called out to a child and a dog scampered past the open door.

Pitt waited.

"I suppose . . . I suppose our paths just . . . diverged," Jago said at last, his eyes wide and dark. He was saying something far less than the truth, and even as he did so he knew that Pitt knew it.

Pitt did not bother to argue.

"I admire your loyalty, Reverend," he said very quietly. "But are you sure that it is as commendable as you think? What about your loyalty to Ada McKinley, who was one of your parishioners, whatever her trade? What about the other women like her? They may be whores, but if you have set yourself as their shepherd, don't you also have a loyalty to the truth, and to the path you've chosen?"

Jago's face was white, the flesh seemed to be pulled tight as though by some desperate inner strain.

"I do not know who killed Ada, Superintendent. I tell you before God, I do not. Nor do I have any reason to believe that Finlay was here in Whitechapel that night, or any other. If I did, I would tell you." He took a deep breath. "As to my friendship with the FitzJames family, it lapsed because of a difference of opinion—of purpose, if you like. Finlay could not understand my taking this calling, nor my wish to devote my life to it. It is not something I could explain, except in terms he did not believe or respect. He thinks I am eccentric, as does his sister."

"Eccentric?"

Jago laughed; this time there was real amusement in his voice. "Oh, not in any admirable sense! She admires the aesthetes, men like Oscar Wilde and Arthur Symons, or Havelock Ellis, who are endlessly inventive, always saying or doing . . . or believing . . . something new. Their purpose is to shock and cause comment . . . and I suppose possibly also to make people think. They see me as an utterly different kind of eccentric. I am a bore . . . the only thing even their moral tolerance will not forgive. It is the one sin that cannot be overlooked."

Pitt searched, but he could see no self-pity in Jago's face, no bitterness whatsoever. For him they had missed the real happiness, not he.

And yet there was still the shadow behind his smile, the awareness of something he would not tell Pitt, something which was full of darkness and pain. Was it knowledge of Finlay FitzJames, or of himself? Or was it possibly one of the other members of the Hellfire Club, either the sensual Thirlstone or the self-satisfied Helliwell?

"Are you still friendly with any of the other members of the Hellfire Club?" he asked suddenly.

"What?" Jago seemed surprised. "Oh! No. No, I am afraid not. I see Thirlstone from time to time, but by chance, not design. I haven't seen Helliwell in a couple of years. He's done nicely for himself, I hear. Married and became respectable—and very well-off. It was what he always wished, once he had had his fling."

"What does Finlay want?"

Jago smiled again, this time with patience. "I'm not sure if he knows. Probably to fulfill his father's ambitions for him, without the hard work and the pressure which they must inevitably involve. I don't think he really wants to be Foreign Secretary, still less Prime Minister. But then I suppose Augustus will die before it comes to that anyway, and he'll be able to relax and be what he truly wants . . . if he can still remember what that is." He stopped. "Maybe Tallulah will marry well and become a duchess, or a great countess. I doubt she has the intelligence to be a great political wife. That requires considerable skill and tact, and a profound understanding of the issues and of human nature, as well as fashion and etiquette and how to be entertaining. She hasn't the discretion, for one thing."

"Might she not acquire it?" Pitt asked. "She's still very young."

"There's no good acquiring discretion once you've marred your own reputation, Superintendent. Society doesn't forget. At least that's not exactly true. It will to a certain extent if you are a man, but not if you are a woman. Depends what you do." He leaned against the pew, relaxing a little at last.

"I've known young men to behave really badly, being drunk and extremely offensive, and their comrades will hold a trial and decide he is guilty of a breach of behavior which cannot be overlooked. Then he will be advised that he should volunteer for some foreign service, say in Africa, or India, for example, and not return."

Pitt stared at him, stunned.

"And he will do so," Jago finished. "Society will discipline its own. Some things are not accepted." He stood upright. "Of course others are, sometimes things you or I might find abhorrent. It depends on how public the outrage is, and against whom. If you want me to say Finlay never visited a prostitute, I can't. But then you know that already. If that were a crime, you could charge half the gentlemen in London. Where else are they to take their appetites? A decent woman would be ruined, and they themselves would not want her afterwards."

"I know that," Pitt agreed. "Is that the issue?"

"No," Jago conceded, looking at Pitt thoughtfully. "But old Augustus has made a great many enemies, you know, people he used and threw away in his rise to power, people who lost because he won. There's more than one family owes its misfortune to him, and a great house doesn't forgive its ruin. There are a few political ambitions which would be helped along if it were known they had destroyed FitzJames. Power is cruel, Superintendent, and envy is crueler. Before you commit yourself to any action against Finlay, be sure it really was he who left the badge in Pentecost Alley and not one of his father's enemies. I . . . I find it terribly difficult to believe it was the man I knew . . . and I knew him well then."

Pitt searched his face, trying to read in it the emotions behind his words, and saw too many conflicting currents, but through them all a certainty of gentleness, and even in his eyes a restraint from judgment.

He rose to his feet.

"Thank you, Reverend. I can't say that you have helped me

greatly, but then I shouldn't have expected it." He bade him good-bye and walked out into the hot street with its noise and traffic, its horses and scurrying people on foot, the clatter of hooves, voices and film of dirt. He felt an even deeper liking for Jago Jones than before, and a conviction that in some fundamental way, he was lying.

"Well, have you learned anything else about FitzJames?" Cornwallis said in exasperation. It was the end of the day, and the sun had already set in an orange ball behind the wreath of chimney smoke that lay over the rooftops. The heat still burned up from the pavements and the smell of horse droppings was pungent where crossing sweepers had shoveled it to one side but no carts had been by to pick it up.

Carriages still bowled along the streets as the lamps came on, electric now along the Thames Embankment. People were beginning to think of the theater and the opera, restaurant dinners and evening parties. The lights of pleasure boats were visible on the river, and the sound of music drifted up.

"No," Pitt answered wearily, standing beside Cornwallis at the window. "Jago Jones won't say more than that they were all wild half a dozen years ago and that he hasn't kept more than casual touch since then. And that's easy to believe, since he's now a priest in Whitechapel . . ." He smiled for an instant. "Not exactly FitzJames's territory. The Foreign Office says he's able, diligent, behaves as well as most young men and better than some. And as soon as he marries suitably, he is likely to get a very good embassy post. He certainly has talent in that direction, and a good deal of charm."

"But you have Rose Burke's identification of him!" Cornwallis insisted, turning away from the window to stare at Pitt. "And the badge, and the cuff link. Have you had that identified as his?"

"Yes."

Cornwallis's face was grave.

"Then, what's troubling you, Pitt? Have you some evidence you haven't told me of? Or are you worried about political pressure?" He shook his head slightly. "FitzJames's friends are increasing their pressure, but it will never stop me from backing you totally—if you are sure he's guilty and you can prove it."

"Thank you, sir." Pitt meant it profoundly. It was a gift beyond price to have a superior whose nerve held under fire, even when his own position might be threatened. He was less certain of his judgment. Did he really have an understanding of how powerful Augustus FitzJames's friends might be and how little innocence or guilt might matter to them, so long as there was every chance it would never be exposed? And had he also considered that FitzJames might also have enemies who were equally powerful? Jago Jones's words rang in his mind and he could not ignore them.

"You haven't answered me." Cornwallis broke the train of his thoughts.

"I wish I had someone else who had seen Finlay in Whitechapel . . . anyone else at all," Pitt replied. "I can't find any evidence of his having been there, that night or at any other time. I'll put Tellman on it tomorrow, as discreetly as possible."

"Doesn't prove anything," Cornwallis continued. "He may usually do his whoring in the Haymarket, doesn't mean to say he didn't go to Whitechapel this time. Have you tried cabbies? Other street women? Local constables on the beat?"

"Ewart has. No one has seen him. But they know him farther west."

"Damn," Cornwallis swore under his breath. "When were the cuff link and the badge last seen by his valet, or anyone whose evidence is reasonably unprejudiced?"

"Valet's been with him for years and has never seen either," Pitt replied.

Cornwallis digested this in silence.

The carriage lamps moved slowly along the street towards them and the sound of wheels and hooves came up through the still air.

"What do you think, Pitt?" he said at last.

"I think he's guilty, but I don't think we've proved it yet," Pitt replied, surprising himself as he said it. "But I'm not sure," he added.

"Well, you'd better make sure," Cornwallis said grimly. "Within the next week."

"Yes sir," Pitt agreed. "I'll try."

CHAPTER

FIVE

Emily spent a very ordinary day, like any other during the London season. She rose at eight and at nine went riding in the Park, where she nodded to a score of acquaintances, all of whom were agreeable enough, but none were particular friends. But the day was fine, the air brisk and sweet, and her horse was an excellent beast. She rode well, and returned a little after ten, feeling invigorated.

Jack had already left for Whitehall and Edward was in the schoolroom, so she ate alone. Evie was in the nursery being cared for by the nursemaid.

She spent the next two hours reading and answering correspondence, of which there was not a great deal. Largely she wasted time. She planned the day's menu, over which she could not consult Jack because he was not there. Next she called the housekeeper and discussed half a dozen domestic matters with her regarding linen, parlor maids' duties, the new scullery maid, the mark on the library carpet and several other things, to discover they had all been dealt with satisfactorily without her advice.

She spoke to her ladies' maid, and found that she too had already solved all the minor problems which had arisen.

"The red ink on the sleeve of my morning dress," she began. She had been leaning over Edward's map of India, admiring it.

"Already done it, m'lady," Gwen said with satisfaction.

"Gone?" Emily was amazed. "Red ink?"

"Yes, m'lady. Mustard does it. Smeared a little mustard over it before it was laundered. Works a treat."

"Thank you."

"An' if I could have a few drops of gin, m'lady, I'll clean up the diamonds in your bracelet. They've got a bit dusty over use. I asked Cook, but she wouldn't give it me without your say-so. Reckon she thought I might drink it!"

"Yes, of course," Emily agreed, feeling utterly redundant.

She fared no better with the nursemaid and the cook.

At noon she left the house in her own carriage and went to call upon her mother, only to find that she was out. She debated whether to go shopping or visit an art gallery, and decided upon the latter. It was extremely boring. The pictures were all very genteel, and to her, appeared exactly like the same exhibition the previous year.

She returned home, where she was joined for luncheon by her grandmother, who demanded an account of her morning and her plans for the remainder of the week. When she had heard them, she dismissed them as trivial, scatterbrained and totally frivolous. She spoke out of envy, because she would dearly have liked to have done the same, but Emily privately agreed with her.

"You should be supporting your husband!" the old lady said viciously. "You should be engaged in some worthy work. I was, at your age! I was on the parish council for unmarried mothers. I can't tell you the number of wicked girls whose futures I helped decide."

"God help them," Emily muttered.

"What did you say?" the old woman demanded.

"How helpful," Emily lied. She did not want a full-scale battle.

At half past three she attended an afternoon concert with the wife of one of Jack's friends, a worthy woman with very limited conversation. She found almost everything "uplifting." At half past four they went together to a garden party and remained for half an hour, by which time Emily was ready to scream. She wished she had paid afternoon calls instead, or gone to a charity bazaar alone, but it was too late.

At half past six Jack returned home in something of a hurry. They dined in haste and then changed before leaving for a theater party with friends they knew only slightly. At half past eleven they had supper, made a great deal of light, very trivial conversation. By a quarter to one she was in bed and too tired to think constructively, but quite sure the day had been wasted.

Tomorrow she would do something with purpose. In the morning she could use the telephone and discover at which social function she could expect to run into Tallulah FitzJames. She would address the matter of helping her, either with her romantic decision regarding Jago and how to effect a satisfactory conclusion or else with clearing her brother of the suspicion of having committed the murder in Whitechapel, or possibly even both.

At a little after two o'clock, having lunched early, Emily dressed in her most gorgeously fashionable afternoon gown: an exquisitely cut pink brocade with a confection of silk at bosom, neck and elbow, and a skirt which moved most flatteringly as she walked. She took an outrageous hat, one by which even Aunt Vespasia would be impressed, and a matching parasol, then set out for a flower show in Kensington where she had ascertained Tallulah was very likely to be.

She arrived at three, alighted from her carriage and immediately saw several ladies of her acquaintance. She was obliged to exchange greetings and to accompany them into the succession of tents and enclosures filled with arrays of flowers and blooming shrubs and trees. Small wrought-iron tables painted white were set between, with two or three graceful chairs by each. Beautifully dressed ladies wandered from arrangement to arrangement, often accompanied by gentlemen in afternoon frock coats, cutaway jackets, striped trousers and shiny, tall hats. Here and there young girls of twelve or fourteen stood primly in flounced dresses, long hair held back with ribbons around their heads, or made faces at each other when they imagined no one was looking.

Emily's heart sank. She had forgotten how crowded flower shows were, how many winding pathways there were between the exhibits, arbors under potted trees, and places between arrays of blossoms and under overhanging boughs where people might talk discreetly or flirt. One could keep assignations with little chance of being seen by those one would prefer to avoid. No doubt that was why Tallulah had chosen such a place. It sounded so respectable. What could be more appropriate for a young lady to attend than a flower show? How feminine. How delightfully innocent. No doubt she could learn much about gardens, conservatories and the tasteful ways of decorating one's formal rooms for dinners, soirées or any other manner of receiving guests. All of which would be the last thing on Tallulah's mind.

Emily asked quite casually if anyone had seen Miss FitzJames, inventing some slight reason for wanting to speak to her—a friend in common, a milliner's name.

It took her nearly an hour before she found her, and then it was by chance. She came around the corner of a large exhibit of late roses and some high-standing, very vivid yellow lilies, and saw Tallulah sitting in an arbor created out of the twined branches of a vine. She was leaning back, her feet on the chair as though it were a chaise longue, skirts draped carelessly, her long, slender throat arched. Her dark hair was beginning to fall a little out of its pins. It was a relaxed, seductive pose, graceful and inviting.

The young man beside her was plainly entranced. He leaned farther and farther forward as she regarded him lazily through half-closed eyes. Emily could completely understand the desire to behave shockingly. She herself had never done anything of the sort, but then she had so far not been severely tempted . . . not yet.

"Why Tallulah! How nice to see you!" she said utterly ingenuously, as if they had bumped into each other walking in the Park. "Aren't the flowers gorgeous? I would never have thought they could find as much as this so late in the year."

Tallulah stared at her in amazement turning to dismay. Such a breach of tact was inexcusable. Emily should have withdrawn, blushing and suitably taken aback.

Emily stood precisely where she was, a bland smile on her face.

"I always think August is a difficult season," she went on cheerfully. "Too late for one thing and too early for another."

"There seems to me to be plenty of flowers," the young man said, pink-faced. He straightened his tie and collar as if he were trying to appear to be doing something else.

"I am sure there are, sir," Emily agreed, fixing her eyes on his hands. "To men there always seem to be plenty of flowers." She let the remark hang in the air, with its double meaning, and turned to Tallulah, her bright smile back again. "I have been thinking quite hard about the matter you discussed with me the last time we had an opportunity to talk together. I would so like to be of assistance. I am sure something could be done."

Tallulah continued to stare at her, but gradually the lightness died out of her face. She straightened up, ignoring her gown and the angle to which it had slipped. "Are you? It is much worse, you know? It is all much worse."

The young man realized that the conversation had proceeded beyond anything of which he was aware. He rose and excused himself, doing it with surprising flair, in the circumstances, and with a bow took his leave.

Tallulah readjusted her gown, her face now very somber.

"I saw Jago again," she said quietly. "Not for very long. It was a charity bazaar. I knew he would be there, for his wretched church, so I went. He looked through me as if I were some naughty child he was obliged to be civil to, as one does when other people's children misbehave and one cannot do anything because their parents won't permit it." She screwed up her face. "Suffering with a weary and tolerant look. I was so angry I could have slapped him!"

Emily saw the pain in Tallulah's eyes and the struggle to know whether she should deny it or try to face and overcome it. It was so much easier to pretend it was only anger she felt, not pain.

Emily sat down where the young man had been. The scent of the flowers was heavy in the air. She was glad of the very slight breeze.

"Are you sure you don't want him simply because he's unattainable?" she said frankly.

Tallulah thought about it in silence. She sat down again where she had been before, only this time more decorously, her feet on the ground.

"Are you attracted to a man who adores you?" Emily would not be put off.

"No," Tallulah said immediately. Then she smiled. "Are you?"

"Not in the slightest," Emily confessed. "He has to be at the very least unsuitable, but better he should need to be won as well. The harder the battle, the more the prize is worth. Men are the same, of course. It is simply that we are better, on the whole, at disguising it and pretending to be uninterested, when we are actually enthralled."

"Jago is not enthralled," Tallulah said glumly. "At least not by me. I might have a better chance of engaging his emotions if I were a fallen woman and he thought he could save my soul!"

"Is that what you were about just now?" Emily asked with a smile. "Falling?"

But Tallulah was too hurt to be amused.

"No, of course not," she said tartly. "I was merely bored. It was all words and ideas. If you knew Sawyer, you'd know that. Everything's a pose with him."

Emily sat back a little farther, making herself comfortable. It was very warm in the bower, and the perfume of so many petals a trifle clinging.

"Why don't you simply forget Jago?" she asked without pretense at subtlety. "The thought of him is only causing you distress. A challenge is excellent, but not one you can't win. That's just depressing. Anyway, what would you do if you had him? You couldn't possibly marry him. He hasn't any money! Or do you just want your revenge on him because he despises you, or you think he does?"

"He does."

"So you want revenge?"

Tallulah stared at her. With the sunlight dappled on her face she had a kind of beauty, one born of courage and a fierce vitality.

"No, I don't. That would be horrible." Her voice sharpened in frustration. "You really don't understand at all, do you? Jago is the best person I've ever known! There's an honor in him, and a gentleness unlike that in anyone else I've ever met. He's honest." She leaned forward. "I don't just mean he doesn't take things that aren't his, I mean he doesn't even want to. He doesn't lie to other people, but he doesn't lie to himself either. That's rare, you know? I lie to myself all the time. All my family does, mostly about why they do things. They say they had to, when what they mean is they wanted to so they looked around for an excuse. I've seen it all the time."

"So have I," Emily admitted. "But I'm not sure I could live with anyone who always spoke the unadulterated truth. I don't think I want to know it, and I'm quite sure I don't want to hear it. It may be very admirable, but I would sooner admire it from a distance . . . quite a large distance."

Tallulah laughed, but there was no happiness in it. "You are deliberately misunderstanding me. I don't mean he's tactless, or cruel. I just mean he has a sort of . . . light inside him. He's . . . whole. His mind doesn't have lots of different pieces, like most people's, all wanting different things, and lying to each other so you can try to have everything, and telling yourself it's all right."

"How do you know?"

"What?"

"How do you know that?" Emily repeated. "How do you know what is inside him?"

Tallulah was silent. Two girls in pink and peach walked past them, deep in conversation, heads close together, the brindled light in their hair. "I don't know why I'm explaining all this to you!" Tallulah said at last. "It doesn't really fit into any words. I know what I mean. I know that he has a kind of courage that most people haven't. He faces what really matters, without evasions and excuses. His beliefs are whole." She stared at Emily. "Do you understand me at all?"

"Yes," Emily agreed quietly, dropping the challenge from her voice. "I only wanted to see if you really care for him as much as you think. Wouldn't you find him a little serious? After a while might not so much goodness become a trifle predictable, and then ultimately become even boring?"

Tallulah turned her head away, her profile outlined against the bank of blossoms. "It really doesn't matter. He's never going to look at me as anything but Finlay FitzJames's rather shallow sister who wastes her life buying dresses that cost enough to keep one of his Whitechapel families in food and clothes for years." She looked down at her exquisite skirt and smoothed it over the flat of her stomach. "This cost fifty-one pounds, seventeen shillings and sixpence. We pay our best maids twenty pounds a year. The scullery maids and tweenies get less than half that. I saw it in the household accounts. And I have a dozen or more dresses as good as this one."

She shrugged and smiled. "And yet I go to church on Sundays and pray, and so does everyone else I know, all dressed in clothes like this. It isn't that Jago would tell me I'm wrong. If no one buys them, then the people who make them have no trade. He just wouldn't be bothered with me, because I care so much what I look like. But then for an unmarried woman that's what matters, isn't it." It was not a question but a statement of fact.

Emily did not argue, nor did she bother to mention money or family influence. Tallulah knew the rules as well as she did.

"Would you marry him?" she asked softly, thinking of Charlotte and Pitt. But Charlotte was different. She had never been the socialite that Tallulah was. Her wit was far too acerbic, her outspokenness seldom—not often—funny. She was not intentionally outrageous; she was a genuine misfit. And to be honest, it was not as if she had had so many other good offers. She rather put people off.

Although in spite of her father's wealth, if Tallulah continued to behave as she had done this afternoon and the other evening in Chelsea, she might not receive any offers in the future. There were many women whom people found vastly entertaining but did not marry.

Tallulah sighed and looked up at the flowers overhead, her expression a strange mixture of wistfulness and horror, and a kind of desperate laughter at herself.

"If I were to marry him, I would have to live in Whitechapel, wear gray stuff dresses and be happy ladling out soup to the poor. I should have to be polite to the self-righteous women who think laughter is a sin and love is telling people what they ought to do. I would eat the same food every day, answer my own door, and always watch what I said, in case it offended anyone. I'd never be able to go to the theater again, or the opera, or dine in restaurants, or ride in the Park."

"Worse than that," Emily put in. "You'd have to ride on the omnibus, crammed in with other people, fat, out of breath and smelling of onions. You'd have to do most of your own cooking, and count your money to judge whether you could buy a thing or not, and the answer would usually be not." She was thinking of Charlotte's early years, before Pitt's last promotion. Some of them had been hard. But they had shared so much that Emily now looked back on that time with a kind of envy. She seemed to have shared more with Jack before he had won his seat in Parliament, when there was still so much to work for, and victory was uncertain, and a long way away. He had needed her so much more then.

"It wouldn't be so bad as that," Tallulah argued. "Papa would make me an allowance."

"Even if you married a parish priest, instead of his choice for you?" Emily said skeptically. "Are you sure?"

Tallulah stared at her, her eyes wide and dark brown, nearly black.

"No," she said quietly. "No, he'd be furious. He'd never forgive me. He'd like me to marry a duke, although an earl or a marquis might do. I don't think his ambition has any ceiling, to be honest. If I thought about it harder, it would frighten me. Nothing ever stops him, he just finds a way around it. People have tried to stand up to him, but they never win."

Distant laughter sounded somewhere behind them, and a girl giggling. It really was getting very hot.

"Have you?" Emily asked.

Tallulah shook her head. "I've never needed to."

"Would you, to marry Jago?"

Tallulah turned away. "I don't know. Perhaps not. But as I said, it doesn't matter. Jago wouldn't have me."

"Perhaps that's just as well," Emily said deliberately. "That you don't have to make up your mind what you really want: to be rich and have pretty gowns, parties, trips to the theater, and marry whoever your father tells you . . . or marry a man you really love and admire, and trust, and help him in his life's work—in comparative poverty. I don't suppose you'd ever actually be hungry, and you'd always have a roof over your head—but it might leak."

Tallulah swung around on the seat to stare at her in a flash of temper.

"I don't suppose your roof leaks, Mrs. Radley!" she snapped. "Even if Jack Radley's would, I'll lay any odds the late Lord Ashworth's doesn't!"

It was a reference to Emily's first husband and his very considerable wealth. Emily might have resented the gibe, but she knew she had provoked a retaliation, and she accepted it as fair.

"No it doesn't," she agreed. "But whether I even took a decision or not is beside the point. The thing is for you to recognize the reality of what your choices are. No one has everything. No relationship does. Look at Jago carefully. Look at whoever else there is, and decide what you want . . . then fight for it."

"You make it sound simple."

"That part of it is."

"No, it isn't." Tallulah sat forward and leaned over, putting her hands up over her cheeks. It was a gesture of deep and troubled thought.

An elderly couple walked by, heads close together in earnest conversation, the woman's parasol trailing, the man's hat at a rakish angle. She said something and they both laughed.

"If this wretched business with Finlay doesn't get solved soon," Tallulah went on suddenly, her voice low and filled with anger and fear, "and the police don't stop asking everyone questions about us, then it won't matter anyway. We'll all be ruined, and nobody will speak to any of us unless they have to. I've known it to happen. A story comes out. It is whispered around, and suddenly no one sees you. You are invisible. You can walk down the street and everyone is looking the other way. You talk to people and they don't hear you." Her voice was rising with the fear inside her. "Restaurants where you dine frequently find they are full whenever you call. Dressmakers are too busy to see you. Milliners have nothing to suit you. Your tailors can't fit you in. You call on people and nobody is ever at home, even if the lights are on and the carriages are lined up outside. It is as if you'd died, without being aware of it. It can happen over cheating at cards or welching on a debt of honor. Think what it would do over being hanged for murder!"

This time Emily did not rush in so quickly. It was much too painful an issue to challenge beliefs, or call it self-examination. She would like to have thought beyond doubt that of course Finlay was innocent; it was only a matter of waiting until Pitt found the proof. But she had known Pitt long enough, and seen sufficient cases of human tragedy and violence, to have any such comfortable illusion. People one loves, people one imagines one knows, can have aspects to their nature which are full of uncontrollable pain or anger, dark needs even they barely understand.

"If they are still investigating him, then they have not yet proof," she said aloud, weighing her words carefully.

"It means they still think he is guilty, though," Tallulah responded instantly, her eyes brilliant. "Otherwise they'd leave him alone."

The heat in the arbor was motionless. Distant laughter sounded yards away, although it was merely around the corner. The clink of glass and china came clearly above the buzz of conversation. But they were both too intent on the matter at hand to think of refreshment.

"Do you know why?" Emily asked quietly.

Tallulah's mouth tightened. It was obviously something she had thought about and the answer troubled her.

"Yes. There were belongings of his found where this woman was killed, a badge from that ridiculous club he used to belong to, and a cuff link. He told them about it. He said he lost both of them years ago. He hasn't seen them, and neither has anyone else." Her face tightened. "Some sordid little policeman came and questioned his valet, but he's only been with us for a few years, and he'd never seen them at all. Finlay certainly didn't have them that night." She stared at Emily, defying her to disbelieve.

"Nothing else?" Emily asked without changing her expression from one of strictly practical enquiry into fact.

"Yes . . . actually, some prostitute says she saw a man going into the woman's room, and swears he looked like Finlay. But how can they take her word against his? No jury ever would!" She searched Emily's eyes. "Would they?"

Emily could feel the fear in Tallulah as powerfully as the heat of the sun or the clinging scent of the flowers. It was more real than the distant chatter or movement of color as a woman in an exquisite gown drifted by. But was it fear of social ruin, fear of being unjustly convicted, or fear that perhaps he was not innocent at all?

"I wouldn't have thought so," Emily said cautiously. "Where was he that evening?"

"At a party in Beaufort Street. I can't remember what number, but nearer the river end."

"Well, can't he prove it?" Emily said with a rush of hope. "Someone there must remember him. In fact, probably dozens of people do. Surely he's said so?"

Tallulah looked deeply unhappy.

"Wasn't he there?" Emily asked.

"Yes . . . yes he was." Tallulah's face creased with confusion and misery. "I saw him there myself. . . ."

A waiter strode by, holding aloft a tray of chilled drinks in long-stemmed glasses which chinked as they touched each other. In the distance someone laughed.

Emily realized there must be far more to the story, something very ugly and very private. She did not ask.

"But you cannot say so," she concluded the obvious.

Tallulah turned to her quickly. "I would if I thought anyone would believe me. I'm not trying to protect myself. I'd clear Fin in a second, if I could! But it wasn't that sort of party. They were all taking opium, and that kind of thing. I was only there for about half an hour, then I left. But I did see Fin, although I think he was already too far gone to see me. The place was full of people, all laughing and either drunk or in a daze."

"But you saw Finlay . . . definitely!" Emily said with conviction. "You weren't drunk . . . or . . . or on opium?"

"No." Tallulah took a shaky breath. "But, you see, when Papa asked where I had been, in front of Mama, and the servants, and Mama's doctor . . . I said I had been somewhere else. No one would believe me now. They'd think I was just lying to protect Fin! And who wouldn't think so? If I were them, that's what I'd think."

Emily would like to have argued, said something comforting, but she knew that Tallulah was right. No one would take her testimony seriously.

Tallulah looked down at her hands lying on her skirt. "Damnation!" she said fiercely. "Isn't this a mess!" She clenched her fists. "Sometimes he's so stupid I could hate him."

Emily said nothing. She was thinking hard, searching for any thread she could grasp that might help. This was a practical problem. It would not be solved by indulging emotions, however justified.

"I remember I used to think he was marvelous," Tallulah went on, as much to herself as to Emily. "When I was young he used to have such exciting ideas. He would invent games for us, turn the whole nursery into another world, a desert island, a pirate ship, the Victory at Trafalgar, or a palace, or the Houses of Parliament." She smiled and her eyes were soft with the memory. "Or a forest with dragons. I'd be the maiden and he'd rescue me. He'd be the dragon as well. He used to make me laugh so much."

Emily did not interrupt.

"Then of course he had to go away to school," Tallulah went on. "I missed him terribly. I don't think I've ever been as lonely as

I was then. I lived the whole term time until he should come back home again. To begin with he was just the same, but gradually he changed. Of course he did. He grew up. He only wanted to play with boys. He was still kind to me, but he had no patience. All his dreams were forward and not backward to where I was. It was then I began to understand all the things that men can do and women can't." She looked across at a group strolling past, a man in a tall hat with a young woman on one arm and an older woman on the other with a magnificent feather-trimmed hat, but she did not seem to see them.

"Men can go to Parliament or become ambassadors," she went on. "Join the army or the navy, become explorers or bankers or deal in stocks or imports and exports." She shrugged dramatically. "Write drama, music, be philosophers or poets. Women get married. Men get married too, but only as an incidental. I realized that when I understood what Papa expected of me and what he hoped for Fin. He would like to have had more sons. Mama was always sorry for that. I suppose it was her fault."

Emily had a suddenly bleak picture of family life at the Fitz-Jameses', a little girl realizing with a rush of coldness how small a part of her life was in her own control, how restricted her choices compared with those of her brother. Her mother's success or failure depended on how many sons she bore, and it was not something she could help. Perhaps Tallulah would be the same . . . a failure. Only one thing of importance would be asked of her, and she might not manage to do it.

Emily's own life was the same. She had married a man who wanted sons to carry on his title, but she had not felt the same pressure. She could not recall even doubting herself. But then she had had no brothers.

"Sometimes when Fin was home from school there'd be some terrible quarrels." Tallulah was still staring into the distance, living the past. "Papa would call him into his study, and Fin would come out white-faced. But it was always all right in the end. Nothing terrible ever happened. I was very frightened at first. I remember I sat on the landing behind the stair rail and looked down into the hall, waiting for him to come out of the study, terrified he'd been beaten or something. I don't know what I really expected. But it never happened. It was always all right."

Someone laughed in the distance, but she barely seemed to hear it.

"Fin and Papa still made their plans. Fin went back to school, then to University, then into the Foreign Office. If this goes away without any scandal, he'll be posted to a really good ambassadorship, probably Paris. He'll have to get married first, but that won't be difficult. There are dozens of suitable girls who'd be happy to have him."

She took a deep breath and turned to look at Emily, her eyes bright with tears.

"I wish I could help, but I don't even have any idea what I could do! He won't talk about it to me, but I know he's frightened. Mama won't talk about it either, except to say it will be all right because he can't be guilty and Papa will see that he isn't blamed for something he couldn't possibly have done."

Emily had a picture of a frightened woman, loving her son but knowing startlingly little about him, seeing in her heart only the child she had known so many years ago. She did not see the present man who lived in a world outside her experience, with appetites beyond her emotional or physical imagination, a woman clinging to decency because it was what she lived by, perhaps even lived for. What did Aloysia FitzJames know of reality beyond her very handsome, safe front door?

No wonder modern, outrageous Tallulah could not speak to her or share her fears. It would be cruel and completely pointless even to try. Who did Tallulah talk to? Her society friends who were all totally occupied in seeking suitable marriages? The convention-defying aesthete set who sat up all night talking about art and meaning, the idolatry of the senses, the worship of beauty and wit? Jago? But he had time only for the poor. He did not see the loneliness or the panic behind her extravagant dresses and defiant face.

"We'll do something," Emily stated with absolute determination. "To begin with we'll deal with this badge which they say is his. If he didn't leave it there, then someone else must have, either by accident or deliberately."

"Deliberately?" Tallulah stared at her. "You mean they stole it and put it there to try to get Finlay hanged?" She shivered in spite of the heat, which was now so intense there was a fine dew of perspiration on her brow and Emily could feel the muslin of her own gown sticking to her uncomfortably.

"Is that impossible?" she asked.

Tallulah hesitated only a moment. "No, no it isn't," she answered with a catch in her voice. "Papa has quite a few enemies. I've come to realize that more lately. They might want to strike out at him where it would hurt the most, and where he was most vulnerable. Finlay does behave like a fool sometimes. I know that." She shook her head a little. "I think he's half afraid of being an ambassador, and then going into Parliament, in case he doesn't live up to all Papa's expectations for him. It's almost as if he wanted to do something to prevent it, even before he really tries. Not really," she added quickly, with a fleeting smile. "Just at moments when he's . . . when he has no confidence in himself. We all get times like that."

"Who in particular?" Emily pressed, flicking her hand sharply to shoo a fly away.

Tallulah thought for a moment. "Roger Balfour, for one. Papa just about ruined him in a business deal with the army—over munitions, I think. Peter Zoffany. I used to like him. He told wonderful stories about living in India. I think he rather liked me too. I thought Papa might marry me to him, but then he used him to get to somebody else and there was a terrible row and I never saw him again. But Fin would never do anything like that." She did not add any assurance, which made it the more absolute.

She looked at Emily with a frown.

"Does it matter who? All we could do would be tell the police. I wouldn't mind telling Mr. Pitt if he comes again, but I wouldn't tell that other miserable-faced man. I think his name was Tellman, or Bellman, or something like that. He looked at me as if I were a leper. He'd only think I was trying to protect Finlay anyway."

"No, I don't suppose it matters," Emily conceded. "That club badge is the thing. If we could throw doubt on that, it would weaken this case a great deal."

"But they've got it!" Tallulah protested. "What doubt could there be? It has Fin's name engraved on the back. He told me. Anyway, I've seen it."

"What is it like?" Emily asked quickly. "What is it like exactly? Do you remember?"

"Certainly. About that size." She held her finger and thumb apart about three quarters of an inch. "Round. Gray enamel, with 'Hellfire Club, 1881' on the front in gold letters and a pin across the back. Why?"

"And where was his name?"

"On the back, under the pin. Why?"

"Written how?"

"What do you mean?"

"Copperplate, Gothic, Roman?"

"In . . . copperplate, like a signature, only neater." Her expression quickened. "Why?" She drew in her breath. "Are you thinking we could duplicate it? Have another one made? But what could we do with it?"

"Well, if there are two," Emily was still juggling ideas in her mind, "it will at least raise doubts as to which one is real. One of them has to be false! Why not the one found in the prostitute's room? At least it would prove that someone could get a false one made and put it wherever they wanted to."

"Yes it would," Tallulah agreed with alacrity, sitting forward. "Where should we put it?"

"I'm not sure." Emily was still thinking. "I suppose somewhere it could have fallen accidentally, so Finlay couldn't find it. At the back of a drawer, or in the pocket of something he never wears."

"But if we find it," Tallulah pointed out, "they will know that we put it there, or they might do."

"Obviously we can't find it," Emily agreed. "But we can arrange for the police to search again, and they can find it themselves."

"How can we do that?"

"I can. Don't worry about it." Emily was certainly not going to explain that Superintendent Pitt, in charge of the case, was her brother-in-law. "I'll think of a way."

"Won't they check up on all of us, to see if we had the copy made?" Tallulah went on. "I would! And Tellman may be a horrible little man, but I've a feeling he's awfully clever, in his own way. And Mr. Pitt might come back again. He speaks beautifully, even though he's a policeman, but underneath the good manners I don't think he'd be fooled either."

"Then it's your job to see that you and your mother can account for your time, and if possible that Finlay can too," Emily said decisively. "There's nothing we can do about your father. I'll take care of getting another badge made. You must draw it for me, as precisely as you can, the right size, with the writing exactly like the other one."

Tallulah was alarmed. "I'm not sure if I remember exactly."

"Then you'll have to find out, from Finlay, without him realizing why you want to know. Don't ask any of the other members. They might know what you are doing, and even if they wouldn't intentionally betray Finlay, they might to save themselves, even without meaning to."

"Yes . . ." Tallulah said with increasing conviction in her voice. She rose to her feet, stopping for a moment as the heat and the dizzying perfume overcame her.

Emily stood also.

"Yes. I'll start straightaway." Tallulah straightened her shoulders. "I'll draw the badge for you and send it in the post. You'll receive it tomorrow. Emily . . . thank you! I don't know why you should befriend me like this, but I'm more grateful to you than I can say."

Emily dismissed it as gracefully as she could. It embarrassed her, because she had done it out of boredom and her own sense of having done nothing valuable for months, and of being unnecessary to anybody.

They parted at the entrance, surprised to find that everyone else was gone too. It was already well into the hour appropriate for final calls, or even returning home if one was thinking of an early dinner before the opera or the theater.

Tallulah was as good as her word, and in the midday delivery the following day, Emily received a letter from her, hastily and sprawlingly written, and accompanying two rather good sketches of a badge, both front and reverse. One was in minute detail, larger than scale so it could be seen easily; the other was less exact but of precisely the same size as the original. The materials were also described. With it was a five-pound note, neatly folded, to cover the cost, and Tallulah's repeated thanks.

Emily had already decided where she intended to go in order to get the badge made. One or two friends had from time to time had need of a discreet and skilled jeweler who was able to either copy a piece or maybe reproduce it from a drawing or photograph. One had accidents. An original piece had been pawned and sold against a debt one did not care to mention to one's husband and which could not be met from a dress allowance. One misplaced things sometimes. There were even occasions when it was not advisable to wear an original. A jeweler unknown to the rest of the family, and who knew how to keep his own counsel, was a friend to be treasured.

Of course, Emily did not tell him who she was. But he was used to ladies who veiled their faces and whose names did not appear in any social register, even though both their clothes and their manners suggested that they should. He accepted the commission without demur and promised to have it completed for collection in two days' time. Emily thanked him, paid him half the price, and promised the rest on completion.

She returned home only just before Jack arrived, coming into her boudoir looking harassed and apologetic.

"I'm sorry," he said earnestly, and indeed he did look very disturbed about something. His usually immaculate jacket was a trifle crooked and his eyes were tired.

"What is it?" she asked, touched with a moment's anxiety. "What's happened?" She rose to her feet and went over to him, her eyes searching his face.

"The Home Secretary has called a meeting this evening," he said ruefully. "I have to be there or no one will put my point of view. I'm sorry, but it really does matter."

"Of course you have to," she agreed, overwhelmed with relief.

"But I promised to take you to the opera. We have the tickets, and I know how much you wanted to see it."

She had completely forgotten. Beside Tallulah's troubles it was so unimportant. What was an evening's entertainment compared with the fears and the loneliness she had seen only an hour or two ago?

"Never mind," she said, smiling at him. "It is a matter of priorities, isn't it? Perhaps I shall go and see Charlotte, or something like that. The opera will play again." She saw the apprehension iron out of his face and felt a sharp twinge of guilt. She already knew exactly what she would do with the late afternoon and evening.

"Thank you, my dear," Jack said, touching her gently on the

cheek. Standing so close to him she could see the fine lines of tiredness around his eyes and mouth and she realized with a jolt how hard he was working, for the first time in his life, at making a success of something which was a challenge to him. It was something which he cared about for himself and for her, and which he feared might be beyond him. He had grown up a younger son, handsome and idle, with a charm which enabled him to live quite easily on those who found his company such a pleasure he could move from one to another of them and never have to think further ahead, or behind, than a few weeks.

Now, because he loved Emily and wanted to fit into her life and her circle, he had looked for depths in himself and discovered them. He had committed himself to a difficult task in which failure was more than possible, and many vested interests were ranged against him. The time of charm without battles, smiling his way out of conflict, was past.

She wanted to reach up to kiss him, but she knew it was not the right time. He was weary. There was a busy, arduous and not entirely pleasant evening ahead of him, and already his mind was straggling with its problems, anticipating them and what he would say or do.

She caught his hand and held it, feeling his fingers close around hers in a moment's surprise and warmth.

"Don't be silly," she said quickly. "I'm not going to sulk over an evening at the opera when what you are doing is really important. I hope I'm never so shallow. I do know what matters, you know."

He smiled, his eyes lighter with amusement, and for a moment his tiredness vanished.

"I do!" she said fiercely. "More than you know!"

As soon as Jack had left for his engagement, Emily herself dressed for the evening in one of her older gowns, something she did not intend to wear again, then took the second carriage and directed the coachman to Keppel Street in Bloomsbury.

When they arrived she alighted, gave instructions that they should wait for her, and knocked on Charlotte's door. As soon as it was answered, by Gracie, she swept in and went straight through to the parlor, where Charlotte was mending one of Jemima's pinafores.

"Please listen to me," Emily said. She sat down in Pitt's chair without bothering to arrange her skirts. "I know the case Thomas is working on at the moment. I have quite a good acquaintance with the sister of his chief suspect, and I know a way we might be able to prove his innocence." She ignored Charlotte's surprise. "Believe me, he would be very grateful. It is not a man he would wish to prosecute, but unless someone can show that he was there at the time, he may have to."

Charlotte put down her sewing and stared at Emily with gravity and growing suspicion.

"I assume from your manner that you already have a plan as to how we shall do this, when the police have failed to?" she said guardedly.

Emily swallowed, then took a deep breath and plunged in.

"Yes I have, actually. He does not really remember where he was, but his sister, Tallulah, was at a party, and she saw him there."

"Oh yes?" Charlotte said skeptically. "And why has she not told the police this?"

"Because nobody would believe her."

"Except you, of course." Charlotte picked up her sewing again. The matter was not of sufficient sense to keep her from it.

Emily snatched it away.

"Listen to me! This really matters!" she said urgently. "If Finlay was seen at this party, in Chelsea, then he could not have been in Whitechapel murdering a prostitute. And if we can prove it, we will not only save Finlay from disaster, we will save Thomas from having to arrest the son of one of London's wealthiest men!"

Charlotte retrieved the sewing and put it away tidily.

"So what are you suggesting? Why can . . . Tallulah? . . . Tallulah . . . not find some of the other people who were at this party and have them swear that Finlay was there? What does she need you for? Or me?"

"Because she has already denied being at the party," Emily said exasperatedly. "Please pay attention! She was only there for a few minutes, perhaps half an hour at the most, and she does not remember who else was there either."

"It seems altogether an extremely forgettable party," Charlotte said with a wry expression too close to laughter for Emily's temper. "Do you really believe all this, Emily? It's ridiculous. She doesn't remember anyone there except him, and he not only doesn't remember anyone at all, even his own sister, he doesn't even remember being there himself!"

"They were taking opium," Emily said furiously. "The place was a . . . a shambles. When Tallulah saw what it was like she left. She didn't remember the other people because she didn't know them. Finlay didn't remember because he was out of his senses."

"That last part I can believe," Charlotte conceded dryly. "But even if it is all true, what could we do?"

"Go back to the house where the party was and see if it really happened and if it was as she said," Emily replied, although as she heard herself, it sounded increasingly foolish. "Well . . . we could at least see if there had been a party that night and if anyone remembered seeing either Tallulah or Finlay. It would prove something."

"I suppose we might find someone . . ." Charlotte said dubiously. "But why doesn't Tallulah go herself? Presumably at least she knows these people? We don't." Her eyes narrowed. "Do we?"

"No! No, of course not!" Emily denied it hastily. "But that is precisely why we would be better. We are important witnesses."

"Where is it?"

"Beaufort Street, in Chelsea. You'd better change into something a little more formal, as if you were going to a party."

"Since everyone seems oblivious of their surroundings, it hardly seems worth it," Charlotte answered. But she did rise to her feet and go towards the door. "I'll be down in a few minutes. I hope you know what you are doing."

Emily did not answer.

Half an hour later they were in the carriage, turning from the river into Beaufort Street.

"What number?" Charlotte asked.

"About here," Emily replied.

"What do you mean 'about here'?" Charlotte said. "What number is it?"

"I'm not sure. Tallulah didn't know."

"You mean she didn't remember, I suppose," Charlotte said sarcastically. "If Thomas arrests anyone in that family they can plead insanity and get away with it. Come to that, so could we."

"We are not doing anything to get arrested for," Emily retorted sharply.

Charlotte did not reply.

Emily called out for the driver to stop and, with a challenging look at Charlotte, she alighted, rearranged her skirts, and walked across the pavement towards the front of a house where three other carriages appeared to be waiting. By the time she reached the door, Charlotte had caught up with her.

"What are you going to say?" Charlotte demanded. "You can't just ask if they had an orgy here last Friday and do they know who was here!"

"Of course not!" Emily whispered. "I'll say I forgot something . . . a glove."

"Doesn't sound to me like an affair where they wore gloves."

"Well, I'd hardly go home without my shoes!"

"If you could go home without your memory or your wits, why not the odd shoe?" Charlotte said waspishly.

Emily was prevented from replying by the door's opening and a footman's staring down at her. He was in full livery, and stood a full head above her.

"Good afternoon." Emily smiled dazzlingly at him, swallowed convulsively, and began. "I was at a party last Friday evening, and I believe I may have left behind me, er . . . my . . ."

The footman's stare would have frozen milk.

"I believe that would have been at number sixteen, madam. This is number six." And without waiting for any further remark he stepped back and closed the door, leaving Emily on the step.

"I gather sixteen has something of a reputation," Charlotte said with a reluctant smile.

Emily said nothing. The color was burning her face in a mixture of embarrassment and anger.

"Well, come on." Charlotte touched her arm. "Having come this far, we might as well finish it."

Emily would dearly liked to have gone back to the carriage and never returned to Beaufort Street in her life. The look on the footman's face would haunt her dreams.

"Come on," Charlotte said urgently. There might even have been laughter in her voice.

Reluctantly Emily obeyed, and they made their way up the street towards number sixteen. This time it was Charlotte who rang the bell.

The door was opened by a young man with an open-necked shirt, possibly silk, and dark hair which flopped over his brow.

"Hello?" he said with a charming smile. "Ought I to know you? Forgive my absentmindedness, but there are occasions when my mind is absolutely absent. Off on travels to another world where the most fantastic things happen." He regarded her with candid, friendly interest, waiting for her reply as if his explanation had been utterly reasonable.

"Not very well," she said, sketching the truth. "But I think I may have left my glove here last Friday. Silly place to wear gloves, I know, but I told my father I was going to the opera, so I had to dress as if I were. I came with Tallulah FitzJames," she added, as though it were an afterthought.

He looked completely blank. "Do I know her too?"

"Slender, dark," Emily chipped in. "Very elegant and rather a beauty. She has a . . . well, a long nose, and very fine eyes."

"Sounds interesting," he said approvingly.

"I'm sure you know her brother Finlay," Charlotte said, making a last attempt.

"Oh! Fin . . . yes, I know him," he agreed. "Do you want to come in and look for your glove?"

They accepted and followed him into a wide hallway, and then through a series of rooms all decorated in exotic styles, some strongly Chinese, some Turkish or mock Egyptian. They pretended to look for the glove, and at the same time asked the young man more about Finlay FitzJames, but beyond establishing that he had been there several times, they learned nothing else. The young man had no idea whether the Friday of the murder in Whitechapel was one of those occasions or not.

They thanked him and left, without a glove.

"Well, it could be," Emily said as soon as they were on the pavement. "It was certainly the sort of party she described, that much at least is true."

"You believe her, don't you?" Charlotte said seriously.

"Yes, I do. I really want to help. I know what it feels like to be suspected of something you didn't do . . . something you could be hanged for."

"I know," Charlotte said quickly, taking her arm. "But you really didn't do it."

"I don't think he did either," Emily replied. "I'm going to do everything I can to help!"

The following morning Emily wrote a hasty note to Tallulah outlining what she further planned and asking if Tallulah would come with her. If so, would she send a reply with the messenger who delivered the letter.

An hour later a note was returned in Tallulah's scrawling hand saying that most certainly she could come. She would meet Emily at seven o'clock at St. Mary's Church, Whitechapel, and from there they could follow their campaign. As requested, she would be dressed very plainly indeed, in order to be inconspicuous, taken by a casual observer to be a maid on her day off, perhaps visiting her family.

Emily was nervous sitting in the hansom clipping smartly eastward from her own highly fashionable street with its elegant windows overlooking wide, clean pavements, private carriages with liveried coachmen and footmen, its front doors and side entrances for servants and tradesmen. The surroundings changed as she came through the City itself. There were more business premises and shops. The traffic became heavier. There was far more noise. The hansom had to stop frequently where the roads were congested.

Gradually she moved beyond the banks and trading centers and under the great shadow of St. Paul's, closer to the river. It was a balmy summer evening. There would be pleasure boats out, perhaps music, but she could not hear it above the clatter of hooves and wheels.

Soon she was on the Whitechapel Road. It was narrower, grayer, the buildings high and small-windowed, the footpaths sometimes mere ledges where people scurried by, heads down, with no time to stroll or chatter. The traffic was different also. Now there were carts and drays, wagons, even a herd of pigs blocking the road and making everyone stop for several minutes. The smell of manure was sharp in the air.

She alighted at St. Mary's Church and paid the cabby quickly, before she lost heart and changed her mind. What if she couldn't find a hansom back again? What if she had to walk? How far would it be? Would people take her for a street woman? She had heard that perfectly respectable women had been arrested by the police for being alone in the wrong places . . . even in the West End, never mind here. What would Jack think? He would never forgive her. And who would blame him? Would he understand that she had come to try to help clear the name of a man who faced ruin for a crime he did not commit? Charlotte would have done the same. Not that that was any mitigation.

Where on earth was Tallulah? What if she did not come?

Emily would have to go home again. It was still broad daylight. In fact, it was sunny and quite warm. She did not need to hug her shawl around her as if it were midwinter.

"Are you lorst, luv?"

She spun around. There was a short man with an ugly, friendly face staring at her. His cap was on crookedly and he had gaps in his teeth. There was a smear of dirt across his broad nose.

"No . . . thank you." She gulped, then forced herself to smile back. "I'm looking for someone, but she doesn't seem to be here yet. This is Saint Mary's Church, isn't it?"

"Yeah, that's right. Yer ain't lookin' fer Mr. Jones, are yer? The Rev'rent? 'Cos 'e's up Coke Street wi' Maisie Wallace. She lorst 'er little girl yest'dy. Scarlet fever. She's taken it 'ard, an' 'e gorn up there ter sit wiv' 'er."

"I'm sorry," Emily said quickly, her own fears vanishing. She thought of Evie at home asleep in her clean, quiet nursery in the afternoon sun, with someone to watch over her all the time, and Edward, his fair head bent over his books as he had been when she left. "I'm very sorry."

"Bless yer, luv, it 'appens. 'Appens every day ter some poor soul."

"I suppose so. That doesn't stop it being like the end of the world when it happens to you."

"Course it don't. Yer sure yer all right, now? You in't from 'round 'ere, are yer?" His eyes narrowed with concern. Suddenly she realized what he might imagine—an elopement, or far worse, a respectable woman fallen on desperate times and taking to the streets as an attempt to meet impossible debts . . . or worst of all, perhaps, seeking an illegal abortion. She forced herself to smile cheerfully and frankly at him, meeting his worried eyes.

"Yes, I am all right," she said firmly. "But if she doesn't come, perhaps you can tell me where I could get a hansom to take me home again? I have the fare," she added hastily.

"Right 'ere's as good as any place," he answered. "Or yer could try Commercial Road. That way!" He pointed, stretching out his arm. "Well, if yer all right then, I'll get 'ome ter me tea. Gor' bless yer."

"And bless you too," she said with warmth. She watched him walk off and turn down an alley to the left, and wondered what he did and what family he was going back to.

She was still facing the way he had gone when a hansom stopped a dozen yards away and Tallulah scrambled out, paid, and came hurrying towards her. She looked untidy, very different in a navy stuff dress with no frills, and a gray shawl.

"I'm sorry I'm late!" she said breathlessly. "I had to tell so many lies to get away without Papa thinking there was anything odd. Sometimes I get so tired of being told what to do. And now Mama has agreed I really must accept the next remotely reasonable offer of marriage if there's a title, whether there's money or not. Papa is going to insist." Almost unconsciously she glanced at the church, then back at Emily again, her eyes dark with foreboding. "Of course there won't be one, if Finlay's charged. Do you really think we can do anything?"

"Of course we can," Emily said boldly, taking her arm. "And I do believe you about seeing him at the party."

Tallulah looked at her curiously.

"What I mean is," Emily said quickly, "I am not merely accepting your word, which is pleasant but of no use. I went there yesterday evening and met a young man. He had no idea who was there on that occasion, but he does know Finlay."

"How does that help?" Tallulah asked, standing in the middle of the footpath, her face creased with anxiety.

"Well, it doesn't prove he was there, but it shows he could have been, and that you at least know the place. And presumably you could prove that you were not where you told your father you were . . . if you had to?"

"Well . . . yes . . ."

"Good. And about Jago," Emily proceeded to the next subject. "That may be hard, but we'll try. But first we must find those wretched women who say they saw Finlay that night. They must be wrong. They saw somebody like him—that's all. Maybe it was only a gentleman with fair hair. There can't be many 'round here, but there must be thousands in London."

"Yes, of course there must," Tallulah agreed. She glanced up the street ahead of her. "Isn't it grim around here! I think Old Montague Street is that way." She gave a little smile. "I asked the cabby."

"Good." Emily started off at a brisk walk, Tallulah by her side. "I didn't think to."

They crossed the road and went up Osborn Street, then sharp right into Old Montague Street. The collected heat of the day shimmered up from the gray cobbles and the smell of middens and drains was thick in the air. Emily found herself wanting to hold her breath, but of course it was impossible. Memories flashed back to her of going with Charlotte into a filthy house—it seemed like years ago—and finding a sick woman huddled under old blankets in the corner. The pity she had felt was almost as sharp now as it had been then, and the wish that she had never known, so it would not hurt.

A dray passed them, the horses' flanks lathered with sweat. Two women were shouting abuse at each other. It seemed to be an argument over a pail of oysters. An old man was asleep in a doorway, or perhaps he was drunk. Half a dozen children played a game with a little heap of stones, balancing them on the backs of their hands and then tossing them into the air, shouting and cheering when someone performed the maneuver with particular skill.

Opposite Pentecost Alley the sweatshop was still busy. The windows were open and they could see the women's heads bent over the needles. They had many hours to go yet before they could leave and go home for the short night before half past four, and time to return. Some of them actually lived there.

Tallulah stopped and looked at Emily. Now that it came to the moment, both found their courage evaporating. Could they really go into this brothel and ask to speak to one of the women? How would they know which one? Perhaps it was all rather ridiculous.

Emily drew in a deep breath. "Come on. If we stop now, we'll never do it."

Tallulah stood rooted to the spot.

"Is Finlay innocent or guilty?" Emily whispered fiercely. "Did he strangle that poor woman and leave her?"

"No! No, of course he didn't!" Tallulah clenched her fists and strode forward up the steps with Emily behind her. There was a wooden door at the top, streaked with damp. It was closed, but there was a tarnished brass bell beside it. Tallulah yanked on it hard.

Nothing happened, and she tugged again, still facing it, and not looking at Emily. She was shivering, in spite of the close heat.

A few moments later the door creaked open and an enormous woman with a bloated face peered out.

"We got one room, duck. Can't take two o' yer. This is an 'ouse o' business."

"We don't need a room, thank you," Tallulah said politely. Emily, standing a step behind her, could see her hands clenched into fists, nails biting into the palms. "We've come to speak to one of your

... residents. We're not quite sure who, but she saw a young man the night poor Ada McKinley was murdered, and we need to speak to her."

The larger woman's naked eyebrows shot up. "Wot fer? Yer in't rozzers, so 'oo are yer?"

"We used to work with Ada," Emily put in before Tallulah could speak. "I was a ladies' maid in the same house. Lula here was laundress. My name's Millie."

Tallulah gulped. "That's right. May we speak to her, please?"

"Well, that'd be up to Rose. I'll ask 'er." And with that she closed the door again, leaving them standing waiting.

"That was brilliant," Tallulah said with admiration. "Now we'll just have to hope Ada was in service at some time."

"It's a good chance," Emily replied. "If not, we'll just have to pretend we got the wrong person."

"If she'll see us," Tallulah added.

They waited in silence the few moments until the fat woman returned, this time smiling. She ushered them in.

"That's Rosie's room," she said, pointing to a door some way along the passage.

"Thank you." Tallulah straightened her shoulders and obeyed, knocking sharply on the indicated door. As soon as she heard an answer, she opened it and went in, Emily hard at her elbow in case she should change her mind.

Inside the room was opulent in a garish way, lots of red and flounces, a huge bed with tattered red-pink curtains tied back with cord. That would have done for strangling someone, Emily thought grimly. She wondered if that was what he had used, if Ada had had the same.

Rose herself was a handsome woman, probably in her middle thirties. There was no paint on her face at this hour, and she had had a good day's sleep. Emily could see that in other circumstances, cleaner, properly dressed, she could have been beautiful. Now she was looking at them curiously, leaning back a little in the one chair in the room.

"So you knew Ada, poor cow?" she said coolly. "Wot yer want wi' me? I can't 'elp yer. If yer cared so much abaht 'er, w'ere was yer w'en that bleedin' butler done 'er, eh?"

Tallulah looked blank, her face white, her eyes almost hollow.

Emily made a quick guess at what she meant.

"She didn't tell us," Emily said aloud. "It was all dealt with without any of the rest of us knowing, until it was too late. Did you really see the man who killed her?"

"Yeah." Rose shifted position slightly, easing herself backwards. "Why? Wot's it ter you? Yer know 'im? It were some toff from up west."

"We work up west," Emily pointed out. "Did you see him clearly?"

"Yeah, more or less." Rosie's eyes narrowed. "Why'd you care?"

Emily made another guess. They had not much to lose.

"We hoped you hadn't, not to know him for sure, beyond question, because we hoped it might be our butler. You see, he's done it again, and this time he might have been caught, if anyone had believed Ada then."

Suddenly they had Rose's true attention.

"D'yer reckon? I'd love to get that swine, fer Ada. Bleedin' bastard."

"But are you sure it was this other man?" Emily said doubtfully. "Did you hear him speak?"

"Nah! Jus' saw 'im goin' past like."

"Could it have been our butler?"

"Yeah, course it could. Were 'e out that night?"

"Yes," Tallulah said quickly. She was still standing rigid in the middle of the floor, as though to move might bring some catastrophe on her.

Rose let out her breath in a long sigh, her eyes bright.

"Geez, I'd love ter get that son of a bitch. Maybe it were 'im? We could nail the sod proper!"

"What about what you've told the police?" Emily asked.

Rose shrugged. "Don't matter. I in't said anythin' in court yet. They can't do me fer it. I didn't swear ter nuthin'. It were just me and one rozzer in an 'ansom. I thought it were 'im, now I'm not sure. Nan in't sure anyway, so I'm only goin' wi' 'er."

Tallulah let out her breath in a long, silent sigh. At last her shoulders relaxed a little, although her back was still stiff and her feet rooted to the spot.

"Thank you," she said with passionate sincerity. "Thank you very much."

When they were outside again they walked rapidly back along Old Montague Street without speaking, or even looking at each other, until they reached the corner of Osborn Street and turned down towards the Whitechapel Road. Then Tallulah stopped abruptly.

"We did it," she said almost in a squeak. "We did it!" She threw her arms around Emily impulsively and hugged her so fiercely that for a moment Emily could not draw breath. "Thank you! Thank you more than I can say! Not just for helping me to defend Fin, but for showing that it wasn't really evidence against him." She let go and stepped back a bit, her eyes bright with tears. She sniffed. "If you hadn't had the courage, I'd still be at home pacing the floor, or out at some wretched party, pretending to enjoy myself, and all the time worried sick he'd never prove he was innocent."

"Then let us go and address the next problem," Emily said resolutely. "If Finlay is not involved, and there is no charge brought against him, then your father will have you married to the next suitable person whose admiration you attract. Are you prepared for that to happen?"

"I shall probably have to be," Tallulah replied, the happiness draining out of her. "Jago really does despise me. I'm not being falsely modest, you know."

"Then we must change that," Emily declared, too elated with her victory to consider defeat in anything. "Or at least we must try." She started walking again towards the church of St. Mary's and Tallulah followed reluctantly.

They reached it just as the Reverend Jago Jones came out and almost strode past them, so intent was he upon his errand. It was only that Emily stopped and let out a cry that drew his attention. He swung on his heel and stared at her.

"Are you all right, ma'am?" he asked with concern puckering his brow.

She was startled by his face, then instantly knew she should not have been. She had expected something blander, handsomer, less urgently alive. She had expected someone she could manipulate and outwit. Instead she faced a man whose intelligence she knew instinctively and whose will would not easily be subverted by flattery or irrelevance. Now that she had drawn his attention, what could she possibly say?

"Yes . . . thank you." She made it almost an apology. "We were in the area . . . because . . ."

He glanced at Tallulah and did not recognize her. He looked back at Emily, waiting for her to continue.

"Because of the death of poor Ada McKinley . . ." Emily went on desperately. "It touches us closely . . . because . . ."

"Because my brother is suspected of the crime," Tallulah finished.

"I don't think . . ." he began, then frowned, studying her face in the light. "Tallulah?" His voice was high-pitched with incredulity. Even as he said it he could not completely believe. It was a question rather than a statement.

"Hello, Jago." Her voice was rough with emotion. "Did you not know they suspected Finlay?"

"Yes. Yes, I did know, but I can't believe he's guilty. It's too . . ." He did not finish. Whatever he had been going to say, he changed his mind. His face hardened, the pity or the tenderness forced out of it. "There really isn't anything you can do here. You had better go home before it gets dark. I'm going 'round to Coke Street to serve out soup, but I'll walk with you up to a place where you can get a hansom first. Come on."

"We'll help you with the soup," Tallulah offered.

He dismissed the idea contemptuously. "Don't be ridiculous! You don't belong here. You'll get dirty, your feet will hurt standing, and the people will smell and it will offend you. You'll be tired and bored." Anger hardened in his eyes and his mouth. "Those people's hunger is not entertaining. They are real, with feelings and dignity, not something for you to come to look at so you can tell your friends."

Emily felt as if she had been slapped. Tallulah had not exaggerated his scorn of her.

"Why do you imagine you are the only person who can wish to help from a genuine desire, Mr. Jones?" Emily said tartly. "Is compassion solely your preserve?"

Tallulah's mouth dropped.

Jago drew in his breath sharply and the skin tightened across his cheeks. It was too dark to see if he blushed.

"No, Miss . . ."

"Radley," Emily supplied. "Mrs. Radley."

"No, Mrs. Radley, of course not. I have known Miss FitzJames for several years. But I had no right to judge you by her past nature. I apologize."

"I accept your apology," Emily said with considerable condescension. "But you should extend it to Tallulah as well. It was she who offered to help. Now, if you would lead the way, we shall come with you. I am sure more hands would make the task easier."

Jago smiled in spite of himself, and obeyed, moving to the outside of the narrow footpath and walking beside them towards Coke Street.

He was right. The work was hard. Emily's feet hurt, her arms ached and her shoulders and back felt as if they would never adjust to their natural position again. The people were noisy and the smell of hot, unwashed bodies and stale clothes was at times almost sickening. But far more than that she was oppressed by the hunger, the hollow eyes in the lamplight, the spindly limbs and skin pitted and dark with ingrained dirt. She saw tired women with sickly children and no hope. She looked across at Tallulah and saw the shock in her eyes. In the space of a couple of hours, poverty had become a word with a whole realm of meaning. It was reality, pain, people of flesh and blood who loved and had dreams, who got frightened and tired just as she did, only it was most of the time, not merely once or twice a year.

And Jago Jones had become different also, not an idealization but a man of flesh and spirit who also felt, who was occasionally clumsy and dropped things, whose knuckles bled when he scraped them against the wall while maneuvering the cart that carried the soup, who laughed at a child's silly joke, and who turned away to hide his grief when he was told of a woman's miscarrying her baby.

Emily watched him and saw his contempt for Tallulah slowly soften as she worked to help, stifling her disgust at the smell of dirt and stale sweat, and smiling back at people with blackened or missing teeth, at first with an effort, at the end almost naturally, forgetting the gulf between them.

When the last person was fed they tidied away the empty churns and began slowly to push the cart back to the house where it was kept and the food was cooked. It all came from donations, sometimes from wealthy people, sometimes people with little more themselves.

At quarter past nine, in the dark, they walked side by side to the church. Then Jago insisted on accompanying them until they should find a hansom.

"Why did you really come to Whitechapel?" he asked Tallulah. They were passing under a gas lamp, and in the pool of light his expression was innocent. There was no guile in him, or expectation of a particular answer. Emily was interested that he had no thought that she might have come to see him. She liked him even better for his modesty.

"I wanted to help Finlay," Tallulah answered after only a moment.

Emily longed to tell her to be quiet. Jago Jones would not approve of their going to see Rose Burke about her testimony. She pretended to trip, and caught hold of Tallulah's sleeve, jerking her hard.

"Are you all right?" Jago said quickly, putting out his hand to steady her.

"Yes, thank you." She stood upright again, smiling, although they were past the lamp now. "It wasn't a very clever idea really. There isn't anything we can do. But we thought if we saw the place, we might think of something."

Jago shook his head but forbore from comment. He could be tactful when he chose.

Tallulah glanced at Emily as they moved under the next light. She seemed to have understood the hint.

Jago found them a hansom on Commercial Road, and after helping them in, bade them good-bye and thanked them with a wry smile, then turned and walked away without looking back.

Tallulah swiveled to face Emily, although they could barely see each other in the darkness inside the cab.

"I know even less than I did before," she said, her voice tight with confusion and weariness. "I know I love Jago, but I don't think I could live here. It smells so awful! Everything is so . . . dirty! Who could I even talk to? How can he bear it?"

Emily did not answer, because there really was nothing to say, nothing to argue about or rationalize. There was only the decision to be made, and no one could help with that.

Emily collected the new Hellfire Club badge and met Tallulah, by arrangement, at a dog show held by the members of the Ladies' Kennel Club. It was somewhere they could both go quite comfortably without comment, and meet and compare notes, as if on the scores of dogs of every breed and color and size. Tallulah was in a gorgeous gown of daisy-patterned muslin with white satin ribbon trim. No one would have recognized her as the woman who had helped ladle soup in Coke Street the previous evening. She looked carefree, full of laughter and grace, until she saw Emily. Then she excused herself from her friends and came over, her hand held out, her face tense and shadows of unhappiness in her eyes.

Without comment Emily put her hand into Tallulah's and passed over the badge, then as quickly withdrew. "What's the matter?" she asked. "Has something new happened?"

"No. I . . ." Tallulah shook her head. "I just love this dog show. Look at them all. Aren't they beautiful and intelligent?"

"The people or the dogs?"

"The dogs, of course!" She brushed her fingers against the soft fabric of her skirt. "And I love this dress."

"You look wonderful in it," Emily said honestly.

"Can you see me wearing it in Whitechapel? It probably cost more than Jago makes in a year. Maybe two years."

"Nobody can decide for you," Emily replied under her breath, smiling and nodding to the wife of another member of Parliament who walked by leading a Great Dane and trying to look as if it were not leading her. "The one thing you must never do is blame someone else because you have chosen the wrong way. Be honest with yourself. If you want your life as it is, with money, fashion, a husband you may not love, then take it." She smiled and lifted her hand in a gesture of acknowledgment to the wife of a cabinet minister she loathed. "But if you want Jago, with all that that means, don't attempt to change him or blame him for being what he is."

"Don't you expect to change a husband a little?" Tallulah said reasonably. "Why should I be the one to make all the accommodations?"

"Because that way doesn't work," Emily said with eminent practicality. "It is no good dealing with what you think is fair, only with what is real. Anyhow, would you want Jago to accommodate you by changing his beliefs? What would that make of him?"

"I thought marriage was supposed to improve men, at least a little," Tallulah protested. "Are we not meant to be a gentler and civilizing influence? Isn't that what we are for? To have children and to provide an island of peace and purity and high ideals away from the clamor and conflict of the world?"

Emily bit her tongue so she did not reply too savagely.

"Did you ever know a man who wished to be civilized and improved?"

"No," Tallulah said with some surprise. "All the men I know wish to be supported, admired and obeyed. That is certainly what Papa wants and insists on. In return he provides for us, advises us and, on occasion, protects us."

"Of course," Emily countered with a smile. "Sometimes we may behave in such a way as to cause a man to wish to civilize and improve himself. But that is a different proposal altogether. It is one thing to ask for something, it is quite different to accept when offered it."

Tallulah was prevented from continuing the discussion by the intervention of a group of ladies who came across to them, leading two spaniels and a setter. The conversation was turned over to dogs.

Emily remained only another ten minutes or so, then excused herself and went to her carriage. It was agreed that Tallulah would place the badge immediately on her return home. Now it was necessary for someone to provoke Pitt into searching again, in order for it to be found. She gave her coachman Charlotte's address in Bloomsbury and sat back to compose some sensible way of introducing such a suggestion into a conversation. Naturally she would not tell Charlotte why; that would place too great a strain on her loyalties, and Emily had no wish for Pitt to be told. At this point it could defeat everything.

It was a beautiful afternoon, warm and still with that mellow tone of sunshine one gets only in the late summer, a sort of gold in the air, a heavy perfume of flowers, and the knowledge that in a month's time the first leaves would yellow, but would ripen and the nights begin to chill, and to darken earlier.

Charlotte was in the garden inspecting the young chrysanthemum plants and admiring the asters in bloom, great shaggy heads of purple and magenta. "It's perfectly beautiful," Emily said sincerely.

Charlotte looked at her skeptically. "Is that what you came to say?"

"No, of course not." She wondered for an instant if picking a quarrel might divert Charlotte's attention from what she had come to say, and decided it would not. It was extremely difficult to think of a way of having Charlotte persuade Pitt to search again for the badge without Charlotte's realizing exactly what Emily was doing, and why.

"I've just come from the dog show," she said tentatively. "I saw Tallulah FitzJames there. She looks terribly worried. I feel so helpless to know what to say to her. Does Thomas really think her brother is guilty? Did you mention . . ." She stopped.

"That we went to Beaufort Street?" Charlotte said with wide eyes. "No, of course I didn't! What could I say? That Finlay's sister says she saw him at a party, but she can't remember who else was there because nobody remembers anything about the whole event, except where it was held, and when?"

"I suppose it wouldn't help," Emily agreed unhappily.

They walked side by side very gently down the lawn towards the apple tree and past the honeysuckle, which was still in bloom. The late afternoon began to send a heavy sweetness into the air.

"All it would really do," Charlotte said gently, "is show that Tallulah is a loyal sister."

"It's the badge, isn't it?" Emily seized her opportunity. "That's what makes it look so bad for him. How could it be there if he wasn't?"

They had reached the end of the lawn and stood together in the sheltered sun.

"If he's not guilty," Emily continued, as though thinking aloud, "then either this is a most hideous mischance or he has a terrible enemy. And from what Tallulah says, that is not impossible. At least," she hurried on to prevent Charlotte from interrupting, "they are Augustus's enemies."

"You think they stole his badge, murdered someone, and left it at the scene?" Charlotte asked with incredulity. "Isn't that a terrible risk to take with your own life, simply to injure someone else? What if they were caught and hanged themselves?"

Emily drew in her breath and let it out slowly.

"Someone so very arrogant is probably quite sure in their own minds that they will not be caught. And I hadn't thought of their stealing Finlay's badge . . . why not simply have another one made? It wouldn't be very difficult. Then leave that one there."

"But what if the police found the original? Or Finlay did himself?" Charlotte reasoned.

"The club disbanded years ago. He probably hasn't any idea even when he last had it, let alone where."

"But they looked for it . . . Thomas did."

"Did he look for it himself?" Emily pressed. "Or did he simply have a constable do it, thinking that if Finlay knew where it was he would produce it quickly enough?"

"Perhaps a constable, I don't know."

Late swallows dipped and darted after tiny flies. The light was lengthening and turning gold, casting heavy shadows from the apple tree.

"Well, ask him," Emily said, trying not to sound desperate. "After all, if he found another badge, it would make things much easier, wouldn't it? For Thomas, I mean. Then he wouldn't have any real evidence against Finlay, and he wouldn't be in the wretched position of having to charge him! He wouldn't be caught between the pressure from the establishment and the Home Office, and it would stop the newspapers suggesting that he is letting Finlay off because of who he is. I know the sort of thing they will say."

"I suppose you might be right," Charlotte said thoughtfully. "I'll mention it to him."

Emily linked her arm in Charlotte's and they began to walk back up the lawn towards the house. She did not trust herself to say anything further.

CHAPTER

SIX

While Emily was involved with helping Tallulah, Pitt had been searching further into the character and associations of the FitzJames family. He had sent Tellman to learn what he could to add to their knowledge of the history of the other members of the Hellfire Club, as being those most likely to have had the badge, either intentionally or by accident. In spite of their appearance of a life far removed from frequenting the brothels of Whitechapel, it was quite possible that they did so. Married men in Helliwell's status had been known to. Thirlstone was certainly not beyond suspicion.

And much as Pitt would like to have believed that Jago Jones was all he proclaimed, he might have all too human weaknesses, and if he gave in to them, where better to turn than to a prostitute whose company would be so natural in his pastoral labors; no one would question it. He could explain it even to himself. He would be far from the first man of the cloth to find his relationship with a beautiful and intelligent parishioner slipping helplessly beyond the bounds of propriety into a physical hunger which he had not denied. He lived an abstemious life, lonely and full of hardship and self-discipline. It was not difficult to understand. He had been a man of both appetite and indulgence in his Hellfire days. What had changed him, and so completely?

And what had gone so hideously wrong that he had killed Ada? Had she said or done something unforgivable? Had she laughed at him . . . mocked him with his own frailty? Was she the instrument by which he had betrayed himself, the serpent and Eve in one? Or had she simply threatened to expose him? Had she asked for money, continuous blackmail money? Rose Burke and Nan Sullivan had both said she was greedy, with an eye to opportunity.

It was possible, and the more Pitt thought about it, the more the idea hurt him. He had liked Jago Jones, admired him, but the possibility could not be ignored. He had liked other men before and found them guilty.

He could not like Augustus FitzJames, and the further he delved into the probability of his having enemies who might hate him enough to have gone to these lengths to ruin him, the less did he find to like.

The further back Pitt went in the search into Augustus's past, the less easy it became to trace with any clarity. He had apparently inherited no money from his father, a somewhat feckless landowner in Lincolnshire who had mortgaged his holdings to the hilt. Augustus had served a short time in the merchant navy, largely on the Far Eastern routes. He had returned home shortly after the Second Opium War in 1860 with sufficient money to begin investing, an art which he exercised with skill amounting at times to genius.

Now he possessed a financial empire of enormous size and complexity, with tentacles stretching across the breadth of the Empire. He had investments in India, Egypt, the African expeditions of Cecil Rhodes, and the new expansions in Australia. Frequently his interests cut across those of others to their disadvantage.

Pitt heard several stories both of Augustus's generosity and of his ruthlessness. He seemed never to forget a friend or an enemy, and there were anecdotes of his cherishing a grudge over decades and repaying it when the perfect opportunity presented itself.

He lacked polish. He had no social grace, but even so he had been attractive to women. Aloysia had married him for love, and he had been far from her only suitor. Other men, with more humor, with more charm, had sought her hand. She certainly had not needed the money. At that time her own fortune was greater than his. Perhaps there was something in his energy, his driving ambition and the inner power that drove him which attracted her.

Finlay had not only his mother's broader face and easier, more graceful manner, it seemed he also had her more malleable nature and slower intellect. He appeared altogether a more likable man, a little self-indulgent, but that was not unnatural at his age, or with the pressure of expectation placed upon him.

Ewart grew more insistent that Finlay was innocent and that it was some enemy of Augustus who had deliberately implicated him. And where he had dismissed it before, Pitt now began to entertain the idea with some seriousness.

"The valet said he's never seen the cuff links," Ewart argued as they were sitting in Pitt's office in Bow Street. "They could have gone missing years ago, as Finlay says."

"How did one get down the back of the chair in Ada's room?" Pitt asked, although he knew what Ewart would answer.

Ewart screwed up his face. He still looked tired and harassed. His suit was rumpled and his tie a little crooked. There were shadows around his dark eyes as though he habitually slept poorly.

"I know he said he'd never been to Whitechapel," he replied, shaking his head. "But it was an understandable lie, in the circumstances. He could well have been there years ago. He could have been drunk at the time, and completely forgotten it."

That was true—Pitt did not argue. He could also understand Ewart's reluctance to think Finlay guilty. The evidence was not conclusive, and if they charged him it would be a hard fight and a very ugly case. To lose it would be an embarrassment from which neither of their careers would recover easily.

"And the badge?" Pitt was almost thinking aloud, Charlotte's words to him the previous evening turning over in his mind.

"He said he'd lost it years ago," Ewart reminded him. "I daresay that's true. Certainly we can't prove the club has ever met in, say, five . . . six years. All the members say it hasn't, and I'm inclined to believe them. They don't seem to have any connection anymore. Helliwell is married and doing well in the City. Thirlstone has taken up with the aesthete group. And Jones has taken the cloth and gone to the East End. Frankly, if it isn't one of Augustus FitzJames's enemies, I'm inclined to think it could be Jones. Perhaps he and Finlay had some old quarrel?"

Pitt leaned farther back in his large chair. The desk was between them, meticulously polished, and inlaid with green leather.

"And he waited six years to murder a prostitute and blame Finlay for it?" He raised his eyebrows.

"All right, that's ridiculous, put like that. The cuff link's an accident. Finlay was there once. The badge was put there deliberately by someone, for whatever reason we'll discover in time."

Pitt put forward Charlotte's idea. "If someone really hated Augustus FitzJames enough, perhaps the badge we found was not the original one, but a copy someone had made in order to implicate him?"

Ewart's face lit up. His clenched fist thumped very gently on the desktop. "Yes! Yes, that's the most likely solution so far! It could well be what happened." Then his eyes shadowed. "But how could we prove that? I'll start my men searching for a jeweler straightaway, but he'll probably have been well paid to keep silent."

"We'll start by searching Finlay's rooms again for the original," Pitt replied, although he had scant hope of succeeding. "I've no idea whether it's the truth or not, but any good defense counsel would put it forward as a suggestion, to indicate reasonable doubt. That may be its main relevance to us."

Far from being disheartened, Ewart was elated.

"But it is reasonable doubt!" he said fervently. "Unless we have more, there's no point in arresting him, whatever we believe."

"No," Pitt conceded, and it was a concession. He could not help wondering how much Ewart's unwillingness was belief in the possibility of Finlay's innocence, and how much merely cowardice, a dread of the battle that lay ahead, even the threat to his own career, the myriad small struggles and unpleasantnesses which would lie ahead if they pursued Finlay FitzJames for the murder. Augustus would be fighting for his social and political life. There would be no mercy, and no rules, except those forced upon him by circumstance.

He went personally to supervise the further search of the FitzJames house for the original badge. He took two constables with him, and was admitted at first with reluctance, then with appreciable surprise when he explained his purpose.

It took them a little under three quarters of an hour, then the badge was discovered in the inside pocket of a jacket the valet said he could not remember Mr. Finlay's having worn, which was extremely thin at the elbows and a little frayed at the collar. It was apparently kept only for sentimental reasons, and then at the back of the wardrobe. It was comfortable, something for him to use on summer walks, when it did not matter if it were to get torn or grass stained. He had not had opportunity for such indulgence in some time. It could have been there all the time. There was fluff caught on the pin, and a tiny scratch across the face of the enamel.

The explanation was given by Miss Tallulah FitzJames, who happened to be there that morning, writing letters to certain of her friends and answering invitations.

Pitt stood in the morning room turning it over in his hand. It was exactly like the one in police custody. Certainly as he looked he could see no difference, except a slight variation in the careful copperplate writing of the name, Finlay FitzJames, under the pin at the back. It was written by a different hand. But then it would be. What he really needed was one of the other club badges to compare it with, to see which was the original and which the copy. There was no other way of telling.

But the other members denied still having theirs.

"What's the matter, Superintendent?" Tallulah asked, looking at him with a faint flicker of concern in her face.

"I now have two badges for your brother, Miss FitzJames. One of them is a duplicate. I need to know which one, and why it was made, and by whom."

She stared at him without blinking. "This one is the original. The one you found in Pentecost Alley is a duplicate, made by one of my father's enemies in order to ruin us."

He looked at her. She was dressed in white with ribbons and an underskirt of pale blue. She was a trifle thin, and it made her look fragile and very feminine, until one saw the strength of her features and the burning will in her eyes.

"Do you really believe your father has enemies who would murder a woman in order to revenge themselves on him?" he asked.

Apparently she had already considered the question. Her answer was quiet, her voice grating with pent-up emotion, but nonetheless unhesitating.

"Yes, Superintendent, I do. I think perhaps you do not realize quite how powerful he is, or how much money he has made in the last thirty years. Envy can be very cruel. It can take you over and swallow up any decent judgment and feeling you have. And . . . and some people do not . . ." She bit her lip. "Do not consider the death of a prostitute to be a great sin. I'm sorry, that is a horrible thing to say." She winced, and he had a sudden conviction that she meant it. "But it is true," she finished.

He knew it was true. Had it not been in Whitechapel, so soon after those other, most fearful of all murders, the newspapers would hardly have bothered with it.

"Perhaps you had better make a list of these people, Miss Fitz-James, and what you know, or believe, of their reasons. I shall ask your father also for a similar list."

"Of course."

Pitt thanked the two constables who had helped in the search, then left the FitzJames house and walked along Devonshire Street towards the Park. He bought two ham sandwiches from a seller on the corner and ate them as he crossed the Marylebone Road and turned up York Gate, across the Outer Circle and through the trees. It was a balmy day. The Park was full of people strolling and fashionable ladies parading, and courting couples. Children were playing with hoops and riding sticks with horses' heads and several tried to fly kites in the lazy air, but there was too little wind to lift them.

Nursemaids in prim uniforms wheeled perambulators or took their small charges by the hand. Some of them sat on seats together, swapping gossip while children ran around. Old gentlemen sat in the sun and relived past glories. Young girls giggled and talked about each other. In the distance a band was playing songs from the music halls.

Pitt could not have argued with Ewart as to why he found it hard to believe that any enemy of Augustus FitzJames should murder a prostitute and lay the blame on Finlay in order to exact a revenge on his father. There was no single argument against it. He simply did not believe in such deliberate machination. In his experience robberies were sometimes carried out this way, but not murder. With violence, the convolutions, the attempts to lay blame elsewhere, came afterwards. However callous this supposed enemy, Pitt found it hard to conceive of him deliberately committing a crime for which he himself could be hanged, could it be traced to him.

And yet he also had to admit that there was something deliberate about it. The badge and the cuff link were extraordinary. How

196 • PENTECOST ALLEY

could a man be careless enough to leave two such pieces of evidence behind him?

He must try harder with Helliwell and Thirlstone and, much against his will, with Jago Jones. Finding another badge to compare with the two he had now might be crucial to Finlay's guilt or innocence.

"Good heavens, Superintendent!" Helliwell said irritably when Pitt approached him as he was walking down Birdcage Walk after a long and excellent luncheon in Great George Street. "I really cannot help you. I have no idea about Finlay FitzJames and his current behavior." His expression darkened. "I thought I had already explained to you that we were friends in the past, but the present is an entirely different matter. I wish I could tell you some definitive fact that would clear his name, but I am not in a position to. Now I have business for which I am a trifle late. You must excuse me." He quickened his pace.

Pitt quickened his also.

"I have found a second Hellfire Club badge," he said at Helliwell's elbow.

"Indeed." Helliwell kept on walking and did not turn. He did not ask where it had been found. "I cannot see how that concerns me. If it is mine, it was lost years ago, and it could be anywhere."

Pitt studied his face, but in the afternoon sun it looked a little red with exertion, and perhaps self-indulgence over the port, but there was not the discomfort of lying on it. He was annoyed, but if he was afraid, he hid it with consummate skill, a subtlety quite different from the rest of his character.

"No," Pitt replied. "It was not yours. It was apparently also Mr. FitzJames's."

This time Helliwell did stop, swinging around. "What? That makes no sense! We had only one each. What . . . what are you saying?"

"That someone has made a second badge, Mr. Helliwell. I would very much like to see yours so I can tell which is the original."

"Oh!" Helliwell let out his breath in a gusty sigh. "Yes. I see. Well, I still can't help you, and frankly I am beginning to find this constant questioning a trifle irritating." He turned to look at Pitt to allow him to understand that he was not apprehensive, but his anger was very real and increasing. "FitzJames was a friend of my rather immature days, which I have now left behind me, and what he may or may not be doing now is none of my concern. Although I find it almost impossible to believe he had anything to do with the death of a prostitute in the East End. It can only be a catalog of mischance that has led you even to imagine such a thing. You would be far more profitably employed looking into the unfortunate woman's own acquaintances, her enemies, or debtors.

"Now, as I said, I have an appointment, and I must hurry, or I shall keep Sir Philip waiting. Good day, Superintendent." And with that he swiveled smartly on his heel and strode away without looking back, or to either side of him.

Mortimer Thirlstone was harder to find. He was not involved in political or public life, and his comings and goings were dependent only upon his whim of the moment. Pitt discovered him at an artist's studio in Camberwell, and it was mid-afternoon before he was able to speak with him. It was a bright, airy room, and several young men and women sat around in earnest discussion. There were paintings on every stretch of wall, and windows in most unexpected places, never as intended by the original architect. Nevertheless the impression was surprisingly pleasant, one of startling color and space, splashes of yellows and blues, shimmering scenery. And it was more an impression, as if seen through half-closed eyes, than a photographic image.

"Oh dear," Thirlstone said wearily, leaning against a windowsill and staring at Pitt. He was dressed in a loose-sleeved white shirt with a floppy collar and an enormous bow at the neck. It was all very affected, but he seemed quite unconscious of it.

"Good afternoon, Mr. Thirlstone." Pitt was about to continue when Thirlstone straightened up.

"Not you again," he said, his eyes darting around the room as if to seek a way of escape. "This is getting frightfully tedious, my dear fellow." He faced Pitt suddenly. "What am I possibly to tell you? I knew Finlay years ago. He was a decent young man, but a bit of a rake. I suppose we all were . . . then. But I see nothing of him now, not a thing. Pleasant enough, you know, but a complete Philistine. Doesn't know old gold from plate. Sometimes I think he's color-blind!"

"I wanted to know if you could find your old Hellfire Club badge, sir," Pitt asked, looking at his agitated face and wondering why he was so uncomfortable. This should not be embarrassing. Pitt was not recognizable as police.

"I told you, I haven't got it anymore!" Thirlstone replied with a frown, his voice sharpening with exasperation. "What can it matter now?"

Pitt told him about the two badges with Finlay's name on them.

"Oh." Thirlstone looked disconcerted. He swallowed, seemed about to speak again, then changed his mind. He moved uncomfortably, as if something in his loosely fitting shirt still scratched his skin. "Well . . . if I . . . if I have it, I'll bring it to you. But it's not likely." He shook his head abruptly. "I really can't imagine Finlay would do such a thing, but people change . . ."

A statuesque young woman walked by, running her fingers through her mane of hair. A man by the farther window was sketching her, and she knew it. "I think you'll find us . . . oh . . ." Thirlstone shrugged. "I don't know. Really. I have no idea." He glanced at the woman, and back to Pitt. "Not pleasant to be disloyal, but I can't tell you anything."

Pitt wished he could think of some question which would crack the façade and let him see beneath to what these men really knew of each other, what relationships there had been, the rivalries, the

bonds which held, and the jealousies which divided, the secret feelings underlying the outward behavior.

"Did Finlay have one particular friend among you?" he asked casually, as if he had thought of it only as he was about to leave.

"No," Thirlstone said instantly. "We were all together . . . well
. . . er, possibly he was a little closer to Helliwell. More in common,
maybe." Then he blushed, as if it had been a hand of betrayal, but it
was too late to take it back.

"Did he have more money than the rest of you?" Pitt enquired.
"His father is extremely wealthy."

Thirlstone looked relieved.

"Ah . . . yes. Yes, he did. Certainly more than Jago or I. And I
suppose more than Helliwell too."

"Was he generous?"

A curious expression crossed Thirlstone's face, a mixture of bitterness and wry, almost careful regret. He obviously disliked talking
about it at all, and that might have been some kind of guilt, or simply that Thirlstone regarded that as an aesthetically wasted time and
preferred to live in the present.

"Was he generous?" Pitt repeated.

Thirlstone shrugged. "Yes . . . quite often."

"He gambled?" It did not matter, except as a blight on his character, but Pitt wanted to keep the conversation going.

A burst of laughter interrupted his thought, and they all turned
to look at the little group who had occasioned it.

"Yes. We all did," Thirlstone replied. "I suppose he gambled
rather more. It was in his nature, and he could afford it. Look, Superintendent, none of that is relevant now. I really have no idea
who killed this woman in Whitechapel. I find it difficult to believe it could have been Finlay. But if you have proof that it was,
then I shall have to accept it. Otherwise I think you are wasting your time—which is your privilege—but you are also wasting
mine, and that is precious. I have not seen my old club badge in

years, but if I should come across it, I shall bring it to Bow Street and pass it in."

"I would appreciate it if you could look for it, Mr. Thirlstone. It may prove Mr. FitzJames's innocence."

"Or guilt?" Thirlstone said, staring at Pitt with an intense gaze.

Charlotte had visited her mother during the day, and was full of news to tell Pitt when he returned home. Most of it cheerful and interesting, variations of the colorful gossip about the theater relayed by Caroline.

But when Charlotte saw Pitt's face as he came in at a quarter past seven, tired, hot and struggling with a confusion of thoughts, she realized this was not the time.

"Did you look again for the badge?" she asked as they sat over dinner. The children had already eaten and were upstairs getting ready for bed. Gracie, with her newly learned reading skill, was preparing to share with them the next chapter of *Alice Through the Looking Glass*. It was their favorite time of the day.

Both kittens were asleep in the laundry basket in the corner of the kitchen by the cooker, and everything was tidy and cleared away, except the dishes they were actually using, and they could wait until Gracie came down again.

"Yes," Pitt answered, looking up and meeting her eyes across the table. The sunlight was low, coming straight in through the large windows onto the table and the scrubbed floor. It made bright patterns on the far wall and gleamed where it caught the china on the Welsh dresser. It shone red on one of the copper-bottomed saucepans hanging up. "And we found it."

Charlotte swallowed. "Does that mean he is innocent?"

He smiled. "No, it just means there are two badges, so one of them is presumably a fake."

"Well, mustn't it be the one that was found in Pentecost Alley?

The other one must have been where you found it, mustn't it? Where did you find it?"

"In the pocket of an old jacket he apparently hasn't worn for years."

"Well then?"

He ate another mouthful of the cold chicken pie. It was very good indeed, so were the fresh tomatoes with it, and the cucumber.

"Thomas?" she prompted, her face puckered.

"Somebody had a copy made and put it either in Ada McKinley's bed in Pentecost Alley or else in Finlay FitzJames's pocket in Devonshire Street," he replied with his mouth half full.

"And don't you know which?" She was beginning to remember Emily's words yesterday, and her eagerness that Pitt should search again. Most unpleasant thoughts crossed her mind. She forced them away. "Surely you can tell, can't you?" she said more urgently, her own pie now forgotten.

"No, I can't." He frowned at her. "Not unless I can compare them with one of the original ones belonging to the other members. The writing is just a little different on the two I have. Presumably the first ones were all made by the same jeweler. The writing which does not match will be the copy."

"Doesn't it have . . ." she began, then realized the answer to her own question, and stopped.

"What?" he asked.

"It doesn't matter. It doesn't make any sense," she denied.

"Either someone had a copy made to prove him guilty when he was innocent," he explained. "Or to prove him innocent when he is guilty, or they fear he is. That could be any member of his family, or Finlay himself."

"Yes," she said cautiously, then looked down at her plate. "Yes, of course it could." She did not add what was in her thoughts. It was screaming in her mind, but she did not dare put words to it, even to herself. "Would you like another tomato?" She half moved from the table. "I have several more. They're really very good."

As soon as Pitt had left the following morning, and she had given Gracie instructions for the day, Charlotte took a hansom cab to Emily's house. By quarter past nine she was being shown into the morning room by a startled parlor maid, who said she would go and see if Mrs. Radley was at home. That meant she was. Had she been out riding she would have said so immediately. Although Charlotte was prepared to wait even if Emily were out for the entire day.

Emily appeared within ten minutes, still in a loose satin peignoir and with her fair hair loose in curls Charlotte had envied all their lives. She came towards Charlotte smiling, as if to kiss her on the cheek.

"Emily!" Charlotte said quickly.

Emily blinked. "Yes? You look very fierce. What's happened? Is it something to do with Grandmama?"

"No, it is not. Why did you ask me to have Thomas search the FitzJames house again for that Hellfire Club badge?" She faced Emily with a stare which should have turned her to stone.

Emily hesitated only a moment, then sat down casually in one of the green chairs.

"Because if he found it, it would prove that Finlay FitzJames is innocent, which will be much better for Thomas," she answered blandly, looking up at Charlotte standing above her. "Wouldn't it? Augustus FitzJames is a very powerful man, and not fearfully pleasant. Of course, if Finlay is guilty, then he should be arrested and tried, and all that. But if he isn't, then it would be much better for everyone, and for Thomas in particular, if it could be proved so before any charges are made. Isn't that all fairly plain?"

"Very plain indeed." Charlotte did not back away an inch. "Do you know him?"

Emily's eyes widened, very clear and blue in the morning sun coming through the long windows.

"Who? Augustus FitzJames? Only by repute. But I'm sure I'm right. Jack has mentioned him several times. He is very powerful, because he has a great deal of money."

"Finlay FitzJames?" Charlotte kept her voice under control with an effort.

"No," Emily answered, still with an air of innocence. "I've met him once, but only very briefly. Just to say how do you do, not much more. I doubt that he would recognize me again."

Charlotte was looking for the connection. It had to be somewhere. She knew Emily well enough to tell when she was being evasive. There was guilt in every line of her body, the wide gaze of her eyes. She sat down on the seat opposite and faced her.

"Is he betrothed to anyone?"

"I don't think so; I haven't heard that he is." Emily did not ask why Charlotte wanted to know. In Charlotte's mind, that was the final piece of evidence. She was lying about something. Her fears were confirmed.

"Tallulah?" she said between her teeth. "Do you care really about her so much you would coerce me into asking Thomas to search again on her account?"

Emily blushed. "I told you, Charlotte . . . if Finlay is innocent, it will be—"

"Rats! You knew that badge was there, because you or Tallulah put it there! Have you any idea of what you've done?"

Emily hesitated on the verge of admitting or denying. She still had not given herself away, not completely.

"Augustus FitzJames does have some very ruthless enemies, you know."

"And some very ruthless friends as well, it seems!" Charlotte said furiously. "Did you have the badge made yourself, or did you just suggest it to . . . Tallulah?"

Emily squared her shoulders. "I really think that as a policeman's wife, Charlotte, I should not discuss that with you. You would feel obliged to tell Thomas anything I told you, and then I might place myself, or my friends, in an embarrassing situation. I am quite certain Finlay is innocent, and I did what I believed to be right—for him, and for Thomas. You know that the identification is nonsense."

"What identification?" Suddenly Charlotte was less confident. Emily was certainly irresponsible, probably even criminal, and totally stupid; but it seemed she also knew something which Charlotte did not, and perhaps Pitt did not either. "What identification?" she repeated.

Emily relaxed. The sun through the morning room windows made an aureole of gold around her hair. The pleasant clatter of domestic chores sounded from beyond the door. Somewhere a girl was giggling . . . probably a between-maid.

"The identification of the other prostitute who said she saw Finlay there in Pentecost Alley the night of the murder," Emily answered.

"What?" Charlotte felt her stomach tighten and for a moment she could hardly breathe. "What did you say?"

"It wasn't a proper identification," Emily explained. "She doesn't really know if it was Finlay or not. She would be perfectly willing to say it was the butler, if it came to trial."

"What butler?" Charlotte was stunned, and now confused as well. "Whose butler? Why would she say it was a butler?"

"The butler who got Ada pregnant," Emily explained. "Which was how she lost her position and finished up on the streets," Emily explained.

"And just how do you know that?" Charlotte's voice dropped and became icy.

It was too late for any possible retreat.

"Because I spoke to her," Emily replied in a small voice.

Charlotte sat down abruptly. She felt a little dizzy.

"You shouldn't be so disturbed," Emily said reasonably. "You and I have both involved ourselves in cases before, and it has always ended more or less right. Remember the Hyde Park Headsman—"

"Don't!" Charlotte winced. "Have you forgotten what Jack said to you after that?"

Emily paled. "No. But he doesn't know about this. And I didn't do anything dangerous . . . well, not really. There wasn't anybody violent around. I was only looking for information to clear Finlay. I wasn't pressing anyone who could be guilty."

"Don't be idiotic!" Charlotte said. "If you clear Finlay, then someone else is guilty. It may be someone around there. In fact, it probably is. Except, of course," she added scathingly, "since you put the club badge there, Finlay could be as guilty as Jack the Ripper. The real badge was the original one, found with the poor woman's body. Or didn't you think of that?"

"Yes, of course I did. But that didn't mean that Finlay put it there!" Emily said. "We both know that he was nowhere near Whitechapel that night. He was at a party in Chelsea."

"We don't both know it!" Charlotte said. "All we really know is that Tallulah says she was there, and she says she saw him!"

"Well, I believe her! And without an identification it's the only piece of evidence that connects him with Whitechapel at all. Anyone could have stolen it, or found it years ago, and used it to revenge themselves on Augustus. After all, why on earth would Finlay kill a woman like Ada McKinley? Or anybody else, for that matter?"

"Somebody did," Charlotte said pointedly.

"Far more probably someone who knew her," Emily argued, leaning forward a trifle. "A rival, or someone she stole from or someone she hurt. She may have quarreled with someone, one of the other women, or some man she made fun of, maybe someone who was once in love with her, and she betrayed him by doing what she did." She took a deep breath. "Charlotte . . ."

Charlotte stared at her, waiting.

"Charlotte . . . please don't tell Thomas about the badge. He'd never forgive me. And he might not understand why I did it. I really do believe that Finlay is innocent."

"I know you do," Charlotte said gravely. "You wouldn't do anything so absolutely idiotic otherwise."

"Are you going to tell Thomas?" Emily asked in a very small voice.

"No," Charlotte answered, more out of pity than good sense. "At least, not unless I have to. He . . . he may discover whatever he needs to know before there's any need."

"Thank you."

Indeed, Pitt did discover at least part of it when he and Ewart went back to Pentecost Alley late in the afternoon. Nan Sullivan was as indecisive as on the previous time Pitt had seen her, but he still had every confidence in Rose Burke. The change in her stunned him.

"I dunno," she said, looking first at Pitt, then away. They were sitting in the kitchen, a large, chipped enamel pot of tea on the table, odd pottery cups around. The cooking range made the place hot and airless. No one wanted to open the window onto the stinking yard below with the fumes from the midden and the pigsty next door.

"What don't you know?" Pitt demanded. "You were quite sure when you saw him from the hansom in Devonshire Street. You were certain enough then you were ready to hang him yourself."

"I were ready to 'ang whoever done 'er," Rose corrected stubbornly. "That in't ter say it were 'im. I only saw 'im fer a minute, an' the light weren't good."

"Are you afraid, Rose?" Pitt tried to keep the anger out of his voice, or the stinging contempt he wanted to put into it.

"No!" She glared at him, ignoring Ewart completely. "No, I in't afraid. Wot's ter be afraid of?"

"Threats from someone," he replied. "The man you identified belongs to a very powerful family."

" 'E may do, but 'e in't spoken ter me," she said with a curl of her lip. "If that's wot yer think, yer wrong . . . dead wrong. I jus' want yer ter get the right man, the man wot really done 'er, poor little cow." She fiddled with her spoon, slicking it against the cup. "An' I think as it could be the butler wot got 'er into trouble in the first place. 'E done it again, an' this time 'is mistress might not be so quick ter believe 'im. 'E got reason ter wanner get rid o' Ada. Geezers like the one wot yer showed me in Devonshire Street don' come down ter Whitechapel. They get their bits o' pleasure up the 'Aymarket way, an' Windmill Street."

"That's true," Ewart conceded.

"You said Ada sometimes went up there," Pitt pointed out.

"Sure. But I never said as she brought 'em 'ome 'ere!" she said with derision. "She in't that daft. If she 'ad 'a', like as not that Costigan'd 'a' took more'n 'alf 'er money. An' why would one o' them gents foller 'er 'ere? Wot for? She weren't that good. There are plenty more w'ere she come from, an' ter them, one tart's as good as another."

"Are you now saying it was this butler you saw?" Ewart interrupted quickly, leaning forward over the table. "Describe him!"

"No I in't sayin' it were 'im," she said cautiously. "I'm sayin' as it might 'a' bin. Geez! Don't yer care 'oo yer top, long as it's someone?"

"I care very much," Pitt replied between his teeth, holding on to his temper. "I find your certainty then, and your change of mind now, suspicious. It makes me wonder if someone has been changing it for you, either with threat or with promise."

"You sayin' as I bin paid ter lie?" she asked angrily.

"No." Ewart was placating. "Nobody's saying you're lying, Rose. We simply have to be sure. Nothing can bring back Ada, and it's a man's life we are talking about. A wrongful accusation would be in its way a second murder."

"Well, mebbe I could lie 'baht somethin' as don't matter," she said carefully, this time looking at Ewart. "But not ter get some poor sod cropped, 'ooever 'e is. Ter tell the truth, I were upset that Ada were killed." She lifted her shoulders very slightly, a gesture of apology and resignation. "I were sort o' angry an' scared, an' too quick ter make up me mind. I wanted someone caught an' topped, 'cos it made it feel better fer the rest o' us. Safer, like." She took a breath and turned to Pitt again. "I wan'ed ter think as I knew 'oo it were. Now I've 'ad time ter think better, I can see as that's stupid. It's gotta be the right sod, not just any poor bastard as looks a bit like 'im. 'Asn't it?"

"Yes," Pitt conceded grimly. "Yes, it has to be the right one."

"Of course." Ewart moved his arm as if to pat her shoulder, then changed his mind. "Of course it has," he added gently.

They left Pentecost Alley and Pitt rode back in the hansom with Ewart.

"We'd better find this butler," he said wearily. "Even if it is only to eliminate him."

"I think he's our man," Ewart replied, his voice loud with conviction, his face set hard, staring straight ahead as they moved west along the Whitechapel High Street. "Stands to reason. He got Ada with child. That time he got away with it. Lied to his employers. Now he's done it again and she was going to come back and tell the whole story. Finish him."

"She told the whole story the first time," Pitt pointed out. "What had she to gain from telling it again?"

"Revenge," Ewart replied, as if the answer were obvious. "He was responsible for her ruin. Oldest motive in the world."

Pitt looked sideways at him. Ewart was a good policeman. His record was excellent. He was in line for more promotion. This was an extraordinary lapse in his thinking. He had been laboring under some emotion right from the start. Was it pity or disgust? Or was it some fear that Augustus FitzJames would set out to ruin whoever accused his son of such a crime, guilty or innocent, and even Ewart's long-standing reputation would not be enough to save him?

Of course it would be unpleasant. But bringing a charge against anyone had its tragedy. There were always innocent people hurt, people who simply loved a husband or a son. They would be overwhelmed by events, and then when all the tumult and the public pain was over, they would be left with its grief.

"What good would that do?" Pitt asked him, watching Ewart's face with its black eyes and the lines of anxiety around his mouth. "Ada had already told her story. Dead, she simply reinforces it. If he killed anyone, it would be the present girl, before she tells her employer. The judgment had already been made between Ada and this man, and she had lost. She might have killed him, but he had no cause to kill her."

Ewart's expression hardened, and a flicker of something like fear shadowed across his features, or perhaps it was anger. He was very tired. His hands shook a little. He must hate having a superior like Pitt put in to take over his case because he was deemed incapable of handling a politically sensitive case. Any man would, and Pitt would have himself.

And Ewart was doing a better job of being politically appropriate than Pitt was. He was searching for any answer but the explosive one.

In his position Pitt would have resented both the man who was brought in and the superior who made the decision.

"I agree with you," he said quietly. "The evidence against Fitz-James is poor. The identification is useless. The cuff links were lost years ago, and the club badge is suspect. It won't stand alone, now we've found a second one in his possession. We've got to go back to the beginning. We should look more closely at Ada's life, and also at FitzJames's, to see who could be implicated."

Ewart turned to face him. "Implicated?" he asked slowly. He seemed almost too tired, too stunned by blow after blow to think.

"If FitzJames has enemies so virulent they would put evidence at the scene of the murder to incriminate him," Pitt started to explain, "then . . ."

Ewart straightened up a little, realization in his face.

"Oh yes. Of course. Do you want me to do that? I'll start tomorrow."

"Good," Pitt agreed. "I'll continue with Ada." It was all ugly, and confusing. He must, as he had said, go right back to the beginning.

Pitt arrived home late, and was startled to find Emily's great-aunt by her first marriage, Lady Vespasia Cumming-Gould, sitting in his parlor sipping a tisane and talking to Charlotte. He had flung the door open, about to speak, until he saw her, and he stopped.

"Good evening, Thomas," Aunt Vespasia said coolly, her silver eyebrows raised. As always, she looked exquisite; her face, with its marvelous bones and hooded eyes, had been refined by time and her character marked into it. It was no longer the mere loveliness of youth but a beauty which was the whole structure of a life, fascinating and unique.

She had given him permission to call her by name as a relative. He used it with pleasure.

"Good evening, Aunt Vespasia. How very pleasant to see you."

"And surprising also, to judge by the expression upon your face," she retorted. "No doubt you are hungry, and would like to dine. I believe Gracie has your meal prepared."

He closed the door and came into the room. He was hungry and extremely tired, but he was not willing to forgo the pleasure of her company, nor the interest of her conversation. She would not simply have called because she was passing by. Vespasia never did anything casually, and she did not pass by Bloomsbury on the way to anywhere. He sat down, glanced at Charlotte, then faced Vespasia.

"Are you acquainted with Augustus FitzJames?" he said candidly.

She smiled. "No, Thomas, I am not. I should be offended if you imagined I had called upon you because I was a friend of his and aware that you were investigating that sordid affair in Whitechapel which seems to implicate his son."

"No one who knew you would suppose you would try to exert influence, Aunt Vespasia," he said honestly.

Her silver-gray eyes widened. "My dear Thomas, no one who knew me would suppose me a friend of a nouveau riche bully like Augustus FitzJames. Please do sit down. I find it most uncomfortable staring up at you."

He found himself smiling in spite of his weariness and the confusion in his mind, the sense of having achieved nothing in all the time and effort he had spent. He sat down opposite her.

"But I do have some compassion for his wife," she went on. "Although that is not why I called. My principal interest is in you, and after that, in John Cornwallis." She frowned very slightly. "Thomas, if you charge Finlay FitzJames, be extremely careful that you can prove your case. His father is a man of great power and no clemency at all."

Pitt had judged as much, but it was chilling to hear it from Vespasia. She was not a woman too arrogant or too foolish to be afraid, but it was a very rare occurrence indeed, and when he had seen it in the past, it had been of the power of secret societies rather than of individuals. It increased his sense of misery and the darkness of thought which surrounded the murder in Pentecost Alley.

Charlotte was looking at him anxiously.

"It begins to appear," he began carefully, "as if Finlay FitzJames may not be guilty. Certainly the evidence against him has largely been withdrawn, or explained away."

"That is very unclear. I think you had better say what you mean," Vespasia commanded.

He told her about the badge, and then finding the second one in

Finlay's possession, and his inability to obtain any of the other original ones with which to compare them to identify the copy. He did not notice Charlotte's pink cheeks or averted eyes, he was too absorbed with laying out the evidence for Vespasia.

"Hmm," she said as he concluded. "Not very satisfactory, but I suppose rather obvious, except for one thing."

"What thing?" Charlotte said quickly.

"One wonders why Augustus did not have the copy made immediately," Vespasia answered. "And then require a more thorough search. It could have been done within the first couple of days. If he were going to do it at all, why wait until the discomfort increased? Unless, of course, it was to teach Finlay a lesson, make him thoroughly frightened for a while, and so perhaps more obedient."

"Why couldn't Finlay have done it himself?" Charlotte asked, then looked down as if she regretted having spoken.

"Because he panicked and hasn't the brains," Vespasia replied simply.

Pitt recalled his first meeting with Finlay.

"But he didn't seem panicked," he said honestly. "He was startled, upset, even shocked, but he didn't seem in a sweat of fear at all. If anything, I would say his fear grew as time went by, and we continued to suspect him."

"Curious," Vespasia admitted. "What other evidence had you?"

Pitt noted that she spoke of it in the past, and smiled ruefully.

"Identification by witness," he replied, then told her the story of Nan Sullivan and Rose Burke and their subsequent retraction.

Vespasia considered for several moments before she commented.

"Not very satisfactory," she agreed. "That could mean any of several things: possibly she spoke the truth in the beginning and has been persuaded to withdraw it by pressure from someone else, threat of injury or promise of reward; or that her own sense of self-preservation has overcome her hatred or her anger; or conceivably she has decided the information is worth more if kept to herself and used at some future date for profit." She frowned. "Or it is possible she is telling the truth, and it was a mixture of fear and desire to see someone caught and punished for Ada's death which made her act impulsively in the first place, and on reflection she realized she was not prepared to perjure herself with an identification she was genuinely not sure of. The story of the butler is tragic, and no doubt true, but obviously irrelevant to her death."

"Do you still think Finlay did it?" Charlotte asked very quietly, anxiety puckering her brows. "I mean ... is the evidence really wrong, or has his father very carefully removed it, or invalidated it?"

Pitt considered for several moments.

"I don't know," he said at last. "I think if I have to make a decision I would say he did not, but I'm not certain."

"That is most unfortunate." Vespasia was simply stating a fact, but not without sympathy. "If he is innocent, then either he has an exceedingly vicious enemy or an extraordinary series of events has combined to make him appear guilty, which, my dear Thomas, seems unlikely."

"Yes, it does," Pitt confessed. "I suppose I return to the very unpleasant task of trying to find the FitzJames family's enemies." He sighed. "I wish I even knew whether it was Finlay's own enemy or his father's. He seems a fairly harmless young man, a great deal more ordinary than he would probably wish to be ..."

"A great deal," Vespasia agreed with a rueful smile. "I think his sister has more chance of doing something genuinely interesting, but she may well be married out of that before she has the chance. At the moment she is singularly flighty and doesn't appear to have a thought in her head except to enjoy herself, preferably without thinking of anything with the least meaning beyond the following day. But she does it with such fervor, I have hope she may stumble upon something she will care about, and that will make all the difference."

Charlotte opened her mouth and then closed it again.

Pitt wondered what she had been going to say. Usually when it was tactless, it was also pertinent. He could ask her after Vespasia had left.

"But he has the arrogance of those who sense their limitations," Vespasia went on, regarding Pitt seriously, "and who fear they may be smaller than their ambitions, or the expectations of others for them. Who were the other members of this rather juvenile club? One of them would seem to be in the ideal position to provide the model for the badge, and also to be familiar with Finlay's habits to the degree where he could implicate him successfully."

Pitt repeated their names.

Vespasia looked blank. "Thirlstone means nothing to me. I have heard of a James Helliwell. He might have a son by the name of Herbert . . ."

"Norbert," Pitt corrected.

"Indeed. Or Norbert either," she conceded. "But he is a very pedestrian sort of man. Sufficient means to be comfortable, and too little imagination to be uncomfortable, unless he sat upon a tack! And Heaven knows, there are as many Joneses as there are Browns or Robinsons. Jago Jones could be anyone at all . . . or no one."

Pitt found himself smiling. "Helliwell sounds like the man I met, very concerned with how he was perceived by others, particularly his parents-in-law, and as you say, beginning to be very comfortable, and unwilling to let anything disturb that. He is no longer so keen to defend Finlay, in case some of the notoriety sticks to him as well. Although he certainly did not wish me to continue investigating Finlay."

"An enemy?" Charlotte said dubiously.

"Insufficient nerve," Vespasia dismissed him, looking at Pitt, her eyes wide.

"I think so," Pitt agreed, remembering Helliwell's red face and his fidgeting manner, his keenness to disclaim any association. "Certainly he hasn't the honor to be loyal once it becomes costly."

"Thirlstone?" Charlotte asked.

"Possibly." As he said it he was seeing Jago Jones's passionate face. He was a man who had the courage, the fire and the conviction. But had he the cause? "I think . . ." he said slowly, "that I should look more closely into why Ada was the victim. Why was it someone in Whitechapel, rather than the West End? It seems irrational. Perhaps there is a reason there which may lead us to who it was."

Vespasia rose to her feet, and Pitt stood instantly also, offering her his hand.

She accepted it, but leaned no weight on it at all.

"Thank you, my dear. I wish I could say I felt easier in my mind, but I do not." She regarded him very gravely, searching his eyes. "I fear this is a most ugly case. Be careful, Thomas. You may trust John Cornwallis's honor and his courage absolutely, but I suspect that his understanding of the deviousness of the political mind has a long way to go. Do not allow him to let you down by expecting of him a skill he does not possess and a loyalty which he does. Good night, my dear."

"Good night, Aunt Vespasia," he replied as he stood watching while she kissed Charlotte lightly on the cheek. Then, head high, she swept through the parlor door towards the front entrance and her waiting carriage.

He began early the next morning, not exactly with enthusiasm, but with a renewed determination. Ewart was already directed to pursue further details of both Augustus and Finlay FitzJames. Tellman was investigating the other members of the Hellfire Club. Pitt himself went back to Pentecost Alley to speak again with the women who had known Ada last.

It was an inappropriate hour of the morning to find them, but he could not afford the time or the patience to wait until the afternoon, when they would naturally get up to begin the day.

Of course, the sweatshop over the road was thrumming with industry, doors open because they had been at work for several hours by nine o'clock, and it was already hot.

Pitt went up the steps to the wooden door of the tenement and knocked. He had to repeat it several times before the door was finally opened by a bad-tempered-looking Madge, her large face creased with irritation and weariness, her eyes almost disappeared in the folds of fat in her cheeks.

"What the 'ell time o' day jer think this is?" she demanded. "Ain't yer got no . . ." She squinted at him. "Oh, it's you! Wotjer want this time? I dunno nuffink more ter tell yer. An' neither do Rose ner Nan, ner Agnes."

"You might do." Pitt pushed against the door, but her vast weight was rocklike.

"Yer in't goin' ter crop that bastard, so wot's it matter," she said contemptuously. "Yer show o' duty don't impress me none."

"Somebody killed Ada," he insisted. "And he's still out there. Do you want me to find him, or not?"

"I wanna be young an' pretty an' 'ave a nice 'ouse an' enough ter eat," she said sarcastically. "W'en the 'ell did wot I want matter a sod ter anyone?"

"I'm not going away, Madge, until I know everything about Ada that I can," he said levelly. "If you want a little peace to conduct your business and turn a profit, you'll humor me, whether you think it's worth it or not."

She did not need to weigh the issue. Wearily she stepped back and opened the door. She heard him close it with a heavy thud, and led him back into the small room she used as a kitchen, sewing room, and somewhere from which she could listen for calls of distress or sounds of violence.

Pitt asked her every question he could think of about Ada's life. What time she got up, how she dressed, when she came and went, if Madge knew where to, or where from, who with, whom

she had met. He wanted any mention of friends or enemies, however vague, any names of clients or of possible allies. He asked her
to estimate Ada's income from her wardrobe, her behavior, her
gifts to anyone else.

"Well," Madge said thoughtfully, sitting on a stool and staring
down at the stained table. "She were generous, w'en she 'ad it, I'll
give 'er that . . . anyone'd give 'er that. An' she done well in the last
couple o' months. Got them new boots the day she were killed.
Pleased as punch she were wi' them. Marched up an' down in 'em
showin' 'em orff. Lifted 'er skirts ter let me see 'em. Mother-o'-pearl
buttons they 'ad." Her face tightened. "But I s'pose yer know that,
seein' as 'ow yer came 'ere that night an' found 'er!"

Pitt thought back to the boots which had been so laboriously
buttoned together. They were beautifully made. He had not given a
thought then to their cost.

"Yes, I remember them. Did she usually have boots of such
quality?"

She laughed sharply. "Course not! Make do and mend, like the
rest o' us. No, she done well recent, like I told yer." Her eyes narrowed till the fat in her cheeks almost obscured them. " 'Ere, are yer
sayin' as she done summink wrong ter get that money?"

"No," he assured her. He leaned forward, elbows on the table.
"But I'd like to know where it came from. Did it start when she
changed from her old pimp to her new one?"

"Yeah," she conceded. "Abaht then. Why? Bert Costigan in't
that much better, if that's wot yer thinkin'. 'E's a fancy-lookin' sod,
but 'e in't that clever. Never liked 'im meself." She shrugged. "But
then I never liked any o' them. They're all swine, w'en it comes ter
it. Bleed yer dry. An' w'ere was 'e w'en she needed 'im, eh?" She
sniffed and the slow tears trickled down her enormous cheeks.
"Gawd knows. Not 'ere!"

He woke Rose and Nan also, and asked them all the same
questions, and received the same answers. By that time Agnes was

up anyway, and he asked her too, but she contributed nothing to his knowledge, except when he demanded a physical description of Ada, whose face he had never seen except disfigured by death. Her hesitant words were of limited use, but he discovered in Agnes a ready pencil which produced a sketch which was more of a caricature than a portrait, but highly evocative. He could see the character of a woman of humor, even spirit. It was extraordinarily alive, even on the lined notebook page. He could imagine her walk, the angle of her head, even her voice. It made her death immeasurably worse, and her torture something he could not bear to think of.

He went back to Bow Street and ate a cold mutton sandwich and a mug of tea at about six o'clock. He wrote down carefully in order the notes he had taken, and he began to see a pattern in Ada's behavior. She had obviously worked her own patch in Old Montague Street and then the Whitechapel Road in the early evenings, and sometimes late as well, but there were regular times when she was absent, excellent times for her trade when one would have expected her to take full advantage of the opportunities.

One answer leaped to mind. She had gone to a more profitable area. Was this the influence of Albert Costigan, a more ambitious man, and she had been only too willing to try to improve her situation? Was it possible that in this new guise she had met either one of Finlay's enemies or one of his father's? Was it even remotely worth searching?

So far neither Tellman nor Ewart had discovered anything of relevance.

He spent the evening, and the later part of the following day and the one after that, walking the prostitutes' beats around the West End, Windmill Street, the Haymarket, Leicester Square and the streets and alleys close by. He saw thousands of women much like Ada, some gorgeously dressed, parading like peacocks, others less so, some in little more than gaudy rags. Many, even in the gaslight after dark, still looked long past their prime, raddle-cheeked, slack-bodied. Some were country fresh, come to the city to seek their fortune and finding it in the accommodation rooms in hasty fornication with strangers, often their fathers' or even grandfathers' ages.

And there were also children, eight or ten years old, running after men, pulling at their sleeves and whispering dirty words in hope of exciting their interest, or thrusting into their hands lurid, pornographic pictures.

Side by side with them were the theater crowds, respectable women, even wealthy ladies on their husbands' arms, arriving at or leaving the performance of some play or concert.

Pitt tried every contact he had in the rooming houses, the pimps and madams he knew, but no one owned to recognizing his picture of Ada or knowing her name other than from the news that she was dead. Since Finlay FitzJames's connection had not been mentioned, the newspapers had made little of it. No one knew of the broken fingers and toes except Lennox, Ewart, Cornwallis and himself.

He was close to defeat when it occurred to him to try away from the West End and into the Hyde Park area. He had one more personal acquaintance to try, a huge, complacent and unctuous figure known as Fat George. He ruled his prostitutes with a rod of iron and the threat of his right-hand man, Wee Georgie, a vicious dwarf with a filthy temper, and quick to use the long, thin-bladed knife he always carried.

He found Fat George in his own house, an extremely well-appointed, classically proportioned building off Inverness Terrace.

Fat George did not rise; his enormous body was almost wedged into his chair. It was a warm day and he wore a loose shirt, newly laundered, his greasy gray curls sitting on the collar.

"Well now, Mr. Pitt," he said in his whispering, wheezy voice. "What brings you to call on me so urgently? Must be something terrible important to you. Sit down! Sit down! Haven't seen you since that ugly business in the Park. Long time solving that, you were. Not very clever, Mr. Pitt. Not very efficient." Fat George shook his head and his curls caught on his collar. "Not what we pay our police force for. You're supposed to keep us safe, Mr. Pitt. We should sleep easy in our beds, knowin' as you're out there protectin' us." If there was humor in Fat George's black eyes, it barely showed.

"We can only solve crimes after they've happened, George, not before," Pitt replied, accepting a seat. "There are a good many around here you could have prevented. Do you know anything about this woman?" He passed over Agnes's sketch.

Fat George took it in his pale-skinned, freckled hand, his fingers swollen so the bones were invisible.

"Yeah, I've seen her," he said after several seconds. "Smart girl, ambitious. Like to have her meself, but she's greedy. Wants all her money for 'erself. Dangerous, that, Mr. Pitt. Very dangerous. She the one that got killed up Whitechapel? Should've seen that coming. Don't have far to look, likely."

"Don't I?"

"Not clever, Mr. Pitt." George wagged his head, pushing out his lower lip. "Losin' your touch, are you? Try 'er pimp, fellow called Costigan, so I hear."

"Very public-spirited of you, George, and very quick to blame one of your own," Pitt said dryly.

"Gives me a bad name," George wheezed sententiously. "Bit o' discipline is all very well. Necessary, or you'd be walked all over. Can't 'ave that. Girls'd be cheatin' you left and right. But stranglin' is overdoin' it. Brings people like you around, an' that's all very nasty." He coughed and his vast chest rumbled with congestion. The room was hot, the high windows all closed, giving it a musty air in spite of its cool colors, gracious lines and at least half a dozen potted palms placed here and there.

"So why didn't Costigan discipline her?" Pitt asked, eyebrows raised. "Killing her would seem to defeat his own purpose. Only a fool destroys his own livestock."

George made a gesture of distaste. "Oh, very crudely put, Mr. Pitt, very crude indeed."

"It's a crude trade, George. What makes you think this Costigan even knew Ada was sneaking up west occasionally and then keeping her earnings?"

Fat George shrugged, and his ripples of fat shook all down his body. "Maybe he followed her? Natural thing to do."

"If he was following her," Pitt reasoned, "he'd have known the first time she left Whitechapel, which was several weeks ago."

Fat George rolled his eyes. "How do I know?"

"Maybe someone told him?" Pitt suggested, watching George's face.

There was a very slight flicker, a tightening of the sallow skin, enough for Pitt.

"You told him, didn't you, George." It was not a question but a statement. "She was on your patch, but refusing to pay you either, so rather than let Wee Georgie at her, and risk unpleasantness for yourself, you told her own pimp and let him deal with it. Only he went too far. Not your fault, of course," he finished scathingly. "When did you tell him?"

The room was becoming suffocating, like a jungle.

George raised colorless eyebrows. "The day she were killed, but I'm hardly to blame, Mr. Pitt. Your tone in't polite. In fact, most unjust. You're an unjust man, Mr. Pitt, and that isn't right. Expect the police to be just. If justice itself don't . . ."

Pitt stood up and shot him a look of such contempt Fat George left the rest of his complaint unfinished.

"Costigan a trouble to you, was he?" Pitt said bitterly. "A threat?"

"Hardly!" Fat George tried to laugh, broke into a wheeze, and ended coughing again, his massive chest heaving as he fought for breath.

Pitt had no sympathy for him at all. He turned on his heel and walked out, leaving George purple in the face, gasping for air, and furious.

Pitt took Constable Binns with him when he went to see Albert Costigan later that afternoon. He knew the area and found him without difficulty in the rooms he rented in Plumbers Row, just the other side of the Whitechapel Road from Pentecost Alley. It was narrow and gray on the outside, like all the other tenements, but inside was well furnished, even comfortable. Costigan liked to do nicely for himself, and his expensive tastes showed in the small extras: engraved glass gas mantels, a new carpet, a very nice oak gate-legged table.

Costigan himself was of average height, with large, pale blue eyes, good nose and white teeth. His brown hair was brushed back in waves from his brow. At a glance, before one noticed the defensive, aggrieved expression in his face, the aggressive angle of his body, he was not unlike Finlay FitzJames. Had chance given him the same wealth and self-confidence, the education of manner, they could have passed for cousins.

Pitt had no evidence against Costigan, except Fat George's words, which were worth nothing as testimony. What was the oath of one pimp against the oath of another? And even a search of Costigan's rooms would be unlikely to reveal anything of use. It would be natural enough for him to have Ada's possessions, and very easily explained.

"Yer still lookin' fer 'oo killed poor Ada?" Costigan said accusingly. "Yer got nothing, 'ave yer?" His contempt was quite open.

"Well, I've got some ideas," Pitt answered, sitting down on the largest and most comfortable armchair and leaving Binns standing by the door.

Costigan remained standing also, looking resentfully down at Pitt. "Oh yeah? What's that then?"

"We think it's something to do with her going up towards Hyde Park," Pitt replied.

Costigan stopped fidgeting from one foot to the other and stared at Pitt.

" 'Oo said she went up there? I never did."

"Are you going to tell me you didn't know?" Pitt asked innocently. "Not very efficient of you, Mr. Costigan. One of your girls going up to the expensive end of town, getting custom up there, and you didn't know about it? Don't suppose you saw much of the money then?" He smiled. "That would be good for a few laughs around here!"

"Course I knew!" Costigan said quickly, lifting his chin a little. "Take me for a fool! I'd beat the 'ell out o' any girl wot cheated me like that! But I wouldn't kill 'er! That'd be stupid. Can't sell a girl wot's dead, now can yer?" His large, bright eyes did not leave Pitt's. They were aggressive and triumphant, as if he had won some contest between them.

Pitt glanced around the room and back at Costigan again. It was not difficult to believe he had made a good deal of money out of someone. He could be telling the truth, except for what Fat George had said, and that could be a lie, simply to damage a business rival.

"Did you send any other girls up there?" Pitt asked, his hope beginning to fade.

Costigan hesitated, trying to decide whether to lie or not.

"No . . . just Ada. She 'ad class, she 'ad." He looked sorry for himself. He glanced at Binns in the doorway, scribbling down what he said.

"Class?" Pitt said dubiously.

"Yeah!" Costigan's head jutted forward. "Dressed nice. 'Ad 'er 'air nice. Could make men laugh. They like that. Some girls is pretty, but stupid. Ada 'ad brains, an' a quick tongue." He squared his shoulders, staring at Pitt, bragging. "An' like I said, she dressed nice. Good enough fer up west. Not like some o' them tarts around 'ere wot look like they in't got no idea wot a lady looks like."

At the doorway Binns let out a grunt.

Costigan took it for disbelief.

"She did, an' all!" he said angrily. "Red an' black dress, she 'ad, good as any o' them tarts up the 'Aymarket way, an' new boots wi' pearly buttons on 'em. Cost a fortune, boots like that. Tarts around 'ere don't 'ave nothin' like them."

"Boots?" Pitt said very slowly, a sudden lift of excitement in his chest, at the very same moment as the weight of tragedy struck him.

"Yeah, boots," Costigan snapped, quite unaware of what he had said.

"When did you see them, Mr. Costigan?" Pitt asked, glancing at Binns to make sure he was writing everything down.

"Wot? I dunno. Why?"

"Think!" Pitt ordered. "When did you see the boots?"

" 'Oo cares? I seen 'em." Costigan was flushed now, his eyes over-bright. His hands were clenched at his sides and there was a thin line of perspiration on his upper lip.

"I believe you saw them," Pitt accepted. "I think you went up to the Hyde Park area, perhaps with a view to breaking into trade there, or perhaps you already suspected Ada was doing a little independent work, and you saw Fat George. And Fat George told you that Ada was indeed working up there, and doing quite well. You realized she was cheating you, and you came back here and faced her with it. She told you she didn't need you and to whistle for your share. You tried hurting her a little bit, only she defied you. You lost your temper and in the quarrel you killed her. Possibly you didn't intend to when you started, but your vanity was wounded. Maybe she laughed at you. You held her too hard, and before you thought about it, she was dead."

Costigan stared at him, too appalled to speak, his face contorted with fear.

"And when you realized she was dead," Pitt went on, "you put a garter 'round her arm and buttoned the new boots to each other, to make it look like some customer with a fetish, a taste for sadism or ritual, and you left."

Costigan swallowed convulsively. His mouth and lips were dry, his skin ashen.

"You were seen," Pitt went on, wanting now to finish it as quickly as possible. "I think if we ask Rose Burke, she'll identify you. And perhaps Nan Sullivan will remember your coat. She used to be a seamstress and she has a very good eye for a cotton. Albert Costigan, I'm arresting you for the murder of Ada McKinley . . ."

Costigan let out his breath in a gasp of despair and collapsed into the chair, still too horrified to speak.

CHAPTER

SEVEN

"Thank heaven." Cornwallis leaned back in his seat in the box at the theater and glanced across at Pitt. Charlotte and her mother, Caroline, were sitting on the farther side, both leaning forward over the balcony watching the people coming and going in the stalls below them. The performance was halfway through. Caroline's new husband, Joshua Fielding, was the star. Pitt had been uncertain how Cornwallis would react to the news that Pitt's mother-in-law had remarried, and to an actor so much her junior. But if Cornwallis found it extraordinary, he was too courteous to show it.

It was also impossible to tell what he thought of the play itself, a deeply emotional and rather daring drama which raised several controversial issues. If Pitt had been aware of that in advance, he would not have invited his superior. With Micah Drummond it had been different. He knew him well enough, both his passions and his vulnerabilities, to be quite aware what would offend him and what would not. Cornwallis was still a stranger. They had shared far too little, only this one case, which, as it now turned out, seemed to be very ordinary and to have delivered none of the dangers it had threatened at first. Pitt really need not have been called in. But of course they could not have known that initially.

Cornwallis ran his hand over his head and smiled ruefully. "I confess, I thought this case was going to be most unpleasant," he said with a sigh of relief. "We were extremely fortunate it turned out to be the poor woman's own pimp—in a sense, almost a domestic matter." There was a very fine wrinkle across his brow. He did not look as at ease as his words suggested. He was immaculately dressed in evening suit and snow-white shirt, but through his elegant clothes there was a tension visible in his body, as though he were not entirely comfortable.

Charlotte and Caroline were still peering over the balcony rail, shoulder to shoulder, staring down.

"Was it just mischance that we were led to suspect FitzJames?" Cornwallis asked quietly, so his words would not be overheard. It was as if he did not want to discuss the subject but felt compelled to.

"I'm not sure I believe in mischance of that sort," Pitt replied thoughtfully. He too was relieved it had in the end so easily proved to be Costigan, but there were facets of the case which were troubling, too many questions Costigan's arrest and charge did not answer.

"Which was the real badge?" Cornwallis asked, as if reading his thoughts. "The first or the second? Or were they both, in the sense that FitzJames had them both made?"

There was laughter from the next box, and an exclamation of surprise. From everywhere came the buzz of conversation.

"I don't know," Pitt replied. "Helliwell had the first badges made, and he says he has forgotten who the jeweler was and cannot find his own."

"And the other two members?" Cornwallis pressed.

"They also claim never to have known the name of the original jeweler and to have lost their own badges." Pitt shrugged. "I rather suspect FitzJames had the second one made to try to prove his innocence, or at least to throw question on his guilt."

"Then the badge you found in Pentecost Alley was his?" Cornwallis said quickly, swiveling around to face Pitt, all attempt at casualness abandoned. "What has that to do with Costigan? I don't understand."

"Neither do I," Pitt admitted. He was about to continue, when there was a knock on the door of the box and a moment later Micah Drummond came in. He greeted Charlotte and Caroline, then as soon as formalities were over, turned to Pitt and Cornwallis. He was a tall, lean man with a gentle, aquiline face. Grace of manner and long habit of command masked a natural shyness.

"Congratulations," he said warmly to both men. "A potentially very unpleasant case handled smoothly. And you managed to keep most of it out of the papers, which was just as well. I've heard murmurs that FitzJames is very pleased." He laughed abruptly. "I suppose 'grateful' would be too strong a word for such a man, but he'll remember it. He may prove an ally in the future."

"Only if our enemies happen also to be his," Cornwallis said dryly. "He's a man to remember an offense and forget a service. Not that our conduct of the case was in any sense intended to be a service to him!" he added quickly. "If Pitt had proved his son guilty, I'd have had him arrested as soon as Costigan, or anyone else."

Micah Drummond smiled.

"I'm sure you would. I'm still delighted it didn't prove necessary." He glanced at Pitt, and then back again at Cornwallis. "There is nothing we can do if tragedy strikes one of the prominent families, but it's a most wretched thing to have to deal with."

Pitt's mind flew back to the tragedy which had affected Eleanor Byam, who was now Drummond's second wife. The tension and the pain of that experience, the ultimate terrible outcome, and Pitt's understanding of Drummond's own emotions, had forged a bond between them which was still absent from his respect for Cornwallis.

Drummond swung around to exchange a few words with Charlotte and compliment Caroline on Joshua's performance, then he excused himself and left.

Pitt turned to Cornwallis and was about to resume their conversation when there was another brief tap on the door and Vespasia sailed in with her head high. She looked marvelous. She had chosen to make a great occasion of the event, and was dressed in lavender and steel-gray silk. On anyone else it might have been cold, but with her silver hair and the diamonds at her ears and throat, it was magnificent.

Pitt and Cornwallis automatically rose to their feet.

"Quite fascinating, my dear," Vespasia said to Charlotte. "What an entrancing man. Such a presence."

Caroline blushed, realized she was doing it, and blushed the more.

"Thank you," she said almost hesitantly. "I think he is doing it rather well."

"He is doing it superbly," Vespasia admonished. "The part could have been written for him. I daresay it was! Good evening, Charlotte. Good evening, Thomas. No doubt you are pleased with yourself? Good evening, John."

"Good evening, Lady Vespasia." He bowed very slightly to her. He looked at once pleased and uncomfortable. Pitt glanced at him, and saw from his expression that he was already aware that Vespasia was in some distant way related at least to Charlotte. He was not surprised to see her, as he must otherwise have been.

"Quite extraordinary," Vespasia went on, with a very slight lift of one shoulder and without offering any explanation of what she was referring to. She turned back to Caroline with a charming smile. "I'm so glad I came. Please don't consider it in the slightest way a reflection on the fact that the alternative was the opera, which was something Wagnerian and fearfully portentous, to do with gods and destiny. I prefer my doomed love affairs in Italian, and to do with human frailty, which I understand, rather than fate, which I do not, and predestination, which I do not believe in. I refuse to. It negates all that humanity is, if it is to be worth anything whatever."

Caroline opened her mouth to say something polite and changed her mind. It was not necessary, and no one, least of all Vespasia, expected it.

"And I could not abide to sit and watch Augustus FitzJames preen himself," Vespasia continued. "I don't know whether he is really fond of Wagner or only considers it the correct mark of good taste, but he attends every one, and always on the first night, with his wife wearing half a South African diamond mine 'round her neck. The sight of his face would be worse than sitting in a box listening to Brünnhilde screaming for four hours, or Sieglinde, or Isolde, or whoever it is. But it would be interesting to look around the audience and see if anyone is in a particularly filthy mood."

"Would it?" Pitt said confusedly.

She looked at him with shadowed silver eyes. "Well, my dear Thomas, someone has tried very hard to ruin Mr. FitzJames's family and has apparently failed. That wretched little man Costigan may have killed the girl, but do you really suppose it was his own idea to implicate young FitzJames? Where on earth would such a man acquire a club badge and a cuff link with which to do it? Do you imagine they could be acquainted?" She did not ask it sarcastically. She was considering the possibility.

"I don't know," Pitt replied. "It doesn't seem likely, but there is a lot yet unanswered. I'm going back to question him again tomorrow. From what we have at the moment, it doesn't seem to make sense that Finlay FitzJames had anything to do with it at all, either directly or indirectly."

"Then how did his badge and cuff link get there?" Charlotte asked curiously. "Do you suppose Ada stole them?"

"I don't know," Pitt repeated. "Perhaps Finlay left them behind some other time, or someone else did." Jago Jones's face flitted into his mind with a sharp, unhappy thought.

"I wish I felt it was purely a mischance," Vespasia said with a little shake of her head. "At least I think I do. I really find Augustus

FitzJames one of the most displeasing men I have ever known. There is much in him I can understand, but he has the soul of a bully."

There was a faint tinkling of a warning bell. Here and there a box door opened. A dozen women moved in a drift of colored silks. A score of men rose to their feet, and slowly the audience began to make their way back to their seats. The noise of chatter dropped to an intermittent hum.

Vespasia smiled. "It has been delightful to see you, but for once I have come to the theater principally to see the performance. I intend to be seated when the curtain rises again." And she bade them all farewell and left in a rustle of shadow-dark silk and the scent of jasmine.

Cornwallis sat down again and turned to Pitt.

"We need to know where those possessions of FitzJames came from and how they got to Ada's room," he said just above a whisper. "Now that Costigan is charged, FitzJames is going to want to know who tried to implicate him and whether they used Costigan or not. Your job isn't over, I'm afraid." He frowned and leaned a little closer as the lights went down. "It was a pretty wild chance, implying FitzJames was in a place like Pentecost Alley. How did he even know he couldn't account for his time? Most young men of his age and station spend their evenings in company. The chance that he was alone, and couldn't remember where he was, was . . . God knows . . . one in a hundred!"

He dropped his voice even lower as the curtain rose on the stage. "I have a very unpleasant feeling, Pitt, that it was someone close to him. And you had better find out, if you can, which of the two badges was the original." He sighed. "And if Finlay had the second one made, or his father did continue to overlook it, there's nothing we can do about it anyway." His tone was sharp with anger and regret. He did not need to say how deeply he hated the compromise of his principles it required.

Further conversation was prevented by the necessity of courtesy that he watch the second act. Not to have done so would have hurt Caroline. They settled down to enjoy it, Charlotte glancing at Pitt, her eyes anxious, Caroline absorbed in the stage, and Cornwallis sitting back, his brow smoothed out, the Pentecost Alley case temporarily set aside.

"I dunno!" Costigan said desperately. "I dunno anyfink abaht it!"

He was sitting in his cell in Newgate and Pitt was standing by the door staring at him, trying to fathom whether he was speaking the truth or still lying—either by habit or with some hope of evading punishment. It was pointless. He would hang for having killed Ada. Anything else would simply be for the record, to solve the remaining mystery.

His dejected figure was hunched up and seeming far smaller without his well-cut clothes and crisp shirt. He wore an old gray jacket now and it was rumpled, as if he had not bothered to hang it up while he slept. Looking at him, Pitt found it hard to be brutal and tell him the truth, which was foolish. He must know it. There could never have been any other outcome, once he had admitted seeing the boots. He was caught, and he had understood that, with all it meant, when he had seen Pitt's face and realized his own admission.

Even so, there was something of a different level of reality once it was put into words. All hope was killed, even the faint whisper thread of denial, of not having faced it yet.

"I dunno," Costigan repeated, staring at the ground between his feet. "I never saw the bleedin' badge, or the cuff link. I swear ter Gawd."

"The cuff link was down the back of the chair," Pitt agreed. "But the badge was underneath her body, on the bed. Come on, Costigan! How long could it have lain there without anyone noticing it? The thing had a pin on it half an inch long, and it was unfastened."

Costigan's head came up. "So it were 'er last customer! Stands ter reason. 'Ow do I know 'ow it got there? Mebbe 'e showed it to 'er? Or she were braggin' as 'ow she nicked it, and were showin' it ter 'im!"

Pitt thought about it for a moment. The first suggestion was not likely, simply because it required the extraordinary coincidence of someone's placing Finlay's belongings in Ada's room the very night she was murdered, and by Costigan, without premeditation. Costigan's discovery of her cheating, and his loss of temper, could not have been foreseen.

Or could they? Could someone possibly have paid Fat George to tell Costigan that day, specifically? And then watched Costigan to see what he would do, followed him back to Whitechapel and . . .

"Wot?" Costigan demanded, watching Pitt's face. "Wot is it? Wot d'yer know?"

No. No one of power and intelligence, no matter how they hated FitzJames, would place themselves into the hands of Fat George by using him in such a way. It was far too convoluted, depending on too many people: Fat George, Costigan himself, and some other person to place the evidence. No one would take that risk.

"Nothing," he said aloud. "Did Ada steal? You suggested maybe she was showing the badge to someone. Didn't you teach her not to steal? It's dangerous. Bad for business."

Costigan stared up at him, his skin white, eyes frightened.

"Yeah, course I did. But that don't mean she always listened, do it? I taught her not to cheat neither, but she still did. Stupid cow!" His face filled with regret, which was more than self-pity. There was a genuine sadness in it. Perhaps old Madge was right and he had been attracted to Ada himself, perhaps even fond of her. That would have made her betrayal hurt the more, a personal issue, not just a financial one. It would explain why his temper had been so violent, the sense of having the emotions he gave so rarely twisted and turned against him. It was truly a domestic affair.

"Did you ever know her to steal before?" Pitt asked, the edge of anger gone from his voice.

Costigan was staring at the floor again. "No. No, she were smart,

Ada were, too smart to steal from a customer. Treated 'em well, she did. Lot of 'em came reg'lar. She were fun. Made 'em laugh. She 'ad class." Tears spilled over his eyes and ran down his cheeks. "She were good, the stupid bitch. I liked 'er. She should never 'a' cheated me. I were good ter 'er. Why'd she make me do it? Now she's finished both o' us."

Pitt was sorry. It was a stupid, futile tragedy of greed and wounded feelings, the ungoverned temper of a foolish man whose ambitions outstripped his ability. And both of them had been used by a cleverer and crueler man in Fat George, and perhaps an even subtler and more callous man beyond him.

"Do you know FitzJames?" he asked.

"No . . ." Costigan was too sunk in his misery to be angry. He did not even look up. He was no longer interested.

"Did anyone ever mention him to you? Think!"

"No one 'cept you," Costigan said wearily. "Wot is it with you an' FitzJames? I dunno 'ow 'is things got inter Ada's place. Somebody stole 'em an' left 'em there, I s'pose. 'Ow do I know? Go ask 'is friends, or 'is enemies. I only know it in't me."

And Pitt could get no more from him. There was no punishment he could possibly receive worse than that for which he was already destined. And there was no reward that would be of the slightest use to him now. Apart from that, Pitt believed him that he had no further knowledge.

He left Newgate and walked out of the humid stone building into the heat of the August afternoon. But it was a long time before the sense of chill left him, the deep coldness inside from the presence of despair and unreachable misery.

By half past five he was back in Devonshire Street and requesting the cheerful butler for the opportunity to speak to Mr. Finlay FitzJames. He was granted it immediately, and was conducted over yards of finely polished parquet floor into the library, where both Finlay and Augustus were sitting near the open window which looked onto the garden. Past the tangle of honeysuckle flowers and stems, it was easy to see a glimpse of pale muslin as Tallulah pushed herself gently back and forth in a swing seat, her eyes closed, her face up towards the sun in a most unfashionable manner. No wonder her complexion had far more color than was deemed fit.

"Something further, Superintendent?" Augustus said curiously. He closed his book, a heavy tome whose lettering was too small for Pitt to read upside down, and left it on his lap, as though to resume any moment.

"Very little," Pitt replied, glancing at Finlay, who was watching him with interest. Now that Costigan had been arrested and charged, he was completely relaxed, almost arrogant again. He was very casually dressed, his thick hair brushed back from his face in heavy waves, his expression polite and confident.

"Then why have you come, Mr. Pitt?" he asked, looking up without moving or offering Pitt a seat. "We know nothing whatsoever about the whole miserable business; which, if you remember, is what we told you in the first instance. I'm sure neither my father nor I wish to be informed detail by detail of your progress, or lack of it. It is all very pedestrian, and rather shabby."

"It is shabby," Pitt agreed, resenting Finlay's arrogance bitterly, almost as if he himself had not despised Costigan just as much. He sat down uninvited. "But it is not pedestrian," he added. "It is most unusual."

"Is it?" Finlay's eyebrows rose. "I would have thought prostitutes were quite often beaten or killed, especially in the East End."

Pitt had difficulty in controlling his voice so it did not show. The indifference to death infuriated him: anyone's death, Ada's, Costigan's, anyone's at all.

"That sort of motive is quite common, Mr. FitzJames." He tried to speak unemotionally, but he could not keep the shadow of sarcasm out of his voice. "But it is extraordinary to find at the scene of such a murder the personal possessions of a man like yourself, when you have no connection whatever with the victim or with the crime."

"Well, as you now know, Superintendent, I do have no connection with it." Finlay was smiling, his eyes bright. "It was her own pimp. I thought we had agreed that was beyond question. If you've come here to ask me how a badge, which looks like mine, came to be there, I had no idea in the beginning, and I still have no idea."

Pitt clenched his teeth.

"And does that not bother you, sir?" he asked, staring levelly at Finlay's handsome face and wide, complacent gaze. "The badge was in the bed, with the pin open. It could not have been there more than a very short time, half an hour at the very most."

"If you are suggesting that Finlay was there half an hour before the murder," Augustus interrupted icily, "then you are not only mistaken, Superintendent, but you are impertinent, and beginning to exceed your authority and trespass upon our goodwill."

"Not at all," Pitt answered. Finlay might not know why Pitt had come, but surely Augustus must now guess. Why was he pretending to be angry and obtuse? Pitt had not expected thanks, but neither had he expected this prickly pretense. "I am quite satisfied his account of his day was exactly true. The mistaken identification of him as having been in Pentecost Alley is easy enough to understand . . ."

Augustus was not interested, and certainly not about to be placed in obligation to an inferior who had done no more than his duty.

"If you have a point, Superintendent, please arrive at it. If you wish my thanks, I am obliged you handled the matter with discretion. I trust you do not expect further of me than that?"

It was grossly offensive.

"I did not expect even that!" Pitt snapped. "I perform my duty for myself, for no one else. There was no personal favor involved to consider. Similarly, I find it my duty to discover who could have placed your son's belongings at the scene of a crime, presumably with the intention of having him at the very best involved in a scandal and his reputation damaged—at the worst hanged." He said the word distinctly and with pleasure. "I would have expected you to wish the answer known even more fervently than I do."

Augustus's eyes narrowed. He had obviously not anticipated such a retort, and his reaction was unprepared.

"And if the Hellfire Club badge which was discovered in your pocket, sir," Pitt went on, turning to Finlay, "was your original one, then someone has gone to a great deal of trouble to see you blamed. It also raises the question not only why they had a second badge made with your name on it, but how they knew to make it so exactly similar to the first! The only way even a jeweler can tell them apart is by the very slight variation in the script behind the pin."

Finlay's composure disappeared. He looked pale and the confidence went from his eyes, leaving them glittering and nervous. He turned slowly and looked at his father.

For a moment Augustus was also caught off balance. He had no answer ready. His resentment that Pitt should have caused him discomfort was hard in his mouth, the tightening of his lips.

Finlay drew breath to speak, looked back at Pitt, then at his father again, and changed his mind.

"Did you have the badge made yourself, sir?" Pitt asked. "It would be understandable in the circumstances, and not require any explanation before the law."

"N-no," Finlay stuttered, then swallowed. "No, I didn't." He looked profoundly unhappy now.

A long clock by the far wall chimed the quarter hour. Through the window Tallulah was still visible in the swing seat.

"I did, Superintendent," Augustus said at last. "As to the first badge, I can only presume it was lost or stolen years ago, as my son has already said. Similarly the cuff link. No one has seen that in five years either. One can only presume the same person had both of them."

"And chanced to use Ada McKinley's services and leave them both there, either on the same occasion or on two separate occasions?" Pitt finished, unable to keep the disbelief from his voice.

Augustus's features were expressionless, except for a swift flicker of rage there, and then gone again.

"It would seem so," he said coldly.

Pitt turned to Finlay.

"Then that narrows down the possibilities a great deal," he reasoned. "There cannot be many of your acquaintances who had the opportunity to find by chance, or to steal from you, two such intimate articles and then accidentally to lose them in Pentecost Alley the night of Ada's murder."

"The cuff link could have been there for any amount of time," Augustus pointed out, his face tight with anger. "You said it was hidden from view, down the back of a chair. It might have been there for years."

"Exactly," Pitt agreed. "And the badge could only have been there since the previous customer. Any new person in the bed must have felt it."

"All very puzzling," Augustus granted. "But it is not a problem with which anyone in my family can assist you. And frankly, since you know beyond question who killed the wretched woman, I would have thought you had better pursuits with which to occupy your time. Are you not rather a senior officer to be concerned with the possible theft of a cuff link and a badge, neither of them intrinsically worth more than a guinea or two, and perfectly easily replaced? My son is not pressing charges against anyone, nor have we at any time even reported the loss, much less requested that you investigate the matter." He picked up his book again, although he kept it closed. "Thank you for your concern, but we would all rather you bent your efforts towards preventing some of the violence that mars our streets, or protecting our more valuable property from thieves. I am obliged to you for calling, Superintendent." He reached with the other hand towards the bell to summon a servant to show Pitt out.

"I am not concerned with the property," Pitt answered, still sitting where he was. "Only with the use made of it, to try to incriminate you." He looked at Finlay. "You appear to have a very powerful and very bitter enemy, sir. The police would like to give you all possible assistance in discovering who that is and, if necessary, prosecuting them."

Finlay was white, a fine beading of sweat on his skin. He swallowed as if he had something caught in his throat.

"I have many enemies, Superintendent," Augustus cut across him, but his tone was guarded. "It is the price of success. It is unpleasant, but I am not afraid of it. The attempt to ruin my son has failed. Should they try anything further, I will deal with it myself with whatever defense is appropriate to its nature. I always have. I appreciate your concern for our well-being and your interest in justice." This time he reached the bell. "The footman will show you out. Good day to you."

Pitt remained unsatisfied about the issue, but he could not afford the time to pursue it any further, nor could he think of any useful line of enquiry. If Augustus had had the second badge made, that was explained, but not how the first one had been put in the bed in Pentecost Alley, or how it had come into the possession of whoever had left it there. Pitt could not believe both that and the cuff link had ended in the same room accidentally.

Possibly it was an enemy of Augustus FitzJames who sought this brutal and devious way to have his revenge, but it seemed more likely the opportunity had arisen for an enemy of Finlay. The other members of the Hellfire Club seemed the obvious choice. Why had they disbanded? Tedium? A sudden maturity? Some opportunity for one of them to advance himself, for which sobriety and a better reputation were necessary, and that had brought all of them to a realization that it was time to abandon such self-indulgence?

Or had there been a quarrel?

Pitt could not get rid of the idea that it was a quarrel, and that Jago Jones was the one with the obvious opportunity to leave anything in Ada's rooms. Yet Jago's face when he had first questioned him about the murder still sprang to his eye, and the horror in it when he had told him that Finlay's badge had been found in the bed.

Did Finlay actually know who had tried to incriminate him, and did he also know why? Was it possible that he planned his own revenge, perhaps with his father's help?

Why would he not simply tell Pitt and allow him to deal with it? A prosecution for theft, or even for simply leaving another man's belongings in a prostitute's room, would ruin Jago Jones. It would ruin Helliwell. His very proper parents-in-law would be scandalized by such a thing. Polite society would cease to know him. It would be long, drawn out and acutely painful. The victim would suffer every moment of it, both in anticipation and in retrospect. What punishment could be crueler or more effective than that?

If Augustus did not choose to effect it, then there must be some reason. To stay his hand and hold the threat forever over someone? To ask for some favor in return, something so big it would be worth forgoing the present pleasure?

Could taking his vengeance rebound upon himself or his family? Was the glamorous and flighty Tallulah in some way vulnerable?

It did not occur to Pitt as a possibility that Augustus would forgive the offense.

August ended in suffocating heat and passed into early September. The trial of Albert Costigan was due to begin. Two evenings before it opened, Pitt went back to Whitechapel to see Ewart and the police surgeon, Lennox. They met, not in the police station, but in a public house off Swan Street, and ate a supper of cold pigeon pie washed down with cider and followed by plum cake.

They talked of agreeable things. Lennox told a funny story about one of his patients a little farther west who had recently acquired a bathtub and invited all the neighbors to behold it.

Ewart was elated because his eldest son had won a place at University and passed his first-year exams. Pitt was surprised that the boy had had sufficient education in Whitechapel for such a thing to be possible, but he forbore from saying so. Then Ewart explained that he had been able to send him to boarding school, where he had received excellent tuition.

"Makes all the difference to a man, education," he said with a sad little smile, both bitter and sweet, and Pitt wondered what wealth of sacrifice had made it possible for a man on Ewart's pay. His wife too must have forfeited a great deal. It gave him a view of Ewart he had not even considered before, and he admired him for it. He must have saved all his life. But he did not comment on it. It would have been intrusive. He smiled at Ewart, and Ewart looked away and avoided his eyes, as though embarrassed. The murder in Pentecost Alley was not even touched upon until they left the public house and walked gently towards the river and the shadows cast by the huge edifice of the Tower of London. The evenings were drawing in. The air was still balmy but night came far sooner and there was a sense of autumn approaching, a fading of flowers, a dustiness of the ground too long without hard, soaking rain.

They stopped on the grass mound under the Tower and stood looking towards the river. The pall of soot and smoke was behind them. The light was soft and apricot gold over the shining sheet of water, hazy in the distance, softening the line of the farther shore. Tower Bridge was just above them. Downstream there was nothing more barring the way to the open sea.

"Are you going to mention the badge and the cuff link?" Pitt asked Ewart. The subject had to be discussed. They were to testify the day after tomorrow.

"Don't see any point," Ewart replied guardedly, looking sideways at Pitt. "Doesn't seem to have any relevance to what happened."

"I went back to FitzJames," Pitt said, squinting into the sun. The reflection off the water was becoming brighter, a vivid daub of color, almost silver where it touched the slight ripples of a passing pleasure boat, darker at the widening edges where it spilled across the shore. "I asked him if he had made the second badge himself."

"Always thought he had." Lennox pursed his lips. His face still looked melancholy, even in the calm, golden air of evening. The light picked out the fine lines around his mouth and eyes, worn into his flesh by the strain of pity or distress. Pitt wondered what private life he had; where his home was; if he had anyone there to care for, anyone with whom he could laugh and share the beautiful and good things, or to whom he could tell at least some of the things that hurt him.

Ewart was talking to him, and he had not heard.

"What did you say? I'm sorry, I wasn't listening."

"FitzJames admitted it?" Ewart pressed. "Then that solves it, doesn't it! Stupid, perhaps, but understandable. There's no point in making any mention of it. It only raises questions we can't answer, and which don't matter now. I daresay he did go there sometime, and lost them then. Point is: it wasn't that night, and that's all that matters."

"It wasn't Finlay who had it made," Pitt argued. "It was his father."

"Comes to the same thing." Ewart dismissed it, but a look of loathing crossed his face for an instant and was suppressed.

"Costigan swears he doesn't know anything about them," Pitt said quietly into the balmy stillness. It still bothered him. It did not make any sense. He could understand Ewart's feeling. He shared it.

"Maybe he doesn't," Lennox said quietly. "I still think FitzJames had something to do with Ada—if not her death, then at least as a customer. I don't believe anyone stole those things from him. Who would? Except Ada herself."

"One of his friends, or supposed friends," Ewart responded after a moment. "Maybe one of the original club members. We don't know what they really felt about each other. Could have been a lot of envy there. Finlay had more money than any of them, more opportunities in life. He's going on to hold high office someday. They are not." There was an anger, almost a viciousness, in his voice that was startling in the golden summer evening. Pitt thought of how easily Finlay's opportunities had been bought, and at what cost Ewart's son's had been, the countless small things that had been given up to pay for it. It was not surprising Ewart felt resentful at Finlay's waste of it.

"We'll never know." Ewart caught himself and the emotion died out of his voice. It became bland again, professional. "We never do know all of a case. There are motives, small actions unexplained in even the best of them. We have the right man. That's all that really matters." He pushed his hands into his pockets and stared over the water. One or two barges had already lit riding lights and they drifted, almost without undulation.

"It's part of the crime," Pitt said, unsatisfied. "Someone put those things there, which means if it wasn't Costigan, then someone else was present. A good defense counsel is going to ask who it was and raise reasonable doubt."

Lennox stared at him, his face half shadowed, half gold in the dying sunlight. There was surprise in him and a mixture of alarm.

Ewart frowned, his mouth tight, eyes black.

"They'd never get him off," he said slowly. "He's guilty as the devil. It's all perfectly plain. She cheated him and he found out. He went to her to have it out, she wasn't giving in, maybe told him to take himself off. They quarreled and he lost his temper. Sadistic little swine. But then what kind of man lives off the prostitution of women anyway?"

Lennox let out a little grunt, sad and savage. His shoulders were hunched hard, as if all his body muscles were locked. There was utter loathing in every part of his face in the half the sun caught. The other half was almost invisible.

Pitt guessed what he felt. He was the one who had examined Ada's body, touched her, seen precisely what had been done to her. He must have imagined her alive, perhaps he even knew what pain she had experienced with the wrenched and dislocated joints, the broken bones, the terror as she struggled for breath. His own pity for Costigan drained away as he watched the younger man's emotions raw in his face.

Pitt sighed. "What I'm really thinking of is that FitzJames knows who it was who tried to incriminate him, or believes he does, and will take his own revenge," he said quietly.

Ewart shrugged. "If we can't work it out, why should they?" He laughed with surprising bitterness. "And if he succeeds, and gets caught, I, for one, shall not mind."

The western sky was burning with the last embers, spilling fire across the water and casting them into black shadows from the Tower and the span of the bridge. The tide was running faster. But the air was still warm, and there were just as many people out strolling, some alone, some arm in arm with others. The sound of laughter came from somewhere just beyond sight.

Ewart shrugged. "We can't stop them, sir." The "sir" distanced him from Pitt, in a sense closing the subject. "If they know that much, they'll almost certainly have the right person, and I'd say they deserve it. It's a filthy thing to do, trying to get a man hanged for a crime he didn't commit."

His face was hard and weary, the light accentuating the lines. "Anyway, if you think you can stop Augustus FitzJames from execut-ing his own form of justice on his enemies, pardon me for saying it, sir, but you just aren't living in the world as it is. If there's a crime committed, and we know about it, it is our job to try to sort it out. But a private hatred between gentlemen is not our business."

Pitt said nothing.

"We can't take the whole world on our backs," Ewart went on, hunching himself as if he had become cold. "And it would be over-stepping ourselves if we imagined we can do anything about it, or that we even should."

"He refused our help," Pitt said. "I offered and he refused, very firmly."

"Doesn't want you looking into the family too closely," Lennox said with an abrupt laugh. "Costigan might have killed the girl, but Finlay's conduct won't bear too close an investigation if he wants an ambassadorship." He spat the word out as if his teeth were clenched, although it was now too dark to see, and he had turned away from the light.

"Well, if that's so," Ewart said tartly, "you'd be best to leave it alone. He won't thank you for ferreting around in Finlay's life to find out who has cause to hate him, and why. You'd no doubt turn up some pretty shabby behavior, and Augustus'll direct his vengeance at you. And perhaps the law too. You've no cause to investigate Finlay now. We've got our man. Leave it alone, sir, for everybody's sake!"

Lennox let out a little gasp as if he had stubbed his toe on a stone, but he was not moving.

Ewart was right. There was no legal ground for pursuing the subject, and Augustus FitzJames had made it unmistakably clear that he did not wish police assistance. Unless Pitt could deduce the answer from the information he already possessed, he was not going to resolve it.

"Then I'll see you in court the day after tomorrow," he said resignedly. "Are you going back that way?" He gestured towards the Queen's Stairs.

"No, no, I'll go home," Ewart answered. "Thank you, sir. Good night."

"Yes, I'll come." Lennox moved with Pitt, and they walked in companionable silence over the grass and down towards the steps and the water, then back up again to Great Tower Hill. It was almost dark.

They gave the evidence as precisely and exactly as they could, trying to rob it of emotion, and failing. Lennox in particular was white-faced, his voice high-pitched with the tension in his throat, his lips dry. Ewart was more practical, but a sense of triumph and relief came through his composure, and a hatred for the viciousness and the greed and the stupidity of it all.

There was not a large crowd. It was not a particularly interesting case. Albert Costigan was a name unknown outside the immediate area of the Whitechapel Road. Ada McKinley was merely an unfortunate woman who ran the risks of her trade and had met with a fate no one would have wished on her; but at the same time, no one was surprised, and only a few grieved. Pitt saw Rose Burke there the first day, and Nan Sullivan, surprisingly handsome in black. He did not see Agnes. If she came, he missed her in the crowd. Nor was old Madge there. Perhaps, as she had said, she never left the house.

None of the FitzJameses attended, but then he had not thought that they might. As far as they were concerned, as soon as Finlay was exonerated that was the end of the matter. Thirlstone and Helliwell had never wanted anything to do with it from the first.

But Jago Jones was there, his startling face with its intensity making him extraordinary, in spite of his faded clothes, and no mark to distinguish him as a priest, no high white collar, no cross or sign of office. His cheeks were gaunt, hollowed under the high bones, and his eyes were shadowed as if he had slept badly for weeks. He listened intently to every witness. One might have thought from the attention he gave it that judgment was his, not the jurors', and he in the end must answer for it.

It crossed Pitt's mind to wonder if Jago was the priest chosen to try to save Costigan's soul before his last, short walk. Would he be the one to seek a confession from him in the hours before execution, then to go those terrifying final steps to the gallows at eight o'clock in the morning? It was a task he would not have wished on anyone at all.

What were they to say? Something about the love of God, the sacrifice of Christ for all men? What would the words mean to Costigan? Had he ever in his life known what love was—passionate, unconditional, wide as the heavens, love which never faded or withdrew and yet was still just? Did he even understand the concept of sacrificing in order that someone else might benefit? Would Jago be speaking in a language that Costigan had never heard, of an idea as remote to him as the fires that burned in the stars?

Perhaps there was nothing more to do than speak quietly, look at him and meet his eyes without contempt and without judgment, simply as another human being aware of his terror and caring about it.

As Pitt stared across the courtroom at the inexorable process of the law, there was a ruthlessness about it which frightened him also. The wigs and gowns seemed as much masks for the men behind them as symbols of the majesty of justice. It was supposed to be anonymous, but it seemed merely inhuman.

There was very little defense Costigan's lawyer could offer. He was young, but he made a considerable effort at suggesting mitigating circumstances, a woman who was greedy and who cheated, even by the standards of behavior accepted by her own trade. He suggested it was a quarrel which had gone beyond control. Costigan had not meant to kill her, only to frighten her and dissuade her from her behavior, bring her back to their bargain. When he saw that she was insensible, he had panicked and thrown water over her to try, vainly, to bring her back to consciousness, not realizing at first that he had killed her.

The broken bones, the dislocations?

The cruelty and perversion of a previous customer.

No one believed it.

The verdict was never truly in doubt. Pitt knew that, looking at the jurors' faces. Costigan must have known it too.

The judge listened, picked up his black cap and pronounced the sentence of death.

Pitt left the courtroom without any sense of achievement, simply a relief that it was finished. He would never know all that had happened, never know who had placed Finlay FitzJames's belongings in the room in Pentecost Alley or why so many lies were told about them. He would never know what thoughts were so harrowing in the mind of Jago Jones.

After the statutory three weeks Albert Costigan was hanged. The newspapers reported it but made no further comment.

The Sunday after that Pitt was in the Park with Charlotte and the children. Jemima was dressed in her very best frock, Daniel in a smart new navy-and-white suit. It was mid-October and the leaves were beginning to turn. The chestnuts, the first to break into bud in spring, were already limpid gold. The softer sunlight of early autumn flickered through them. The beeches showed fans of bronze amid the green. It would not be long till the first frosts, the raking up of leaves and the smell of wood smoke as bonfires consumed the waste. In the country, rose hips would be scarlet in the hedges, and hawthorn berries crimson. The grass would not need cutting anymore.

Pitt and Charlotte walked slowly side by side, indistinguishable from a hundred other couples enjoying one of the last really warm days of the year. The children ran around, laughing and chasing each other, largely pointlessly, simply because they had energy and it was fun. Daniel found a stick and threw it for a puppy that was dancing around them, apparently lost by its owner, at least for the time being. The dog ran for it and brought it back triumphantly. Jemima seized the stick and took a turn, hurling it as far as she could.

Over in the distance near the road a barrel organ was playing a popular tune. A running patterer abandoned the news and sat on the grass eating a sandwich he had just bought from a peddler a hundred yards farther along. An old man sucked on a pipe, his eyes closed. Two housemaids on their day off told each other tall stories and giggled. A lawyer's clerk lay under a tree and read a "penny dreadful" magazine.

Charlotte took Pitt's arm and walked a little closer. He shortened his step so she could keep pace with him.

It was several minutes before Pitt recognized in the distance, striding across the grass, the upright, military figure of John Cornwallis making his way purposefully between the strollers. When he was within twenty yards the expression on his face made Charlotte stop and turn anxiously to Pitt.

Pitt felt a chill run through him, but knew of no reason why he should be afraid.

Cornwallis reached them.

"I'm sorry, Mrs. Pitt," he apologized to Charlotte, then looked at Pitt, his face pale and tight. "I'm afraid I must interrupt your Sunday afternoon." He obviously intended it to be the cue for Charlotte to excuse herself and leave them alone, withdraw to a discreet distance, out of earshot.

She did not do so, but instead held more tightly to Pitt's arm, her fingers curling around and gripping.

"Is it a matter of confidence of state?" Pitt enquired.

"Dear God, I wish it were!" Cornwallis said with passion. "I am afraid by tomorrow everyone else in London will know."

"Know what?" Charlotte whispered.

Cornwallis hesitated, looking at Pitt with concern. He wanted to protect Charlotte. He was unused to women. Pitt guessed he was acquainted with them only at a distance. He did not know other than convention taught him to expect.

"Know what?" Pitt repeated.

"Another prostitute has been murdered," Cornwallis said huskily. "Exactly like the first . . . . in every particular."

Pitt was stunned. It was as if suddenly he had lost his balance, and the grass and trees and sky dissolved and shifted around him.

"In a tenement on Myrdle Street," Cornwallis finished. "In Whitechapel. I think you had better go there, immediately. Ewart is on the scene. I shall find Mrs. Pitt a hansom to take her home." His face was ashen. "I'm so sorry."

CHAPTER

EIGHT

Pitt stood in the doorway of the room where the body had been found. Ewart, gray-faced, was already there. From down the corridor came the sound of hysterical weeping, shock and terror still in the rising, desperate tones, long drawn out as she lost control.

Pitt met Ewart's eyes and saw in them reflection of the horror he felt himself, and the sudden knowledge of guilt. He looked away.

On the bed lay a young woman, small, almost like a child. Her hair spilled out around her, one arm flung over her head, her wrist tied with a stocking to the left corner bedpost. There was a garter with a blue ribbon around her arm. Her yellow and orange dress was drawn up, exposing her thighs. Her legs were naked. Like Ada McKinley, there was a stocking knotted tightly around her throat. Her face was purple, mottled and swollen. And like Ada, the top half of her body and the bed around it was soaked with water.

With knowledge sick in his stomach, Pitt looked down at the floor. Her boots, black and polished, were buttoned to each other.

He lifted his eyes and met Ewart's.

The weeping along the corridor was calmer, the fear subsiding into the long, broken sobs of grief.

Ewart looked like a man who awoke from a nightmare only to

find the same events playing themselves out in reality, from which there is no more awakening. There was a muscle twitching in his temple, and he clenched his hands to keep them from shaking.

"Are her fingers and toes broken?" Pitt found his voice creaking, his throat was tight, his mouth dry.

Ewart swallowed. He nodded imperceptibly, not trusting himself to speak.

"Any . . . other evidence?" Pitt asked.

Ewart took a deep breath, his eyes on Pitt's, wide, filled with knowledge of what they both dreaded.

"I . . . I haven't looked." His voice shook. "I sent for you straightaway. As soon as Lennox told me it was the same, I . . . I just left it. I . . ." He took another breath. "I went outside. I felt sick. If there's anything here, I want you to be the one to find it, not me. At least . . . not me alone. I . . ." Again his eyes searched Pitt's. There was a sheen of sweat on his upper lip and on his brow. "I did look around a bit. I didn't see anything. But I haven't searched, not properly, not combed it, down the backs of chairs, under the bed."

The unasked questions hung in the air between them, the consuming fear and guilt that they had made an appalling, irretrievable mistake, and Costigan had not killed Ada, and whoever had had struck again, here in this room. Was it Finlay FitzJames? Or Jago Jones? Or someone else they had not even thought of, out there in the darkness of the October streets, waiting to strike again, and again . . . like the madman who had called himself Jack the Ripper two years ago.

Pitt turned and looked at the girl on the bed. She had thick, dark hair, naturally curly. She was small-boned, almost delicate. Her skin was very white, unblemished over her shoulders where the top of her dress was low cut, creamy white on the flesh of her thighs. She must have been young, seventeen or eighteen.

"Who was she?" Pitt asked, surprised at the catch in his voice.

"Nora Gough," Ewart replied from just behind him. "Don't know much about her yet. Can't get any sense out of the other women here. All hysterical. Lennox is trying to calm them down now. Poor devil. But I suppose that's what doctors are for. He was just along the street, half a mile away. Been there all evening with a patient." He sniffed. "At least he's not too late to help them, for what it's worth."

They could both still hear the sobbing from the room along the passage, but it was muted now, the high note of hysteria gone from it. Better to let Lennox go on doing what he could than to go now and try to gain evidence from women too terrified to make any sense.

"Then we'd better look through this room," Pitt said wearily. It was a job he hated, and it was unlikely to provide anything he wanted to know. In fact, he dreaded what he might find. The one man who could not possibly be guilty was Costigan.

"I'll start with the bed," he said to Ewart. "You start over there with the cupboard and the box chest. Anything unusual, anything at all. Any letters, papers, anything that might not have belonged to her, borrowed or stolen. Anything expensive."

Ewart did not move. Pitt wondered for a moment if he was so drowned by his horror he was incapable of functioning. His skin was bleached of color, as if he were already dead, a sort of waxen look.

"Ewart," he said more gently. "Start with the box chest." At least that way he could keep his back to the body.

"No . . . I'll . . . I'll do the bed," Ewart replied, not quite meeting his eyes. "It's . . . my job. I'm . . . all right." His voice was thick, fighting so many emotions he seemed torn apart by them, sharp and high among them a white-hot anger.

"Begin with the box chest," Pitt repeated. "I'll do the bed and the chairs."

Ewart still remained motionless. He seemed to want to speak, and yet he was unable to find the words, or perhaps to make the decision to say whatever it was. He looked like a man facing despair.

They stood a few feet away from each other in the quiet room, the girl's body almost within arm's length. The air was stale, closed in. Dusty light coming in through the window showed the bare places on the rug.

Out in the street an old-clothes seller was shouting.

"Do you know something about the death of Ada McKinley that you haven't told me?" Pitt asked, hating doing it.

Ewart's eyes widened a little. "No."

Pitt believed him. Whatever he had been fearing, it was not that question; his surprise was too genuine.

"Are you afraid Costigan was the wrong man?"

"Aren't you?" Ewart asked.

"Yes, of course I am. Who was it? Finlay FitzJames?"

Ewart winced. "No . . ." he said quickly, too quickly for thought.

Pitt turned away and began to search the bed. Lennox had already examined the body. It did not matter if he disturbed her now. It was irrational to be gentle but it came automatically, as if somehow the shell that was left was still a human being, capable of knowing pity or dignity.

He found a handkerchief under the pillow on the farther side, white, like the sheet, and to begin with he thought it was merely the corner of a slip a little crookedly on. Then he pulled and it came away. It was of fine lawn, the hand-stitched hem rolled to a tiny edge, embroidered with letters in one corner. The writing was Gothic, hard to decipher at first glance. Pitt made it out. "F.F.J." He had almost known it would be, but it still gave him a lurching sensation high in his stomach and a tightening in his throat.

He looked across at Ewart, but he had his back turned, going through the contents of the chest, linen and clothes piled on the floor beside him. He was apparently unaware that Pitt had stopped.

"I've found a handkerchief," Pitt said in the silence.

Ewart turned slowly, his face expectant. He met Pitt's eyes and saw in them what he dreaded.

"Initials," Pitt said, answering the question that had not been asked. "F.F.J."

"That's ... that's ridiculous!" Ewart said, stumbling over his tongue. "Why on earth would he leave a handkerchief behind? Who leaves a handkerchief in a prostitute's bed? He didn't live here!"

"I suppose someone who had occasion to blow his nose while he was with her," Pitt replied. "A man with a cold, or whom something caused to sneeze. Dust, perhaps, or her perfume?"

"And he put it under the pillow?" Ewart said, still fighting against it.

"Well, he wouldn't have a pocket conveniently," Pitt rejoined. "Anyway, it is not ours to reason why at the moment. Keep on looking. There may be something else."

"What? Are you saying he left something else here too?" Ewart's voice rose, almost in panic. "He'd have nothing left if he went on leaving things around Whitechapel at this rate."

"Not something belonging to Finlay FitzJames," Pitt said as calmly as he could. "Anything else at all. Perhaps something to indicate another man. We've got to search the whole room."

"Oh. Yes, of course we have. Er ..." Ewart turned back to the box chest without saying anything more and resumed taking the things out and opening them up, shaking them, running his fingers through them, then folding them and placing them on the pile beside him.

Pitt finished searching the bed and moved on to the floor around it. He lit the candle on the table, then placed it in the shadows on the floor and knelt down to peer beneath. There was very little dust, a few threads of cotton, mostly white, and a boot button which he only found by running his fingers carefully over the surface of the floor, searching the cracks of the boards. There were also two hairpins and a straight pin such as dressmakers use.

Towards the foot of the bed he found a piece of bootlace, a button such as might come off any man's white cotton shirt, and another button, leather, handmade, unlikely to belong to anyone in White-chapel unless he had been given a man's casual coat from some charity collection.

He straightened up with them in his hand.

Ewart had finished the box chest and was looking through the small dresser, his hands searching quickly, expertly.

Pitt began on the chairs, lifting up the cushions, exploring down the back and sides and finally turning them upside down and exam-ining the bottoms. He found nothing more to which he could con-nect any meaning.

"Anything?" Ewart asked him.

Pitt held out the buttons.

"Shirt," Ewart said to the first. "Could belong to anyone at all. And it could have been there for months." He took the second, rolled it between his fingers and thumb, then looked up and met Pitt's eyes. "Quality," he said dubiously. "But again, could be any-body's. Could be a tramp in a charity coat." There was a challenge in his voice, daring Pitt to say it was FitzJames's. "Are you going to see the women here? They seem to be in control of them-selves now."

Indeed it was considerably quieter. The light had almost gone and there was no sound from the bottle factory over the road. A horse and trap went by. Someone shouted.

"Yes," Pitt replied. "We'll see what they know."

He led the way along the passage to the kitchen at the back of the house. It was surprisingly large with a black stove in the center of the far wall and a grimy window facing straight onto the backs of houses in the next street. There was a table with odd legs in the center, patched together from two previous pieces of furniture, and half a dozen assorted chairs. Four of them were now occupied by women ranging in age from approximately twenty to over fifty, although with age, drink and paint, it was impossible to be sure.

They all looked tragic and absurd, with powder and rouge streaked by tears, hair falling out of pins, eyes swollen with weeping. And at the same time they looked younger, and more human and individual with the shell of business cracked away.

Lennox was standing half behind one of the women, one hand on her shoulder, a cup of tea in the other, holding it out for her. He looked pale and tired, his nose accentuated by the deep lines scored down the sides of his mouth. He stared at Pitt warningly. His voice was hoarse when he spoke.

"Good evening, Superintendent. If you want to question these women, they are ready to answer you. Just don't tell them details you don't have to, and be a little patient. It isn't easy to remember, or to find words, when you are terrified."

Pitt nodded and turned to Ewart. "You could try the neighborhood. See if anyone else has noticed anything unusual, if they can remember a face, someone coming or going at about . . . ?" He looked at Lennox enquiringly.

"Between four and five," Lennox answered, then smiled in bitter mockery of himself. "Not medical brilliance, Superintendent. Observation of witnesses. Pearl heard Nora calling out in the corridor at about four o'clock. She'd just got up and was asking Edie if she could borrow a petticoat."

Pitt looked at the woman Lennox indicated. Pearl was pale-faced with flaxen hair of extraordinary beauty, sheer as spun glass and reflecting the light of the candles like wheatsilk, a patch of luminosity in the room. Edie was heavy and dark with olive skin and handsome, liquid brown eyes.

"And you lent her a petticoat?" Pitt asked.

Edie nodded. "She 'ad ter pin it, as she in't 'alf my size, but she took it any'ow." She sniffed and controlled herself with an effort.

Lennox turned to another woman, dark, narrow-eyed, with a pretty mouth. She looked ashen, the rouge standing out on her cheeks, her hair lopsided where she had run her fingers through it, pins sliding out.

"Mabel can answer that."

"Me first customer'd just gorn," Mabel replied, her voice hardly more than a whisper. "I were goin' past Nora's door an' I looked in. Dunno 'ow I knew she were by 'erself. Quiet, I s'pose." She frowned, as though the puzzle mattered. "I saw 'er lyin' on the bed wif 'er 'and up ter the post. I reckoned as 'er customer'd bin keen on that kind o' thing, an' left 'er like that. I even said summink to 'er . . ." She sniffed and swallowed with a painful constriction of her throat. Her body was shaking so uncontrollably her fingers skittered on the table.

Lennox moved across behind her and put his hands on her shoulders, holding her against him as if to give her of his own strength. It was a gesture of extraordinary gentleness. She might have been a friend of long standing, not a street woman he had only just met.

It steadied her, like a ray of sanity in the chaos.

"Then I saw 'er face," she said quietly. "An' I know as it 'ad 'appened to 'er too. The same one as got Ada McKinley'd got 'er too. I s'pose I must 'a' yelled. Next thing everyone were there, an' all yellin' an' callin' out."

"I see. Thank you." Pitt turned to Ewart. "You'd better find out what men were seen coming or going from this building between four and five. Get descriptions of all of them and compare them with each woman and her customers. Get times as near as you can. Any man at all. I don't care if they're residents, pimps, or the lamplighter! Everyone."

"And the other time?" Pitt asked Lennox.

"Yes sir."

Ewart departed and Pitt concentrated on the four women present. The last one, Kate, was still sobbing, pushing a wet handkerchief into her mouth and gasping for breath. Lennox went back to the stove and made another cup of tea, passing it to her, closing her stiff fingers around it awkwardly as Pitt began questioning Pearl, sitting on a rickety chair at right angles over the table from her.

"Tell me all you can remember from just before you saw Nora at almost four o'clock," he prompted.

She stared at him, then began hesitantly.

"I 'eard Nora come inter 'er room an' call ter Edie abaht a petticoat, but I din' 'ear wot Edie said. I were busy doin' me 'air ready fer the evenin'. I finished, and went aht. I got a customer real quick, one o' me reg'lars . . ."

"Who was that?"

"Wot?"

"Who was he? What does he look like?"

She hesitated only a moment, glancing at Edie, then at Mabel.

"Jimmy Kale," she answered. " 'E come 'ere most Sundays. Not always ter me. Sometimes one o' the other girls."

"And what does he look like?"

"Tall, skinny. Got a long nose. Always sniffin'."

"Did he come to Nora?" Pitt asked.

"Yeah, I reckon so. But 'e wouldn't've 'urt 'er! W'y would 'e? 'E don't even know 'er, 'cepting ter . . ." She stopped.

Pitt accepted that that was not knowing her in any sense that mattered.

"Go on. How long was Jimmy Kale with you?"

" 'Alf hour."

"Then what?"

"I 'ad a cup o' tea wi' Marge over the road. She come 'ere sometimes. 'Er old man knocks 'er around summink terrible."

"Was she here between four and five o'clock? Would she come in through the door at the front and past Nora's room?"

She shook her head.

"Nah, she come across the wall an' up them areaway steps on the outside. That way 'er 'usband don' see 'er, and nob'dy takes 'er for one o' us." She laughed abruptly. "Poor cow. She'd be better orff if she was! Anybody beat me like 'e do 'er, I'd stick a shiv in 'is guts."

"When did she go?" Pitt ignored the reference to knives.

"When Mabel started ter yell. Rest o' the noise don't matter, but she knew that were different. We all did . . ." She swallowed and her throat tightened. She started to cough and Lennox moved to her side, taking her hand and patting her firmly on the back. The human contact seemed to comfort her, the warmth of touch which demanded nothing of her. She took a shuddery breath. For a moment she hovered on the edge of abandoning herself to the comfort of weeping and clinging to someone.

Lennox removed his hand and passed over the cup of tea.

She straightened up again.

"We knew as summink were terrible wrong," she said levelly. "Kate 'ad Syd Allerdyce wif 'er. 'E come ter the door wif 'is pants rahnd 'is ankles. Proper fool 'e looked too, fat as a pig and red in the face. In't 'alf so la-di-da caught like that, 'e weren't." The dislike was heavy in her face. She did not forget a condescension, or forgive it. "Angie from upstairs were at the end o' the alley wi' a pail o' water. She dropped it and it went all over the place. I suppose someone cleared it up. I dunno. I din't. An' Kate come out o' 'er room wif a shawl rahnd 'er. S'pose 'er customer were still there. Edie went inter Nora's room an' saw 'er there, an' Mabel still yellin'. Edie 'it 'er rahnd the face ter stop 'er, then come out an' sent Kate fer the rozzers."

"Did you see Nora's customer?"

"Nah. I were busy meself."

"Where is your room, compared with hers?"

"Next ter it."

"What did you hear?"

" 'Ear? Everythink! 'Eard Syd wheezin' an' groanin' like 'e was climbin' a mountain. 'Eard them two bloody cats fightin' in the alley—"

"Do you mean cats or women?" Pitt interrupted.

She glared at him. "Cats! Furry thin's wot eat mice an' squeals like all the devils in 'ell 'alf the night. Geez! Don't they 'ave cats up west w'ere you come from? 'Ow d'yer keep the mice down? Or don't you 'ave them neither?"

"Yes, we have them. I have two cats, actually." He thought with a sudden surge of pleasure of Angus and Archie curled up asleep in their basket by the kitchen range. But they didn't have to battle anyone for their food and milk. "What else?"

" 'Eard Shirl upstairs screamin' at someone out the front," Pearl replied. "Yellin' like a stuck pig, she were. Worse'n the cats. Reckon someone bilked 'er. An' someone dropped a tray down the stairs. 'Ell of a row. Then there was Mabel an' 'er customer, laughin' like fools they was. Reckon as 'e were drunk out o' 'is wits. 'Ope yer got paid well, Mabel?"

"Course," Mabel said with conviction.

It flicked through Pitt's mind that she had probably taken all the man had, but that was his affair, if he chose to take chances. He imagined the cacophony of sound that must have gone on during the hour Nora Gough was murdered. She could probably have screamed herself hoarse and been lucky to have been heard above the general clamor.

And yet Edie's screams of horror had been distinguished quickly enough.

He looked at Lennox.

Lennox pursed his lips and shook his head very slightly.

"No way to tell," he said quietly. "She may have known him, and by the time she realized what was happening, it was too late."

Pitt said nothing. He turned to the other girls.

"The names of your customers?" he asked. "Kate?"

"Bert Moss come just before five. Early, but Sundays is different. 'As ter get 'ome fer 'is tea. Then Joe 'Edges. 'E were still 'ere, like, w'en Mabel started to yell."

"With you at that moment?"

"Yeah. Look, 'e din't do it! I brung 'im in! 'E weren't never by 'isself 'ere!"

Pitt nodded and turned to Mabel.

"Dunno. I never asked." She shrugged. "Don't matter."

"He wasn't anybody you've had before?"

"No. Never seen 'im in me life."

"When did he come, and when did he leave?"

" 'E come at quarter after four, near enough, an' left abaht ten minutes afore five. I were jus' takin' 'im aht an' goin' back ter the street w'en I saw Nora's customer goin' . . ." Her face blanched. "Gawd Almighty! D'yer think that were . . ."

She slumped forward suddenly and Pitt thought she was going to be sick. She started to gasp for breath and her chest heaved.

"Stop it!" Lennox said smartly. "There!" He grabbed the tea from Pearl and thrust it into Mabel's hands. "Drink it slowly. Don't gulp it."

She tried to take it but she was shaking so badly, her fingers stiff, that she could not hold it.

Lennox steadied it, his hands over hers, keeping it from spilling.

"Drink it," he told her firmly. "Concentrate, or you'll get it all over you. Hold it still!"

She obeyed, sipping slowly, focusing her attention on it. Gradually her breathing began to subside and become normal again. After several minutes she sat up and put the now empty mug on the table in front of her.

"What did he look like?" Pitt asked her more gently.

"Look like?" She stared across the table at him. " 'E were, I dunno. Orn'ry. 'E 'ad fair 'air, all sort o' wavy."

"What kind of clothes?" Pitt could feel himself cold inside. "What was he wearing, Mabel?"

"Din't really look much." She stared at him in horror, and he knew the other pictures that were in her mind, herself on the bed in Nora's place.

"Expensive?" Lennox said, his voice cutting the silence.

Pitt glanced at him, but it was the same question he would have asked. It was in all their minds, it had to be.

"Yeah. Men around 'ere in't got nuffink like that."

"Would you know him if you saw him again?" Pitt asked, thinking back to Rose Burke, and her face as she had stared at Finlay Fitz-James coming out of the front door in Devonshire Street.

"I dunno." Mabel was terrified. It was there in her white, clammy skin and shivering body. "I sees 'undreds o' men. In't their faces wot I look at. It's money wot matters at the end, in' it? It's only money as gets yer food an' yer rent."

"Thank you," Pitt acknowledged, rising to his feet and pacing three steps across the kitchen floor, and back again. "Do you know anything else about your regular customers? Where do they live? What do they do? How can I find them?"

"Wo' for?" Kate looked at him narrowly.

"In case they seen 'oo done Nora, yer stupid cow!" Edie said. "Wot yer think?" She swung around to Pitt. "It's yor job to get this bastard wot's doin' girls 'round 'ere! Please, mister! First 'e done poor Ada over on Pentecost Alley, now 'e done Nora. 'Oo's next? An' next arter that?"

Pearl began to cry again, softly, like a lost child.

"Geez, Edie!" Mabel said desperately. "Why yer gotter say summink like that?"

Edie swung around. "Well, it weren't that rotten little swine Costigan, were it? 'E bin 'anged by the neck till 'e were dead and stuck six feet under, in't 'e?" She jabbed her fingers towards the wall and the darkness outside. "It's some bastard wot's still aht there, i'n it? Some bastard wot could come in 'ere an' be yer next customer, eh? Poor Nora's, weren't it? 'Oo's gonner 'elp us if the rozzers don't, eh? I dunno 'oo 'e is. D'you?"

"Did anybody see anyone else here this afternoon?" Pitt asked one more time. "Anyone at all?"

Pitt took down everything else they had to say, but it added nothing more. At midnight he left Ewart and a white-faced Constable Binns to continue searching for the customers the women had named and question them as to who they had seen and what they had heard. That was work for the local station.

Lennox had taken the body of Nora Gough in the mortuary wagon, and tomorrow he would perform an autopsy on her. Not that Pitt expected it to tell him anything different from the brief, sad story he already knew.

He arrived home at five minutes to one to find Charlotte standing in the hall, the parlor door open behind her, her face pale, eyes wide.

He closed the door. He had forgotten until this moment that he was still dressed in his Sunday best and had no coat with him. He had expected to be home long before this. Neither had he eaten.

"Was it the same?" she asked huskily.

He nodded. "Exactly the same." He walked past her into the parlor and sat down in his easy chair, but forward, leaning on his knees, not relaxing.

She came in and closed the door with a click, then sat opposite him.

"You never told me what the first was like," she said quietly. "Perhaps you should."

He knew she did not mean that she could see any answer he did not, simply that the process of explaining would clarify his own mind, as it had so often before. There was no better way to learn what one meant than by trying to explain it to someone else who was not afraid to say they did not understand.

Carefully, hating every detail, he told her about finding the body of Ada McKinley, what it was like, what had been done to her. He watched her face, and saw the pain in it, but she did not look away.

"And this time?" she asked. "What was her name?"

"Nora Gough."

"And it was exactly the same?"

"Yes. Broken fingers and toes. Water. Garter with the ribbon 'round her arm, the boots buttoned together."

"That couldn't be chance," she said. "Who knew about all those things, apart from whoever did it?"

"Ewart, Lennox, he's the police surgeon, Cornwallis, and the constable who was first called. And Tellman," he answered. "No one else."

"Newspapers?"

"No."

"The women in the same house could have talked," she pointed out. "People do, especially about something that frightens them. To share it diminishes it . . . sometimes."

"Even they didn't have all the details," he said, remembering what Rose Burke had actually seen. "They didn't know about the fingers and toes. In fact, Binns and Tellman didn't either."

She was sitting forward also, her knees close to his, her hands only inches away.

"Then it was the same person, wasn't it," she said softly. There was no criticism in her voice, nor did he see fear in her eyes, only sorrow.

"Yes," he answered, biting his lip. "It must have been." They neither of them added that it could not then have been Costigan, but it hung in the air between them, with all its dark pain and guilt.

Charlotte put her hands over his and held them.

"Was it Finlay FitzJames?" she asked, searching his eyes.

"I don't know," he said frankly. "I found a handkerchief under Nora Gough's pillow with his initials on it. They aren't common. But it doesn't prove he was there tonight." He took a deep breath and let it out in a sigh. "But her one customer tonight was seen. He was fair-haired and well-dressed. In other words, a gentleman."

"Does Finlay FitzJames have fair hair?"

"Yes. Very handsome hair, thick and waving. And they mentioned that particularly tonight."

"Thomas . . ."

Her voice had changed. He was aware she was about to tell him something he would not like, something which she found extremely difficult.

"What?"

"Emily was absolutely sure Finlay FitzJames was innocent. She knows his sister . . ."

He waited.

"She saw him the night Ada was killed, you know?" She looked up, her brow furrowed, her eyes dark and wide.

"Emily saw Finlay?" He was incredulous. "Why on earth didn't she say so?"

"No . . . no, Tallulah saw him!" she corrected him. "She couldn't say so because she had already lied to her father about where she was, saying she was somewhere else!" She was speaking more and more rapidly. "It was a pretty debauched affair. People were drinking too much and smoking opium, or taking cocaine and things like that. It was in Chelsea, on Beaufort Street. She wasn't supposed to be there. Her father would have taken an apoplexy if he'd known."

"That I can believe," Pitt said fervently. "But Tallulah saw Finlay there? Are you sure?"

"Well, Emily is sure. But Tallulah didn't think anyone would be-lieve her anyway, when she is his sister and had already told every-one she was at Lady Swaffham's party."

"But someone else must have seen him!" Pitt said with a strange, almost frightening sense of exhilaration. Perhaps at least he had not been wrong about Finlay. "Who else was there?"

"That's it. Tallulah didn't know anyone, except the person she went with, and she hardly knew him. He was drunk half out of his senses, and doesn't even remember going."

"Well, people must have seen Tallulah!" he insisted, gripping her hands without realizing it.

"She doesn't know who to ask. Parties like that are . . . well, they are held in private houses. Apparently people drift from one room to another. There are screens for privacy, potted palms, people half drunk . . . you could come and go and no one would know who you were, or care. Even the host himself didn't know who was there."

"How on earth do you know that?" he demanded, trying to envision such an affair. "Did Emily tell you? And I suppose Tallulah Fitz-James told her?"

Her face fell. "You don't believe it, do you?"

He shook his head. "No, I don't think so. I believe Tallulah could have been to such an affair, and so could Finlay. But I don't believe she saw him at one the night Ada McKinley was killed. As proof of his innocence, it's worth nothing."

"That's what Tallulah thought. But it proved it to Emily."

Suspicion in his mind was sharpening.

"Why are you telling me this now, Charlotte? Are you saying Finlay has to be innocent? You said it proved it to Emily—not to you!"

"I don't know," she said candidly, looking down and then up at him again. She was very pale, very unhappy. "Thomas . . . it was Emily who had the second Hellfire Club badge made, and Tallulah put it in Finlay's belongings so you would find it."

"She did what?" His voice rose to a shout. "What did you say?"

She was very pale, but her eyes did not waver. She spoke very quietly indeed, almost a whisper.

"Emily had a second badge made so Tallulah could put it in Finlay's wardrobe."

"God Almighty!" he exploded. "And you helped her! And then had me go and look for it! How could you be so deceitful?" That was what hurt, not the laying of false evidence, the muddying of a case, but the way she had deliberately deceived him. She had never done such a thing before. It was a betrayal from the one place he had never expected it.

Her eyes widened in horror, almost as if he had slapped her.

"I didn't know she'd done that!" she protested.

He was too tired to be angry, and too aware of his own guilt over Costigan, and his need for Charlotte and the loyalty, the comfort, she could give him, even the sheer warmth of her physical presence.

She was waiting, watching his face. She was not afraid, but there was hurt and anxiety in her eyes. She understood the pain in him. Her fingers crept over his, soft and strong.

He leaned forward and kissed her, and then again, and again, and she answered him with the confidence and the generosity she had always had.

He sighed. "Even if I'd known, it wouldn't have altered the evidence against Costigan," he said at last. "Actually, Augustus Fitz-James said he'd had the damn thing made. I wish I knew why he said that."

"To stop you investigating any further," she answered, sitting back again.

"But why?" He was puzzled. To him it made no sense.

"Scandal." She shook her head. "It's scandalous having the police in the house, whatever they are doing there. I suppose you have to go back and see him tomorrow?"

"Yes." He did not want to think of it.

She rose to her feet. "Then we'd better go to bed while there's still some of tonight left. Come . . ."

He rose also and turned off the gas, then put his arm around her, and together they went up the stairs. At least for a few hours he did not have to think of it.

In the morning Pitt got up early and went to the kitchen while Charlotte woke the children and began the chores of her own day. Gracie cooked him breakfast, glancing at him every now and then, her eyes narrowed, her little face pinched with anxiety. She had already seen the morning newspapers and heard there had been a second murder in Whitechapel. Charlotte had quite recently taught her to read, so she also knew most of what was being written, and she was ready to defend Pitt against anyone and everyone.

The afternoon editions would probably be worse, when there was more news to relate, more details, more accuracy from which to draw blame.

She clattered around, banging the crockery and leaving the kettle to whistle, because she was furious with the people who blamed Pitt, and frightened in case they made things even harder for him, and frustrated because she did not know what she could do to help. She did not even know whether she should mention it or not.

"Gracie, you'll break it," Pitt said gently.

"Sorry, sir." She dropped the kettle with a crash. "It just makes me so mad, sir. It in't fair! What've they done about it? Nuffink! They wouldn't know 'ow ter begin, they wouldn't. Stupid little article, 'e is, 'ooever wrote them things. It in't responsible." She was using longer words these days. Reading had changed quite a lot of her vocabulary.

Pitt smiled in spite of the way he felt. Gracie's loyalty was peculiarly warming. He hoped he could live up to the high image she had of him. But the more he thought of it, the more afraid he was that he had made an irreparable mistake with Costigan, that it was something he had overlooked, that he should have seen and understood, which had sent him to an unjust execution.

He ate his breakfast without even being aware of what it was, and rose to leave just as Charlotte and the children came in. Gracie had hidden the newspapers. Even so, Jemima at least was aware that something was wrong. She looked from Charlotte to Pitt, then sat down.

"I don't want any breakfast," she said immediately.

Daniel hitched himself onto his chair, reached for the glass of milk provided for him and drank half of it, wiped the white ring off his mouth with his hand, then announced that he did not want any either.

"Yes you do," Charlotte said quickly.

"There's a man out in the street," Jemima said, looking at Pitt. "He knocked on the door and Mama told him to go away. She was very rude. You told me I should never speak to anyone like that. She didn't say please . . . or thank you."

Pitt looked up at Charlotte.

"A man from one of the newspapers." She forced a smile. "He was impertinent. I told him to go away and not to knock on the door again or I'd bring the dog."

"And she told a fib," Jemima added. "We haven't got a dog."

Daniel looked frightened. "You wouldn't give him Archie, would you? Or Angus?" he said anxiously.

"No, of course I wouldn't," Charlotte assured him. Then, as his face did not clear, she went on. "I wasn't going to give him a dog, darling, I was going to tell it to bite him!"

Daniel smiled and reached for his milk. "Oh, that's all right. Archie could scratch him," he said hopefully.

Charlotte took his glass from him. "Don't drink all that now or you won't eat your porridge."

He forgot about not wanting breakfast, and when Gracie passed him his porridge bowl he was happy enough to take it.

Jemima was more concerned. She sensed the unhappiness in the air. She fiddled with her food, and no one chastised her.

Suddenly there was a ring on the doorbell, and the instant after, a loud knocking. Gracie slammed down the kettle and marched towards the hall.

Charlotte looked at Pitt, ready to go after her.

Pitt rose to his feet. "I've got to face them sometime," he said, wishing he could put it off until he had something to say that would explain it, some answer or reason. There were no excuses.

Charlotte started to speak, then stopped.

"What is it?" Jemima asked, looking at her mother, then at her father. "What's happened? What's wrong?"

Charlotte put her hand on Jemima's shoulder. "Nothing you need to worry about," she said quickly. "Finish your breakfast."

The front door opened and they heard a man's voice, then Gracie's answer, high-pitched and furious. A moment later the door banged shut, and then Gracie's feet marched back down the corridor. For a small creature, she could make a lot of noise when she was angry.

"Cheek of them!" she said, coming into the kitchen, her face white, eyes blazing. "Who do they think they are? Write a few words and think they have all the brains in London! Nothing but a tuppenny upstart." She turned the tap full on and the jet hit the spoon in the sink and rebounded back, soaking the top half of her dress. She drew in her breath to swear, then remembered Pitt was in the room and choked it back.

Charlotte stifled a laugh that was too close to hysteria.

"I assume that was a reporter from the newspaper, Gracie?"

"Yes," Gracie conceded, dabbing at herself with a tea towel and not making the situation appreciably better. "Worthless little item!"

"You'd better go and put on a dry dress," Charlotte suggested.

"Don't matter," Gracie responded, putting the tea towel down. "It's warm enough in 'ere. Won't come to no 'arm." And she began rummaging furiously in the flour bin and then the dried fruit bin, looking for ingredients for a cake which would not be baked until mid-morning, but the physical activity was a release for the pent-up tension in her. She would probably pound the dough for bread to within an inch of flattening it altogether.

Pitt smiled a trifle weakly, kissed Charlotte good-bye, touched Jemima on the top of the head and Daniel on the shoulder as he passed, and went out to begin the day's investigation.

Jemima turned wide eyes to Charlotte. "What is it, Mama? Who's Gracie angry with?"

"People who write things in the newspapers when they don't

know the whole story," Charlotte replied. "People who try to make everyone upset and frightened because it sells more papers, regardless of the fact that it may make a lot of other things worse."

"What things?"

"What things?" Daniel echoed. "Is Papa frightened and upset? Is he people?"

"No," Charlotte lied, wondering frantically how to protect them. Which was worse: trying to pretend everything was all right when it obviously was not, and only making them feel more frightened because they were lied to; or telling them something of the truth, so at least it made sense and they were part of the family? They would be worried and frightened, but not by the formless horrors of imagination and the feeling that they were alone and not trusted.

Without having made a conscious decision, she found herself answering.

"There has been another lady died in Whitechapel, just the same as the one a little while ago. It looks as if perhaps the wrong man was punished. People are very upset about it, and sometimes when you are angry or frightened, you want to blame someone. It makes it feel less difficult."

Jemima was puzzled. "Why does it?"

"I don't know. But you remember when you walked into the chair and stubbed your toe?"

"Yes. It went all blue and yellow and green."

"Do you remember how you felt?"

"It hurt."

"You said it was my fault." Daniel's eyes narrowed and he looked at his sister accusingly. "It wasn't my fault. I never put the chair there! You weren't looking where you were going."

"I was!" Jemima said indignantly.

"You see?" Charlotte interrupted. "It's easier to be angry than to admit you were clumsy."

Daniel beamed with triumph. For once his mother had actually taken sides and he had won the argument.

Jemima looked cross. A flash of temper lit her eyes and she glared at him.

"The point is," Charlotte went on, realizing her example had not been a fortunate one, "that when people are upset, they get angry. They are upset now because another lady has died, and they are frightened that they may have punished the wrong man, so they feel guilty as well. They are looking for someone to be angry with, and Papa seems like a very good person, because he was the one who thought the man they punished was the one who did it. Now it looks as if he wasn't."

"He made a mistake?" Jemima asked, the furrow deep between her fine, soft brows.

"We don't know yet. It's too difficult to understand. But it is possible. We all make mistakes sometimes."

"Papa too?" Jemima asked gravely.

"Of course."

"Will they get very angry with him?"

She hesitated. Was it better to be forewarned? Would a comforting lie rebound on her later and make the hurt even worse? Or was she adding an unnecessary fear, expecting far too much of them? She wanted above everything to protect them. But what was protection? Was it lies or truth?

"Mama?" There was the beginning of fear in Jemima's voice. Daniel was watching her carefully.

"They may do," she said, meeting the solemn eyes. "But they will be wrong, because he has done the best anyone can do. And if there has been a mistake, then it was everybody's, not just his."

"Oh," Jemima replied. "I see." She turned back to her breakfast and continued eating, very thoughtfully.

Daniel looked at her, then back at Charlotte, took a deep breath, and resumed his meal also.

"I'll walk to school with you today," Charlotte said decisively. "It's a lovely day, and I'd like to." If there were other newspapermen waiting outside, or remarks of any sort in the street, she would not have Gracie involved in a full-scale battle with Daniel and Jemima in the middle. She would have to keep a very firm bridle on her own temper.

And as it happened the real unpleasantness did not occur until the afternoon editions were out, and then it was extremely ugly. Someone had given the press a very lurid account of Nora Gough's murder, with a detailed description of the signs and symptoms of asphyxiation by strangling. This time the broken bones, the boots and the water were not omitted. Nothing was spared, and all was naturally likened to the murder of Ada McKinley as well. There were large pictures of Costigan looking frightened and sulky, only now instead of interpreting his scowl as viciousness, they called it terror of the judgment of the law, as used to crush the common man before the wheels of perjured justice. Pitt's name was sprinkled liberally in every article and he carried the blame for Costigan's hanging far more prominently than he had ever won the praise for his original arrest.

Charlotte walked out of the front door and along the road bitterly aware of curtains twitching and whispered words behind them. The tea parties she would not be invited to, the people who would not see her in spite of her being directly in front of them, the sudden urgent engagements declared when she approached, did not worry her. All her fury was for Pitt and the children. She would have defended them to the last blow, if only there were someone to strike at!

As it was, she strode along the road with her head high, ignoring anything to the right or left of her, and swung around the corner almost knocking over old Major Kidderman, who was taking his dog for a stroll.

"I'm sorry," she said hastily. "I beg your pardon." She was about to continue when he spoke.

"Tribulations of command, my dear," he said quietly, touching his hat. "Hard, but there we are." And he smiled at her shyly.

"Thank you, Major. That's very . . ." She did not know what she meant . . . wise . . . kind. Both sounded wrong. "Thank you," she said lamely, but she smiled back at him with a sudden and very real warmth.

She collected Daniel and Jemima from the school and made the return journey. A pinch-faced young woman crossed the road away from them, her expression one of acute distaste. A woman with three children hurried past, avoiding Charlotte's eyes. The little girl, in a frilly dress, stopped to speak to Jemima and was told sharply to come along and not waste time.

On the corner a newsboy was shouting the latest headlines.

"Police 'ang the wrong man! New murder in Whitechapel! Costigan innocent! Read all abaht it! Another 'orrible murder in Whitechapel!"

Charlotte hurried past him, averting her eyes. Not that he would have offered her a newspaper or expected her to buy one. She was walking so rapidly both children had to run to keep up with her, and she raced up the steps and pushed the door open with such force it swung back and banged against the stopper on the floor.

Gracie stood at the kitchen door, a rolling pin in her hand. She was so angry she could hardly speak. Her face filled with relief when she saw Charlotte.

Charlotte burst out laughing, and the instant after it turned to tears. It was several frightening moments for the children before she could control herself and wipe the tears away. She sniffed, and searched for a handkerchief.

"Go and wash your hands ready for tea," she ordered. "Then you can read a story. I'll find *The Wind in the Willows* for you."

Pitt's day was far less pleasant. He went first to the Whitechapel police station, to see if any more news had come in, before he went to see Finlay FitzJames. There was nothing. Everyone he saw looked pale-faced and unhappy. They had all been equally sure Costigan was guilty. Few of them actually liked the rope, but they accepted it. It had always been the price of crime. Now they felt a peculiar kind of guilt by association. It was their force which was being blamed, not only in newspapers, but by ordinary people in the street. A constable had been spat on, another shouted at and followed by a crowd of angry youths. Someone had thrown a beer bottle and it had shattered on the wall beyond Constable Binns's head.

This morning in the sharp, chilly daylight, they were very sober, and very confused.

Ewart came in badly shaven, a cut on his cheek and dark circles under his eyes, the skin paper-thin and looking bruised.

"Anything new?" Pitt asked him.

"No." Ewart did not even turn his head to meet Pitt's eyes.

"Any report from Lennox?"

"Not yet. He's working on it now."

"What about the other witnesses?"

"Found two of them. Very unhappy." Ewart smiled bitterly. "Not easy to explain to your wife—or your sister, in Kale's case—that the police want to talk to you because you might have been witness to a murder in a brothel. Don't imagine Sydney Allerdyce will have a decent supper on the table for years!" There was no regret in his voice; in fact, there was a kind of satisfaction.

"Did they see anyone?" Pitt pressed the only point which mattered.

Ewart hesitated.

"Who did they see?" Pitt demanded, wondering what Ewart was hiding and fearing he knew. "FitzJames?"

Ewart let his breath out in a sigh. "A young man with thick, fair hair, well dressed, average height," he replied. He looked quickly at Pitt, trying to read his face. "Doesn't have to be him," he added, then a look of anger flickered for a moment, anger with himself for having voiced the thought.

"Well, it wasn't Albert Costigan," Pitt said, before anyone else could. "Did they see any other people coming or going?"

"No. Anyway, not that they could remember. Just the women who live there."

"What about other nearby residents, people out in the street, coming or going? Any peddlers, other prostitutes? Did anyone see anything?" Pitt pressed.

"Nothing that helps," Ewart said irritably. "Questioned a drayman who was loading a few yards along most of the time. He only saw people in the street. No one go in or out. Spoke to a couple of prostitutes, Janie Martins and Ella Baker, who were out looking for custom. They saw no one except the men they picked up, and they weren't close to the house—in fact, Ella's wasn't in Myrdle Street at all."

"Well, someone both came and went! Nora Gough didn't do that to herself! Go back and try again. I'm going to see the Fitz-Jameses. I imagine they'll be expecting me."

Ewart laughed sharply, and there was anger and fear in it. He turned his back, as if conscious of having left his emotions naked, and continued writing the report he had been working on when Pitt came in.

The door in Devonshire Street was opened by the same highly agreeable butler as before, but this time he looked very grave, although it did not mar the pleasantness of his features.

"Good morning, Mr. Pitt, sir," he said, opening the door wide to allow Pitt in. "The weather is delightful, is it not? I think October is my favorite month. I imagine it is Mr. FitzJames you wish to see? He is in the library, sir, if you will come this way?" And without waiting for a reply he led the way across the parquet floor and past a magnificent painting of a Dutch harbor scene of the city of Delft, and then into a smaller hallway off which was the library. He knocked at the door and entered immediately.

"Mr. Pitt, sir," he announced, then stood aside for Pitt to enter.

Augustus was standing in front of the fireplace, although there was no fire lit. Pitt had never seen him on his feet before. He had always conducted their conversations without rising. He looked round-shouldered and was beginning to run a little to paunch. His suit was extremely well cut, his collar high and stiff, and his long face with its dominant nose wore a belligerent expression.

"Come in," he ordered. "I assumed you'd be 'round here, so I waited for you. Now you are going to tell me you hanged the wrong man. Or are you going to protest that last night's crime was committed by someone else, a second lunatic in our midst?"

"I am not going to claim anything, Mr. FitzJames." Pitt held his temper with great difficulty. Seldom had he wanted to lash back at anyone so much. It was only the absolute knowledge that it would rebound on him which held him from it.

"I'm surprised you gave so much to the newspapers," Augustus said tartly, his eyes wide, a curious mocking in them. "I would have thought that for your own protection you would have told them as little as possible. You're more of a fool than I took you for."

Pitt heard the fear threaded through his voice. It was the first time it had been audible, and he wondered if Augustus knew it himself. Perhaps that was why he was so angry.

"I have not spoken to the press at all," Pitt replied. "I don't know who has, and if it was one of the women who live in the house in Myrdle Street, there is nothing anyone can do about it. We would be better employed in discovering the truth, and proving it, than in regretting the public knowledge of this second crime and its likeness to the first."

Augustus stared at him, startled as much by his abruptness as by the bitter truth of what he said. It jarred him from the present confrontation back to facing his own jeopardy and the reality of it. There was no time to waste in recrimination, especially against the one person who could most hurt or help him. The effort it cost him to cover his feelings was obvious in his stubborn features.

"I assume it was like the first?" he said slowly, his eyes searching Pitt's. "I did not hear all those details in the reports of the McKinley woman's death."

"They were not published," Pitt replied.

"I see." He straightened his shoulders. "Who else would know of them?"

"Apart from whoever killed her"—Pitt allowed a shadow of irony to pass over his face—"myself, Inspector Ewart, the constable who was first on the scene, and the police surgeon who examined her."

"Other women in the house?"

"Not so far as we know. They would have no occasion to go into her room."

"Are you sure?" Augustus demanded, a lift in his voice, as if it could have been hope. "They were there. Perhaps they saw her, and told . . . I don't know . . ." He twitched his shoulder irritably. "Whatever men they associate with! Perhaps this was deliberately copied?"

"Why? Costigan couldn't be blamed for it," Pitt pointed out. "Out of all the people involved in the entire story, he is the only one who is unquestionably innocent of Nora Gough's death."

"Sit down, man!" Augustus waved his hand in a sharp gesture, like hitting something. However, he remained standing, his back to the empty fireplace, his hands behind him. "I don't know the reason. Maybe it's no more than to discredit the police and make fools of them."

"People don't murder women in order to make fools of the

police," Pitt answered, remaining on his feet. "There's a personal reason for killing her, very personal indeed. Her fingers and toes were dislocated or broken, Mr. FitzJames. That is acutely painful. It is a form of torture." He ignored Augustus's wince of distaste. "It was done while she was tied up with her own stocking. Then she was doused with water, and her boots were buttoned together, and her garter slid up onto her arm. You don't do that to someone without a very violent passion burning inside you, not some secondhand reason of wanting to make someone else look foolish."

Augustus's face was very pale, almost gray, and his heavy nose and narrow mouth were pinched, as though in a matter of hours he had aged a decade.

"I agree, Superintendent, it is obscene. Not the behavior of a civilized man. You are looking for some animal who is less than human. I wish I were able to help you more than I can, but it is not my area of knowledge. I assume this time you did not find anything belonging to my son?" There was certainty in his voice. The question was rhetorical.

"I am sorry, Mr. FitzJames, but we found this." Pitt pulled the monogrammed handkerchief out of his pocket and held it out so Augustus could see the lettering.

For a moment he thought Augustus was going to faint. He swayed a little on his feet and let go his clasped hands to grasp the handkerchief in one hand, then had to extend the other hand also, to maintain his balance. He did not touch it.

"I . . . I see the letters, Superintendent," he said in a hard, tight voice. "I acknowledge they are unusual. That does not mean the article belongs to my son. It most certainly does not mean that he was the person who placed it there. I hope you perceive that as clearly as I do?" For once there was no threat in his tone, instead a mixture of pleading and defiance, a will to do all he could to avert the disaster which now hung so closely over his family.

Pitt had it in his heart to be sorry for him, despite his own personal dislike. He wished he could be surer of what he felt about Finlay's guilt.

"I know that, Mr. FitzJames," he acknowledged quietly. "The difficulty is to discover who could have put your son's possessions so deliberately first at the scene of Ada McKinley's murder, and now at the scene of Nora Gough's . . . and why. I am afraid it may be necessary to look far more closely at those people who consider themselves your enemies. It is beyond reason to suppose your son was selected by chance."

Augustus drew in his breath, then let it out again in a sigh.

"If you say so, Superintendent." Then his eyes narrowed. "May I ask you how it has happened that you were able to obtain a conviction against Albert Costigan when it now appears he cannot have been guilty? I . . . I do not mean to imply criticism. I believe it is something we require to know . . . I require to know. This tragedy now threatens my family imminently."

"I am afraid it does." Pitt took the button out of his pocket and proffered that also.

Augustus picked it up and examined it.

"Very ordinary," he pronounced, looking up at Pitt. "I don't think I have any like that myself, but I know a dozen men who do. It proves nothing, except possibly that someone of good taste was there." His face tightened. "Sartorial good taste, anyway."

"There were also witnesses," Pitt said, adding the final blow. "The dead woman's last customer was a young man of average height with thick, fair hair, and he was well dressed."

Augustus did not bother to argue or point out how many young men might answer that description.

"I see. Naturally I have already asked my son where he was yesterday late afternoon. I assume you will wish to hear it from him in person?"

"If you please."

Augustus rang the bell and, when the butler appeared, sent him to fetch Finlay.

They waited in silence.

Finlay arrived within moments. He came in and closed the door behind him. He was casually dressed; obviously he had changed since returning from the Foreign Office, if indeed he had been there at all. He looked frightened, his face blotchy, as if he had drunk too much the previous evening and still suffered the aftereffects. He glanced first at his father, then at Pitt.

"Good afternoon, Mr. FitzJames," Pitt said quietly. "I'm sorry to disturb you, but I am afraid it is necessary I ask you to tell me where you were yesterday afternoon from approximately three o'clock until six."

"Well, I wasn't in Myrdle Street!" There was a catch in Finlay's voice, as if he were undecided whether to be angry, indignant, self-pitying, or to try to play it lightly, as if he were basically unconcerned. Only fear came through.

"Where were you?" Pitt repeated.

"Well, at three o'clock I was still in the Foreign Office," Finlay answered. "I left at about half past, or a trifle after. I went for a walk in the Park." His chin came up and he met Pitt's eyes so directly Pitt was almost sure it was a lie. "I intended to meet someone, on business, but he didn't turn up. I waited around for a while, then I walked to a restaurant where I had an early supper before going to the theater. I was nowhere near Whitechapel."

"Can you substantiate any of that, sir?" Pitt asked, almost certain before he spoke that he could not. If he could, Augustus would have said so at the outset, and he would have done so triumphantly. He could have dismissed Pitt, not sought for help. The fear in his voice was his answer.

"No, I don't think so. The . . . the matter was a favor for a friend, a rather stupid matter he had got himself into," Finlay overexplained. "Money, and a woman, all very sordid. I was trying to help him settle the matter once and for all without ruining anyone's reputation. I didn't particularly want to be seen by anyone I knew. Didn't stop and speak to anyone."

"I see." All Pitt saw was the futility of it. "Is this your handkerchief, Mr. FitzJames?" He offered him the handkerchief found under Nora Gough's pillow.

Finlay did not touch it.

"It might be. I have at least half a dozen like that, but so has almost everyone I know."

"With 'F.F.J.' in the corner?"

"No, of . . . of course not. But . . . one can . . ." He swallowed. "One can have any initials sewn into a handkerchief one wishes. It doesn't mean it was mine. I suppose you found it somewhere near this new corpse? I thought so. I can see it in your face." His voice was rising. "Well, I didn't kill her, Superintendent! I've never heard of her, and I've never been to Myrdle Street! Some . . . madman . . . is trying to ruin me, and before you ask, I haven't the faintest idea who . . . or why! I . . ." He did not finish what he had been going to say. "Perhaps you should look at Albert Costigan's friends? Someone is trying to incriminate both of us, Superintendent. Make us look like murderers, and you as an incompetent . . . indirectly a murderer too." There was challenge in his eyes and a small, bright victory. "I think it is as much in your interest as in mine to find out who it is and bring him to justice. If I could help you, I would, but I have no idea where to begin. I'm sorry."

"We'll begin with a reconsideration of anyone who might believe they have cause to dislike you, Mr. FitzJames," Pitt answered. "And proceed with those in whose professional or personal way you might stand. And perhaps a reexamination of the original members of the Hellfire Club."

"I can't do that!" Finlay said intensely, all the momentary elation vanished. "We were good friends. They simply are not that kind of person, not remotely. Friends of one's youth are . . . well . . . it is not one of them, I assure you. I'll consider all the other possibilities, and then make a list for you."

"So shall I," Augustus added. "You will have our fullest cooperation, Superintendent." The ghost of a smile touched his humorless mouth. "Our interests are common, at least in this instance."

Pitt could only agree.

"And somewhat urgent," he added wryly. "Thank you, sir." He turned to Finlay. "Mr. FitzJames, good day."

CHAPTER
NINE

The following day the outcry in the newspapers was far worse. It was not only the less reputable publications that were printing sensational headlines, but even *The Times* itself questioned the justice of Costigan's trial, and through that, not only the efficiency of the police but their probity as well.

Farther into the paper there was another article reexamining the evidence put forward. It suggested very plainly that some of it was morally suspect and had been a matter of desire rather than fact. The whole case might have been conducted with more intention of finding a culprit quickly, and without embarrassment to the Force for its ineptitude, including those who had rested their political reputations in backing it, than a genuine concern for justice. Costigan had been the victim of these two less than admirable forces.

Several less reputable newspapers actually suggested that the officers in charge had been either threatened or bribed in order to close the case quickly. Pitt was likened to the unfortunate Inspector Abilene who had been unable to solve the previous outbreak of murders in Whitechapel, and Commissioner Warren, whose retirement the failure had forced upon him.

Several letters were printed raising a plea that Costigan should be pardoned posthumously, and his family, if they could be found, paid a handsome reparation for his wrongful death.

Pitt folded them up after reading them. Gracie snatched them from him and would have put them on the fire, except that she knew that so much paper ash would block it from drawing air, and she would only have to clean the whole thing out and re-light it.

Charlotte said nothing. She knew Pitt already understood every-thing there was to say about it, which was little enough. She knew he had acted honestly. To say so now would only suggest that there could be a question about it. Her greatest concern was to protect Daniel and Jemima. There was nothing she could do to save Pitt any of the hurt ahead except share it with him, and at the same time try not to show it too much.

She debated whether to allow the children to go to school, or if perhaps it would be better to keep them at home, at least for today. Then they would not overhear the remarks or have to endure the torments and the questions of other children or of people in the street. She could not be there all day to argue back or to explain to them what people meant, why they were angry, and why they were wrong.

She could even take them to her mother's house for a while. They would be safe there, anonymous. A week or two away from school would not do any harm. They could catch up when this horri-ble business was over, and the truth was known.

But what if it was never known? What if it was like the Ripper all over again, and never solved? It could happen. Pitt was clever. He never gave up. But he did not solve all his cases. He had never failed with a murder yet, but there had been robberies, frauds, arson, where nothing was recovered and no one caught.

If she took them to Caroline's, she would have taught them that when things are unpleasant, and when you are afraid, then run away and hide. It may disappear, and you won't have to face it.

But if you do have to, it is twice as hard. You have not only told other people you are a coward, you have believed it yourself.

"It's time for school." She heard her own voice saying it before she knew she had made up her mind. She looked across and saw Pitt's eyes on her. She could not read his face. She did not know whether he approved her decision or not. "I'll walk with you again. Come on."

Pitt spent the day in Whitechapel, and it was one of the worst days of his life. He questioned all the women in the tenement in Myrdle Street again, trying to learn anything further about Nora Gough. Could she possibly have known Ada? Had she quarreled with anyone? Had she known Costigan? Had she lent or borrowed money? Was there anything at all which could provide a motive for her death?

Her pimp was a huge, avuncular man with curly black hair and a filthy temper. But he could also account for his whereabouts all the relevant day, with unimpeachable witnesses. And he seemed genuinely distressed by Nora's death. She was his best girl, earned him the most money and gave him no trouble.

In the early afternoon as Pitt was walking along Commercial Road East there was an ugly gathering of men and women outside one of the larger public houses. Someone started to shout. "Let's 'ear it for Bert Costigan! Three cheers for Costigan!"

" 'Ooray for Costigan!" another yelled, and the chorus was taken up all around.

" 'E were a martyr ter the rich wot comes dahn 'ere ter use our women!" a thin man said loudly.

"An' murder 'em!" someone else added to a loud cheering.

" 'E were innocent!" a woman with pale hair chimed in. "They 'anged 'im fer nuffin'!"

"They 'anged 'im fer bein' poor!" a fat man said furiously, his face twisted with rage. "It's them as oughta be 'anged!"

"Nah then! Nah then!" The landlord came to the door, a cloth in his hand, his apron askew. "Don' want no trouble 'ere. Go orff 'ome with yer! Don' talk daft."

A young woman with a missing front tooth pushed her way forward aggressively. " 'Oo a' you callin' daft, eh? Bert Costigan were 'anged fer summink 'e din't do! That's nuffink wif you, is it? Pay yer money an' drink up, an' never mind if yer gets 'anged fer some rich bastard 'oo comes dahn 'ere from 'is fancy 'ouse up west, an' murders our women! Tha's all right, is it?"

"I din't say that!" the landlord protested. But by now there was more shouting and pushing and a youth was knocked over. Instantly a scuffle began, and within moments half a dozen men were throwing punches.

Pitt moved in, trying to force them apart and see that no injury was done, especially to some of the women who were now screaming. He took it to be fear, only to discover—too late, when he was in the thick of it—that it was rage and encouragement.

Someone was yelling Costigan's name like a sort of war chant.

Pitt was being battered from all sides. The landlord was in the middle of it somewhere.

A police whistle shrilled and someone screamed.

The fight grew worse. Pitt was knocked off his feet and would have fallen over except that the landlord cannoned into him from the left, and both of them landed on top of a sprawling youth with red hair and a bloody nose.

More police arrived, and the mêlée was broken up. Three men and two women were arrested. Eight people were hurt more or less seriously. One had a broken collarbone. Two had to be sent to the surgeon for stitching.

Pitt left feeling severely bruised—and with his collar torn, one elbow ripped out of his jacket, and thoroughly covered in dirt and several bloodstains.

Naturally it all made the evening newspapers, along with much comment and criticism, and renewed calls for a pardon for Costigan and questions about the whole structure and justification of the police force in general, and Pitt in particular.

Comparisons were drawn between this case and the previous Whitechapel murders two years ago, flattering to no one.

More riots and the breakdown of public order were predicted.

Pitt returned home at about seven o'clock, worn out, bruised in mind and in body, uncertain even which way to turn next. He had no idea who had murdered either of the women, or where Costigan or Finlay FitzJames fitted in, or if they did at all.

He recognized Vespasia's carriage outside in the street and was not sure whether he was pleased or sorry. He did not want her to see him at his worst. He was ragged, dirty and exhausted. Her good opinion of him mattered very much. He would far rather she thought of him as able to rise above such crisis and failure as this. On the other hand, it would be good to hear her advice—in fact, just to see her and know her strength and resolve. Courage was just as contagious as despair, perhaps more so.

What took him by surprise when he went into the parlor was to find Cornwallis there as well, looking grim and extremely shaken.

Charlotte stood up immediately, even before Pitt had time to greet anyone.

"You must be tired and hungry," she said, going directly to him. "There's fresh hot water upstairs, and dinner will be ready in half an hour. Aunt Vespasia and Mr. Cornwallis are staying. There will be time to talk to them." It was almost a dismissal, but he was glad enough to accept it. He knew his clothes carried the stench of the middens, the spilled beer, the dust of the street where he had fought, and the stale sweat of frightened, jostling people. Even the fear and the anger seemed to cling to him.

He came down again thirty minutes later, still exhausted and stiffening, bruises darkening on his face, but he was clean and ready to face the inevitable discussion.

It began as soon as the first course was served. None of them wished to pretend.

"There are two ways we must approach this," Cornwallis said earnestly, leaning a little forward. "We must do all we can to discover, and prove, who killed this second woman. And we must show that the arrest of Costigan was based on solid evidence, fairly obtained, and his trial was conducted honorably." His lips tightened. "I don't know how we can prove that we did not conceal evidence that would implicate anyone else." His voice dropped and his eyes fixed on the flowers in the blue bowl in the center of the table. "I fear perhaps we did—"

"I have no love for Augustus FitzJames," Vespasia interrupted firmly, looking at Pitt, then at Cornwallis. "But making public the evidence against his son is likely to provoke a hysterical reaction which will not only be unjust, but will almost certainly make it a great deal harder to discover the truth. And whatever my personal feelings towards him, and indeed whatever his own morality, I do not wish to see him punished for something he did not do. Even if no one will punish him for what he did," she added ruefully.

Cornwallis regarded her gravely, weighing what she had said, then he turned to Pitt. "Just how much is Finlay FitzJames implicated in this second crime? First tell me what you know, then give me your opinion." He began to eat his small portion of fish slowly. From his expression of intense concentration on Pitt, it was impossible to tell if he was even aware of what was on his plate.

Pitt told him exactly what he had found in Nora Gough's room and what Finlay had said about his whereabouts.

The dishes were removed and steak-and-kidney pie and vegetables served. Gracie came and went in efficient silence, but she knew who Cornwallis was, and she watched him with the utmost suspicion, as if she feared that at any moment he might pose some threat to her beloved family.

Cornwallis seemed unaware of her keen little face so often turned towards him. His attention never left Pitt.

"And your opinion?" Cornwallis prompted the moment Pitt concluded.

Pitt thought hard. He was acutely aware that Cornwallis would value what he said, possibly base his actions and his own judgments upon it.

"I really believed Costigan was guilty," he answered after a moment. "It wasn't proved beyond any doubt whatever, but he admitted it. I never did understand why he was so brutal with her. He denied that to the end." He remembered Costigan's face with a sick churning in his stomach. "He was a nasty little man, pathetic and vicious, but I didn't sense in him the streak of sadism which would have driven him to break or dislocate her fingers and toes."

"She cheated him out of part of her earnings," Cornwallis said dubiously. "He considered she belonged to him, so it was a kind of betrayal. Weak men can be very cruel." His face tightened. "I've seen it in the navy. Give the wrong man a little power and he'll abuse those below him."

"Oh, Costigan was abusive, all right," Pitt agreed. "But the garter, the boots! It all seems more than just ordinarily vicious. It doesn't seem like hot temper . . . more like . . ."

"Something calculated," Charlotte supplied for him.

"Yes."

"Then you had doubts that Costigan was guilty?" Cornwallis said with anxiety pinching his face but no sense of accusation. He had spent his life in naval command, and he gave without question the same loyalty to his crew that he expected from them in return. On such trust he had faced, and would face again, whatever the forces of nature and the guns of battle could offer.

"No." Pitt met his eyes candidly. "No, I didn't then. I just thought I hadn't read him very well." He tried desperately to clear his mind and remember exactly what he had felt as he had talked to Costigan, seen his face, felt his terror and self-pity. How honest had he been? How much was he influenced by relief and an inner determination to prove the case so they could all escape the shadow of having to pursue Augustus FitzJames's son?

"He never denied killing her," he went on, staring across the dining room table at Cornwallis. The food was almost ignored. Gracie was standing by the kitchen door, a clean cloth in her hand for holding hot dishes, but she was listening as intently as any of them.

"But he always denied torturing her," Pitt continued painfully. "And no matter how hard I pressed, he always denied knowing anything about FitzJames, or the badge, or the cuff link."

"Did you believe him?" Vespasia asked quietly.

Pitt thought for a long time before replying. There was silence in the room. No one moved.

"I suppose I did," Pitt said at last. "As it wouldn't have gone on worrying me. At least . . . I didn't believe he could have done it alone, or that he had any reason to."

"Then we're back to where we started," Cornwallis said, looking from one to the other of them. "It doesn't make sense. If it was not Costigan, and there can be no doubt it is not him this time, then who can it be? Is it someone we have not thought of? Or can it be what I think we are all dreading, and FitzJames is guilty of both crimes?"

"No, he isn't guilty," Charlotte said, looking at the table in front of her.

"Why not?" Vespasia asked curiously, setting down her fork on her plate. "What do you know, Charlotte, which makes you speak with such certainty?"

Charlotte was thoroughly uncomfortable, and Pitt knew why, but he did not intervene.

"Tallulah FitzJames saw him the night Ada McKinley was killed," Charlotte replied, lifting her eyes to meet Vespasia's.

"Indeed?" Vespasia said with caution. "And why did she not say so at the time? It would have saved a great deal of trouble."

"She couldn't say so because she was somewhere she should not have been," Charlotte replied unhappily. "And she had already lied about it, so no one would have believed her anyway."

"That does not surprise me overmuch." Vespasia nodded. "But it would seem that you believe her. Why?"

"Well . . . actually, Emily does." Charlotte bit her lip. "It was Emily she told. Finlay really is a pretty good wastrel, and not a particularly worthy person. But he didn't kill Ada."

"Was no one else at this place who would testify?" Cornwallis asked, looking at Charlotte, then at Pitt. "Why did they not come forward? Surely Finlay would have asked them to? Or if he really did not remember where he was, why did his sister not ask them to speak? The whole issue could have been cleared up immediately!" He was puzzled and there was an edge of anger in his voice.

Vespasia turned to Charlotte, food now entirely forgotten. "Just what sort of a place was this that no one is prepared to admit having been there? I confess, my curiosity is aroused. Do we live in such a very squeamish age? I cannot think of anywhere whatever that a robust young man would be too delicate to admit having attended. Was it a dogfight, or a bare-knuckle boxing match? A gambling den? A brothel?"

"A party where they drank too much and took opium," Charlotte replied in a very small voice.

Cornwallis's expression darkened.

Vespasia bit her lip; her eyebrows arched. "Stupid, but not so very extraordinary. I would not deny having been in such a place if I could save a man's life by admitting to it."

Charlotte said nothing, but Pitt knew that it was not doubt so much as indecision as to how she could phrase what she meant.

Cornwallis, who did not know her, was watching Vespasia.

"Then if we could find these people," he said decisively, "we could at least clear FitzJames of the first crime, and by inference, of the second also." He turned to Pitt. "Did you know this? Why didn't you mention it before?"

"I only learned it when it seemed already irrelevant," Pitt replied, and saw Charlotte blush.

Cornwallis observed the exchange, as did Vespasia, but neither of them made comment.

"At least it solves one question," Cornwallis resumed, sitting back and taking up his fork again.

"Now it remains to discover why someone placed his belongings at the scene, and of course who, but those two are basically the same question. The answer to one will provide the answer to the other. Surely that must be one man."

He looked at Vespasia, then Pitt. "I find it hard to imagine it could be someone living in Whitechapel and an associate of either woman. It must be someone who hates FitzJames profoundly, a personal enemy of an extraordinary nature. Which brings us back to investigating FitzJames, but that is unavoidable."

"Could it be some form of conspiracy?" Vespasia asked, also now eating her steak-and-kidney pie. Charlotte was very good at a suet crust.

Both men looked at her.

"You mean one person to kill the woman, the other to provide the evidence, and perhaps even to place it?"

Pitt did not believe it. It was too complicated, and far too dangerous. If there had been anyone else involved that Costigan knew of, he would have said so. He would not have gone to the rope alone.

But Cornwallis's eyes were on Vespasia.

Charlotte cleared her throat.

"Yes?" Pitt asked.

She was acutely uncomfortable, but there was no escape. Now they were all looking at her.

"It isn't really proof that Finlay was at the party," she said very slowly, her face pink. She avoided Pitt's eyes. "You see . . . I think almost everyone there was so preoccupied with their own enjoyment, and so . . . so affected by whatever they were drinking, or otherwise taking, that the evidence would not really be a great deal of use. One could have taken a troop of dancing horses through there and no one would have been sure afterwards whether it happened or they had imagined it."

"I see." Cornwallis accepted it with good grace but could not mask his disappointment. "But you believe the sister? She was sober enough to be sure she saw him there?"

This time she met his eyes.

"Oh, yes. She was only there for a very short while. When she realized what was going on, she left."

"And did Emily tell you all this?" Vespasia enquired innocently.

Charlotte hesitated.

"I see." Vespasia said nothing more.

Charlotte kept her gaze on her plate and began to eat again, very slowly.

Gracie had retreated into the kitchen.

"I must answer this question of having Costigan pardoned," Cornwallis said grimly. "Although I am not sure how much of it rests upon me, other than to take the blame for the prosecution. A pardon will be up to the judge and the Home Secretary, possibly the Queen. I wish to God we'd waited another week. Then the poor devil would still be alive and we could pardon him to some effect!"

Pitt did not approach the subject of hanging. It was one about which he felt profoundly, but this was not the time. And no doubt others would do so in the all-too-near future.

"Could Costigan be guilty, and this be a second murderer, copying the method of the first?" Cornwallis asked, looking at Pitt but without any hope or belief.

"No," Pitt answered unhesitatingly. "Unless it is one of us, and that is as close to impossible as matters. Only Constable Binns, Inspector Ewart, and Lennox, the police surgeon, knew the details of the first."

They all waited expectantly, Cornwallis leaning forward, back stiff, Vespasia with her hands resting on the table edge.

"Binns was patrolling his usual beat and was attracted by the panic of a witness leaving Pentecost Alley," Pitt said in answer to the unspoken question. "Ewart was at home with his wife and family, and Lennox was called from another case he'd been attending. It was close by, but he'd been with the patient all evening. Hadn't left them at all until he was sent for."

"That seems to make it plain," Cornwallis said bleakly.

Charlotte stood up and cleared away the plates, some unfinished. Then, with Gracie, she brought in the rice pudding, which was golden on top, sprinkled with nutmeg. There were stewed plums to go with it.

"Thank you," Cornwallis accepted, then winced as his mind returned to the problem. "It seems all we can do is present a brave face, make no excuses, no accusations until we have absolute proof; blame no one else; and keep on investigating both FitzJames and the material evidence around Nora Gough's death, exactly as we would if we had no suspects at all. Pitt, I would prefer it if you handled the Fitz-James end of the case. It is extremely sensitive and will no doubt get worse. I would like to think the newspapers would leave us alone, but it would be quite unrealistic to expect it. I am afraid we have enemies, and they will not lose such an opportunity to strike at us. I'm sorry." He looked distressed. "I wish I were able to offer you more protection . . ."

Pitt forced himself to smile.

"Thank you, sir, but I am quite aware of the restrictions upon you, or anyone in your position. There is no defense."

And so it proved. Pitt interviewed everyone he felt might be of the slightest assistance regarding the FitzJames family, and anyone so injured by them, intentionally or not, that they might wish revenge.

He enquired both personally and professionally, and learned a great deal about Augustus FitzJames and the nature of his financial empire—and the means whereby he had forged it and now maintained it. It was ruthless. There was no deference paid to loyalties or friendships, but it was never outside the law. He settled his debts to the letter, never above. He seldom lent, but when he did, he expected repayment to the farthing.

He was a cold man, yet apparently not unattractive to women, and had been known to carry on affairs with several acquaintances. But in his circle he was far from the only one, and it had never provoked scandal, and most certainly never a divorce. No one's reputation had been marred.

As Cornwallis had foreseen, the press became more strident. Costigan was rapidly becoming elevated to the status of a folk hero, a martyr to the inefficiency and corruption of the police, whose creation some were now beginning to say had been a mistake. Pitt's name was mentioned several times. One agitator even suggested that he was personally responsible for having placed the evidence which incriminated Costigan and of having removed evidence which would have implicated someone else, a man of breeding and money, able to purchase his immunity.

It was slanderous, of course, but the only defense of any value was to prove him wrong. And that Pitt was so far unable to do.

He was sitting in his office in Bow Street late in the afternoon of the third day after Nora Gough's death when Jack Radley came to see him. He was formally dressed, as if he had just left the House of Commons, and in spite of the smooth, handsome lines of his face, he looked tired and harassed. He closed the door behind him and walked over to one of the chairs.

"It's not very good, Thomas," he said thoughtfully. "They raised it in the House this afternoon. A great deal was said."

"I can imagine." Pitt pulled a rueful face. "The police have enemies."

"You have personal enemies too," Jack replied. "Although they are not all where you might have expected."

"Inner Circle," Pitt said unhesitatingly. He had been invited to join the ranks of that secret society, and had declined. Quite apart from the members he had exposed at one time and another, that was a sin for which he would not be forgiven.

"Not necessarily." Jack's dark blue eyes widened. His usual carefree, half-amused expression was absent. There were unaccustomed lines of anxiety between his brows and from nose to mouth. He leaned back in his chair, but his attention was still absolute, and there was no ease in his body.

"If it were not so damned serious, it would be quite funny watching them decide which side to be on," he went on. "Those who are either friends of FitzJames, or afraid of him, find themselves on the same side as you, no matter how much they may dislike it. And those who, for whatever reason, don't want to see the chaos which a police or judicial error of this sort made public can cause are also very uncertain where to lay the blame, and so the majority of them are keeping silent."

"So who is speaking out?" Pitt asked, tasting the irony of it. "Fitz-James's enemies who are powerful enough not to need to be afraid of him? Perhaps we'll find the killer among them? Or at least the man who put young FitzJames's belongings there for us to find."

"No." Jack did not hesitate. There was complete certainty in his voice. "I'm afraid your most vociferous enemies are those who believe Costigan was wrongly convicted, and that it was largely a matter of a new appointee placed to deal with politically sensitive cases, listening to the voice of his masters, and making a scapegoat of a wretched little East Ender in order to protect some idle and lecherous young blueblood. Although FitzJames's name didn't appear in the newspapers, no one has mentioned him, and I daresay only a very few know who it is who is actually suspected."

"How do they know anyone is suspected at all?" Pitt asked.

"They know who you are, Thomas. Why would you have been

called into the case at all if it were not either politically or socially sensitive? If it were simply another squalid little domestic murder—in other words, had there been no suspicion of anyone except Costigan, or his like—then why were you brought in . . . the very night it was discovered?"

Pitt should have seen that. It was obvious enough.

"Actually"—Jack stretched his legs and crossed his ankles—"very few people have any idea who is involved, but word gets around. I imagine FitzJames has called in a few old debts, so some very surprising people are defending the police." He gave a little grunt of disgust. "It's entertaining, in a fashion, knowing how much they loathe having to defend you. But their only alternative is to come out in the liberal view and question hanging."

Pitt stared at him. It was indeed an irony that the people Pitt most disliked, and disagreed with, were forced into defending him; while those with whom his natural sympathies lay were in the vanguard of the attack.

"Except Somerset Carlisle," Jack said with a sudden smile. "He's a dyed-in-the-wool liberal, and he's defending you without qualm or question, and at some cost to his own political reputation. I suppose you know why?"

It was one very oddly sweet memory in the present bitterness.

"Yes, I know why," Pitt replied. "I did him a favor several years ago. A rather absurd affair in Resurrection Row. He was acting in a matter of conscience, although I don't think anyone else would have seen it that way. He's a trifle unorthodox, but a man who is committed to his beliefs. I've always liked Somerset Carlisle. I'm . . . I'm very glad he's on my side . . . whether he's able to do any good or not." He found himself smiling, even though he was not quite sure why, perhaps simply at the thought of the strange, unmentioned and rock-firm loyalty which stretched from one bizarre tragedy to another.

It flickered through Pitt's mind to tell Jack that Emily at least was certain that FitzJames was innocent. Then he thought of all the questions Jack might ask as a result of that remark, and he preferred not to answer them, at least at present, so he said nothing.

"I am afraid the Palace is displeased," Jack added, his eyes on Pitt's face. "I suppose some busybody had to tell her?"

Pitt was surprised. "Does that make any difference?"

"I didn't know you were so politically innocent, Thomas! She isn't likely to intervene, but the mere mention of her name will alter things. It will send a goodly number of people scurrying around interfering and making themselves important. It just makes it all more prominent, more difficult . . . gives more people an excuse to make comments. And it will certainly be fuel to the columnists in the newspapers, as if these weren't enough already."

"I haven't sensed the terror there was two years ago," Pitt said cautiously. "It seems to be more . . . anger!"

"It is," Jack agreed. "Anger, and a lot of talk of political and police corruption." He uncrossed his legs and leaned forward. "I'm sorry. I would very much rather not have had to tell you this, but my silence won't alter it, only rob you of the modicum of defense forewarning might give you." He looked straight at Pitt, suddenly a trifle self-conscious. "And for what it is worth, I don't believe you made an error of judgment of this proportion, and I know damn well that you are as honest as it is possible to be. We all delude ourselves a little, see what we want to see, or expect to see, but you less than most of us. And I've never known you to take advantage of another man's misfortune." And before Pitt could stumble towards an answer, Jack rose to his feet, gave an awkward little mock salute, and went out.

That morning Charlotte made the decision to pack some clothes and take Daniel and Jemima to their grandmother, not because she was running away but because she intended to do something about the situation. If Emily knew Tallulah FitzJames socially, and was privy to her secrets, indeed had established a considerable trust, then this was the obvious way to help Pitt. To do that effectively would take time, and she must be free to do whatever was called for. She could not afford to be worrying about her children's welfare.

Caroline welcomed her in but looked extremely anxious. The whole house seemed at once familiar and oddly different since her marriage to Joshua Fielding, like an old friend who has suddenly adopted quite alien dress and mannerisms. She too had changed. All the conventions she had followed since childhood were abandoned, with pleasure, but new ones had taken their places.

The decorations Charlotte had grown up with had gone. The sense of solidity, of dignified servants running an establishment to a precise regime, had vanished altogether. Charlotte regretted it at the same moment that she smiled to see her mother so happy. The old order had had a kind of safety in it. It was familiar, full of memories, most often happy ones.

The antimacassars were gone from the backs of the chairs. She had laughed at them as a child, but they were part of the continuity, the sameness which made the house comfortable. Instinctively she looked at the wall for the dark, rather drab still-life pictures her father had been given by his favorite aunt. He had hated them—they all had—but they had kept them there for Aunt Maude's sake.

They were gone. So was her father's walking stick from the umbrella stand. Of course it was. There was no real reason why it should not have been given away when he died, it simply had been overlooked.

It was oddly painful, like a tearing up of roots, something broken.

There were new things here as well: a Chinese vase on the hall stand. Caroline always used to hate chinoiserie. She had thought it affected. There was a red lacquer box as well, and half a dozen playbills. A silk shawl of brilliant colors hung carelessly from the newel post. There was nothing wrong with any of it. It was simply strange.

"How are you?" Caroline asked, looking at her with concern. She hugged the children, then sent them through to the kitchen for cake and milk so she could speak to Charlotte alone.

"I saw the newspapers. It's frightful. And so terribly unjust." A wry amusement filled her face. "Although since I have been married to a Jew, I am a great deal more aware of instant judgments than I was in the past, and how incredibly stupid they can be. I used to be so careful of what people would think. Now most of the time I simply do what I want to and be the person I want to be. One moment it's marvelous, and the next it terrifies me and I am afraid I shall lose everything."

Charlotte looked at her mother with amazement. She had never thought of her as so aware of her own vulnerability, or so calculated in her risks. She had imagined her love for Joshua had overwhelmed all knowledge of what the cost to her might be. And she was wrong. Caroline was perfectly aware. She had chosen intentionally, and without denying the risk.

Maybe she would understand Charlotte's own fear for Pitt now far more intensely than she had believed. She had never considered they were alike. Perhaps in that she was wrong. They were different generations, with all the values and experiences that that meant, but their natures held more in common than ever separated them. The excuses she had prepared vanished.

"Will you look after Daniel and Jemima for me for a few days, please?" Charlotte asked, following as Caroline led the way into the old, familiar withdrawing room. "I dare not leave them at home. Gracie would do anything necessary for them, but she is so furious with everyone who criticizes Thomas she might start a fight in the street, before I could stop her, especially if the children are frightened or upset. And anyway, it is not fair to expect her to comfort them if appalling things are said about their father."

"Where will you be?" Caroline asked, her expression conveying that her willingness need not even be questioned. She sat down and indicated one of the other chairs for Charlotte.

"Emily knows the sister of the man Thomas suspects may be behind it all," Charlotte started to explain, sitting a little sideways, ignoring her skirts. "At least his family and his enemies are. I must do something to help. I can't just sit at home and commiserate. Mama, they are attacking him at every side! Liberal writers and politicians, the very people who should be most on his side, because he agrees with them, are accusing him of corruption."

Her voice was rising and she could hear it herself, and yet her emotion was too strong to govern. "They are saying he had Costigan charged and convicted to satisfy people's fears after the other White-chapel murders two years ago, and didn't care whether it was the right man or not. He should have investigated the well-born young men who use prostitutes instead of their own class of women, and that the establishment don't care what happens to the poor, as long as it doesn't cause a scandal in their own circles. If—"

"I know," Caroline interrupted. "I know, my dear. I read the newspapers now. Of course it is facile and stupid, and bitterly unjust. But did you not expect them to say something of the sort?"

"I . . ." Charlotte leaned forward and rested her chin on the heels of her hands. Here in these half-familiar surroundings, the old shapes within the new colors, she could so easily remember her first meeting with Pitt, how he had infuriated her, made her think. Even at her angriest she had never been able to dislike him. He had shown her new worlds, a different kind of pain, of joy and of reality from the safety of the dreams she had known before. She could not bear to see him so vilified, all he had built so carefully destroyed, and by people who thought they were fighting for justice and compassion. Well-meaning, and so desperately wrong.

"It is beside the point at the moment," she answered, swallowing down the ache in her throat which threatened to choke her. "I can't prevent that. I can go to the FitzJames house, with Emily, and learn a great deal more about them, in a way Thomas never could. I'm going to visit Emily, right now."

"Of course," Caroline agreed. "I shall see that Daniel and Jemima are perfectly all right. I . . . I suppose there is no point in saying to you, be careful?"

"None at all," Charlotte replied. "Would you?"

"No."

Charlotte smiled briefly, then rose, hugged Caroline, and went out to the front door. In the street she turned sharply towards the thoroughfare where she would find a hansom. She had no intention of taking care of herself, but she was going to be meticulously careful of every piece of information she acquired and every step she took to obtain it.

"Of course," Emily agreed immediately when Charlotte asked her. She had gone straight from Caroline's house to Emily's. "But if we are to achieve anything of value, we must see Finlay as well as Tallulah. We had better go later this afternoon, when he is likely to be home from the Foreign Office. Although frankly, I'm not sure how much work he really does. And it had better be before he dresses and goes out for the evening."

"Yes, that makes sense," Charlotte acquiesced, although it would be hard to master her impatience until then. "We must get some sure evidence of Finlay's having been at this wretched party," she went on. "If we can at least prove his innocence of the first crime, then we can prove the reason Thomas didn't prosecute him was that he knew he was innocent, and that who he was had nothing to do with it."

They were in Emily's favorite room, the small sitting room which opened into the garden, with moss-green carpet and yellow floral curtains. It always seemed to feel warm, whether the sun was shining or not. There was a vase of chrysanthemums on the low rosewood table.

"The next thing," she continued, "will be to find out who could have killed both women. They lived near enough to each other, they might have known some of the same people." She bit her lip, caught between suppressing the fear—not giving it words—and the slight comfort of sharing it.

"Do you suppose it's another lunatic, Emily?"

"Not unless I have to," Emily said with a bleak smile. "Let's try to clear Finlay first. And have some luncheon. We can plan what we are going to say. Better to be prepared, and hunger won't help."

They arrived in Devonshire Street at a quarter past four, and were received by Tallulah in her own boudoir, the sitting room specifically for ladies. She was delighted to see Emily, but taken aback when she saw that she was accompanied by someone else, and a stranger.

"My sister, Charlotte," Emily introduced them. "I was sure you would not mind my bringing her. She is most resourceful, and I thought she might help us with the dilemma we face. She is already familiar with something of the circumstances."

Tallulah looked a little startled. She had obviously not considered that Emily might have confided their situation to anyone else.

Emily ignored her expression and plunged on, looking innocent. "It has come to the stage when we must prove the matter once and for all." She shook her head a little and her face was full of sympathy. "You are going to have to admit that you were at that wretched party and that you saw Finlay."

"No one will believe me!" Tallulah said with exasperation, glancing at Charlotte nervously, then back to Emily again. They were all seated in small, floral-covered easy chairs, but Tallulah hunched herself uncomfortably on the edge of hers. "We've been over all that," she protested. "If it would have been the slightest use, I would have said so in the beginning. Do you think I would have allowed Finlay to be suspected at all if I could have helped it? What kind of a person do you think I am?" Her eyes were very bright, as if filled with tears, and her hands were clenched in her lap.

Charlotte wondered whether it was Emily's opinion which hurt her or some other, perhaps that of Jago Jones. There was so much they did not know about Tallulah, about Finlay, about all the emotions which seethed below the surface of polite exchanges between those who lived beneath one roof, who seemed to share so much of daily life, of heritage, of status in the world and in society, who had known each other all their lives and yet had so little idea of what mattered or what hurt.

Emily was thinking how to phrase her reply so it did not make a fragile situation worse.

"I think you are frightened for a brother you love," she answered at length. "As I would be. I love my sister, and would do anything I could to save her from an unjust punishment." She smiled apologetically. "I might even go to some lengths to mitigate a just one, were it necessary. As she would for me . . . as she has done." She looked at Tallulah gently. "But because I care so much, I would also be unable to think as clearly as I might were it someone less close to me."

She waited, watching Tallulah.

Slowly Tallulah relaxed. "Of course. I'm sorry. This is such a nightmare. And I have not been myself lately." She looked at Emily, as if her last remark were not merely a figure of speech but something she meant more literally.

Emily perceived the difference.

"Who have you been?" she said, not quite jokingly.

"Someone much more virtuous," Tallulah replied, also as if she were not quite certain if she were serious or not. "Someone who doesn't go to exciting parties, or waste time, or wear very expensive and fashionable clothes." She sighed. "In fact, someone really pretty tedious. I'm trying to be good, and all I'm being is a bore. Why is being good such a list of things you mustn't do? And it's almost everything that's any fun. Being virtuous seems to be so . . . so bland! So . . . gray!"

"Doing good works can be gray," Charlotte replied, remembering something Aunt Vespasia had said. "Being good isn't, because that involves feeling, caring about what you do. It isn't a bloodless sort of thing at all. Selfishness is gray, in the end. It may not look it to begin with, but when you realize someone is essentially interested only in themselves, and if they even have to choose between what they like and what you need, you will lose. That's gray. Cowardice is gray . . . the people who run away and leave you to fight alone when it looks as if the danger is real and you might not win. Liars are gray, people who tell you what you want to believe whether it's true or not. It's generosity, courage, laughter and honesty which are really the bright colors."

Tallulah smiled. "You say that as if you really mean it. Mama thinks I'm trying to mend my reputation. Papa thinks I'm being obedient. Fin hasn't even noticed."

"Does any of that matter?" Emily asked.

Tallulah shrugged.

"No, not really."

"And Jago?"

Tallulah tried to laugh and failed. "He thinks it's a pose, and very silly. If anything, he despises me even more for being artificial." Her face was full of pain and confusion. "I don't know how to be better, except by behaving as if I were. What does he expect me to do?" She took a deep, shuddering breath. "I think he wouldn't really like me no matter what I did." Suddenly she was angry, the pain of rejection flaring up inside her. "And anyway, I don't want to be liked! Who on earth wants to be liked? It's a pale, tepid sort of thing! I like rice pudding!"

"Why?" Charlotte said suddenly.

Tallulah turned to look at her. "I beg your pardon?"

"Why do you like rice pudding?" Charlotte repeated.

Tallulah could not hide her impatience. "Because it tastes pleasant. What on earth difference does that make? It hardly matters, does it?"

"I know that you meant you like rice pudding because you were contrasting a bland and unimportant feeling with one of passion and intensity," Charlotte explained, trying for a few moments to put her own desperate need to help Pitt from the front of her mind and think wholly of Tallulah. "But the point I am trying to make is that the liking you are thinking of is purely subjective. What you mean is not that you like rice pudding but that you enjoy it. You like the way it makes you feel."

Tallulah stared at her without comprehension. Only inbred good manners kept her from saying something dismissive.

"When we speak of affections for a person," Charlotte continued as she would have to Jemima, "we might be speaking only of the way they make us feel, but if it is really a love, or even liking, we should also be speaking of some concern for what they feel. Isn't love supposed to be an unselfish thing? A placing of someone else's well-being before your own?"

There was complete silence in the room. It was a typical boudoir of a young woman of fashion and a good deal of money, where she could receive her visitors in privacy. It was richly decorated in florals, all pinks and blues with dashes of white. Actually, for someone of Tallulah's originality, it was surprisingly conventional. Perhaps she had not been allowed to decorate it herself. From what Emily had said of her, Charlotte would have expected something more inventive, perhaps Oriental, or Turkish, or even a touch reflecting the current fascination with ancient Egypt, not these conventional flowers.

"I . . . I suppose so," Tallulah said at last. "I hadn't thought of it like that. . . ."

Charlotte smiled. "Yes, you had. Your concern for your brother is unselfish. You are prepared to get into a considerable amount of unpleasantness yourself in order to clear him of suspicion. It will not enhance your reputation—with society in general, or Jago in particular—if you admit to having been at that party. Nor will your father be inclined to view it favorably. You may well find your freedom curtailed, or your dress allowance cut short or even suspended altogether."

Tallulah was very pale. "Yes," she said softly. "I know. But that's different." Her hands clenched in her lap. "Fin is my brother. I've known him all my life. If I don't stand by him, who will?"

"Probably no one," Charlotte said honestly. "But please don't think so lightly of liking someone. It's terribly important. It is a kind of loving, you know, and one that frequently lasts a lot longer than romance. You can fall out of love, as well as in. Most of us do, especially if you don't actually like the person as well. It doesn't always grow into love by any means, but sometimes it does."

Tallulah blinked and frowned.

"Would you care to spend the rest of your life with someone you didn't actually like?" Charlotte added.

"No, of course not." Tallulah looked at her closely, as if trying to judge what kind of woman she was. "Would you marry someone you merely liked, and who no more than liked you?"

Charlotte had to smile broadly. "No, I wouldn't even entertain the idea. I married highly unsuitably because I loved my husband wildly, and still do."

"Well, Jago doesn't love me," Tallulah said with flat desperation. "And the whole discussion is pointless because he doesn't even like me either."

"Don't give up yet," Emily cut in. "Merely not going to parties and being extravagant is not enough. It is negative, a case of not doing things. Your heart isn't in it, and he knows that. You must find something to do that you care about, a cause to fight for. We'll think about it after we have won this battle. We have a pretty big cause in these terrible murders. If no one is going to believe you, then we must find someone else who was there, and sober enough to recall seeing Finlay, or if not Finlay, then at least seeing you. That would prove you were there. It might push someone's memory. Are you willing to do that?"

"Of course I am." Tallulah was very white, but she did not hesitate. "As soon as he comes home, we shall speak with him." She reached for the bell and rang it. When the parlor maid answered, expecting a request for tea, Tallulah asked her to inform them as soon as Mr. Finlay should come in.

"Yes, miss. Is there any message?"

"Only that there is something most urgent I have to see him about," Tallulah replied. "It concerns him, and it may be of service to him. Please be sure to let him know immediately, and then tell me."

The maid had no sooner gone than there was a knock on the door, and before Tallulah had time to respond, it opened and Aloysia FitzJames came in. She was a handsome woman with a quiet, well-bred manner. There was a serenity in her face, as if she deliberately closed out that which was ugly and, by strength of will, created her own world.

"Good afternoon," she said as they rose to greet her. "How pleasant of you to call." It was now considerably after the appropriate hour for formal calls, or even informal ones. Their presence needed some explanation.

"Mama," Tallulah began, "these are my good friends, Mrs. Radley and her sister, Mrs. . . ." She was obliged to hesitate, not having been told Charlotte's name.

"Pitt," Charlotte supplied.

It was a moment before Tallulah realized what she had said. She glanced at Emily, saw the consternation in her face, turned to Charlotte and saw it there also. Anger flamed up inside her, a sense of betrayal which she held in check only with extreme difficulty.

Aloysia noticed nothing.

"How do you do, Mrs. Radley, Mrs. Pitt," she said with a smile. "Tallulah my dear, are your guests remaining for dinner? I think now would be an appropriate time to inform Cook."

"No." Tallulah forced out the word between clenched teeth.

"They have previous matters to attend to which would make that impossible."

"What a shame," Aloysia said with a slight shrug.

"It would have been pleasant to have an interesting conversation over the dinner table. Men tend to talk about politics so much of the time, don't you think?"

"Yes indeed," Emily agreed. "My husband is in the House. I hear a great deal too much of it."

"And your husband, Mrs. Pitt?" Aloysia enquired.

"We already know Mrs. Pitt's husband," Tallulah said viciously. "He is a policeman!" She turned to Charlotte. "I imagine you hear about all manner of things over the dinner table? Thieves, arsonists, prostitutes . . ."

"And murderers . . . and politicians," Charlotte finished with a bright, brittle smile. "Usually they are separate, but not invariably."

Aloysia was totally bemused, but she did not falter. She had kept up a calm, agreeable conversation in worse circumstances than this.

"I feel very sorry for these women that have been killed," she said, regarding Emily and then Charlotte. "Perhaps if we could make prostitution illegal, then such things wouldn't happen?"

Tallulah stared at her.

"I don't think it would help, Mrs. FitzJames," Charlotte said quite gently. "There isn't much point in making a law you can't enforce."

Aloysia's eyes widened. "Surely the law must be a matter of ideals, Mrs. Pitt? We cannot call ourselves a civilized or a Christian people if we make laws only on those issues where we feel we have control. All crime must be against the law, or the law is worthless. My husband has said that many times."

"If you pass a law against something, that defines it as a crime," Charlotte argued, but still with perfectly conceded patience. "There are a multitude of things which are sins, such as lying, adultery, malice, envy, ill temper, but it would be completely impractical to make them against the law, because we cannot police them, or prove them, or punish people for them."

"But prostitution is quite different, my dear Mrs. Pitt," Aloysia said with conviction. "It is utterly immoral. It is the ruination of good men, the betrayal of women, of families. It is unbelievably sordid! I cannot believe you really know what you are talking about . . ." She took a deep breath. "Neither do I, of course."

"I hold no advocacy for it, Mrs. FitzJames," Charlotte replied, suffocating an intense desire to giggle. Tallulah was so furious she could scarcely contain herself. "I simply believe it is impossible to prevent. If we really wished to do so, we would have to address the issues which cause prostitution, both the women who practice it and the men who use them."

Aloysia stared at her.

"I have no idea what you mean."

Charlotte gave up. "Perhaps I am not very good at explaining myself. I apologize."

Aloysia smiled charmingly. "I'm sure it doesn't matter. Perhaps you will come again one day? It was charming to have met you, Mrs. Radley, Mrs. Pitt." And with that she made some comment about the weather and excused herself.

Tallulah glared at Emily, pointedly ignoring Charlotte.

"How could you?" she said furiously. "I suppose you contrived my acquaintance right from the beginning. You must have found my confidences very entertaining, if not particularly instructive."

She swung around on Charlotte. "It still hasn't cleared your husband of the blame for hanging the wrong man, has it? Are you here now trying to help him hang the person you believe to be the right one this time?"

Emily opened her mouth to explain, but Charlotte cut in before her. "If what you say is true—and I believe you—then it is certainly not your brother. Is it not as much in your interest as mine that he should be cleared, and that beyond question? Proving he was somewhere else the first time would be an excellent start, but proving that someone else is definitely guilty would be even better. That would remove the slightest speculation." She took a deep breath. "I would have thought you would also be very keen to know who it is that is so determined to incriminate him. I would, if he were my brother . . . or indeed anyone I cared about."

Tallulah regarded her with intense dislike, which only gradually softened as she realized the truth of what Charlotte had said.

"We all have the same interests, even if it is for slightly different reasons," Emily pointed out practically. "And I assume we all believe that Finlay is innocent?"

"Yes," Charlotte answered.

"I know he is," Tallulah agreed.

Emily smiled charmingly. "Then shall we pretend that we are still friends, at least for the time being?"

Tallulah accepted with surprising grace, considering her rage only a few moments earlier.

When Finlay arrived home he came almost immediately to the boudoir and was startled to see two other women there. He did not know Charlotte, and he did not remember Emily. Tallulah introduced them, omitting Charlotte's surname but being surprisingly gracious about her, speaking of her desire to help as if she had been aware of it from the beginning.

Finlay looked doubtful, although there was a flicker of humor in his eyes.

Charlotte returned his gaze, trying not to peer at him with the curiosity she felt. He must already be sensitive to the speculative thoughts of others, intrusive, on occasion prurient, considering the crime of which he was suspected.

He was a handsome man, but he had not the kind of looks she found appealing. She could not see in him the strength she admired, or the width of imagination which excited her. She thought she saw something vulnerable in him, something which should be guarded from injury, because it would not recover, would not heal.

He turned away from Charlotte. The name meant nothing to him, and she herself did not spark his interest.

"Thank you for your confidence," he said dryly, touching Tallulah lightly on the shoulder. It was a familiar gesture, but one of affection, and perhaps gratitude. "Are you really prepared to face what Papa will say if you tell him you were there? It may not be very easy to find anyone else willing to admit it. I can't remember anything. Except I know perfectly well I wasn't anywhere near Pentecost Alley. The first thing I can remember clearly was having a cracking headache the next morning. It could be that most other people will feel the same way." His face looked bleak. "I couldn't swear before a jury as to who was there."

"Some of the others might have been soberer than you, Fin," Tallulah pointed out.

He gave a halfhearted laugh, glancing at Emily with a smile. "Well, I can give you a list of the sort of people who were likely to have been there. I can ask them if they were and if they remember seeing me. I daresay one of them might own up to it."

"It's me they need to have seen," Tallulah pointed out. "Then people will believe me when I say I saw you. It won't have to be public. At least . . ." She looked at Charlotte. "Will it? I mean, it is not as if the whole of society will have to know?"

"Or the Foreign Office?" Finlay added. "Although I'm not sure how much difference that will make now." He pushed his hands into his pockets and paced across the floor and back again. "None at all, if they charge me with killing Nora Gough. Or even if they suspect me of it and no one else is charged." He looked hopeless. There was a kind of blank fear in his eyes, as if he knew disaster was inevitable but he still did not understand where it had come from, or how it had happened to him.

"Someone is very determined to incriminate you, Mr. FitzJames," Charlotte said gravely. "They took your belongings and put them at the scenes of two murders. It must be someone who hates you with almost insane passion—"

"Or hates my father," Finlay interrupted. "I can't imagine any-one hating me so much. A few people dislike me, naturally. And quite a few might be envious of the family wealth, or opportunity. I daresay there are several who don't think I deserve my position, let alone an ambassadorship in the future." He looked at Char-lotte, then at Emily. "But I haven't ravished anybody's wife, welched on any debts, stolen anything, or . . . well, anything." He stood at the far side of the room staring at them, defiant and help-less, as if an ugly reality had come to him, drying up what he had been going to say.

"Well, perhaps it is your father," Charlotte agreed. "But there is another point, Mr. FitzJames. Whoever it is has considerable knowl-edge of you. He had your original club badge and your cuff link. And not only that, but he knew you were unable to account for where you were that night. There would have been little point in trying to blame you if you had been at dinner with your family, or with friends, or at the opera, for example. All of which were pretty likely. How did he know that you weren't?"

Finlay stared at her, a terrible comprehension dawning in his face.

Charlotte waited.

Emily stared at him too. No one spoke.

"What?" Tallulah demanded, her voice high and sharp. "Who is it, Fin?"

Finlay looked straight ahead of him, his face pasty, his eyes full of fear.

"Who?" Tallulah said even more sharply.

"Jago," Finlay replied in a whisper, then coughed, avoiding turn-ing his head towards her. "I saw Jago Jones that afternoon, and I mentioned to him that I was going to a party in Chelsea. I said where it was. Joked about it not being the sort of thing he would go to, be-ing so self-righteous these days. He—"

"That's impossible!" Tallulah said abruptly. "That's a wicked thing to say . . . and stupid. You know perfectly well Jago would never hurt anyone . . . let alone . . ." She stopped. Her voice filled with tears, and her face was so white she looked about to collapse.

"Of course not," Emily said quickly, and without conviction. "But he may have mentioned it, unwittingly, to someone else . . ."

"Who?" Tallulah demanded, swinging around in panic, her eyes glittering with tears. "Why would he tell anyone about Finlay going to some drunken party? Who would Jago know that had ever even heard of Fin?" She turned back to her brother again. "Who else did you tell? Someone must have invited you? Think!" Her voice was rising, angry and raw with pain. "Don't stand there like a . . . a fool. Anyone could have seen you there and left early. For the love of heaven, Fin, use your brains!"

"I don't know!" He shouted back at her. "If I knew, don't you think I'd tell you? For God's sake, Tallulah, I'm the one they'll hang . . . not bloody Jago!"

"Stop it!" Charlotte said sharply. "They aren't going to hang you if we can prove you couldn't be guilty. But we've got to use our wits. Turning on one another won't accomplish anything. Control yourself, and think."

Finlay stared at her, his mouth open.

"She's right," Tallulah said grudgingly. "Anyone who was there could have seen you and the state you were in. Or simply known you well enough to be sure you couldn't remember the night, and neither would most other people."

"And there's also the fact that most people would be unwilling to admit they were there either," Emily added.

"Try your friends," Charlotte instructed. "Surely one of them at least will have the honor to own up to you having been there, and having seen you, if not at the relevant time, at least earlier. He may know who else was there at the beginning."

"What are you going to do?" Tallulah asked, mainly of Charlotte, but including Emily.

Charlotte's mind was racing ahead.

"I assume you are going to do something?" Tallulah continued. "After all, the question is as urgent for you as it is for us . . . at least almost."

"Hardly," Finlay said bitterly.

"Oh, yes it is," Tallulah argued with a flash of temper. "If we never find who did it, you will be ruined because of the mystery and the whispers. Nothing bad will happen to you, but neither will anything good."

"I know that!" Finlay said, self-pity sharp in his voice and his face.

"And Mrs. Pitt's husband will be ruined as well," Tallulah finished. "Because he hanged the wrong man and never caught the right one."

Finlay looked up at Charlotte, his eyes wide, then a tide of scarlet rushed up his cheeks.

"Pitt! Pitt—of course." His voice was thick. "I never connected it! I never even thought of policemen as having wives, let alone ones who could pass for ladies!" And he began to laugh, a thin, sharp note of hysteria creeping into it and rising up the scale, louder and more shrill.

Tallulah looked as if she would like to have hit him.

"I'm sorry," she said to Charlotte, her face pink. "I shall send a message as soon as I learn anything which could be of value."

"So will we," Emily promised a trifle mendaciously, then she and Charlotte took their leave.

"He's frightened," Emily said as soon as they were seated in her carriage and moving along Devonshire Street.

"So would I be," Charlotte replied vehemently, "if I knew I had an enemy prepared to go to these lengths to have me hanged." She shivered, for a moment uncontrollably, cold deep inside her. "He has tortured and killed two women just to destroy Finlay. To hate anyone that much is insane."

Emily hugged her arms around herself.

"What are we going to do next?" she asked very quietly.

"I don't know. Try to see if there is any connection between Ada McKinley and Nora Gough, I suppose. Why did he choose them? Why not somebody else?"

"Maybe it didn't matter who it was," Emily said miserably. "Maybe there isn't a reason. It could just as easily have been any-one." She looked even more wretched. "What if it is Jago Jones?"

"If it is, it will be terrible," Charlotte replied. "But we shall have to live with it."

CHAPTER

TEN

Emily returned home determined to do all she could against the injustice she felt hung over the head of Finlay FitzJames. Perhaps it was more for Tallulah's sake than for his, but she had sensed the fear in him, and the complete bewilderment. She would have sworn before any authority in the land that he had no idea how his belongings had come to be in Ada McKinley's room, nor who had put them there. That it had been done in order to see him blamed for her death was the only certainty in the grim, chaotic picture.

There was an enemy somewhere, just out of sight, an implacable enemy, verging on insanity with hatred. Over what? It did not seem as if Finlay had any idea, and the more she considered that, the more did it seem certain that it must be his father's enemy rather than his own.

The following morning she approached Jack over breakfast, beginning as soon as he sat down.

"I have been thinking a great deal about Thomas's present case," she said before he had even reached for the dish with the bacon. "I feel we must do anything whatever that we can to help." She took a small serving of scrambled eggs and a slice of toast. "Finlay FitzJames is not guilty, we know that—"

319

"No we don't," he said sharply. "He may very well be guilty. The only person we know is innocent is Albert Costigan, poor devil."

With a sudden sinking inside, Emily realized she had led herself into a trap. Naturally she had told Jack nothing whatever about her trip to Beaufort Street. He would disapprove fiercely, he would have to. In the past he might very well have attended such a party himself, but things were very different now; he was a Member of Parliament and a respectable family man with a reputation which was of great value.

"Oh." She tried hastily to think of some way to retreat. No argument to justify her statement came to her mind. There was nothing but to deny it. "Perhaps I spoke more in hope than reality. I . . ." She had better not mention Tallulah. That could lead to complications. "I cannot believe Thomas would make such a mistake. . . ."

He lifted two poached eggs out of the dish onto his plate.

"You mean Costigan was guilty?" he asked, raising his eyes and looking very directly at her. She was still taken aback by how very beautiful his eyes were.

"No . . . no, what I meant was that Thomas wouldn't let Finlay FitzJames go just because of who he is. He wouldn't think he had to be innocent, and not follow it up, because . . ." She stopped. He was looking at her with patient disbelief.

"Do you know Finlay FitzJames?" he asked.

"I've met him." She never lied outright. There was all the world of difference between deceit and discretion. "But only twice, and both times by chance. I don't know him."

"But there is no doubt in your mind that he is innocent." He made it a statement, not a question.

"I . . ." She held a quick debate with herself. Justice and help for Tallulah were extremely important. It was a question of right and wrong. Her honesty with Jack, the trust between them, was also important, more important than she had thought even five minutes ago. "I know his sister," she added.

"And she has told you something which makes you believe his innocence," he observed.

She had not expected him to be so perceptive.

"Yes," she agreed with considerably less confidence.

"What?"

"Pardon?"

"What did she tell you, Emily?"

"Oh! Just that she saw him somewhere else at the time. Thomas knows about it. It isn't exactly proof."

"Obviously," he said with a tight smile. He took a mouthful of egg and bacon.

She relaxed a little and ate some of her own scrambled eggs, and buttered her toast. There was no sound but the faint, crisp sound of the knife.

"Where did she see him?" he asked.

Her heart sank.

"At a party."

"That's hardly an explanation. Don't make me pull teeth, Emily. What sort of a party? A drunken one, I presume, and no one else remembers whether they were there themselves, let alone who else was?"

"Yes." She kept the answer simple. Everything new she added only got her into further trouble. She was realizing with surprise how much it would hurt if Jack were to lose his trust for her, or his respect. Perhaps she should confess to going to Beaufort Street before he found out?

"Did she tell Thomas this?" he asked.

"She didn't think anyone would believe her. She'd already lied about being somewhere else."

"But you believe her?"

"Yes."

"Would there be any point in asking why?"

"Not really."

He returned to the bacon and eggs. She was not sure whether he believed her or not.

"Do you know Augustus FitzJames?" she asked hopefully.

He did not look up, but his lips curved in amusement, almost as if he were about to laugh.

"Fishing?" he enquired.

"Yes, fishing," she admitted. "Do you?"

"Slightly. And no, I don't know who it is who hates him so passionately he is prepared to sink to this level to revenge himself on him. But I shan't stop looking, for Thomas's sake."

"Thank you." She took a deep breath. "Is he really so awful?"

"Augustus? Yes, I think so. From everything I can learn, he's not gratuitously cruel, he simply doesn't care. He has a great sense of family—of dynasty, if you like. Which is odd for one who comes from such a relatively ordinary background. Perhaps that's why. Money has bought him all he has, and he thinks it can buy everything. He's right more often than I would wish."

"But you are finding out who his greatest enemies are?"

"Of course. Do you think I don't care about Thomas as much as you do? But there is also a pretty grave job of defense to be made in the House. The attacks are mounting." His eyes were troubled, dark shadows behind the honesty.

"He's going to be all right, isn't he?" Now she was really afraid, not for Tallulah or Finlay FitzJames, but for Charlotte, perhaps even for Jack too, if he made his connection obvious. She could not ask him how far he was prepared to go. Anyway, looking at his face she knew the answer. There would be no limit. If necessary, Jack would jeopardize his own career, even lose it, before he would deny Pitt.

Before he replied, she smiled at him, radiantly, absolutely, the tears spilling over and running down her cheeks.

He reached across and took her hand, turning it over and kissing the palm very gently.

"I don't know," he confessed, then held her fingers very tightly.

Cornwallis looked harassed. He invited Pitt to sit down but was too tense to do so himself. He paced back and forth across the carpet in his office, stopping every now and then, forcing himself to stand still. He did not mention that the campaign to pardon Costigan was gaining momentum, but they both knew it. Nor did he say that several questions had been asked in the House of Commons, and not only was Pitt held to blame for an exceedingly ugly stain on British justice, but he himself was also.

"Have you learned anything?" he asked quietly. There was no anger in his voice, and certainly no accusation. He was a man in whom crisis brought out the strength. His loyalties were plainest when tested to the bitter end.

"Nothing useful," Pitt said honestly. "I have spoken again to Thirlstone and Helliwell, but no one will admit to any serious quarrel, although a pattern of dislike is becoming plain. They didn't part friends, but I have no idea yet why. In fact," he added ruefully, "I'm not honestly sure if it even matters."

"What about Jones?" Cornwallis asked. "You didn't mention him." His face tightened and it obviously pained him to say what he was about to. "I know he is a man of the cloth, and very obviously doing fine work in Whitechapel, but that doesn't mean he is not capable of personal hatred of a man like FitzJames. You don't know what old wrongs may be in the past, Pitt." He jammed his hands into his pockets, pulling them out of shape. "Nor is any man invulnerable to hungers and loneliness that can overwhelm one at times. He has chosen a path of service and self-denial, but he is a young man. It can happen that we ask too much of ourselves and find our weaknesses sharper than we can bear."

Pitt heard the emotion in his voice, and the urgency. Was he speaking entirely of Jago Jones? He had spent long, lonely years at sea himself, with all the isolation of command. The responsibility for the lives of every man on his ship, with no one else to turn to for six months at a time.

"I know," Pitt answered quietly. "Please God it is not he, and I believe it isn't, but I know it is not impossible. I'll see him. Then I'm going back to the most straightforward way, start again at the beginning with the evidence in the death of Nora Gough. I want to know more about her."

"Does anything connect the two victims?" Cornwallis asked, starting to pace again, then stopping in a square of sunlight. "Apart from the same occupation and neighborhood?"

"I don't know. I'm going to see Ewart again. He must have found something by now."

"He's a good man," Cornwallis said seriously. "I've been looking into his record. Everyone speaks well of him, not just because of the success he's had professionally but personally as well. His reputation is excellent. Quiet, conscientious, good family man. Works extremely hard and saves his money." Cornwallis's voice lifted with surprise. "He has three sons and a daughter. Daughter married well, to a farmer somewhere in Kent. Doing very well. His oldest son has a place in University, and the other two look set the same way. That's a remarkable achievement." He did not add "for an ordinary policeman." Tact held his tongue, but he meant it. "We couldn't have a better man with us."

"Yes," Pitt agreed. "He's a good man. You know, he never thought FitzJames was involved with Ada McKinley. He always believed it was someone local. Perhaps he was right. It might have been exactly the domestic tragedy he had said. I should have listened to him more closely, paid more attention to his judgment. He never thought the connection with FitzJames mattered, and perhaps it doesn't. I'll see him tomorrow."

"Then the core to this doesn't lie with FitzJames at all?" Cornwallis said with a frown, more as if he were testing an idea than voicing a conviction. He was standing over by the telescope and the sextant on the wall, and the sunlight caught his face and gleamed on the polished brass surfaces. "What about this handkerchief? It could be his, but is it? Does it have to be?"

"No. Anyone could have had it made."

"And the button?"

"Expensive, but quite easily obtained if one went to any good tailor."

"So it doesn't really mean anything?"

"It doesn't mean FitzJames was there," Pitt corrected. "It means someone would like us to think he was. And that someone wasn't Costigan."

Cornwallis shook his head a little and his eyes were bright with sadness.

"It comes back to Jones again," he said quietly. "He seems to be the common factor, Pitt."

"I know."

"We must face it. Find out exactly where he was when both women were killed. Stay with the evidence. Forget the reason why. He was a member of this wretched club. He lives and works in Whitechapel. He knew Ada McKinley. Perhaps he knew Nora Gough as well." He shook his head fractionally. "I know you think it's out of character with what you have seen of the man, but what do you really know?"

"Not enough," Pitt confessed, the words dragged out of him. "But then I don't think I ever do." He rose to his feet. "I'll see him tomorrow. After I've seen Ewart." He had not the heart to do it that evening. He knew where Jago would be: handing out soup in Coke Street. He did not want to go and question him while he was doing that. He had never wanted to question a man less, or been less willing to find some other face behind the mask. Tomorrow would be too soon. Tonight was unbearable.

———

He found Charlotte solicitous but uncommunicative. She had apparently been out all afternoon, and had at last succumbed to taking the children to her mother's to protect them from the unpleasantness of hearing people's comments in the streets or the gibes and questions of their schoolfellows.

They did not mention the case. He wanted to forget it for an evening. He had no more thoughts, no more clues to explore, nothing more to wrestle with or try to understand. He was happy to sit quietly, think of something calm and sensible, like the garden, or whether Daniel's bedroom should be repainted in a more adult fashion now he was growing up. He was no longer really the age for a nursery. And perhaps it was time to give Gracie another raise.

In the morning he went to Whitechapel early and found Ewart still at his desk. He looked tired and unhappy. Pitt did not need to ask if he had discovered anything of value, the denial of it was in every line of his face and body. He had cut himself shaving, and his features looked pinched.

"I haven't found anything," he said before Pitt asked. "The evidence means nothing." He slid back in his chair, his body crumpled, too tired to straighten. He looked strangely beaten, considering it was Pitt who would take the blame. He might be glad now that the case had been removed from his responsibility.

"I know the button and the handkerchief don't mean anything," Pitt said, then sat down in the only other available chair. "What else do we have?"

"Nothing." Ewart spread his hands. "We've spoken to all the women again. They say they saw only one man: youngish, with fair, wavy hair. Although they are beginning to be less certain even about that. Some are not sure it was fair. As if that mattered a damn!" His mouth turned down at the corners. "Light plays tricks anyway. We are still looking for him. I've got several men on it, but it could be anyone. Could have been some toff from up west, and we'd never find him."

Pitt stared at him. It was extraordinary to hear a man of Ewart's rank and experience speaking with such defeat. If that was the man who had tortured and murdered two women, then they must find him, whatever it took. Did Ewart really still fear that it was Finlay FitzJames, with all the ugliness that would mean, the blame, the accusations of dereliction of duty, of bigotry, even of corruption? He could understand his reluctance, even his shrinking from it—but he could not condone it.

He leaned forward with a jerk. "Well, if he is the man who killed Nora Gough, and Ada McKinley, we are bloody well going to find him," he said more loudly than he had intended. "Someone must have seen him! He came. He went. Have you repeated the descriptions of him from the women in Myrdle Street to the other women in Pentecost Alley?"

"Yes, I have." Ewart was too miserable to respond with an answering anger. "They just say it sounds like Costigan. Which it does."

"Well, has Costigan any brothers, cousins, any relatives at all?" Pitt demanded.

Ewart smiled bitterly. "I thought of that. No, he doesn't. Rose Burke and Nan Sullivan are still convinced Costigan did it."

"And who do they think killed Nora Gough?" Pitt said sarcastically.

"Don't know. Some lunatic who copied Costigan."

"Why, for heaven's sake. He could hardly hope Costigan would be blamed."

"I don't know," Ewart said. "Because they saw Costigan and they want to think he's been topped, finished, out of the way! Whatever they think, it doesn't matter a toss. Somebody was there, a youngish man with thick hair that waves, and no one else came or went, so it has to be him. God knows who he is . . . I don't!"

"No one else came or went?" Pitt repeated.

"That's right." Ewart sounded utterly wretched, as if it were his own personal tragedy he spoke of, not just one more of the regular occurrences he must have seen throughout his career. "Can't get them to move on that."

"Anything else about the man?" Pitt persisted. "Build? Way he walked? Ears? People's ears vary very much. Did anyone notice anything at all? Make them think, remember back."

"Don't tell me how to do my job!" Ewart said angrily. "I have asked them all those things. Nobody took any notice of him. He was just another client."

"Doesn't anybody keep a watch?" Pitt could not afford to let it go. He had nothing else. "Don't these girls have any protection? Even someone to count the customers and make sure they get their fair share of the earnings?"

"Yes . . . and they can only say he was well dressed and had thick hair. Look, Pitt." He forgot Pitt's new rank and addressed him as he used to be, an equal. "I've been over the ground again and again. I've got men out searching for this man, with descriptions. They've tried every other brothel and bawdy house from Mile End to the north, Limehouse to the east, and the Tower to the west. Everybody's seen half a dozen men who answer the description, at least." He started to add something, then changed his mind and bit it off. "There's nothing."

Pitt leaned back, worn out himself. Was it Finlay FitzJames after all? Or was it Jago Jones, in some insane, bitter mixture of hatred of prostitutes, of Finlay, of all his past life and whatever he used to be, and of Finlay's knowledge of him? Or perhaps it was even that Finlay had introduced him to it? Was that the core of his madness—the conviction that somehow Finlay was the one who had led him to discover the sinner within himself, the uncontrollable appetite?

"What is it?" Ewart asked, sitting upright suddenly, knocking a pile of papers with his elbow. "What do you know?"

"Nothing," Pitt answered. "But I shall have to go and speak to the Reverend Jago Jones again."

"Jones?" Ewart said in surprise, leaving the papers where they were. "You think he knows something? I doubt it. Good man, but not worldly-wise. If he knew anything, he'd have told us already." His voice fell flat again, the moment's hope gone out of it. "Anyway, it's a waste of time your going to see him. He won't betray a parishioner, even if he knows for certain who it is. Priest's vows, and all that. Better to compare between Ada and Nora, see who might have known both of them. I've already started." He fished among the fallen papers and pulled out a few. He pushed them across at Pitt. "These are the people who know both the women and dealt with them, one way or another: clothes, hosiery, cosmetics, medicines, food, shoes, even bed linen." He grunted. "Never realized a prostitute went through so much bed linen. See, just a few of them are the same."

"Naturally." Pitt took the paper, although he did not expect it to reveal anything interesting. "I don't suppose there are all that many dealers in such things in a small area like this. Any of them answer the description?"

"Not so far. Most of them are middle-aged and were at home with their families at the time." Ewart relapsed into his hopeless air, leaning back in his chair, slumped over.

"Anything from Lennox?" Pitt asked.

"No. She was killed in exactly the same way," Ewart answered, his face pinched, pain written all through him, and a driving, consuming anger. "Tortured the same. All the details match, even those no one else knows but us. It had to be the same person."

"Anything different at all?" Pitt said quietly. The shabby room was claustrophobic, too small to contain the huge emotions within it.

"No, not a thing," Ewart answered.

"Anything at all found, apart from the button and the handker-chief?" Pitt went on.

"No."

"Odd, isn't it?"

"What?"

"That all the evidence at both scenes implicates Finlay Fitz-James . . ."

"Circumstantial," Ewart said too quickly, then slipped down in his chair again, white-faced.

"I was going to say," Pitt continued, puzzled and unhappy, "that it doesn't seem natural. The more I look at it, the more it seems as if the evidence in both cases was put there by someone specifically so we should find it. Has anyone in either building ever seen Finlay FitzJames before?"

Ewart sat upright with a jolt. "No!" A spark of hope lit in his face. "I'll ask them all again, but I'm sure they haven't. You're right! It's too much of a coincidence to suppose that he came here for the very first time and killed a woman he'd never even met before. Why would he, unless he's mad? He might do it once, if . . ." He swallowed hard, as though his throat were almost closed with the strain. "If he were drunk, or . . . or crazed with . . . with lust, or anger, or whatever grips people. But that once would scare him out of his senses. He'd never come back less than two months later and do it again. Especially when he knows we already suspect him."

He was leaning over the desk now, his face sharp with eagerness. "You've met him, Pitt. Did he seem to you like a man possessed by insanity? Or like a young man who'd occasionally behaved like a fool, lost his self-control in the past, drank a bit too much and couldn't remember the night before, and was terrified he'd be blamed for something he didn't do? Terrified of letting down his family, of having his father despise him and make life exceedingly unpleasant for him for several months, if not years?"

It was exactly how Finlay had impressed Pitt. He could not have worded it more perfectly himself. It was an acutely perceptive characterization of the man he had seen. He had underrated Ewart's judgment.

"You're right," he said aloud. "It comes back every time to someone else trying to blame him." He looked at Ewart steadily. "Were we wrong with Costigan? I was so absolutely sure I was right. I couldn't explain the boots or the garter, but I was sure he killed her."

"So was I," Ewart said quickly, seriously. "I still think so. The boots and the garter must have been the customer before."

"And the second time, with Nora?" Pitt asked. "Not the same customer?"

"No, that'd be done by whoever put the handkerchief and the button there, to add to it looking like the same person." His mouth tightened. "I'm sorry, sir, but it looks like your Reverend. Bit of a fanatic anyway. I mean ... why would a high-living gentleman suddenly give up everything and study to be a minister, then choose to come to work here in Whitechapel?" He shook his head. "People like him don't have to work at all. Take the rest of the old Hellfire Club members ... Helliwell works in the City, but only when he feels like it. Doesn't really have to. Just likes to live high. Got a wife to keep, and I daresay children now. Runs a carriage, big house, servants, gives parties. His wife's dress allowance is probably more than Jago Jones makes in a decade."

Pitt could not argue. Other thoughts raced into his mind.

"And Thirlstone," Ewart went on, an edge to his voice. "Plays at being an artist. Doesn't make any money at it. Doesn't need to. Just enjoys himself. Drifts from one stupid conversation to the next. Walks in the Park, goes to studios and exhibitions. FitzJames wants to be an ambassador or a Member of Parliament, but he doesn't actually work every day, like you or me. Goes to the Foreign Office when he feels like it. A lot of what he does is cultivate the right people, be seen at the right places."

Pitt said nothing. He heard the contempt in Ewart's voice and he understood it, perhaps even shared it.

"But Jones works from morning till night," Ewart concluded. "Sundays as well. I don't know what they pay him, but they don't say 'poor as a church mouse' for nothing. Wears old clothes, eats the same as the rest of 'em 'round there. Probably as cold in winter as they are, worse than I am. Why?"

"I don't know." Pitt stood up. "But you're right, it requires an answer. You had better keep on looking for this man who last saw Nora."

"I don't know who else to question," Ewart protested. "We've spoken to all the women in the building, the people in the bottle factory, local residents, shopkeepers."

"Even the beggars and workers in the street," Pitt said from the doorway. "Keep on trying them. Someone must have seen him. He didn't walk out of there and disappear." He turned the handle. "Unless you've got any better ideas?"

He left Ewart in the dark, untidy office and went back to Myrdle Street. The question of the customer who had disappeared nagged at his mind. He had to be the one who killed her, but the fact that no one admitted seeing him leave was significant. In fact, no one even admitted seeing him arrive. The house was a brothel. There were always people about. It was not only a fact of business, it was part of their safety. Every woman who worked the streets was aware of the dangers of a client who was violent, abusive, refused to pay, or had tastes and demands beyond those she was willing to satisfy.

He walked briskly from the police station along the gray streets filled with traffic: men and women bustling along the pavements, tradesmen, petty clerks, errand boys, deliverymen, peddlers and news sellers. Nora's death was still on every front page, along with protests of Costigan's innocence and the call for reform. Some even asked for abolition of the police because of their failure to catch the first Whitechapel mass murderer, and now a second.

Pitt hurried by, wanting to look the other way and yet drawn to them against his will. His imagination painted lurid headlines. What he saw was even worse. He was spared nothing.

"Police getting nowhere!" screamed one. "Whitechapel lives in terror again!" And another sandwich board read, "Has Jack the Ripper returned? Police helpless!" "Senior policeman Pitt going 'round in circles! Or is he? Does he know something he dare not tell? Who is the Whitechapel murderer?"

He arrived at the house in Myrdle Street tense, miserable and out of breath. No one was up yet. Business had resumed as usual. The demands of debt do not wait upon a decent mourning period, and the fact that a murder had been committed on the premises had not apparently deterred the clientele.

He roused Edie with some difficulty, and she came into the kitchen at the back, her long black hair tangled, her face puffed with sleep, a loose robe wrapped around herself. Her trade had robbed her of any pretension to modesty.

"Yer wastin' yer time," she said sourly, sitting down on one of the hard-backed chairs. "We don't none of us know nuffink as we 'aven't already told yer. We saw no one else come nor go that night 'cept our own customers. We dunno 'oo the geezer was wif the fair 'air wot went inter Nora's room, an' we didn't 'ear nuffink."

"I know." Pitt tried to be patient. "Nobody outside saw him either. Doesn't that strike you as peculiar?"

"Yeah. So wot? Yer sayin' as we got a ghost wot comes in 'ere, strangles Nora, an' goes aht agin?" She shivered, her heavy flesh dragging at her robe. "Yer mad! In't no such fing. Someone's lyin', that's all. Somebody seen 'im. They just in't sayin'."

"Several people," Pitt said thoughtfully. "Why?"

"I dunno. It don't make no sense. I want the bastard caught and topped!" She put her slender-fingered hands up to her face. "Nora were a cheeky bitch, but nobody deserved wot 'appened to 'er. Could've slapped 'er meself a few times. But then reckon as we all get across each other some days."

"Why did Nora get across you?"

Edie pulled a face of self-mockery touched with a kind of humor.

" 'Cos she were pretty, I suppose. An' she could really get the men. 'Ad a way wif 'er." She looked at Pitt with contempt. "I don' mean nicked yer customers. I mean yer own men. Took a few as I fancied."

"Not customers?" Pitt asked. "Not paying men?"

"Geez. Yer can do it for fun too, yer know," she said indignantly. "Well . . . not often, mebbe. But it's good ter 'ave someone 'oo likes yer. No money. Treats yer like yerself, not like they bought yer. Nice ter 'ave jus' a cuddle an' a laugh."

"Yes, of course it is. And Nora would take your man, and other people's?"

" 'Ere, not reg'lar. Just mine once, only a geezer wot I fancied, nuffink def'nite. Made an 'abit of it, and we'd 'a' 'ad 'er thrown aht! She weren't bad, Nora. An' if I knew 'ow ter 'elp yer get 'oo it was as done 'er, I'd bust meself ter do it. Bloody useless lot y'are too." She ran her fingers through her black hair. "Geez! Anyway that little sod Costigan sure as 'ell din't do it. And yer in't caught the real bastard wot did, even though 'e's done it twice now. Gonna wait till 'e does it again, are yer? Catch 'im the third time? Or will it be like in 'eighty-eight, and 'e'll thumb 'is nose at the lot o' yer." She stood up, pulling her robe around her. "I dunno nuffink more, an' I'm goin' back ter me bed. I dunno wot they pay yer for. If I weren't no better at me job than you are, I'd starve."

Pitt roused Pearl and Mabel, and learned nothing else of use. They only repeated what they had already said.

It was lunchtime, and he was hungry. He walked towards the river and the nearest public house, the same one in Swan Street where he and Ewart and Lennox had met two evenings before Costigan's trial.

Was he wrong about Costigan? Could he possibly have been so eager to believe him guilty he had misinterpreted what he said? He had to think back, but he could not remember the words, only his own certainty that it was an admission.

He went to the bar and asked for a pint of cider and a sandwich with cheese and pickle. He took it to a table and sat down, eating without tasting. The room was noisy, packed with porters, draymen and laborers. The smells of sawdust and ale were everywhere, the sounds of voices and occasional laughter. He had been there several minutes and was more than halfway through when a large man with an open jacket stared at him pointedly.

"Rozzer!" he said slowly. "Yer that rozzer wot 'anged Costigan, ain't yer?"

Pitt looked up at him.

"I didn't hang him," he corrected. "I arrested him. The court tried him, the jury found him guilty, and the judge sentenced him." He took another mouthful of his sandwich and turned away.

Several people close by stopped talking.

"That's right!" The man raised his voice. "Stuff yer face. Look the other way from us. Wot der we matter? Jus' poor folks from Whitechapel. 'Ang some poor bastard an' go 'ome ter yer bed." The jeering in his voice grew sharper, uglier. "Sleep easy, do yer, Rozzer? Only Costigan in't gonna wake up agin, is 'e? 'Cos you 'anged 'im! But it don't stop some bloody toff comin' 'ere from up west, usin' our women, and then torturin' 'em an' stranglin' 'em, do it?"

Another man joined in, his face tight with hatred.

" 'Ow much they pay yer, eh? Judas!"

"Judas!" came the cry from half a dozen other throats. No one was eating anymore. All other conversations stopped.

Someone stood up.

The landlord yelled for order and was told to keep his mouth shut.

They moved closer to Pitt's table, faces ugly.

"Wot yer come back 'ere fer, eh? 'Opin' ter be paid agin, are yer?"

"Pay yer every time 'e kills some poor bitch, does 'e?"

" 'Ow much, eh? 'Ow much is one o' our women worth to yer, Rozzer?"

Pitt opened his mouth to speak, and someone hit him. It was a glancing blow, but it shocked him and sent him off balance.

There was a cheer, then someone laughed.

Pitt straightened up onto his feet.

He was taller than the man had expected, and bigger. The man stepped back.

Another man squared up beside him, ready to join him. It was becoming extremely unpleasant. Pitt felt a sharp tug of fear and sweat broke out on his body. He would not go down without a fight, but he would have no chance whatever of beating this many men. They would injure him badly, perhaps even kill him.

The man nearest him rocked gently on the balls of his feet, ready to begin, his eyes moving from one side to the other, his face glistening with the sweat of excitement. Pitt could smell it sharp in the air.

"Go on!" a high voice yelled. "Wot yer waitin' fer?"

The first man glanced sideways to make certain he would not be starting alone. He saw confirmation in the other's eyes and stepped forward, fists high, clenched.

Pitt altered his weight, ready for the first blow.

"Stop it!"

Everyone froze. There was command in the voice. It was not a shout, but it carried across the full extent of the room.

Pitt's breath caught in his throat and almost choked him.

The crowd was elbowed aside and Jago Jones forced his way through. His face was set like iron, his eyes blazing.

"What the devil's going on here?" he demanded, staring at one man, then another.

"No need for you, Reverend," one man said sharply. "You go on about 'elpin' the sick and them as wants yer. We don't want yer 'ere!"

There was a murmur of agreement. Someone stretched out a hand towards him to push. He ignored it.

"In't your business 'ere, Reverend," another man said roughly. "Go on wi' yer own business an' aht o' ours!"

"What are you trying to do?" Jago stared at him without wavering. "Commit another murder and prove we are the ignorant and stupid people the rich would like to believe? Murder a police superintendent who's only doing his job and they'll have the army in here before you can turn 'round."

There was a low grumble of complaint, but one by one they stepped back, or were pulled, leaving Jago facing Pitt.

"Are you finished with your lunch?" Jago asked, but his face made it plain it was an order rather than a question.

Pitt swallowed. There was still a good deal of his sandwich left, and half his cider. He picked up the glass and drained it, then took the sandwich in his hand.

"Yes."

Jago turned to face the way out. For several seconds no one moved. They stood together, belligerently, daring Jago to brave them.

"Are you going to attack me too?" he said with only the faintest catch in his throat. "Is this your idea of courage and intelligence? This how you want the people up west to think of you . . . beasts who set upon priests and policemen?"

There was a growl of anger, but several moved back a step.

Jago led the way through the silent crowd. Their eyes were sullen, and many fists were still clenched tight. No one moved any farther to let them pass, and Pitt actually brushed two of them as he went.

Outside the air was colder and smelled of horse manure and drains, but Pitt gulped it as if it had been as sweet as the bright, clean wind off the sea.

"Thank you," he said shakily. "I . . . I didn't realize the feeling was so deep . . . or so bad."

"There's always someone to take advantage of trouble," Jago replied, striding out along the street back towards St. Mary's Church.

"Political opportunists, or simply people full of hate and failure who need to blame someone for it. You were a natural target. You were a little naive not to have seen it."

Pitt said nothing. Jago was right.

They walked side by side, rapidly. Pitt had come because he could not rid himself of the painful suspicion that Jago was the link between Finlay FitzJames and Whitechapel, between the past and the present. He was the only person who unarguably knew both Ada and Finlay. He probably knew Nora Gough as well. Pitt hated the thought. He hated even more having to broach the subject to Jago, who had just rescued him, possibly at some risk to himself.

Pitt drew breath and was about to ask when Jago stopped abruptly.

They had gone up Mansell Street and were at the corner of the Whitechapel Road. The traffic was heavy, mostly commercial.

"I've got to go and call on a woman whose husband was drowned last week," Jago said as clearly as he could above the rattle of wheels and clatter of hooves. "I'd be careful around here, Superintendent. Don't wait in any place too long. If you have to question a crowd, take some constables with you. I presume you are no further . . ." The rest of what he said was drowned out by a passing dray.

"No," Pitt replied when it had gone. "Not much."

Jago gave him a quick, brilliant smile of sympathy, then set out across the street, dodging between the traffic, and disappeared.

Pitt went to find Lennox. It was just possible there was some fact he might have noticed that he had omitted to mention, some strand of difference, even something he might know about the nature of a man who would do such a thing to another human being.

He found him in a makeshift shelter of half-rotted timber crates by the river stairs. He was treating an old man whose bent body shook with delirium, although whether from fever or the effects of raw alcohol Pitt did not know. Apparently Lennox did not care. He spoke to the man gently, easing him up in his makeshift bed, straightening out the rumpled blankets. He fetched him water and produced from his own pocket half a loaf of bread, which the man took, bit into, then chewed very slowly, barely able to swallow.

Pitt waited until he had finished, and then as he left, walked with him across the alley to the broader street. Every now and then the afternoon sun was overcast by clouds driving up from the east over the river.

"How can I help you, Superintendent?" Lennox asked curiously. He still looked strained, but there was less tension in his body than the last time Pitt had seen him, and less tiredness in his face.

"I'm achieving nothing with this case," Pitt answered frankly. "You examined both bodies. Were there any differences at all in the way in which they were treated?"

Lennox kept on walking, his eyes straight ahead.

"No."

"Nothing at all?" Pitt persisted. "I know the stockings used to strangle both women were their own, and tied in the same way. But then there are only a number of ways you tie a noose to strangle someone. What about the fingers and toes? Were they the same ones broken or dislocated?"

"Yes." Lennox's face was hard and tight, as if he were still feeling in his own mind the pain it must have inflicted. The corners of his mouth were white. There was a tiny muscle ticking in his temple.

"Exactly the same?" Pitt pressed.

"Yes, exactly. If you are trying to say it was two different men committed the murders, then I am afraid I can't help you. I know Costigan is hanged, and I'm sorry. I wish I could comfort you . . . but I can't." He was dogged, head forward, eyes almost blind; so absorbed was he by his emotions, he nearly stepped off the footpath into the road. Only Pitt's hand jerking his arm prevented him. A hansom swept by, the rush of air causing his hair to blow back off his brow.

"What about fingernails?" Pitt said after Lennox had composed himself, but not spoken. The roadway was clear and they set off together, matching step for step until they reached the far side.

"Fingernails?" Lennox asked.

"Yes. One of Ada's was torn where she tried to get the stocking off her neck. She fought, but only for a few moments. Nora had small bruises, and blood in one nail. She was a much smaller woman, very light, yet she seems to have fought for longer."

"Is that a question?" Lennox asked, skirting around a pile of refuse on the pavement.

"Yes." Pitt went around the other side of it. "Why was Nora able to fight longer? That's a difference!"

"I don't know." Lennox looked puzzled, a furrow across his brow. "Maybe he took Ada by surprise? Some people do fight harder than others. No idea why. Same with illness. Some people succumb, die of things you think they should have recovered from quite easily. Others cling onto life and survive illnesses or injuries which should have killed them, would have killed anyone else. It's to do with will, not physical size or strength."

Pitt was waiting for him to go on, but he did not.

"But the medical evidence suggests to you that it is the same person who killed them both?" Pitt said after a minute or two.

Lennox stopped and turned to face him. His eyes were shadowed, confusion and pain in them, his mouth pinched with memory.

"I don't know, Superintendent. All I know is what I see. It is your job to deduce guilt or innocence. I can't help you any more. If I could, and I could point to someone and say 'That is the man,' I would. Surely to God you know that? I have seen two young women tortured, subjected to humiliation and terror and pain, and then killed!" His voice caught in his throat and for a moment he lost control of himself, the emotion within him was so violent. He gasped for breath, swallowing, trying to regain at least mastery of his face.

Pitt put out his hand and took the younger man's arm. He felt the muscles in spasm beneath the cloth of his jacket.

"It's all right," he said quietly. "I'm sorry. I shouldn't have pushed you for more. Of course it's the same person. I . . . I can't bring Costigan back, and I don't seem able to find who it is that really did it. I'm getting desperate."

Lennox drew in his breath as if to speak, then stared at Pitt in utter misery.

"I'm sorry, Dr. Lennox," Pitt apologized. "I've waited too long to face something I dread, but it's time I did. Thank you for your time. I'm sorry to have taken you away from your patients." He let go of him and turned on his heel, walking back towards the Whitechapel Road and St. Mary's Church. It was time to confront Jago Jones.

Actually he found Jago in Coke Street, as he had before, handing out mugs of hot soup to the hungry and the homeless, only this time he was helped by a tired and smut-smeared woman Pitt barely recognized—Tallulah FitzJames. He stopped close to them and watched without attempting to draw their attention. Tallulah looked utterly different from the blithe and brittle woman he had seen in Devonshire Street. Were it not for the individuality of her face, he would never have known her. She was absorbed in what she was doing, although every now and again he saw a fleeting look of revulsion come over her face, and her effort to wipe it away as she reapplied herself to the work of helping, lifting, spooning out.

There was a bay of used clothes in which every now and then she searched, found something, and took it out, passing it to eager hands.

For one grimy child with a runny nose she took a little extra trouble, searching through the drab clothes until she discovered something bright, cheerful, with a pattern of red on it.

"There you are," she said with a smile. She was too tactful to mention its warmth as well. "You'll look really pretty in that!"

The child swallowed and sniffed. She had never even thought of being pretty before. It was a dream, something only for other people.

"Take it," Tallulah urged. "It's yours."

The mother looked up, speechless.

The child had no words. Her eyes widened. She looked up at Tallulah, then took a step towards her, and another, then she threw her arms around her.

For an instant Tallulah froze, her whole body stiff with an instinctive revulsion. Then she made an effort of will which was there in her face only an instant, then gone again. She smiled and bent down, putting her own arms around the child in response.

Then the moment was gone, and she moved on to the next person in line, but a softness remained in her face as if her wide eyes still saw something precious.

The people in the line moved by slowly, one by one. Men were resentful, hating to take charity. Women, gaunt-faced, holding grubby children, had no such pride. To them the cold and hunger of a child was sharper than any diminution of status or confession of need.

When the last mug had been filled and Jago and Tallulah were left alone with the cart, Pitt went over to them. Tallulah was picking up the now-empty sack from which the clothes had been taken. He wondered if perhaps she had brought it herself, a material contribution as well as her labor.

Jago walked over and greeted him civilly enough, but his eyes were wary and tired. Tallulah was some yards away, still tidying up.

"What can we do for you, Superintendent? I don't know anything more than I did last time we spoke."

"Did you know Nora Gough?" Pitt asked quietly. "I didn't have the chance to ask you then."

Jago smiled in spite of himself. "No you didn't, did you! Yes, I knew her slightly. A pretty girl. Very young. Very confident. I think she might well have been one of those who go on to marry and become quite respectable. It happens, you know?" He looked at Pitt to see if he believed it.

"Yes, I know it does," Pitt agreed. "I've seen it a few times."

Jago sighed. "Of course you have. I'm sorry, I didn't mean to patronize you."

"Any reason you say that . . . about Nora?"

"Not directly. Just an impression. She may have said something. Why? Do you think it has any relation to her being killed?"

"I'm looking for anything at all. A handkerchief with Finlay's initials on it was found under her pillow."

Jago cleared his throat sharply, his face suddenly very pale.

"You can't think . . ." He let out a long sigh. "What do you want of me, Superintendent? I know nothing about who killed either woman. I . . . I find it hard to believe it was Finlay, and I would regret it more profoundly than you could know if it were." He did not look at Tallulah. It did not seem at that instant as if her pain was what was uppermost in his mind.

"A man resembling Finlay was the last customer to be seen leaving Nora's room," Pitt went on, watching Jago's face.

"And you think it was Finlay?" Jago asked. "Can't you trace this man? Someone else must have seen him after he left Myrdle

Street. Where did he go? There are all sorts of people around at that time of the afternoon. Why on earth would Finlay come to Whitechapel at that hour? It doesn't make sense. I assume he can't prove where he was, or you wouldn't be here asking me this." He kept his voice low, so Tallulah, who was almost finished, would not hear him.

"No, he can't," Pitt agreed. "And no one saw this man after he left the house in Myrdle Street."

"Who have you asked?" Jago screwed up his face in concentration.

Pitt listed off all the names he could remember of the neighbors he and Ewart had spoken to. "Where were you, Reverend?" he said at the end.

Jago laughed abruptly. "Playing shove halfpenny with half a dozen urchins in Chicksand Street, then I went back to the vicarage for tea, to meet with some charitably minded ladies. I didn't go anywhere near Myrdle Street, and I certainly didn't see Finlay . . . or whoever it was."

"No one saw him leave." Pitt shrugged. "Which doesn't seem possible. Is everyone lying?"

"No." Jago seemed certain. "If no one saw him, then either you've described him so inaccurately they don't recognize him from what you say . . . or he didn't leave."

Pitt stared at him. Perhaps that was true? Perhaps whoever it was had not left at all, but gone up or down the stairs and remained on one of the other floors of the tenement?

Or else he had changed his appearance so much he no longer seemed a young man with fair wavy hair and good clothes.

"Thank you," he said slowly. "At least I know where to try again."

"Be careful," Jago warned. "Remember to take a constable with you. The mood is still ugly. No one liked Costigan when he was alive, but he's a convenient hero now. Anger and despair run deep, and there are always men who are willing to use it, make some poor stupid beggar stick the police for them, take the blame, and leave them to reap the political reward."

"I know." Pitt was eager to start. "Don't worry, I shall be careful. I don't want to be responsible for a riot as well as a hanging." And without waiting any longer he started out towards the Whitechapel Police Station and a constable to accompany him back to Myrdle Street.

CHAPTER
ELEVEN

The day after Pitt had his unfortunate experience in the public house in Swan Street, Charlotte also went to the East End, but not before she had first visited Emily, and then together they had gone to see Tallulah.

"We know it was not Finlay," Emily said decisively, sitting in Tallulah's bay window overlooking the autumn garden. "And unfortunately we also know it was not Albert Costigan. For all our various reasons, we need to know who it was. We must set about it systematically."

"I don't see what we can possibly do that the police haven't," Tallulah said hopelessly. "They have questioned everyone. I know that from Jago. They have even questioned him." It was obvious from her face that the idea of Jago's guilt had not entered her mind. Her conviction of his goodness was so total that anything but the smallest fallibility was impossible.

Charlotte carefully avoided Emily's eyes. The same ugly thought had occurred to both of them, and they had both pushed it aside, but it would not disappear.

"We must apply logic," Emily continued, looking at Tallulah. "Why would you kill anyone?"

Tallulah was startled. "What?"

"Why would you kill anyone?" Emily repeated. "If you were on the streets living from day to day. Make that leap in imagination. What would drive you to do something so extreme, so messy and so dangerous, as to kill someone?"

"If I killed anyone, it would be on the spur of temper," Tallulah said thoughtfully. "I couldn't imagine planning it . . . unless it were someone I was afraid of, and I wasn't strong enough to do it otherwise. But that doesn't apply here, does it?"

"So you might if you were afraid of someone," Emily clarified. "Why else? What would make you lose your temper enough to kill anyone?"

"Maybe if they mocked me?" Tallulah said slowly. "I might hit them, and perhaps it would be too hard. No one likes being made fun of, not if it is something they are very sensitive about."

"Enough to kill?" Emily pressed.

Tallulah bit her lip. "Not really . . . perhaps, if I had a very short temper indeed. I've seen some men get very angry if their honor is questioned, or perhaps their wife or mother insulted."

"Enough to lash out, yes," Charlotte agreed. "But enough to break someone's fingers and toes first, and then strangle her?"

Tallulah stared at her, the blood draining out of her face, leaving it chalk-white. She moved her mouth as if to speak but made no sound.

With a violent jolt of guilt, and anger with herself, she realized that of course Tallulah would not read newspapers. No one would have told her how the women died. She might have assumed it was just strangling, something quick, a few moments' struggle for breath and then oblivion. And now she was, in a sentence, hurled into the reality.

"I'm sorry," Charlotte said quietly. "I forgot you didn't know that. I shouldn't have said it."

Tallulah swallowed hard. "Why not?" Her voice cracked. "Why should you shelter me from the truth? That is the truth, is it? They were . . . tortured?"

"Yes."

"Why? Why on earth would anyone do such a thing? Was it . . . both of them?" Her eyes implored Charlotte to say it was not.

"Yes. I am afraid it was."

"That's horrible!" Tallulah shivered and seemed to shrink into herself, as if the bright, warm room with its charming florals and dainty chairs were cold, in spite of the sunlight through the windows and the low fire in the grate.

"There were other things as well"—Emily glanced at Charlotte warningly—"which seem to suggest it was the sort of crime that has to do with . . ." She hesitated, seeking a way to describe what she meant without further distressing Tallulah, who was not a married woman and was assumed to be still ignorant of many aspects of life. "Relations between men and women," she finished.

"What . . . things?" Tallulah asked, her voice husky.

Emily looked unhappy. "Silly things. People sometimes have . . . odd fancies. Some people . . ." She stopped and looked at Charlotte.

Charlotte took a deep breath. "All sorts of relationships are odd," she said quietly. "Sometimes people like to say hurtful things to each other, or establish a dominance. You must have seen it? Well, between a man and woman these things are sometimes sharper, and take a physical form. Of course, most people are not like that. But it looks as if whoever did this . . . was . . ."

"I see." Tallulah made a brave effort to look unshaken. "So that means it was someone with a very strong cruel streak, and a man who had a . . . a physical relationship with her." She laughed a little jerkily. "Although since that was her trade, it is hardly surprising. But why should he actually kill her?"

"I don't know," Emily replied. "Could she have threatened him in any way?"

"How?" Tallulah was confused. "She was far weaker than he. She must have been."

"Blackmail?" Emily suggested.

"Two of them?" Charlotte was highly skeptical. "Blackmail over what? Because they visited a prostitute? We don't speak of it openly, but we know that men do. If they didn't, then there wouldn't be any prostitutes."

"We know it happens," Emily corrected her, "to someone else! What about if it is your husband? What if he has some of these unusual appetites? If he were important enough, it could ruin him. Let's say he had a very fortunate marriage in view, or already achieved, and was dependent upon the goodwill of his father-in-law for more preferment? Or he needs a son and heir, and his wife is unlikely to give him one if she knows of his behavior?"

"Good," Charlotte agreed. "That makes sense. Why both Ada and Nora? And why torture them? Why not simply kill them and get out as soon as possible? The longer he's there, the more risk he runs of being discovered. Is the torture part of what he does anyway? No, it can't be. No prostitute is going to have her fingers and toes broken whatever you pay her. Tied up, doused in cold water perhaps, but not injured."

Tallulah was still very pale, and she sat hunched in her pretty chair.

"Proof," she said thoughtfully. "She had proof of his behavior, and he tortured her to try to make her give it to him."

"But she didn't . . . because she had given it to Nora for safekeeping!" Charlotte finished.

"What sort of proof?" Emily pressed, but her voice was rising in eagerness. At last there was something which made at least a little sense. "Pictures? Letters? A statement from a witness? What else?"

"Statement from a witness," Charlotte answered. "Paintings wouldn't mean anything; they're not evidence. No one would take photographs of such a thing. I mean, how could you? You have to sit still for ages for photographs. And who writes letters to prostitutes? It would have to be something to do with a witness. Maybe it happened before? Perhaps there are lots of women who know, and she had statements from all of them?"

"Then where are they now?" Tallulah looked from one to the

other. "Does he have them, or did Nora hide them too well from him?"

"What we have to do," Charlotte said decisively, sitting more uprightly, "is to learn all we can about Nora and Ada. That's where the answer is. First we need to have proof they even knew each other. We need to find everything in common in their lives, and then see if we can find any other women who knew this man. They would give us a proper description of him. They might even know his name."

"Marvelous!" Tallulah stood up. "We'll begin straightaway. Jago will help us. He knew Ada McKinley. He'll know where we can start, and he might even help us to gain people's trust so they will talk to us."

"I . . ." Emily looked at Charlotte, uncertain how to say what she needed to without hurting irreparably.

"What?" Tallulah demanded.

Charlotte's mind raced. "Don't you think that would be rather an unfair way to do it?" she said, making it up as she went along.

"Unfair?" Tallulah was confused. "To whom? The women? We're looking for a man who murdered two of them! What has fairness to do with it?"

"Not to the women. To Jago." Charlotte's brain cleared. "He is their priest. He shouldn't compromise his work with the people by being seen to help us. After all, he has to stay there as their friend long after we've gone." She could only think of the hideous possibility that it was Jago himself who had killed the women. Who was more vulnerable to blackmail than a priest with a taste for prostitutes? He could be the one sort of man whose image would not survive the accusation that he had slept with a street woman, or even more than one. His work would be finished, not only in Whitechapel but in the Church anywhere.

"Oh." Tallulah relaxed. "Yes, I suppose so. We had better go alone. We can find it easily enough. I'd rather we went in the daytime." She flushed uncomfortably. "In the evening . . ."

"Of course," Emily agreed quickly. "It will all be sufficiently un-pleasant and difficult without our being considered as rivals."

Tallulah giggled nervously, but it was agreed. They would meet in the early afternoon, proceed by hansom to Old Montague Street, and begin their enquiries—suitably attired, of course.

It was not easy to obtain entrance to the house in Pentecost Alley. Madge answered the door, and remembered them clearly from their earlier visit. They were similarly dressed.

"Wot jer want this time?" she said, eyeing them narrowly through the space between the door and its frame. She looked at Charlotte. "An' 'oo are you, the parlor maid?" She regarded her handsome figure. "You look more like a parlor maid ter me. All got thrown out, did jer? Well it in't no good comin' 'ere. I can't take yer in. On'y got room for one, and that'll be expensive. Works on yer earnin's, though we gotta 'ave rent even if yer don't earn nuffink. Which one of yer wants it?"

"We'll come in and have a look," Charlotte said immediately. "Thank you."

Madge looked at her suspiciously. "Why does a girl wot speaks proper, like you, wanna work the streets 'round 'ere for? W'y don't yer work up west, w'ere you could make some real money?"

"I might," Charlotte agreed. "Let's look at this room first. Please?"

Madge opened the door and let them in. They followed her along the corridor, which was faintly musty smelling, as if lived in too much, with windows that were never opened. She pushed the second door along and it swung wide. Charlotte was in front. She peered in, and instantly wished she had not. It was so ordinary, about the same size as her own bedroom in the house where she had grown up. It was far less pretty, but it had a lived-in air. It was too easy to imagine the woman who had slept here, and conducted her business here, and died here in fearful pain.

She heard Tallulah behind her draw in her breath sharply, and beside her Emily's body stiffened, though she made no sound.

"D'jer wan' it?" Madge asked bluntly, her voice harsh.

Charlotte swung around and saw the huge woman's face tight, red and chapped, her eyes brimming with tears.

"Let's sit down and talk about it," Emily suggested. "Have a cup of tea. I brought a little something to add to it. You've got to let the room sometime."

Without speaking Madge led them to the back of the house and the kitchen.

The room was messy, designed for laundry as well as cooking. A black stove gave off a very slight warmth, its front dull and a fine ash coating the floor around it. The kettle was already on, steaming gently. Perhaps it always was. There were dirty mugs on the board next to the basin and two pails of water standing with lids on. Charlotte guessed the water had to be fetched from the nearest well or standpipe. She hoped they boiled it thoroughly before it was offered for tea. She wished Emily had not suggested it. But then perhaps they would have no other chance to talk, and what was a possible upset stomach compared with the disaster that faced Pitt if the crime was never solved? He would always be thought of as the man who hanged Costigan when he was innocent. Perhaps worse than that, he would think of himself that way. He would doubt his judgment, be awake at night and tear his conscience. And there would be those who would believe he had done it knowingly, in order to protect someone else, someone with the money or the influence to reward him appropriately. He would be suspected of far more than a mere error. Errors could be forgiven; they were a human failing. Corruption was something far deeper; it was the ultimate betrayal, that of self.

The tea was strong and bitter, and there was no milk. They all sat around the table on uneven chairs. Emily produced a small flask of whiskey out of her voluminous pocket and put a generous dash in each mug, to Tallulah's amazement, although she concealed it almost instantly.

"Here's to your health," Emily said optimistically, and lifted her mug.

"Here's to all our health," Charlotte echoed, more as a prayer than a toast.

"What's the area like?" Emily asked with interest.

"S'all right," Madge replied, taking a good swig of her scalding tea and sucking her teeth appreciatively. "That's very civil of you," she added, nodding her head towards the whiskey bottle. "Can make a fair livin' if yer prepared ter work for it."

"Ada did well, didn't she?" Emily continued. "She was bright."

"An' good at it," Madge agreed, taking another slurp.

"Hope they catch that bastard who killed her," Emily said fiercely.

Madge breathed out a long sigh.

"And poor Nora," Charlotte put in with a shiver. "Did you know Nora?"

"Did you?" Madge asked, looking at her narrowly.

"No. What was she like?"

"Pretty. Little, sort o' skinny for some tastes."

Considering Madge's twenty stone that remark was open to personal interpretation. Charlotte felt a momentary desire to giggle, and controlled it only with an effort.

"But good at it?" she asked, hiccuping.

"Oh yes!" Madge agreed. "Though some says as she were gonner quit and get married."

"Do you think that's true?" Tallulah spoke for the first time, her voice hesitant, high in the back of her throat.

"Mebbe." Madge stopped. "Saw 'er around wi' Johnny Voss. 'E weren't bad orff. Could 'a' married 'er, I s'pose. Although 'e were said ter be keen on Ella Baker, over in Myrdle Street. Mebbe 'e switched ter Nora. Edie said she seen Nora kiss 'im good-night abaht a couple a' weeks ago."

"I've kissed people good-night," Tallulah said in response. "That didn't mean they were going to marry me."

"Did you now." Madge looked at her more closely. " 'Ow long yer bin in the trade, duck? Yer wanna watch yerself. This in't no place for beginners!"

"I'm . . . I'm not a beginner," Tallulah said defensively, then stopped with a little squeak of pain as Emily kicked her under the table.

"If yer kissin' people, y'are." Madge stated it as an unarguable fact. "Kissin' is fer family, people as yer care abaht. Customers get wot they paid fer, nothin' more. Yer gotta keep summink as is real, summink as is yer own an' can't be bought."

Tallulah stared at her, two bright specks of color in her cheeks.

"Yer need someone ter look aht fer yer, teach yer 'ow ter be'ave," Madge said gently. "Take the room, an' I'll teach yer."

Tallulah was speechless. The thoughts racing through her mind could only be guessed at.

"Thank you," Charlotte said quickly. "That's very kind of you. That might be a very good idea. We could always look elsewhere. There must be other places in the neighborhood. I suppose poor Nora's room is to let now?"

"I in't 'eard," Madge replied. "But yer could ask. If it's gorn, yer could go an' ask Ma Baines over on Chicksand Street. She's usually got summink free. In't the best, but yer could take it, and then w'en summink better comes up, yer'd be placed ter move on, like. She in't bin 'ere all that long, but I 'eard say she in't bad. Gotta get all yer own clothes. Got yer own, 'ave yer?"

"M-my own clothes?" Tallulah stammered.

"Yeah. Lor', you are the beginner, in't yer?" Madge shook her head. "Still, yer in't got a bad face. Nice 'air. We'll make summink of yer yet." She patted her on the hand comfortingly, then she looked at Charlotte and Emily in turn. "You two can look arter yerselves." She regarded Charlotte. "You got a bit o' flesh on yer. Yer'll do. An' lots o' 'air. Yer face in't bad."

"Thank you," Charlotte said a trifle dryly.

Madge was impervious to sarcasm. She looked Emily up and down.

"Yer not so good, bit thin, but yer got a nice enough face, nice skin. An' men always like yeller 'air, 'specially wot curls like yours do. Look like yer got a bit o' spark too. You'll do."

"Can you tell us where to find this Ma Baines?" Emily ignored the personal assessment and returned to the point.

"Yeah, course I can," Madge responded. "Twenty-one Chicksand Street. Next one up towards Mile End. Anyone will tell yer."

It looked as if they were about to be dismissed any moment, and they had learned too little to give up.

"Ada and Nora knew each other," Charlotte plunged on. "Were they at all alike? Did they have friends in common?"

Madge blinked. "W'y the 'ell der you care?"

"Because I don't want to get my fingers and toes broken and end up strangled with my own stockings," Charlotte answered tersely. "If there's some lunatic around here, I want to know what sort of women he picks on, so I can be a different sort."

" 'E picks on one sort o' woman, duck," Madge said wearily. "The sort o' woman wot sells theirselves to any man wot 'as the money, 'cos she needs ter eat an' feed 'er kids, or 'cos she don' wanna work in the watch factories an' end up wi' phossie jaw an' 'er face 'alf rotted off, or in a sweatshop stitchin' shirts all day an' 'alf the night for too little money ter feed a rat! Layin' on yer back is easy money, while it lasts." She poured more tea from the pot into the mug, and refilled the others, looking hopefully at Emily.

Emily topped them up again with whiskey.

"Ta," Madge acknowledged it.

"Course there is danger," she went on. "If yer wanted life wi'out danger yer should 'a' bin born rich. Yer'll mebbe end up wi' a disease, or mebbe not. Yer'll get beaten now an' agin, slashed if yer luck runs aht. Yer'll get so yer never wants ter see another man in all yer born days."

She sniffed. "But yer'll not be 'ungry, and yer'll not be cold once yer orff the streets an' inside. An' yer'll 'ave a few good laughs!" She sighed and sipped her tea. " 'Ad some good times, we did, Nora an' Rosie and Ada and me. Tol' each other stories an' pretended we was all fine ladies." She sniffed. "I 'member one summer evenin' we took orff an' went up the river in one o' them pleasure boats, just like anyone. All dressed up, we was. Ate 'ot eel pies and sugared fruit, an' drank peppermint."

"That must have been good," Charlotte said quietly, imagining them, even though she did not know their faces.

"Yeah, it were," Madge said dreamily, the tears brimming her eyes. "An' we tol' each other ghost stories sometimes. Scared ourselves silly, we did. Course there was the bad times too. But then I s'pose it's them 'ard times as tells yer 'oo yer friends is." She sniffed again and wiped her hand over her cheeks.

"That's true," Emily agreed. "I'm sorry about Ada. I hope they catch whoever did it."

"Geez, why should they?" Madge said miserably. "They never caught the Ripper. Why should they catch this one?"

Tallulah shivered. Two years afterwards, his name still chilled the body and sent the mind stiff with fear.

Charlotte found herself cold as well, even with the tea and whiskey inside her, and the heat of the small, closed kitchen. There was no other sound in the house. All the women were sleeping after their night's work, bodies exhausted, used by strangers to relieve their needs without love, without kisses, as one might use a public convenience.

She looked at Tallulah and saw a whole new comprehension dawning in her face. She had seen one new world with Jago, feeding the poor, the respectable women, downtrodden by hunger, cold and anxiety. This was another world, altogether darker, with different pains, different fears.

"Do you get many gentlemen down here?" she asked suddenly, the words coming out jerkily, as if speaking them hurt her.

"Men wi' money?" Madge laughed. "Look, duck, any man's money is as good as any other."

"But do you?" Tallulah insisted, her face tense, her eyes on Madge's.

"Not often, why? Yer like gentlemen, yer should go up west. 'Aymarket, Piccadilly, that way. Cost yer ter rent rooms by the hour, though, an' competition's 'igh. Yer'd be better 'ere, beginners like you are. I'll look after yer."

Tallulah was aware of the gentleness in the older woman and it touched her unexpectedly. Charlotte could see it in her face.

"I . . . I just wondered," she said unhappily, looking down at the table.

"Sometimes," Madge replied, watching her.

"Was it a gentleman who killed Ada?" Tallulah would not give up. Her slender fingers were clenched around the cup with its dark tea and odor of whiskey.

"I dunno." Madge shrugged her huge shoulders. "I thought as it were Bert Costigan, but I s'pose it couldn't 'a' bin, now Nora got done the same."

"So it could have been a gentleman?" Emily looked from one to the other of them. "But would it be likely? Wouldn't it maybe be someone who knew them both?"

"Maybe it was a gentleman who knew them both." Charlotte took it a step further. "One who was a bit bent in his ways."

Madge finished the last of her tea and set the mug down with a bang on the hard tabletop.

"Don't you go startin' talk like that 'round 'ere," she said sharply, pointing her finger. "Yer'll only get everyone all scared witless, an' it don't do no good. We all gotta work whether there's a lunatic out there er not. Yer go see Ma Baines. She knows 'er job. She'll find yer a place. An' don't yer go makin' a noise as you leave. My girls is still sleepin', like yer'd be if you'd worked all night." She looked at Emily. "Ta fer the drink. That were nice manners of you." Her face softened as she looked lastly at Tallulah. "I'll 'old the room for yer till termorrer, duck. Can't 'old it arter that, if I gets an offer."

"Thank you," Tallulah answered, but as soon as they were outside beyond the alley she shivered violently, and walked so close to Emily she almost pushed her off the narrow footpath into the street.

They followed directions up to Chicksand Street and found the huge shambling tenement where Ma Baines kept her establishment. They had expected someone else like Madge—obese, red-faced, suspicious. Instead they found a cheerful woman with a large bosom, but narrow hips and long legs. She had rather a plain face and a mass of fading yellow hair tied up loosely in pins which were in imminent danger of falling out.

"Yeah?" she said when she saw the three young women.

"We understand you might have rooms," Charlotte began without hesitation. It was getting towards the time in the afternoon when women began to work.

"This is a workin' 'ouse," Ma Baines said warningly. "Rent is 'igh. I got no place fer sweatshop girls. In't even enough fer a night, let alone a week."

"We know that," Charlotte replied, making herself smile. "Do we look like seamstresses?"

Ma Baines laughed, a sound of generous amusement without bitterness.

"You look like West End tarts ter me, 'cept fer yer dress. They look like maids on their day orff. Terrible respectable, an' abaht as darin' as a vicar's wife."

"We're off duty," Emily explained.

"Aren't never orff duty, luv," Ma Baines responded.

"Are if you haven't a room," Charlotte pointed out. "I don't do my business in the street."

Ma Baines stepped back. "Then yer'd better come in."

They followed her. The place was narrow and stale-smelling, but quite clean, and there was an old carpet on the floor, making their footsteps quiet as they were led to a small sitting room at the back of the house, again reminding Charlotte ridiculously of the housekeeper's room in the house where she had grown up.

Ma Baines invited them to sit, and she herself took the largest and most comfortable chair. It was as if she were interviewing prospective servants. Charlotte felt the desire to giggle coming back, a sort of wild hysteria at the insanity of it. A few years ago her mother would have fainted at the very thought of her daughter's even knowing about such a place, let alone being there. Now she might conceivably understand. Her father would simply have refused to believe it. Heaven only knew what Aloysia FitzJames would think if she knew Tallulah was here.

Ma Baines was talking about rent and rules, and Charlotte had not been listening. She tried to look as if she were paying attention, fixing her eyes on Ma's face.

"That sounds all right," Emily said dubiously. "Although we're not absolutely sure about the area."

"Cost yer more up west," Ma pointed out. "Yer can always go up west from 'ere, long as yer bring back yer share o' yer take an' don' cheat." Her face was still pleasant, but there was a relentless ice-gray in her eyes, cold as a winter sea.

"It wasn't that," Charlotte explained. "It was the murders you've had here. We'd want a place where if we got a bad customer there we could be sure there were other people about to hear us yell." She did not add that she knew there were other people close enough to have helped Ada and Nora, but no scream was heard, and no one came.

"Don't make no difference w'ere yer are," Ma said with a bitter laugh. "There's lunatics everywhere, all depends on luck."

"But there've been two pretty horrible murders here in Whitechapel," Tallulah said, staring at Ma Baines, her voice low and shivery. "That hasn't happened anywhere else."

"Course it 'as!" Ma said abruptly. "Were one just like these w'en I were in Mile End. Six year ago, mebbe seven."

"What do you mean . . . just like these?" Charlotte's voice came out huskily, as if she had something in her throat.

"Jus' the same," Ma repeated. " 'Ands tied, fingers and toes broke or pulled out o' joint, garter 'round 'er arm, an' soaked in cold water . . . all over the place, 'ead, shoulders, 'air."

Tallulah gasped as if she had been struck.

Emily turned and stared at Charlotte.

For seconds there was icy, pricking silence. The floorboards creaked overhead as someone walked across them on the story above.

"Who did it?" Charlotte forced the words out at last between frozen lips.

Ma shrugged. "Gawd knows. 'E weren't never found. Rozzers stopped lookin' arter a while. Jus' like they will this time, w'en they don' find no one."

"What . . . what kind of a girl was she?" Emily asked, her voice also hoarse.

Ma shook her head.

"Dunno 'er name. Forget it. Jus' young, though, a beginner. Probably 'er first week or so, poor little thing. Pretty, 'bout sixteen or seventeen, so they said." Her face pinched with momentary pity. "Funny, but they never made that much fuss about it. Papers din't write it up too much. O' course that were before the Ripper an' all. Still, they're sure as 'ell burns takin' it out on the rozzers this time. Wouldn't wanna be one o' them now." She lifted one broad shoulder. "But then 'oo wants ter be a rozzer anyway?" She looked at Emily. "D'yer want the rooms or not, luv? I in't got time ter sit an' talk wif yer."

"No thank you," Charlotte answered for them. "Not at the moment. We'll think a bit harder. Maybe it's not what we're looking for right now." And she rose to her feet, steadying herself on the arm of the chair a moment. Her knees were wobbling. She made her way back along the corridor and out into Chicksand Street with Emily at her elbow and Tallulah, moving as if in a dream, a pace behind. The cold air hit her face like a slap, and she barely noticed it.

Pitt had slept badly the previous night. It seemed as if half the night he lay motionless in bed, afraid to move in case he woke Charlotte. When she was troubled she slept lightly. When one of the children was ill, the slightest noise reached her and she sat up almost immediately. Since the second murder she had been aware of his nightmares and of the fact that he could not rest. Even if he turned over too frequently, she would be disturbed and waken.

He lay in the dark, eyes wide open, watching the faint pattern on the ceiling from the distant gas lamps in the street through the bedroom curtains. If he slept he dreamed of Costigan's despairing face, his self-loathing and his fear. Why had he all but admitted killing Ada, if he did not? Were his words—"I done 'er"—intended only to mean that in some way he felt responsible for her behavior, and thus for her death, but only indirectly? He had confessed to a quarrel, to striking out at her. Was it possible he had knocked her insensible but not actually been the one to kill her? He had always denied the cruelty, the fingers and toes. He had even denied the garter, which was hardly an offense, and the water.

Why, if it was true? It could hardly make any difference. He would be hanged exactly the same either way. And since the wardens believed it of him, it would not mitigate their treatment of him either.

Certainly he could not have been guilty of killing Nora Gough.

Who was the fair-haired man who had been seen going into Nora's room shortly before she was killed? How could he possibly have left without any one of the dozen or so people around having seen him?

Jago Jones's words swirled around in his head. Surely they had to be the answer . . . either when he left he had looked so different no one had recognized him as the same man or else, simpler still, he had not left!

Was the fair wavy hair a wig? Had he actually left with a different coat on, and different hair? Then what had happened to the coat? Did he carry it? And the wig? His own hair could be any color or texture at all.

Pitt needed to go back and question all the people again, to see if they remembered anyone at all leaving who could have been disguised with a wig.

How could they know that? You can carry a wig in a pocket. Then they would have to have a pocket. A trouser pocket would be too small, it would make a bulge. Perhaps they might remember the coat. Not many people in Myrdle Street had full-length overcoats, let alone well-cut ones.

What about the other possibility, that he had not left at all but had gone to another floor in the same building? He had not thought of looking upwards, to the women on the floor above. They may have continued doing business with whoever was already in the building. The police presence on the floor below would deter new custom, but those already there might well fill in their time pleasantly. They could not leave until the police had gone, from the very natural desire not to be identified. That would need no further explanation.

When he went back to Myrdle Street tomorrow, he must also question all the women on the floor above to get descriptions of all their clients of the night. He should have done it at the time. That was a bad oversight.

He lay staring up at the darkness. Charlotte was breathing evenly beside him. He listened and there was no variation in the soft sound. She was deeply asleep. Or else lying there also pretending to be and not wanting to disturb him, let him know that she too was sleepless, and worried, and frightened.

Cornwallis would back him, but he might not be able to save his job if Costigan were pardoned, or even if he were not. And perhaps he should not be able to. If Pitt had caused an innocent man to be hanged, perhaps he should lose his job. Maybe he was not man enough to fill Micah Drummond's position anyway? He was promoted beyond his ability. Farnsworth would have smiled at that. He never thought Pitt was ready for command . . . not the right background or breeding.

Vespasia would be hurt. She had always had confidence in him. She would be let down. She would never say so, but she would not be able to help feeling it. Most of all, he would have let Charlotte down. She would not say anything either, and in a way that would almost make it worse.

He drifted into uneasy sleep, and woke again with a start.

What if it was Jago Jones, after all, with a fair wig on? He was laughing at Pitt, making the suggestion himself, because he was so sure Pitt could never piece it together, or even if he did, he could not prove it.

It was nearly morning. He was stiff, longing to stretch and turn, even to get up and pace the floor to help him to think. But if he woke Charlotte now she would not get back to sleep again. This would be selfish, unnecessary.

He lay still until six o'clock, and unintentionally went back to sleep.

He woke with a start at half past seven, with Charlotte touching him gently, shaking him a little.

It was half past nine before he was back in Myrdle Street, and highly unwelcome. As usual the women were in bed after a long night, and no one wanted to talk to a policeman and answer questions they had already answered several times. He started on the floor above, disturbing the residents one by one and having to wait while they roused themselves, threw a little water on their faces to startle themselves awake, and then put on a robe or a shawl and stumbled through to the kitchen, where Pitt sat with the kettle on, topping up the teapot regularly and asking endless, patient questions.

"No, I don't 'ave no customer wif fair, wavy 'air."

"No, 'e were bald, like a bleedin' egg."

"No. Even 'is muvver wouldn't 'a' said he were young! Geez, she must 'a' bin dead since Noah landed 'is ark! 'E's fifty if 'e's a day!"

"No, 'e were gray."

"Could he have looked fair in the gaslight?"

"Mebbe . . . but not wavy. Straight as stair rods."

And so it went on. He questioned every woman meticulously, but no one had seen any man who could have answered the description Edie had given of Nora's last customer.

He went back down again, and found Edie herself, by now almost ready to consider getting up in the normal course of her day. It was three o'clock in the afternoon.

"Describe him again," he said wearily.

"Look, mister, I din't even see 'is face, just 'is back as 'e went in!" she said in exasperation. "I din't take no notice. 'E were jus' anuvver customer. I din't know 'e were gonna kill 'er, let alone . . ." She stopped and shuddered, her fat body tight under her robe.

"I know. Just close your eyes and bring back what you saw, however briefly. Take a moment or two. You saw the man who killed her, Edie." He spoke gently, trying not to frighten her. He needed her to clear her mind so she could concentrate. "Describe exactly what you saw. You may be the only way we shall catch him." He tried to keep the desperation out of his voice.

She caught it, in spite of his effort.

"I know," she whispered. "I know I'm the only one wot saw 'im, 'ceptin' them wot 'e killed." She stopped, leaning over the kitchen table, her fat elbows resting on it, pulling her robe tight, her black hair over her shoulders, her eyes closed.

Pitt waited.

" 'E were quite tall, like," she said at last. "Not 'eavy—in fact, 'e looked sort o', well, not thickset. I reckon as I thought 'e were young. Jus' the way 'e stood." She opened her eyes and looked at Pitt. "But I could be wrong. Tha's just wot I felt."

"Good. Go on," he encouraged. "Describe his coat, the back of his head, whatever else you saw. Tell me exactly. What was his hair like? How was it cut? Was it long or short? Did he have side-whiskers, did you see?"

She closed her eyes obediently. " 'Is coat were sort o' gray-green. The collar were . . . were turned up 'igh, over the bottom of 'is 'air, so I reckon 'is 'air must 'a' bin quite longish. I couldn't see the ends of it. Could've bin cut any'ow. Come ter that, could've gorn all down 'is back!" She gave an abrupt, jerking laugh. "An' I din't see no side-whiskers. Reckon 'e din't turn 'is 'ead enough. Beautiful 'air, 'e 'ad, though. Wouldn't mind 'air like that meself. Makes me think o' Ella Baker, wot lives up the street. She got gorgeous 'air, just like that." She opened her eyes and looked at Pitt again. "Mebbe she 'as a bruvver?" she said jokingly. "An' mebbe 'e's a lunatic an' all."

Pitt stared at her.

"She in't got a bruvver!" she said in amazement. "Yer can't think as . . . I don' mean . . ." Then she stopped, her eyes widening with a slow, terrible horror.

"What?" Pitt demanded. "What is it? What do you know, Edie?"

"She an' Nora did fall out summink awful over Johnny Voss . . ."

"Why? Who's Johnny Voss? Is that the man Nora was going to marry?"

"Yeah. On'y 'e were goin' ter marry Ella first . . . at least she thought 'e were. Actual—I thought 'e were too. Then Nora come along . . . an' 'e fancied 'er instead, an' she made the most of it. Well, yer would, wouldn't yer? 'Oo wouldn't sooner be married ter a decent sort o' bloke than make yer way like this?" She barely looked around her, but her gestures drew in the whole shabby, shared room, the tenement, its occupants and their lives.

"Yes," Pitt agreed. There was no need for more words than that. "Thank you, Edie." He left the kitchen and went back to the room in which Nora had died. It was still as she had left it, bed unmade, sheets rumpled, only the pillows were in the center where he had tossed them after finding the handkerchief.

He stood in the center of the floor for several moments, wondering what he was looking for, where even to begin. The bed. The floor around it.

He bent down and began with the floor, peering for anything at all that would bear out his theory. There would be nothing here to prove it, only small things that might help.

There was nothing.

He stood up and threw the bedcovers aside, running his hands gently, very slowly, over the sheets.

He found it on the top sheet, first one, then another, then several—golden fair hairs, very long, sixteen or eighteen inches, and wavy . . . hair that would never come from a man's head, and far too fair for Nora Gough.

Ella Baker, with her hair tucked under her high coat collar, a coat borrowed from a client or a friend, and a pair of men's trousers, perhaps over her own skirts tucked up, just under the coat's length. She would let the skirts down as she left, undo her hair, and she would be invisible. It would explain why this had been more of a fight. She was taller and stronger than Nora, much heavier, but still far short of the strength of a man.

But why on earth would she have killed Ada McKinley? And what was her grudge against FitzJames? That could be anything . . . a slight, an abuse in the past, an injury not necessarily to her but to someone she loved . . . even a child lost. Perhaps she had been employed by the FitzJames family at some point in the past. That was an aspect he had never considered. He should have. A servant abused and dismissed would have a bitter grudge. When he heard about the butler who had got Ada pregnant, he should have looked at all the servants the FitzJameses had ever had. Young FitzJames would not be above seducing a handsome parlor maid and then having his father put her out in the street.

It all looked obvious now.

He left the house rapidly and walked down Old Montague Street and along Osborn Street, where he found Binns on his beat, then they went the few hundred yards' distance to the tenement where he knew Ella Baker lived. He remembered Ewart had questioned her before about the possibility of her having seen the man leave, or of even having seen Finlay FitzJames. Ewart had said she was distressed then, obviously under pressure of extreme emotion. He had supposed it to be the natural terror and pity they all felt, knowing there had been another murder, and the shock and dismay that Costigan should have been hanged for a crime it now looked impossible for him to have committed.

And yet she had allowed him to be hanged. That was a double guilt that must have torn at her.

He banged on the door until the pimp who also lived on the premises came and opened it. He was unshaved and smelled of stale beer.

"What yer want?" he said abruptly, looking at Pitt and not seeing Binns behind him. "Yer too early. Geez, can't yer wait till evenin', yer bastard?"

Binns moved forward.

"Police," Pitt said curtly. "I wish to talk to Ella Baker now!"

The man looked at Pitt's face and Binns's bulky form, and decided against arguing. He allowed them in, sullenly, and led them to Ella's door. He knocked on it and shouted her name.

After a moment or two she came. She was a handsome woman, in a big, clean-cut way. Her features were strong, a trifle coarse. Her glory was her hair, thick, waving, the color of ripe wheat, dark, dull gold. It hung around her shoulders and down her back.

"Thank you," Pitt dismissed the pimp, who went off sullenly, grumbling to himself. Pitt went inside the room and closed the door, leaving Binns standing outside it. The windows were small and two stories up.

"What you want this time?" Ella asked, staring at him, her brow furrowed.

"I can understand your killing Nora," he said levelly. "She took Johnny Voss from you, and your one chance of marrying and getting out of here. But why Ada McKinley? What did she do to you?"

All the blood drained from her face. She swayed, and for several moments he thought she was going to faint. But he did not move to help her. He had been caught that way before, and had someone turn in an instant to a clawing, scratching fury. He remained where he was, his back to the door.

"I . . ." She gasped, choking on the sudden dryness of her own throat. "I . . . I never touched Ada, swear ter Gawd!"

"But you killed Nora. . . ."

She said nothing.

"If I were to pull away that high neck of your dress, I'd see where she scratched you, trying to fight you off, fighting for her life . . ."

"No I never!" she denied, glaring at him. "You can't prove I did!"

"Yes I can, Ella," he said calmly. "You were seen."

" 'Oo seen me?" she demanded. "They're a liar!"

"You stole a man's coat, a good one, well-cut, and hitched your dress up so your skirts wouldn't be seen. You had your hair under the coat. You looked like a man, but your hair was recognized. Not many people have hair like yours, Ella, beautiful, long, gold hair." He watched her white face. "I found strands of it in Nora's bed, where you struggled and she pulled some of it out, fighting for her life . . ."

"Stop it!" she shouted. "Yeah, I killed the greedy little cow! She took my man. Did it deliberate. She knew 'ow I felt abaht 'im, an' she still did it. Proud of 'erself she were. Gloated. Tol' me as she would move up ter Mile End an' 'ave a nice 'ouse, all to 'erself, an' 'ave kids an' never 'ave ter be touched by another drunken layabaht or sleazy sod cheatin' on 'is wife again."

"So you tied her up, broke her fingers and toes, and then strangled her." Pitt said with loathing.

Her face was pasty white, but her eyes blazed.

"No I bleedin' didn't! I 'ad a row wif 'er an' I 'it 'er. We fought an' I 'eld 'er by the throat. Yeah, I strangled 'er, but I never touched 'er fingers an' toes. I dunno 'oo did that, an' I dunno why!"

Pitt did not believe her, he could not. Yet his instincts were hard and bright that she was not lying.

"Why did you kill Ada?" he repeated.

"I din't!" she shouted back at him. "I din't kill Ada! I never even know'd 'er! I thought it were Bert Costigan, jus' like you did. If it weren't 'im, I dunno 'oo it were!"

He remembered with a sickening jolt Costigan's denials that he had broken Ada's fingers and toes, his indignation and confusion that he should even be accused. His eyes looked just like hers, frightened, indignant, utterly bewildered.

"But you killed Nora!" he repeated. He meant to sound certain of it. It was not a question, it was a charge.

"Yeah . . . I s'pose there in't no use denyin' it now. But I never broke 'er fingers, an' I never touched Ada! I never even bin there!"

Pitt had no idea whether he believed her or not. Looking at her, hearing her voice, he felt sure she spoke the truth; but his brain said it was ridiculous. She was admitting killing Nora. Why deny killing Ada? The punishment would be no worse, and no one would believe her anyway.

"I never killed Ada!" she said loudly. "I never did them things to Nora neither!"

"Why did you try to implicate Finlay FitzJames?" he asked.

She looked nonplussed. " 'Oo?"

"Finlay FitzJames," he repeated. "Why did you put his handkerchief and button in Nora's room?"

"I dunno wotjer talkin' abaht!" She looked totally bewildered. "I never 'eard of 'im. 'Oo is 'e?"

"Didn't you once work in the FitzJames house?"

"I never worked in any 'ouse. I were never a bleedin' 'ousemaid ter nobody!"

He still did not know whether to believe her or not.

"Perhaps. But it doesn't make a lot of difference now. Come on. I'm arresting you for the killing of Nora. Don't make it more un-pleasant for yourself than it has to be. Let the other women see you leave with some dignity."

She jerked her head up and ran her hands through her glorious hair, staring at him defiantly. Then the spirit went out of her, and she drooped again, and allowed him to lead her out.

"Well, thank God for that," Ewart said with a sigh, leaning back in his chair in the Whitechapel police station. "I admit I didn't think we'd do it." He looked up at Pitt with a smile. All the tension seemed to drain out of him, as if an intolerable burden had been lifted and suddenly he could breathe without restriction, free from inner pain. Even the fear which had haunted him from the begin-ning was gone. He did not grudge Pitt the respect due him. "I should say you did it," he corrected. "I didn't do much, as it turned out." He folded his hands over his stomach. "So it was Ella Baker all along. I never thought of a woman. Never crossed my mind. Should have."

"She swears she didn't kill Ada," Pitt said, sitting down opposite him. "Or break Nora's fingers and toes."

Ewart was unperturbed. "Well, she would, but that doesn't mean anything. Don't know why she bothers. Won't make any differ-ence now."

"And she swears she didn't implicate Finlay FitzJames," Pitt added. "She says she's never heard of him, and never been in domes-tic service."

Ewart shrugged. "I suppose she's lying, although I've no idea why she should bother. Anyway, it hardly matters." He smiled. "The case is solved. And without any really unpleasant effects. That's a damned sight more than I dared hope for. I always thought FitzJames was innocent," he added quickly, for a moment uncomfortable again. "I just . . . thought it would be very difficult to prove it."

Pitt stood up.

"Are you going to tell FitzJames?" Ewart asked. "Put the family's mind at rest."

"Yes. Yes, I am."

"Good." He smiled, a curious, half-bitter expression. "I'm very pleased. You deserve that."

"Good," Augustus FitzJames said tersely when Pitt informed him that Ella Baker had been arrested and charged with the murder of Nora Gough. "I assume you will charge her with the death of the other woman as well?"

"No. There's no evidence of that, and she doesn't admit to it," Pitt replied. Once again they were in the library, and this time the fire was lit, casting a warmth in the chilly evening.

"Well, I suppose it doesn't matter." Augustus was not particularly interested. "She'll hang for the second one. Everyone will know she committed the first as well, since they were apparently identical. Thank you for coming to inform me, Superintendent. You have done an excellent job . . . this time. Pity about the man . . . er . . . Costigan. But there's nothing to be done about it." His tone was dismissive. He rocked very gently back and forth on the balls of his feet. "Sort of man we're all better without anyway. Filthy trade, living on the immoral earnings of women. Belonged in jail, if not on the end of a rope. Might have finished up there sooner or later anyway."

If Pitt had not been responsible for Costigan's death, he would have retaliated with his opinion of such thoughts, the deep horror they inspired in him, but his own part was too profound.

"Did Ella Baker ever work for you, Mr. FitzJames?" he asked, tangled threads, questions unanswered still tugging at the back of his mind.

"Don't think so." Augustus frowned. "In fact, I'm sure she didn't. Why?"

"I wondered how she obtained your son's belongings in order to leave them at the scene of her crimes, and above all, why she should want to."

"No idea. Stole them, I expect," Augustus said tersely. "Hardly matters now. Thank you for coming yourself, Superintendent. It is good to know the police are not as incompetent as some of our most lurid and ill-informed newspapers would have us believe." He pursed his lips. "Now, if you will excuse me, I have an appointment this evening. Good day to you."

Pitt opened his mouth to protest further, but Augustus had already reached for the bell rope to summon the butler to show Pitt out, and there was nothing more he could say. Augustus was obviously unprepared to discuss the matter any further.

"Good evening, Mr. FitzJames," Pitt replied, and had to leave as the butler opened the door and smiled at him.

CHAPTER
TWELVE

Pitt returned home late and tired, but it was the weariness of victory, even if there were still aspects of the case which puzzled him profoundly and which he feared he would now never resolve. It was already dark and the gas lamps were haloed with mist. There was a damp in the air, and a smell of rotting leaves, turned earth and the suggestion of the first frost.

He opened his front door and as soon as he came in the hallway he saw Charlotte at the top of the stairs. She was dressed in a very plain skirt and blouse, looking almost dowdy, and her hair was coming out of its pins. She came down so quickly he was afraid she was going to slip and fall.

"What is it?" he asked, seeing the eagerness in her face. "What's happened?"

"Thomas." She took a deep breath. She was too full of her own news to notice that he also had something urgent to say. "Thomas, I did a little investigating myself. It was all quite safe . . ."

The very fact that she mentioned safety told him immediately that it was not.

"What?" he demanded, facing her when she was on the bottom step. "What did you do? I assume Emily was with you?"

"Yes." She sounded relieved, as if that were a good thing, something in mitigation. "And Tallulah FitzJames. Listen to me first, then be furious afterwards if you must, but I found out something really important, and terrible."

"So did I," he retorted. "I discovered who killed Nora Gough, and why, and obtained a confession. Now, what did you discover?"

She was startled.

"Who?" she demanded. "Who, Thomas?"

"Another prostitute. A woman named Ella Baker." He outlined how they had assumed it was a man because of the coat, and how she had been able to disappear without anyone's seeing her. They were still standing in the hall at the bottom of the stairs.

"Why?" she asked, her face reflecting none of the sense of victory he expected.

"Because Nora took the man she was going to marry, her escape from the life she had. And maybe she even loved him as well." He put his hands up and touched her shoulders, holding her gently. "I'm sorry if I spoiled your news. I know you want to investigate for my sake, and I am not ungrateful." He bent to kiss her, but she pulled away, frowning.

"Why did she kill Ada McKinley?"

"She denies it," he replied, aware as he said it of the weight of dissatisfaction heavy inside him. It was a thin victory, and the substance of it seemed weaker every hour he thought of it.

"Why?" she asked. "That doesn't make any sense, Thomas. They can't hang her twice!" Her face was very pale, even in the glow of the gaslight from the hall chandelier. "Or three times."

"No, of course they can't," he agreed. "What do you mean 'three times'? There were only two murders."

"No there weren't." Her voice was barely audible. "That's what I was going to tell you that we found out. There was a third, about six years ago . . . a young girl, just a beginner. She had only been on the streets for a week or two. She was killed in Mile End, exactly the same way as the others . . . the garter, the fingers and toes, the cross-buttoned boots, even the water . . . everything. They never found who did it."

He was stunned. For long seconds he stood motionless, as if he had not truly understood what she had said, and yet it filled his mind. Another crime, six years ago, in Mile End. It had to be the same person. Hadn't it? There could not possibly be two . . . three people who would commit exactly the same gruesome, senseless murder, three people unconnected? And who was the first victim? Why had he not heard of her? Why had Ewart not known, and told him?

"I'm sorry," Charlotte said very quietly. "It doesn't help, does it?"

He focused his eyes again, looking at her.

"Who was she? Do you know anything about her?"

"No. Only that she was new on the streets. I didn't learn her name."

His mind was still whirling.

"Couldn't Ella Baker have killed her too?" Charlotte asked. "Maybe she tried to take something from her? Did she say why she wanted to implicate Finlay?"

"No." He turned and walked towards the parlor. He was suddenly cold standing in the hall, and very tired. He wanted to sit down as close to the fire as he could.

She followed him and sat opposite, in her usual chair.

The fire was burning a little low. He put more coal on it, banking it high and prodding it with the poker to make it burn up more rapidly.

"No," he went on. "She denied it. Claimed she had never heard of the FitzJameses, and Augustus said he had never heard of her." He sat back in his chair again. The flames were mounting in the fireplace as the new coal caught, the heat growing, tingling the skin. "And Ewart doesn't care," he added. "He's so damned glad it's over, without having to arrest FitzJames, he doesn't want to know anything more about it."

"And Mr. Cornwallis?"

"I haven't seen him yet. It was late by the time I'd been to the FitzJameses'. I'll tell him in the morning. And speak to Ella Baker again. Perhaps I'd better find out about the other crime first. Six years ago?"

"Yes, about that."

He sighed.

"Would you like a cup of tea?" she asked. "Or cocoa?"

"Yes . . . yes please." He left her to decide which to bring, and sat hunched in his chair in the slowly increasing warmth while the fire strengthened and flames leaped up the chimney.

In the morning he was in the bitter chill of Newgate asking to see Ella Baker, memories of Costigan's face, white and frightened, filling his mind. Of all the duties he ever had to perform, this was perhaps the worst. It was a different kind of pain from that of going to tell the relatives of a victim. That was appalling, but it was a cleaner thing. It would eventually heal. This wrenched him in a way that was always sickeningly real and new. Time did not dull it or inure him in any measure at all.

Ella was sitting in her cell, still dressed in her own clothes, although they were not particularly different from prison garb. He had arrested her before she was dressed for work.

"What you want?" she said dully when she saw him. "Come ter gloat, 'ave you?"

"No." He closed the cell door behind him. He looked at her pale face, hollow hopeless eyes, and the glory of hair over her shoulders. Curiously, although he had seen both Ada and Nora, and seen their broken hands, their dead faces, disfigured in the last struggle, all he could see now was Ella and her despair. "I have no pleasure in it," he told her. "A certain relief because it's over, but that's all."

"So wot yer come for?" she said, still half disbelievingly, although something in his eyes, or his voice, touched her.

"Tell me about the first one, Ella," he replied. "What did she do to you? She was only young, a beginner. Why did you kill her?"

She stared at him with total incomprehension.

"Yer mad, you are! I dunno wot yer talkin' abaht! I 'it Nora, then we fought an' I throttled 'er. I never broke 'er fingers ner toes, ner chucked water over 'er, ner did up 'er boots! I never touched Ada McKinley. I never 'eard of 'er till she were killed. An' as fer another, I dunno wot yer on abaht. There weren't no other, far as I knowed."

"About six years ago, in Mile End," he elaborated.

"Six year ago!" She was incredulous, then she started to laugh, a high, harsh sound, full of pain, dark with fear beyond control. "Six year ago I were in Manchester. Married an' went up there. Me 'us-band died. I come 'ome an' took ter the streets. On'y way ter keep a roof over me 'ead, 'ceptin' the match factory. 'Ad a cousin 'oo died o' phossie jaw. Ter 'ell wi' that. Sooner be 'anged." Suddenly tears filled her eyes. "Jus' as well, eh?"

Pitt ached to be able to say something to comfort her. He felt the terrors closing around her, the darkness from which there was no es-cape, but there was nothing. Pity was no use now and to talk of hope was a mockery.

He smiled in answer to her bitter humor. There was some courage in it. He could admire that.

"What was your husband's name?" he asked.

"Joe Baker . . . Joseph. You gonna check on me?" She sniffed. "A good man, Joe were. Drunk too much, but 'e weren't bad. Never 'it me, jus' fell over 'isself. Stupid sod!"

"What did he do?"

" 'E worked the canals till 'e 'ad an accident an' drowned. Drunk again, I s'pose."

"I'm sorry," Pitt said quietly. He meant it.

She shrugged. "Don' matter now."

———

Pitt went from Newgate to the Mile End police station and asked to see the most senior officer present who had been there over six years. He was shown, by a somewhat puzzled young sergeant, up to the cramped office of Inspector Forrest, a lean man with receding black hair and sad, dark eyes.

"Superintendent Pitt," he said with surprise, rising to his feet. "Good morning, sir. What can we do for you?"

"Good morning, Inspector." Pitt closed the door behind him and took the proffered seat. "I understand you were here in Mile End six years ago?"

"Yes. I see in the newspapers you got our murderer." Forrest sat down behind his desk. "Well done. Damn sight more than we ever managed. Mind, I was only a sergeant then."

"So you did have one exactly the same?" Pitt found it difficult to keep the anger out of his voice.

"Yes. Far as I can tell," Forrest agreed, sitting forward in his chair. "Right down to the last detail. Weren't much in the papers about ours, but I'll remember it for the rest of my life. Poor little thing. Can't 'ave been more than fifteen or sixteen. Pretty, they say, before he did that to her."

"She," Pitt corrected.

"Oh." Forrest shook his head. "Yes . . . she. Sorry, I just had it fixed in my mind all these years that it was a man. Looked like a crime rooted in sex to me, the kind of perverted sex of a man that has to hurt and humiliate before he can get any pleasure. Sort of person who has to have power over someone, see them totally helpless. Evil. Still can't believe it was a woman. Though, s'pose it must be, if she confessed."

"No, she didn't confess, except to the last one, Nora Gough. In fact, she said she was in Manchester six years ago."

Forrest's eyes widened. "Well, it has to have been the same person. Even in London, sink that it is, we can't have two lunatics going around doing that to women."

"Why didn't you tell me about your case?" Pitt asked, trying not to sound accusatory, and failing.

"Me?" Forrest looked at him with surprise. "Why didn't I tell you?"

"Yes. For heaven's sake, it might have helped us! We should at least have known! We could have found out what they had in common and who might have known all three."

"I didn't tell you because . . . Didn't Inspector Ewart tell you? He was on the case!"

Pitt froze.

"I took it for granted that he'd have told you," Forrest said reasonably. "You saying he didn't?" There was disbelief in his face and in his voice. He was watching Pitt as if he could scarcely believe him.

Pitt could scarcely believe it himself. Images of Ewart filled his mind, memories of his anger, his misery, the fear in him.

But there was no point in lying. The truth was obvious anyway.

"No, he never mentioned it."

Now it was Forrest's turn to sit in silence.

"Do you know Ella Baker?" Pitt asked him. "Or know of her? Have you ever heard her name?"

Forrest looked blank. "No. And I know most of the women on the streets around here. But I'll ask Dawkins. He's been here for years and he knows 'em all." He rose to his feet and went out, excusing himself, and returned a few minutes later with a large, elderly sergeant with gray hair. "Dawkins, have you ever heard of a woman, a tart around here, called Ella Baker?" He turned to Pitt. "What did she look like, sir?"

"Tall, ordinary sort of face," Pitt answered. "But very beautiful fair hair, thick and wavy."

Dawkins thought carefully for a moment, then shook his head. "No sir. Nearest to that description is Lottie Bridger, an' she died o' the pox sometime early this year."

"You're absolutely sure, Dawkins?" Forrest urged.

"Yes sir. Never 'eard the name Ella Baker, an' never 'ad a girl on the streets 'round 'ere like you said."

"Thank you, Dawkins," Forrest dismissed him. "That's all."

"Yes sir. Thank you, sir." Dawkins left, looking puzzled, closing the door behind him with a sharp click.

"What does that mean?" Forrest regarded Pitt with open confusion. "Are we saying as this woman didn't do our killing then?"

"I don't know what we're saying," Pitt confessed. "Have you got records of this case I can look at?"

"Course. I'll have them sent for." Forrest excused himself again, and it was a long, frustrating quarter of an hour before he returned with a slim folder of papers. "This is it, sir. Isn't a lot."

"Thank you." Pitt took it, opened it and read. Forrest was right; there was very little indeed, but the details were the same as in the deaths of Ada McKinley and Nora Gough. It was all set out clinically, unemotionally, in fine copperplate handwriting. The name of the victim had an air of unreality: Mary Smith. Was that really her name? Or did they simply not know what to call her? She was new in the area, new to prostitution. There was nothing else said about her, no place of origin, no family mentioned, no possessions listed.

Pitt read carefully from the description of objects found on the premises. No mention was made of anything which could be called a clue. Certainly there was nothing belonging to Finlay FitzJames, or any other gentleman.

He read the statements of witnesses, but they conveyed little. They had seen men come and go, but what else were they to expect in the room of a prostitute. There were no personal details, only that they were fairly young.

It was all insubstantial. No wonder the officer in charge had failed to find the killer. And the officers were Constable Trask, and Constable Porter, with Ewart the inspector in charge. The surgeon who had examined the body both at the scene of the crime and later was Lennox.

Why had neither of them mentioned it to Pitt? He could think of no justifiable answer.

"I don't remember this in the papers," he said to Forrest, who had sat silent throughout, his face furrowed with anxiety.

"It wasn't in," he replied. "Only 'er death, that's all. None o' the details. You know how it is: keep it back, might help to trap someone. They knew something, let something slip . . ."

"Yes, I know," Pitt agreed, but the answer troubled him deeply. It made inescapable the darkest fears in his mind.

When he faced Ewart with it in his office in Whitechapel two hours later, Ewart stared at him blankly, his face stunned, eyes as if mesmerized.

"Well?" Pitt demanded. "For God's sake, man, why didn't you tell me about the first case?"

"We didn't solve it," Ewart said desperately. "There wasn't anything in it that could have helped."

"Don't be ridiculous!" Pitt turned on his heel and walked over to the window, then swung around and stared back at Ewart. "You can't know whether it would have helped or not! Why would you conceal it?"

"Because it only obscures the present." Ewart's voice was rising too. "There's nothing to say it was the same person. It was Mile End, and six years ago. People copy crimes, especially mad people, wicked, stupid people who read about something and it sits in their brains, and they—"

"What newspapers?" Pitt asked curtly. "Most of those details were never released to the papers, which you know as well as I do. I never heard of the case, neither had any of the other people here working on this one. Nobody in Whitechapel connected it with the first one—but you must have. And Lennox!"

"Well, they weren't related, were they?" Ewart said with triumph of logic. "Are you saying now that you aren't sure it was Ella Baker who killed the Gough woman?"

"No I'm not." Pitt swung around and gazed out of the window

again, at the gray buildings and the darkening October sky. "She confessed to it. And I found her hair in Nora's bed, long fair hair. Nora must have pulled it out when they struggled."

"So what's the matter?" Ewart demanded with growing confidence. "I was right. The two cases are unconnected."

"How do you know that Ella Baker didn't kill the first girl, Mary Smith, or whatever her name really was?"

"I don't know. Maybe she did. It hardly matters. We can't prove the first one was her, and she'll hang for this one anyhow."

"And she says she's never heard of Finlay FitzJames," Pitt added.

Ewart hesitated. "She's lying," he said after a moment.

"And Augustus FitzJames says he's never heard of her, either," Pitt went on.

Ewart said nothing. He drew in his breath, and then let it out again silently.

"Was there anything at the scene of the first murder to incriminate Finlay?" Pitt asked curtly.

Ewart looked straight back at him. "No, of course not. If there had been I'd have mentioned it. That would have been relevant. We never had any idea who did it. There was nothing to go on . . . nothing at all."

"I see."

But Pitt did not see. He traveled from Whitechapel back to the center of the City, and went straight to Cornwallis's office.

Cornwallis welcomed him, striding forwards with his hand out, his face alight.

"Well done, Pitt. This is brilliant! I admit, I had lost hope we should have such a satisfactory outcome—and a confession, to boot." He dropped his hand, suddenly realizing something was wrong. The smile faded from his lips. His eyes clouded. "What is it, man? What now? Sit! Sit down." He gestured to one of the large, leather-covered easy chairs, and sat in the other himself. He leaned forwards, his face grave, his attention total.

Pitt told him about the crime in Mile End.

Cornwallis was stunned. "And Ewart has only just told you? That's beyond belief!"

Pitt could think of no easy way to recount what had actually happened without implicating Charlotte, and this was not a time for lies or evasions of any sort.

"Ewart didn't tell me at all," he said grimly. "My wife discovered it, and she told me." He noticed the look on Cornwallis's face, but perhaps Vespasia had made some reference or other, because he did not question what Pitt said.

"But you have spoken to Ewart?" he affirmed, his eyes dark with foreboding.

"Yes," Pitt replied. "He said he didn't mention it because he thought it irrelevant."

"That is inconceivable." Cornwallis was very earnest, his whole face filled with distress. "And Lennox was involved as well?"

"Yes. Although that is easier to understand. He may well have assumed Ewart had told me. It was Ewart's job, not his."

"But why?" Cornwallis said with exasperation. "I can't begin to understand it! Why would Ewart hide that first murder?" His hands were clenched, fidgeting. "All right, he failed to solve it, but that's no shame to him. From what you say, there were no clues to follow. The witnesses saw nothing of value. There was nothing further he could have done. Pitt . . ." He looked wretched, hardly able to bring himself to say what he meant.

"I don't know," Pitt replied to the question that had not been asked. "I can't believe Ewart was involved in a murder, let alone three. But I have to know. I'm going back to the original witnesses to the Mile End case. I know their names and the address where it happened. But it's not my station, and it's not my crime. I need your permission to question Inspector Forrest about Ewart's duties that night."

Cornwallis's face was tight with pain. He had been in command too many years not to know the weaknesses and the fallibilities of man, that courage and temptation can work side by side, and loyalty and self-deceit.

"You have it," he said quietly. "We must know. Go back to the first murder, Pitt. I can't believe Ewart is guilty himself. He certainly wasn't of the second or third, we know that. But if Ella Baker didn't do it, then for God's sake, who did?" He frowned. "Do you believe it is really credible that we have three extraordinary murders, all with the same features of torture and fetishism, the cross-buttoned boots, the water, committed by three different people?"

"It looks like it," Pitt replied. "But no, I don't believe it. It's preposterous. There is something fundamental that we don't yet know, and I have no idea what it is." He stood up.

Cornwallis rose also and went to his desk, writing Pitt a brief note of permission. He gave it to Pitt wordlessly, gripping his hard hand, his own body stiff. He held Pitt's eyes, wanting to speak, to communicate some of the emotion he felt, but there was nothing to say. He took a deep breath, hesitated, then let it out again.

Pitt nodded, then turned and left, going out into the sharp October air to hail a hansom and return once again to Mile End. It was four o'clock in the afternoon.

By quarter past five he had seen the duty rosters for the day of Mary Smith's death. There was no way in which Ewart could have been involved in her murder, just as he could not have been involved in the murders of Ada McKinley and Nora Gough.

Next he left and went to the house in Globe Road where Mary Smith had died. He asked the grayly unshaven landlord for the first witness named in the statements.

"Is Mr. Oliver Stubbs here?"

"Never 'eard of 'im," the landlord said abruptly. "Try somew'ere else." He was about to close the door on Pitt when Pitt put his foot in it and glared at him with such ferocity he hesitated.

" 'Ere, wos' matter wiv you, then? Get yer foot outer me door or I'll set the dog on yer!"

"Do that and I'll close you down," Pitt said without hesitation. "This is a murder enquiry, and if you want to avoid the rope as an accomplice, you'll do all you can to help me. Now, if Oliver Stubbs isn't here, where is he?"

"I dunno!" The man's voice rose indignantly. " 'E scarpered two years gorn. But 'e never done no murder as I knows of."

"Mary Smith," Pitt said tersely.

" 'Oo?" The man's eyes widened. "C'mon! D'yer know how many Mary Smiths there are 'rahnd 'ere? Every tart wot tries 'er hand is Mary Smith."

"Not all of them end up tortured, strangled and tied to a bed," Pitt grated between his teeth.

"Geez! That Mary Smith." The man paled under his stubble beard. "Bit late, aren't yer? That were six, seven years gorn."

"Six. I need to see the original witnesses. Get in my way and I'll find something to arrest you for."

The man turned away and yelled into the dim passageway behind him. " 'Ere! Marge! Come 'ere!"

There was no reply.

"Come 'ere, yer lazy sow!" He raised his voice even more.

There was another moment's silence, then a fat woman with ginger hair emerged from one of the back rooms and came forward.

"Yeah? Wot yer want?" She looked at Pitt with minimum curiosity.

"Weren't yer 'ere six years ago?" the man asked her.

"Yeah," she answered. "So?"

"This rozzer wants ter talk to yer. An' be nice to 'im, Marge, or 'e'll do the lot of us."

"Fer wot?" she said with a sneer. "I in't done nuffink agin the law."

"I don't care," the man replied, coughing hoarsely. "Jus' tell 'im, yer stupid mare. Yer was 'ere. Tell 'im!"

"Are you Margery Williams?" Pitt asked her.

"Yeah."

"You were one of the witnesses the police spoke to about the murder of Mary Smith six years ago?"

She looked uncomfortable, but her eyes did not waver. "Yeah. I told 'em everythin' I know. Wot yer want ter know fer now? Yer sure as 'ell in't gonna catch him."

"You said 'him.' " He looked at her closely. "Are you taking it for granted it was a man who killed her, or could it have been a woman?"

Contempt filled her face. "Wot kind o' woman does that ter 'nother woman? Geez, where do you come from, mister? Course it were a man! Din't yer look at wot I said? They wrote it all down on their little bits o' paper. Always scribblin', they was."

The man stood beside her, looking from her to Pitt and back again.

"They can't have kept it," Pitt said, realizing with surprise how much must have been thrown away once it was regarded as of no use, and the case marked "unsolved" and forgotten. "Tell me what you can remember of the man you saw, and with as much detail as possible."

"Wot in 'ell do it matter now?" She screwed up her face, eyeing him with suspicion and curiosity. "Yer never sayin' yer got someone, 'ave yer? After all them years?" She hesitated another moment, deep in thought. " 'Ere! You sayin' as it were the same one wot done Mary Smith as done the other women in Whitechapel?"

For a moment it seemed such a glaringly obvious conclusion Pitt wondered at the woman's stupidity. Then he remembered with a jolt that the details of this first death had not been published in the newspapers. If she had not seen the body herself, and the police, specifically Ewart, had not told her, then maybe she was unaware of the exact sameness of the method, even to the most bizarre detail.

"Yes," he said simply. "It is possible."

"I 'eard as it was a woman wot done 'em. In't that true then?" She swung around to the unshaven man. "That Davey Watson's a liar! 'E said as it were another tart wot done 'em. Wait till I catch 'im, the bleedin' little sod!"

"It was a woman who killed Nora Gough," Pitt said soothingly. "Now please describe this man for me as closely as you can remember, but don't add anything or leave anything out. Please."

"Right." She shrugged heavy shoulders. "There were four of 'em. All come together. One were dark an' kind o' fancy, arty-lookin', nothin' special abaht 'is face as I can remember. Jus' ordinary, 'cept 'e fancied 'isself or summink. Painter, mebbe!"

There was a clatter somewhere inside the building. A woman swore.

"The second man?" Pitt prompted.

"Pompous as a prater, 'e were, all airs like 'e thought 'e were summink."

"What did he look like?" Urgency was mounting inside him.

"Nuffin' much. Orn'ry as muck, w'en it comes ter it." She stared at him, trying to work out why he cared so much his voice was cracking. "Wouldn't know him agin if he walked in be'ind yer."

"And the third?" he pressed.

" 'Nother self-satisfied sod wot thinks 'e runs the world," she answered. " 'Andsome, though. 'Andsome face, lov'ly 'air, all thick an' waves. Would o' done a woman good, that 'air."

"Fair or dark?" Pitt felt a curious sensation of anticipation as he said it, a clenching in his stomach. Ewart had known all this. He had heard this six years ago. What terror or stupidity had kept him silent?

"Fair," she said without hesitation.

"A gentleman?"

"Yeah, if talk an' clothes makes a gent, then 'e was a gent. I wouldn't 'a' give yer tuppence fer 'im. Nasty little swine. Summit mean abaht 'im, sort o' . . . excited, like 'e were . . . I dunno." She gave up.

"And the last one?" Pitt did not want to know, but he had to, there was no evading it. "Can you remember him?"

"Yeah. 'E really were diff'rent." She shook her head a little, the ginger hair waggling from side to side. "On the thin side, but wi' one o' them faces as yer never forgets. Eyes like 'e were on fire. Inside 'is 'ead . . ."

"You mean a little mad? Or drunk? What?"

"No." She waved a fat hand impatiently. "Like 'e knew sommat inside 'isself wot were so important 'e 'ad to tell everyone. Like 'e were a poet, or one o' them musicians, or summink. 'E din't belong wi' them lot."

"I see. And what happened? Are you saying they came together, or one by one, or how?" He asked even though he knew the answer.

"All come together," she replied. "Then all went ter different rooms. All went orff tergether arter. Close, they was. White as paper. Thought they was sick drunk, till I knew wot they done . . . or wot one o' them done. Reckon as they all knew abaht it, though."

"I see. And do you know which one went in to Mary Smith?"

"Yeah." She nodded. "They all started tergether wif 'er. Then the one wi' the 'air stayed wif 'er. Then they all went back agin. I dunno which one o' them killed 'er, but I'd lay me money it were the one wi' the 'air. 'E 'ad a look in 'is eyes."

"I see." Pitt felt numb, a little sick. "Thank you, Mrs. Williams. Would you testify to that, if necessary?"

"Wot, in a court?"

"Yes."

She thought about it for a moment. She did not consult the man, who stood by sullenly, unimportant.

"Yeah," she said at last. "Yeah, if yer wants. Poor Mary. She din' deserve that. None o' my girls ever did, nor anybody else's neither. I'll see the bastard 'ang, if yer can get 'im, that is!" She gave a harsh, derisive laugh. "That all, mister?"

"Yes, for now. Thank you."

Pitt walked away slowly. It was now nearly six in the evening, and growing dark with the heavy clouds moving in from the east, a sharper wind behind them, smelling of the river, salt and dead fish and human effort.

There was no evasion possible. Margery Williams had described the four young men too precisely for there to be any but the faintest doubt, driven by hope, not reason. It had been the Hellfire Club: Thirlstone, Helliwell, Finlay and Jago Jones. Pitt was crushed by an inner misery. He walked slowly away from Mile End and towards Whitechapel. It would take him half an hour to reach Coke Street. He wished it could be longer.

He was passed by all sorts of people on their way home from offices: clerks with ink-stained fingers and stiff shoulders, some with squinting eyes after staring all day at the black letters on the white page. Shop clerks passed in twos and threes. Laborers would be finishing soon, going home to the piled tenements, each having their own narrow little place where their own people were, their own few belongings.

He crossed the street and only just avoided being struck by a hansom. It was getting dark, and considerably colder.

He turned his coat collar up and increased his pace without being aware of it. He did not intend to get there any faster; he was drawn by emotion, an anger and urgency within.

He was going straight down the Mile End Road, which would become the Whitechapel Road as it crossed Brady Street. From reluctance he had changed to wanting to get it over with as quickly as possible. He was striding along, barely seeing people on either side. The streetlamps were lit. Orange lights were brilliant through the gathering darkness, carriages mere looming shapes with riding lamps on either side, horses' hooves clattering on the wet stones, wheels hissing.

He turned left down Plumbers Row, which led into Coke Street. It was the one time and place he was almost sure of finding Jago

Jones, and he had a deep, perhaps irrational belief that Jago would not lie to him if he was faced with the truth.

He swung around the last corner and saw the cart under the gas lamp, the light shining on its handles, polished smooth where hands had gripped it day after day perhaps for generations. Jago Jones's lean figure in his shabby clothes was still serving hot soup to the last ragged figures. Beside him, working in silent unison, was Tallulah FitzJames.

Pitt watched, leaning against the wall in the shadows, until they were finished and turned to start putting it all away. There was nothing left; there never was.

"Reverend Jones." Pitt moved forward and spoke softly.

Jago looked up. He was no longer surprised to see Pitt. He had been here too often over the last weeks and months.

"Yes, Superintendent?" he said patiently.

"I'm sorry." Pitt meant it. Seldom had he regretted any necessity so much. "I cannot let the matter rest." He glanced at Tallulah, still tidying and packing away.

"What is it now?" Jago asked, his brow furrowed with puzzlement. "I don't know anything else. I have spoken to Ella Baker once or twice, but she was a very self-sufficient woman. She had no need of my counsel." He smiled ruefully. "At least, shall I say, she had no desire for it. I did not know her well enough to be aware of her agony. Perhaps that is my shortcoming, but at least for her, it is too late now."

His face in the lamplight showed nothing but sorrow and a sense of defeat. He moved farther away so Tallulah could not overhear them. "Please don't ask me to question her, Superintendent. Even if she could speak to me, whatever she said would be between her and God. All I could offer would be some shred of human comfort, and the promise that God is sometimes a kinder judge than we expect, if we are honest. And I think too, perhaps, harsher, if we are not."

"Honest, Reverend?" Pitt heard the catch in his own voice.

Jago stared at him. Perhaps he heard more of the irony, some deeper understanding, and pain than before. He half turned towards Tallulah, then changed his mind, or perhaps his belief in what he could accomplish.

"What is it, Superintendent? You say the word as if it had some greater meaning for you."

Pitt had not expected Tallulah to be there. His first instinct had been to have her leave, to face Jago with his knowledge alone. It was a matter of decency, not to confront the man before someone who obviously had the utmost respect for him. Now he realized Tallulah would have to know. It concerned her too closely. Finlay was her brother. Whatever was said here in the dark and the damp of Coke Street would eventually be just as devastating in the withdrawing room of Devonshire Street. The delay would not save her from misery.

"It does, when spoken between the two of us regarding the deaths of Ada McKinley and Nora Gough," Pitt answered his question.

Jago's eyes were unwaveringly steady.

"I know nothing about them, Superintendent."

Tallulah had finished the packing away and moved closer.

"What about Mary Smith?" Pitt asked, and neither did he flinch. "Off Globe Road, in Mile End, about six years ago. Are you going—" He stopped. Jago's face was ashen. Even in the yellow-white glare of the gas lamp he looked like a death's-head. There was no point in finishing the sentence. Jago was not going to lie. A lie would have been grotesque now, an indignity beyond redeeming.

"You were there," Pitt said quietly, trying to ignore Tallulah's eyes, staring at him with dawning horror. "You, Thirlstone, Helliwell, and Finlay FitzJames." He did not make it a question, and his voice left no room for doubt.

Jago closed his eyes very slowly. He was controlling himself with a supreme effort. He looked as if he might fall if for an instant he let go.

"I will answer for myself, Superintendent, but for no one else." He swallowed hard. His clenched hands shook. "Yes, I was there. In my younger days I did many things of which I am ashamed, but none as much as that. I drank too much, I wasted my time and valued things which were of no worth. I cared what people thought of me, not for love. Not respect or honor." He said the words bitterly. "Not whether I hurt people. Not whether my example was good or bad, only to posture and parade, wanting to be smarter and wittier than the next man."

Tallulah was still staring at him, but he seemed oblivious of her, drenched in loathing of the man he had been. She moved a step closer, but still he was unaware.

"Globe Road," Pitt said, bringing him back to the issue, not only because it was what mattered to him but because Jago's other sins, whatever they had been, were not his to judge, nor did he wish to know them.

"I was there," Jago admitted again. "I did not kill Mary Smith." His voice sank to a whisper, hoarse, as if the memory of it were still before his eyes. "But I know what was done to her, God forgive me. I have spent the rest of my life since then trying to repay—"

"Who killed her?" Pitt said gently. He believed it was not Jago, not only because he wanted to, but there was a passion in his face, a torture of guilt and memory, a self-disgust, but also a courage that he had at last spoken the truth and at the same time kept his own kind of honor.

"I will not tell you, Superintendent. I'm sorry."

Pitt hesitated only a moment. There was no real decision to make.

"Reverend . . ." He used the title intentionally. "Mary Smith was not only killed, she was tortured first and humiliated. She was tied to her own bed, with her stocking, intimate garments . . ." He saw the naked pain in Jago's face, but he did not stop. "She was terrified and hurt. Her fingers and toes were either wrenched out of their joints or the bones were broken. She wasn't a practiced whore!" He heard his own voice grating hard. "She was a young girl, just started—"

"Superintendent!" The cry was wrung from Tallulah. She stepped forward and was standing beside Jago, staring at Pitt. "You don't need to go on. We know what happened to the girls in Whitechapel. We accept that Mary Smith was the same, and that it was very terrible. Nobody, no living creature, should be treated that way, and you must find out who did it, and they must be punished—"

"Tallulah!" Jago gasped, trying to push her away. His face was streaked in the damp of the evening, or in the sweat of inner pain. "You don't . . ." He stopped, unable to go on. "You . . ." He drew in a long, shuddering breath, then turned to Pitt. "Superintendent, I understand what you are saying, and I know even better than you do just how . . . how fearful it was. I admit my part in it. I was there, and I helped conceal what was done. For that I am guilty. But I will not say more than that.

"I have done all I can in the years since then to become a man worthy of forgiveness. I began from my own sense of remorse. Now I do it for the love of the task itself. Someone has to care for these people, and my reward in it has been greater than any bound or measure. But I understand that I was an accessory after the fact in a murder, and an accomplice in concealing the truth. There is always a price. May I please take the cart back to the kitchen before I come with you? They will need it tomorrow. Someone will take over what I cannot."

"I will," Tallulah said immediately. "Billy Shaw will help me, if I ask him, and Mrs. Moss."

"Thank you." Jago acknowledged this without looking at her.

"I am not taking you, Reverend," Pitt said slowly. "I don't believe you murdered Mary Smith, and I know you didn't murder either of the two women here at Whitechapel."

Jago stood without moving, confused. Still, he could not bring himself to look at Tallulah. He kept his head turned away from her, unable to bear what he might see in her eyes.

Pitt hesitated.

"Jago," Tallulah said softly, taking him by the arm. "You cannot protect him anymore. It was Finlay, wasn't it? Somehow Papa managed to have it hidden, covered over. He must have bought the policeman."

A rush of memory flooded over Pitt, a score of small impressions. Ewart's pride in his son, the carefully bought education, the daughter who had married well. Such an achievement! But at what price?

He recalled Ewart's eagerness to blame someone else, the look on his face when Augustus's name was mentioned, the strange mixture of fear and hatred. It was hideously obvious now why he had destroyed the statements of the witnesses to the Globe Street murder and marked the case unsolved, and why he had not mentioned it to Pitt. What nightmares he must have endured when he thought Finlay had committed the same crime again, and Ewart again had to conceal it for him, but this time with a superior officer called in and handed the investigation over his head. No wonder he couldn't sleep, couldn't eat, came into the station looking like a man who had opened a door on hell.

And then Pitt had arrested Albert Costigan, and it had seemed indubitable that he was guilty. He had not even denied it himself. Ewart must have thought himself free.

Then there was another crime, in Myrdle Street. A second nightmare for Ewart . . . a second torture of trying to prove Finlay had not done it, of guiding Pitt step by step away from Finlay and towards some other explanation, any other at all!

And Pitt had found Ella Baker. And she too had not denied her guilt.

Tallulah was standing very close to Jago, her arm around him, almost as if she were supporting him. Her face was wet with the settling mist, shadows around her eyes. Shock and misery were stamped deep into the lines of her features. But there was also a strength in her which had never shown itself before, almost a luminosity, as if she had found within herself something which she knew was precious, and indestructible, and, in time, of greater beauty than anything Devonshire Street could give her, or take from her.

"You cannot protect him," she repeated, searching Jago's face.

"Neither can I betray him," Jago whispered, but he leaned a little towards her, half unwillingly, as if he did it against his will but could barely help himself. "I gave my word. I was also to blame. I went. I knew what was in him, the anger, the need for power, and I still went."

"In Finlay FitzJames?" Pitt said.

Jago did not answer him.

Pitt knew there was no more purpose in pressing him. He had not yet sufficient evidence to arrest Finlay for the murder of Mary Smith, not if Jago would not speak. Margery Williams might recognize the four men, but six years had passed. And what was such a woman's testimony against that of Finlay FitzJames and the weight of his father's power?

Would Tallulah go home to Devonshire Street and warn Finlay? Might Pitt even get there and find Finlay gone, possibly to Europe, or even farther? Perhaps to America?

The three of them stood under the gaslight in Coke Street, motionless, Jago and Tallulah close, her arm around him, Pitt opposite. They were all cold. The damp had settled with a clinging, biting chill. Down on the river a foghorn sounded, thin and miserable, echoing across the water.

"Who put Finlay's cuff link and club badge in Ada McKinley's room?" Pitt asked curiously. "Was that you? Or one of the other two?"

"It wasn't me," Jago said with surprise. "I'd stake all I possess, which admittedly isn't much, that it wasn't either of them. Helliwell is terrified he'll be tarred with the brush of disrepute, never mind murder. Thirlstone simply wants to forget the whole thing. The Hellfire Club broke up, and we swore never to see each other again."

Tallulah looked from Jago to Pitt, her brow furrowed.

"It doesn't make sense, Superintendent. The people whom you say killed the women live in Whitechapel. They can't ever have heard of Finlay, much less have his possessions. And why would it be Mortimer, or Norbert either?" Her face was very white, her eyes hollow. "The one person it couldn't be is Finlay himself." Her voice sank to a whisper. "He was guilty the first time, but not the second. I know that, Superintendent, I swear I really know it! I did see him at the party!"

"I believe you, Miss FitzJames. Nor was it Ewart. He was desperate that Finlay should not even be seriously suspected, let alone charged. He may hate your father, he may hate Finlay, but he has everything to lose—his livelihood, his family, even his freedom—if Finlay is proved guilty. And I have a feeling that if that were to happen, your father, far from protecting him, would be the first to destroy him for having failed."

Tallulah said nothing. She could not deny it, but it was too painful to agree. It was one step beyond what she could endure.

Jago's arm tightened around her.

"There is something fundamental that you don't know," Jago said, almost as much to himself as to Pitt. "Something upon which this all turns."

"What is it?" Pitt and Tallulah spoke at once.

"I don't know," Jago confessed. "I just know it exists, it matters terribly."

But as he spoke, Pitt realized the thing that had been unresolved at the back of his own mind.

"Mary Smith," he said aloud. "Such an ordinary name. Too ordinary. Who was she? Who was she really?"

Jago closed his eyes again. "I don't know. She was young. She was very pretty, and very unhappy. God forgive us . . ."

"But it still doesn't make any sense!" Tallulah protested, turning to Pitt. "You found Finlay's things in the women's rooms! Who could have put them there except whoever killed them? Had Mary Smith something to do with both Costigan and Ella Baker?" Her face wrinkled up with confusion. "But they wouldn't kill two women just to blame Finlay! That's insane."

As he stood in the deepening chill, the mist now a halo of light around the gas lamp, another answer came to Pitt's mind, absurdly simple, and tragic. If it was the truth, it would explain everything.

"I must go back to the police station," he said. His voice sounded exactly as it had done moments before, yet he felt utterly different. It was an answer he did not want, and yet it intruded more and more fiercely into his mind, even the few seconds he stood there.

"I will take Tallulah ... Miss FitzJames ... back with me to Saint Mary's," Jago said, his face composed, his shoulders straight.

Pitt smiled, very slightly. It was a warm gesture, but a glimmer where he would have wished a beacon.

"That's a good idea, Reverend. It may be the very best place for her. May I suggest you keep her there, if decency permits?"

"But . . ." Jago started.

"I know where to find you if I should need you," Pitt cut him short. "But I don't think I shall. I know you won't testify against Finlay, and there is no one to testify against you. Keep on with your work here. It does much good. Good night." And he swiveled around and walked away towards the corner. He turned once and looked back. He saw two figures under the lamp, but so closely entwined they could have been one, a man and a woman locked in an embrace for which each had imagined and dreamed and waited, until the reality was sweet beyond hope.

Ewart was startled to see Pitt. He looked up from his desk, his face calm, no suspicion in it, no dread of what was to come.

"Is Dr. Lennox in?" Pitt asked. "If not, please send for him."

"Are you ill?" Even as he asked it, the light died out of Ewart's face. He could see Pitt was not ill, only hurt and darkened in spirit.

"Get me Dr. Lennox," Pitt repeated. "How well do you know him?"

"Er . . . moderately." Ewart's face was pale, the blood slipping out of his cheeks. "Why?"

"What did his father do?"

"What?"

"What did his father do for a living?" Pitt said again.

"I . . . I don't think . . . I've no idea! Why?" He looked genuinely puzzled. "Has he done something he shouldn't? What's the matter, Pitt? You look dreadful. Sit down, man. I'll get you a glass of brandy. Dr. Lennox!"

"I don't want brandy." Pitt hated this. Ewart was being considerate, in spite of the fear which was beginning to take hold of him. Pitt despised a bought man. Ewart had concealed a brutal murder, one of the vilest Pitt had heard of. God knows how many other things he had done at Augustus FitzJames's behest. One coercion, one blackmail, led to another. One fall, and there was no road back, except by admission—and payment in full. And the police would not forgive one of its own for such an act of corruption. Mary Smith, or whoever she was, deserved better than that.

"Get me Lennox!" Pitt repeated between his teeth.

White-faced, Ewart went to the door and disappeared along the passage. He came back a moment later. "He'll be here in fifteen minutes," he said, uncertain whether to sit or to stand, watching Pitt with apprehension.

"I've just been speaking with the Reverend Jago Jones," Pitt said slowly.

"Oh?" Ewart did not know whether to be interested or not.

"About the murder of Mary Smith," Pitt went on. "In Globe Road, six years ago."

Ewart went sheet-white. He struggled for breath and gagged. Very slowly he collapsed back into the chair behind him, feeling for it with fumbling hands.

"Why did you destroy the witnesses' records?" Pitt asked. "I know the answer, but I'll give you the chance to say it yourself, if you have that shred of honor left."

Ewart sat in silence. The torment was plain in his face, as naked as hate and grief and failure and the inner terror that one can never escape, the knowledge of self.

"He offered me money," he said so quietly Pitt could barely hear him. "Money to make a better life for my family. My sons for his. He said it was an accident. Finlay never meant to kill the girl. When he realized what he had done he tried to revive her. That was why they threw the water over her. But of course he'd gone too far. The game had got out of hand and had choked the life out of her. He must have gagged her before she screamed. The marks of it were on her cheeks."

He leaned down and hid his face in his hands. "But he didn't kill the others." His voice was thick, half muffled. "You had the right man. Costigan was guilty, I'd swear to that! And Ella Baker too! God knows how Finlay's things got there. That was one of the worst days of my life, when I saw them. It was like hell opening up in front of me."

Pitt said nothing. He could imagine it: the sudden, sick horror, the fear, the desperate writhing of the mind to find escape, the relentless terror as fact piled upon fact, and the sheer incomprehensible mystery of it.

There was no sound from the passageway outside, nothing but a blur of sounds from the street.

It was a full fifteen minutes of agonized silence in the room before the door opened and Lennox came in. He looked tired. He saw Ewart first, slumped over the desk, then Pitt in the chair opposite it.

"What is it?" he asked. "Is Inspector Ewart ill?"

"Probably," Pitt answered. "Come in and close the door."

Lennox obeyed, still puzzled.

Pitt remained where he was.

"You were the first at the scene of Ada McKinley's death after Constable Binns, weren't you, Doctor?"

"Yes. Why?" He did not look troubled, only surprised.

"And of Nora Gough's death also?"

"Yes. You know I was."

"You examined the bodies before anyone else?"

Lennox stared at him curiously, the dawn of understanding in his weary hazel eyes.

"You know that too."

"Then you went through to comfort the witnesses before we spoke to them?" Pitt continued.

"Yes. They were . . . upset. Naturally."

"Were you first on the scene of Mary Smith's death also?"

Lennox paled, but he kept his composure.

"Mary Smith?" He frowned.

"In Globe Street, six years ago," Pitt said softly. "A young girl, only just taken to the streets, about fifteen or sixteen years old. She was killed in exactly the same way. But was she, Dr. Lennox?"

For seconds no one moved. There was not even the sound of breathing. Then Ewart looked up at Lennox, his face haggard.

But the pain in his eyes was a shadow, a ghost compared with that in Lennox's face, in his whole thin body.

"My sister," he whispered. "Mary Lennox. She was sixteen when that animal did that to her!" He looked down at Ewart. "And you had the evidence and you let him go! What did he pay you that was worth that, Ewart? What in God's name was worth that?"

Ewart said nothing. He was too numb with despair and self-loathing to feel another blow.

"So when you found a prostitute murdered, without the use of a knife," Pitt went on, speaking to Lennox, "and you were the first on the scene, you put Finlay FitzJames's belongings under the body and broke her fingers and toes to look like Mary's, and tied the garter, cross-buttoned the boots, threw water over her, and waited for us to do the rest, hoping Finlay FitzJames would be blamed," Pitt said carefully.

"Yes."

"Where did you get the badge and the cuff link?"

"I stole them from Ewart. He kept them, so they wouldn't be in the evidence," Lennox replied.

"And when Finlay wasn't blamed, and we hanged Costigan, you were first on the scene of Nora Gough's death, so you did it again," Pitt went on. "Did you coach the witnesses too? Persuade them they had seen a man like Finlay at the house?"

"Yes."

Ewart rose to his feet, swayed and almost overbalanced.

Neither of the others moved to help him.

"I must get out," he said hoarsely. "I'm going to be sick."

Lennox stepped back to let him pass. Ewart fumbled for the doorknob, threw the door open and went out, leaving it swinging behind him.

Lennox faced Pitt.

"He deserved to be hanged for what he did to Mary," he said in a low, husky voice. "Are you going to charge Finlay now, or is he still going to get away with it?" The words were torn out of him.

"I haven't enough evidence to charge him," Pitt said bitterly. "Unless Ewart confesses, which he may, or he may recover his composure and realize I have very little proof."

"But . . ." Lennox was desperate.

"I can see if Margery Williams will identify Finlay," Pitt went on. "She might. So might the other two witnesses who saw him. Or there is the possibility Helliwell and Thirlstone may be sufficiently frightened they will speak, especially if they are identified as well."

"You must!" Lennox leaned forward and grasped Pitt, his grip so hard it pinched the flesh. "You must . . ."

He got no further because the door opened and a very worried Constable Binns put his head in.

"Sir . . . Mr. Ewart just went out of 'ere lookin' like 'e 'ad the devil be'ind 'im, sir, an' 'e took them sticks o' dynamite as we took from the—"

Pitt shot to his feet, almost knocking Lennox over, and charged past Binns and out into the corridor. Then he spun around, face-to-face with the two men who were hard on his heels.

"Binns, go and get a hansom. Commandeer one if you have to. Go—now!"

Binns obeyed, ran down the stairs, and they heard his feet clattering on the boards below.

Pitt looked at Lennox. "Give your resignation to the sergeant immediately. Be gone by the time I get back. Just don't tell me where, and I shan't look for you."

Lennox stood motionless, gratitude flooding his face, softening the harsh lines, filling his eyes with tears.

Pitt had no time to say anything further. He plunged down the stairs after Binns and ran through the entrance hall and down the steps into the street. Binns was waiting with a very angry cab-driver standing by the open door of a hansom.

"Number thirty-eight Devonshire Street!" Pitt shouted, and swung himself up and into it with Binns a step behind. "Fast as you can, man! Lives depend on it!"

The cabby caught the tension and the urgency. He cracked the whip and the cab lurched forward. In a few moments it was charging through traffic at considerable risk to everything in its way.

Neither Pitt nor Binns spoke. They were thrown from side to side and clinging onto the handles, in peril of being injured, and there was too much noise to hear anything clearly above the hooves, the wheels, the creak of straining wood, and the yells of outraged coachmen.

When they slowed to a halt in Devonshire Street, Pitt threw the door open and was out onto the pavement, Binns a yard behind him. He raced up the steps and yanked the doorbell, almost pulling it out of its socket, then beat his fists on the door.

Binns was shouting something, but he took no notice.

The door swung open and the agreeable butler looked alarmed.

"Is Ewart here?" Pitt demanded. "Policeman . . . Inspector Ewart! Dark, thinning hair, carrying something, probably a bag!"

"Yes, sir. He arrived a few minutes ago. Called to see Mr. FitzJames."

"Where?"

The butler paled. "In the library, sir."

"Is there a fire there?" Pitt's voice cracked with the unbearable tension.

"Yes sir. What is wrong, sir? If I can—"

He never completed his sentence. The blast from the explosion tore out the fireplace and the outer wall of the library. It hurled the door off its hinges into the hallway and the force of heat and air knocked the men to the floor, bruised and wounded. Pitt was driven back and crashed into the hall table, Binns fell to his knees. There were books and loose papers everywhere and a cloud of gray ash.

There were seconds of silence, except for the settling of stones and rubble, then the screaming started.

Pitt climbed to his feet, unsteadily, dizzy and hurt, unaware of his bleeding hands or the scratches and smears of blood on his face. He stumbled towards the library and peered in. The wreckage of books littered everything except a space in the center where live coals were burning on the carpet. The body of Ewart lay crumpled, drenched with blood, and less than a yard away what was left of Augustus FitzJames sprawled across the pile of splinters which had been the table. One jagged end speared through his chest, but he would no longer care.

Pitt turned back and saw the butler rise to his knee, his face gray with shock. Binns moved forward slightly to help him.

Somewhere beyond the landing a maid was screaming, over and over again.

Aloysia FitzJames stood at the head of the stairs.

Finlay came from the withdrawing room. He looked incredulous, as if he did not believe what he saw. He faced Pitt with anger.

"What in God's name have you done?" he said abruptly. "Where . . . where's my father?"

"He's dead," Pitt answered quietly, the smoke catching in his throat. "So—is—Inspector Ewart. But his records remain. Finlay FitzJames, I arrest you for the torture and murder of Mary Lennox, on the twelfth of September, 1884."

Finlay looked once, in desperation, towards the wreckage of the library.

"He cannot help you this time," Pitt said. "Nor can Ewart. You can put off the time, Mr. FitzJames, but it always comes, one day or another. Have the courage now to face it. It is still not too late at least for dignity."

Finlay stared at him, then his eyes swung wildly, seeking an escape, help, anything but Pitt standing in front of him.

"I can't! I won't! I . . ." His voice rose higher, more shrill. "You can't prove—"

"Ewart confessed before he died."

Aloysia came slowly down the staircase and stood by her son, but without touching him. She looked at Pitt.

"He will come with dignity, Superintendent," she said very quietly. "I will come with him. In the last few moments I have lost everything that I have lived my whole life believing I possessed. But I will not go out of here weeping, and whatever I feel, no one else will know it."

Finlay stared at her, incomprehension turning into rage.

"You can't let him . . ." he began. "Do something!" His voice rose in terror and accusation. "Do something! You can't let him take me! They'll hang me!" He started to struggle, but Binns had hold of him so hard by the arm he would have wrenched it out of the socket had he continued to struggle. "Mother! You . . ."

Aloysia was not listening. She walked slowly down the steps and Binns followed with Finlay, his features tearstained and twisted with rage.

Behind them then, grimed and smeared, but still with an agreeable face, the butler staggered to the door and pulled it closed.

ABOUT THE AUTHOR

Among **Anne Perry**'s fifteen other novels featuring Thomas and Charlotte Pitt are *Traitors Gate*, *The Hyde Park Headsman*, and *Highgate Rise*. She has also written six novels featuring another formidable Victorian investigator, William Monk, including *A Sudden, Fearful Death*, *Defend and Betray*, and, most recently, *Cain His Brother*.

Anne Perry lives in the Scottish Highlands.